Sharing twins is a lifetime commitment
...and double trouble!

Twin Ties,
Twin Joys

Three heart-warming romances from three
favourite Mills & Boon authors!

Twin Ties, Twin Joys

RAYE MORGAN

JOSIE METCALFE

TERESA CARPENTER

MILLS & BOON

All the characters in this book have no existence outside the imagination of
the author, and have no relation whatsoever to anyone bearing the same name
or names. They are not even distantly inspired by any individual known or
unknown to the author, and all the incidents are pure invention.

First published in Great Britain 2011
by Mills & Boon, an imprint of Harlequin (UK) Limited,
Eton House, 18-24 Paradise Road, Richmond, Surrey TW9 1SR

TWIN TIES, TWIN JOYS © by Harlequin Enterprises II B.V./S.à.r.l 2011

The Boss's Double Trouble Twins, Twins for a Christmas Bride and *Baby
Twins: Parents Needed* were first published in Great Britain by Harlequin
(UK) Limited in separate, single volumes.

The Boss's Double Trouble Twins © Helen Conrad 2007
Twins for a Christmas Bride © Josie Metcalfe 2007
Baby Twins: Parents Needed © Teresa Carpenter 2007

ISBN: 978 0 263 88443 2

05-0811

Printed and bound in Spain
by Blackprint CPI, Barcelona

THE BOSS'S
DOUBLE TROUBLE
TWINS

BY
RAYE MORGAN

Dear Reader,

A tough guy from an old romance showing up on your doorstep, a past in Paris, a present in Texas, and a pair of adorable twins in your life—sometimes I wish I didn't just write these things. How fun to actually live them!

On second thought, the emotional highs and lows would surely wear me out pretty quickly. Much better to read about them than try to untangle them in your own life. That is exactly what makes fiction so much fun!

I hope you enjoy the ups and downs of the romance of Darcy Connors and Mitch Carver. Love those Texas guys!

Happy reading!

Raye Morgan

Raye Morgan is a fool for romance—even in her own family. With four grown sons, love, or at least heavy-duty friendship, is constantly in the air. Two sons have recently married—that leaves two more to go, and lots of romantic turmoil to feed the idea machine. Raye has published over seventy romances and claims to have many more waiting in the wings. Though she's lived in Holland, Guam and Washington, DC, she currently makes her home in Southern California with her husband and the occasional son. When not writing, she can be found feverishly working on family genealogy and scrap-booking. So many pictures—so little time!

To the harried but happy mothers of twins everywhere.

CHAPTER ONE

MITCH CARVER hesitated as he came into the bright, shiny new chrome and glass office he'd been assigned. Everything in him was rebelling. How many times had he vowed he would never work here in his family's company? And yet, here he was.

He swore softly to himself, looking at the huge desk, the sleek computer, the neatly stacked books—the shackles of a businessman's life. And then he caught sight of himself in the reflection from the floor-to-ceiling window. He was wearing a suit, for God's sake. The hair that was usually long and untamed, the better to let him slip unnoticed into life on the wild side, had been trimmed short and neat. The beard and mustache were gone. It had been years since he'd looked so conventional. And he hated it.

"You win again, Dad," he muttered dryly. But only for one year. That was all he'd promised.

A sound turned his head. It was coming from what he assumed must be his new executive lounge. He stared at the closed door. He'd been told this entire floor was empty—a clean slate he was to fill with his own entrepreneurial genius, such as it was. Something—or someone—had been overlooked. There seemed to be humming going on.

A feminine voice sang out, low and bluesy.

Mitch cocked an eyebrow. This was interesting. The voice was incredibly sexy.

Then her voice trailed off as though she'd forgotten the words.

He bit back a grin. There was definitely a woman in his brand-new washroom. A stowaway. Maybe a squatter. And if she looked anything like she sounded… The hair on his arms was bristling— always a good sign.

Surely she hadn't been left here on purpose, just for him. But you never did know. This bore looking into and was certainly more interesting than any business he was going to be conducting today.

"Hello," he called out.

There was no answer, but suddenly a weird hush hung in the air.

"Who's there?" he tried again.

Nothing. He frowned. He couldn't leave it at that.

"I'm coming in," he warned, waited a moment for a response, then tried the door. It opened to his touch and there stood a young woman, dripping wet and naked except for a fat, fluffy towel, which was slipping precariously.

"Hey!" she cried, reaching quickly to stop the towel's impending dive toward the cold tile floor.

"You!" he said in turn, wondering for a fraction of a second if he was dreaming. This was a face, after all, that had haunted his sleep for months a year or so ago. A face—and a body—he couldn't forget, even while slogging his way through the Brazilian rain forest or trekking past the hidden villages that dotted the foothills of the Himalayas. He'd known her for how long? Less than forty-eight hours. And yet, out of all the women he'd ever met, she'd stuck in his thoughts like…like the refrain of a low, bluesy song you couldn't get out of your mind.

Yeah, he told himself cynically. A guilty conscience will do that to you.

Guilty for treating a woman such as this like a one-night-stand. Guilty for seducing a woman whose relationship to an old friend had never been made exactly clear. Guilty for letting a strong attraction take over and push away all concerns about anything but his own raging desire. He could try to blame it on the exotic intoxication of a Paris night, but he knew very well it had been his own fault. She'd bewitched him, but he'd asked for it.

"Mitch Carver?" she said, dark eyes wide with shock.

He grimaced. The feeling was mutual. No one liked to face a reminder of his own weakness.

"Darcy Connors," he recalled, noting her confirmation as she nodded, looking numb. "Did I get the wrong office?" he asked her quizzically. "Or are you just passing through?"

She was still staring at him as though she were seeing a ghost.

He shrugged. "Never mind. I'm always happy to share with an old…uh…friend," he said, silently cursing himself for hesitating before the word. "Carry on. I'll just go and…"

"What are you doing here?" she demanded, clutching the towel up to her chin. "I thought you said you'd never come back to Texas."

He wasn't any happier to see her than she was to see him, but he was beginning to feel she was overdoing it a bit. The tragic look she was giving him was hardly fair. After all, he wasn't an ax murderer or anything like that.

"I've said a lot of things I shouldn't have in my time," he admitted. "Things change. Sometimes you've got to eat a little crow. See this?" He gestured toward his mouth. "Covered with feathers at the moment. That was one tough bird."

She frowned as though she was still too surprised

at seeing him to get his little joke. He took in all of her, the dripping hair, the shimmering drops on her thick eyelashes, the creamy skin and those long, lovely, silky legs he remembered from that moonlit night.

That unforgettable moonlit night. For just a moment it flooded back, the soft air, the sound of water parting as the Bateau Mouche moved along the Seine, a distant jazz singer, notes from an accordion, lights making patterns against a set of statues, trees, wrought-iron balconies. She'd shivered slightly and he'd put his arm around her shoulders, pulling her close to keep off the chill. She'd curled up against him and whispered something and he'd laughed, catching her scent and turning….

Wow. Snap out of it, he told himself sharply, remembering exactly why this woman was so dangerous to him. For some reason she'd appealed to his senses in a basic, primal way he couldn't ignore. And looking at her now, he knew nothing had changed. Everything about her seemed to tug at his libido.

And that just didn't make any sense. She wasn't his type at all. She had "happily ever after" written all over her. And he was a "here today, gone tomorrow" type of guy. Oil and water. They didn't mix well and it was dangerous to try. At least that was the way it was in his world.

"So you're not in France anymore," he noted.

She stared at him so intensely, he almost took a step backward, and at the same time, he realized there was one thing that *had* changed. She'd fallen for him that night just as hard as he'd tumbled for her. He'd seen it in her eyes, felt it in every move she made. But that was all gone now. Her gaze was wary and speculative. Her body language was defensive. She looked like a woman who expected to be under attack. And she definitely wished he hadn't shown up on her doorstep.

That triggered his curiosity. He knew why he wanted to stay away from her. But why did she want to stay away from him? Was she angry that he hadn't tried to contact her in the last two years? Or did it have something to do with that same guilt he was feeling?

"No, I'm not in France anymore," she admitted. "I transferred to Atlanta first, but they needed me here, so I packed up again and moved to the San Antonio area. And here I am, in Terra Dulce."

Here she was. Which meant they were going to be working in near proximity for the next year. He nodded, not really sure why that gave him such a feeling of foreboding. After all, when you came right down to it, they hardly knew each other. Just because they'd shared that one night in Paris didn't mean they had to be buddies. They didn't have to see each other socially just because they had both landed back in the same town. They would probably just greet each other in the halls now and then and leave it at that. He wasn't going to be here all that long, anyway. Keep it casual. That was the ticket.

"I heard about what happened to Jimmy," he said softly, mentioning the friend whose Paris apartment was the place he and Darcy had met. Jimmy had been killed in a race car incident just days after Mitch had left France for Brazil. "Sorry I didn't hear in time to make the funeral."

She looked nonplussed for a moment, then nodded.

He could have said more. He could have explained that he was in a South American jail about the time Jimmy was being eulogized, not sure if he was going to make it out alive himself. Of course, he obviously had been released. The odd time in various jails was just one of the minor drawbacks of his chosen line of work. But that seemed a bit much to lay on her at the moment.

Jimmy had been their tie, and at the same time, what might now stand between them. Mitch and Jimmy had been childhood friends. They'd lost touch after high school, but he'd heard that Jimmy was working in Paris, and when he was passing through, he'd looked him up. He'd found his old friend changed and a bit distant, but he'd also found Darcy. She was living with Jimmy but it was never clear to him just what their relationship was, and he had to admit, he hadn't really wanted to know. She had seemed eager to get out of the tiny, cramped apartment so the two of them had left Jimmy behind and taken in the sights and sounds of the French city. Very quickly it had been as though Jimmy didn't exist. For the next day and a half, they had been so wrapped up in each other, nothing else seemed to matter.

"He was a great guy," he said gruffly.

She winced, then nodded again, biting her lip. "Yes. It was a shame." But after a moment, she was issuing a significant look his way. "Do you mind?" she said, nodding toward her towel.

"Oh. Sure. Sorry." He started to close the door, then stopped. "Wait a minute. You haven't told me what you're doing here. I thought this was my new office."

She blinked at him, searching for words. "I… uh…" She shrugged helplessly. "I was the victim of an industrial accident. One of our financial department geniuses dumped his café latte on me."

He stared at her. "From head to toe?" he asked, noting her wet hair.

She nodded. "He was on the second floor catwalk and I was down in the lobby…."

"Okay. I get the picture." He couldn't resist a quick grin. "He must have been really mad at you."

She opened her mouth, obviously to protest his

characterization of the incident, but he held up a hand. "Never mind. I'll leave you to your grooming tasks. Nice to see you again, Darcy."

She'd been turning away but her head snapped back around at that, as though she thought she might have caught a joking reference to her too-revealing appearance and she glared as he quickly closed the door.

Once outside, he stopped for a moment, like a man checking out his body parts after a risky maneuver. Everything was still in one piece. Everything, that was, except his peace of mind. It looked like he was going to have Darcy Connors back in his life, one way or another. And that was something he hadn't counted on. When he'd agreed to come back and work in his family's company he had assumed Darcy was still in Paris. It hadn't occurred to him that she might be working at the home office.

He took a deep breath and told himself things would be different. He wasn't passing through on his way to danger and adventure this time. He had other things on his mind and a better perspective. He wasn't going to let a provocative woman tangle up his emotions. He would keep his libido in check.

But damn! It wasn't going to be easy. There was something about that woman that appealed to him in ways he didn't understand. And that low, sexy voice just knocked him out. *It* appealed to him in ways he understood too well.

Steady, he warned himself.

Straightening his tie, he started for the elevator. He didn't want to be standing here waiting when she emerged.

Darcy was in shock. Mitch Carver was back. The man who had been unreachable, unfindable and unfathomable for the last two years was suddenly back and very much available, and that meant she was finally going to have to do what she'd been unable to do all this time—tell him about the twins.

Of course she had to tell him. But… A feeling very like panic fluttered in her chest. Yes, she was going to tell him, but not right now. She wasn't ready. She hadn't prepared. She'd pretty much accepted that it might never be possible to tell him. And now, suddenly, it was. So how was she going to do this?

She groaned, her shoulders slumping. If only she'd had some warning. Lately it seemed everything came at her so fast, she was never ready. And that meant she always seemed to do the wrong thing. Like this morning. Knowing the office was empty and unused, she'd been sure she would have time for a quick shower before anyone even noticed her missing from her desk on the second floor. And what happened? Mitch Carver showed up to catch her at it. Of all people! She'd never dreamed that could happen.

When she'd heard a Mr. Carver was coming in to take over Property Acquisitions, she'd assumed it was Craig Carver, Mitch's cousin, who she'd heard was transferring from the Dallas branch of the family firm. She'd never met Craig. Unfortunately she couldn't say the same about Mitch.

Closing her eyes, she swayed in silent agony. How was she going to do this? How was she going to tell this man she barely knew that he was the father of her two children? That what had seemed like a romantic interlude, a chance encounter, a fleeting intimacy, had turned into a lifetime commitment? One mistake, one night of letting down her legendary guard, a one-time retreat from a lifetime of caution, and she was destined to pay the price forever. And so was he.

Not that her babies weren't worth it. She couldn't even think about them without smiling. They were her joy, her life. But their father was her dilemma and her complication. And now she had to tell this man who had made no secret of his determination never to settle down, never to live a conventional life, that he had a pair of anchors, whether he liked it or not.

She knew he wouldn't be happy about it. Would he hate her? Hate them? It was clear he wouldn't want to let anything as mundane as children get in the way of his work. She wasn't real clear on just what he did out there in the world. She had the impression he went where people paid for his services, but she was also pretty sure he spent more time using his brain than his brawn. Nevertheless, there was plenty of danger involved, and she knew from what he'd told her that the excitement was intoxicating to him. He loved it. So what was he doing here?

A speedy wipe-down with the towel and then she was slipping into the fresh clothes her friend Marty had supplied: a jersey top and a cute denim skirt. Both were a little large for her slim figure, but they would do.

She rolled the soggy dress she'd worn to work that day in the towel, fluffed her shoulder-length blond hair under the wall hair dryer for a few minutes and peeked out into the office to see who was there.

No one. Super. In just moments she was back on her own floor, her own desk in her sights, when someone called from behind.

"Hey, Darcy!"

It was Kevin, he of the errant café latte. She kept walking, but he caught up with her.

"Hey, I really, really am sorry."

He looked sorry. He was young and bright and he seemed to have something of a crush on her, but he certainly did look sorry.

"Forget it," she said shortly, reaching out to pick up the papers filling her in-box.

"Really Darcy, it was an accident. I just leaned over the rail to look at you and the cup slipped and…"

"Sure, Kevin. I understand. Don't think another thing about it." She began riffling through the papers, though she didn't see a thing. She was wondering where Mitch was—mainly so that she could avoid him. She needed time to think.

"I'd love to make it up to you, Darcy," Kevin was saying, looking puppy-dog hopeful. "I thought maybe I could take you out to…"

Kevin's suggested destination was to remain forever unknown. Before he got the name out, the elevator doors across from her office opened and Bill Monroe, her amiable boss, stepped into their conversation.

"My office, Darcy," he said, cocking a stern forefinger her way. "Right now."

"But…" She glanced at the clock on the wall over the elevator. "I really don't have time this morning. I'm running a little late and I've got people waiting for some research I've been doing and—"

"Forget that," Bill said flatly. "I need to talk to you right away."

There was a grim look on his normally jovial face as he headed for his office. Kevin shrugged dejectedly and disappeared down the stairs. Darcy sighed, stowed her things away and looked up to find Mitch coming toward her.

"Oh, hi," she said awkwardly. It gave her quite a start to have him casually turning up where she wasn't used to seeing him. It also gave her an opportunity to really look at him, and for a moment, that was what she did.

He looked so different, it was a wonder she'd recognized him right away. She flashed back to that weekend in Paris and what he'd looked like then. She'd been sharing a small place with Jimmy ever since she'd arrived in Paris. Apartments were impossible to find in the area near where they both worked at the same company. Their mothers had been best friends, so they'd known each other forever, and it had seemed only natural to share a place.

When she'd heard that Mitch was dropping by, she'd had a few seconds of excitement before she'd reminded herself that he wasn't coming to see her. He probably didn't even remember who she was. So when the doorbell had rung, she'd gone to let him in, not expecting much but pleased to be seeing someone from home. Opening the door, she'd found him standing there and her world had fallen out of the sky.

He'd been completely wild, totally exotic, like a fictional hero. His hair was a long, thick tangle framing his outrageously handsome face. His body had been spectacularly displayed in a tight, clinging shirt and torn jeans that molded to his muscular legs like something that had grown to cover him. He was reeking with attitude and looked like a young freedom fighter, a rebel, a revolutionary, ducking in out of the street to evade a pursuer. Even now, the memory of how provocatively fine he'd looked took her breath away.

She'd fallen for him like a ton of bricks, right there in the doorway to Jimmy's tiny flat. Not that it should have been surprising. After all, even though she hadn't seen him for years, she'd had a crush on him since she'd been a child. Of course, he'd never noticed her in those days.

Only, this time he did.

"Hey," he'd said, looking deep into her eyes.

"Hey yourself," she'd said back, looking dreamily into his.

"What's your name?" he'd asked, proving her theory.

"Darcy," she'd responded, just as glad he didn't remember the awkward girl who'd mooned after him in the old days.

"I'm Mitch."

"I know."

He'd smiled and she'd swooned toward him.

"Want to run away with me?" he asked her softly, leaning even closer.

She'd nodded without hesitation, knowing it was just banter, but answering in all sincerity. "Yes," she whispered.

His gaze had seemed to devour her hungrily and for one long moment, she'd lost herself in his blue eyes.

"Hey, Mitch," Jimmy had called out from the kitchen. "You finally got here."

And she'd pulled back, thinking the moment was over, that the relationship between the two men would be the focus of the rest of the day. But she'd been wrong. The magic that had sparked between them didn't fade. As soon as they got the chance, they'd gone out into the city together, and things had gone from pure delight to rapture.

At first she'd looked on that exciting weekend as a mistake, but one that was just too delicious to really regret—a romantic episode she would treasure forever. It seemed the kind of thing you read about in books or saw in movies. He'd come into her life at just the moment she had felt most lost and lonely and reminded her of what joy in living could be like—and then he'd gone.

And then she'd realized she was pregnant.

She watched as he approached her now, looking so clean-cut and handsome—not a rebel at all. But she knew that exciting body still lay under the suit coat and hints of that crazy untamed spirit still lurked in his eyes if you looked hard enough. The packaging had changed, but he was still the same guy.

Was she still the same girl? Not on your life.

CHAPTER TWO

"WHAT are you doing on this floor?" Darcy asked for lack of anything better to say.

Mitch shrugged. "I got a message from Bill Monroe." He noted the startled look on her face in reaction to that news. "You, too?"

She nodded. A feeling of dread was beginning to build inside her. If this was what she thought it might be…

He inclined his head. "Lead on, McDuff," he muttered.

She bit her lip and led the way into her boss's office. Bill rose and shook hands with Mitch, murmuring a greeting. Still standing, he got to the point.

"Darcy, I hate to lose you. But you've been assigned to the new department Mitch will be heading."

She blanched, though by now she'd been expecting this very thing. "What?" She shook her head.

Surely this wasn't written in stone yet. "No." She turned to Mitch appealingly. "No!" Surely he would do something to stop this.

And he looked as though he wanted to. "Interesting," he said. "But there's been some mistake. You see, I won't need an assistant. I've already got a secretary picked out and—"

"Darcy isn't a secretary. She's a property analyst. And her area of expertise resides smack dab in the center of your new project." Bill dropped an armful of folders on the desk as though that settled the matter. "You can take these with you."

Darcy's heart sank. That meant Mitch was taking over the Bermuda Woods development. She'd been working on that one for months. There was no way she was going to get out of this, was there? She stared into Mitch's eyes and he stared right back into hers. She'd forgotten how gorgeous those eyes were, deep blue and dangerous as the sky on a stormy day. Those eyes were the first thing that had intrigued her when she'd met him in Paris. She winced.

Don't think about Paris, she told herself sharply. Not now.

"You know, I really can't do this," she said, looking at her boss brightly, giving it one last try. "I've got a desk full of work. Mr. Grayson is waiting for my report on the Clemson release."

The older man glowered at her. "Sorry, Darcy," he said stiffly. "You've been assigned to Mr. Carver. You can take it up with the board, but as far as HR is concerned, you're working up there now."

She swallowed hard and tried to smile. The man was droning on, giving Mitch some last-minute instructions on paperwork, but she wasn't listening. This was disastrous. She couldn't work for Mitch. She could barely look at him. Once he'd found out about the twins…

"They want these forms to be filled out before you leave this evening," Bill was saying to Mitch. He sent a regretful look Darcy's way. "I hate to see you go," he told her, "but my loss is Mitch Carver's gain." He smiled at the younger man. "Her expertise is going to be invaluable to you. You'll see that soon enough."

Nice words, but she hardly heard them. She took up the folders and carried them back to her own desk, the one she was going to spend the day clearing out. Mitch came behind her.

"Want me to carry some of those on up for you?" he asked.

When she flashed him a look, he added, "Look, Darcy, I'm not any crazier about this than you are."

She turned on him, thinking if that was really the case, he could have tried a little harder. "You ought to have some pull, being the boss's son and all. Can't you do something about this?"

He grimaced, raking fingers through his thick hair distractedly. "I'm pretty much in the position of the returning prodigal right now. I don't have too many favors owed me. But I'll see what I can do."

"Good." That seemed to be all she wrote as far as rays of hope were concerned. She didn't think holding her breath until she turned blue would be effective at this point. "You've got to do something."

"Do I?" Turning back toward her, he cocked an eyebrow.

"Yes. Of course. You know we can't work together."

"Can't we?"

He looked genuinely puzzled and she realized he had no clue why she might feel that way. Not yet, anyway. Once he knew about the twins, he would understand. She was going to tell him…just as soon as she figured out how.

But that was just the problem. She had no idea what his reaction would be. She knew he didn't want a family. He'd been very clear on the point that night when it had seemed they were opening their hearts to each other. So he wasn't likely to take this as good news. She'd assumed he would resent her dropping this bombshell in his lap—maybe even try to wriggle out of facing it. But he didn't know about them yet, so why was he acting as though he wanted to keep distance between them as much as she did? She could think of only one possible reason—he was

afraid she might want to resume their affair and he
didn't want any part of that.

Just the thought of that sparked a flash of anger,
but she pushed it back. After all, wasn't that exactly
what she was feeling as well?

"I'll do what I can," he was saying, turning to go.
"I'll let you know."

She nodded and watched as he strode toward the
elevator.

"Who's the hottie?" asked a voice at her elbow.

She started, then grinned feebly at Cindy, her of-
ficemate who had come up to stand beside her.

"Looks like he might be my new boss," she said
ruefully.

Cindy laughed, shaking back her thick, ebony
hair. "Oh the agony of it all," she said, amusement
dancing in her green eyes. "Listen, I'm willing to
take your place if it will make you feel better."

"I'll keep that in mind," Darcy said, wishing that
sort of trade was actually possible. But once she'd
heard what Mitch's assigned area would be, she
knew she was on shaky ground for a transfer. This
was her project. Getting *him* transferred would be
more logical. And that hardly seemed likely.

Still, there had to be some way.

Mitch should have felt right at home in the sleek
offices of ACW Properties. His grandfather had

started the company sixty years ago. His father had been CEO of the San Antonio branch ever since he could remember. He'd played in these halls as a child, had part-time jobs here in high school, did a summer internship. And in those days, it had all seemed natural to him.

But his relationship with his father had been destroyed shortly after his freshman year at college. In reaction, he'd rejected every part of the life his family had expected him to follow. Coming back now had been a bitter pill to swallow. It had taken emotional blackmail to make him do it.

Now he was being escorted through the building by Tanya Gayle, the long and lanky director of Human Resources. She'd offered to give him a tour of all the new facilities and from her sideways glances, he had a feeling she was offering a lot more than that. Luckily, once he'd realized he wasn't going to get out of it, he'd had the presence of mind to bring along Paula Pinter, his new secretary and the woman who had baby-sat for him here in the office as a child. There was nothing like the addition of a sweet, gray-haired older woman to tamp down the fires of office romance.

Tanya escorted him into the workout room as though she'd been personally responsible for it herself, explaining as she went how it was company policy that each employee take an extra fifteen minutes at lunch to get in some exercise.

"Really. Who made that decision?"

"Your father, I imagine."

"No kidding."

Mitch raised an eyebrow. That seemed a bit ironic, considering the way his father used to spend his lunch hours in the old days.

The Carvers had always been community leaders. To the outside world, they looked like an ideal family. But the public face had been in many ways a false one. Mitch and his brother Dylan spent part of their youth covering up the truth about their father's drinking and the ugly fights that sometimes tore apart their homelife.

Pushing away bad memories, he glanced around the room, noting a full complement of employees in colorful workout uniforms. And then his eye was caught by Darcy on a treadmill. She had on earphones and was working hard, looking determined. He watched her for a moment. Paula noticed where his gaze was directed.

"That's Darcy Connors," she said helpfully. "She's down here every day, a real role model to us all."

"Yes, she's worked hard to get back that trim and girlish figure," Tanya chimed in. "And she's done a great job. We're all jealous."

Mitch frowned. Get back her girlish figure? Where'd it gone? It had certainly been present when he'd known her before. He turned to ask Tanya what she meant, but Paula had pulled out a bright jersey tank top in the company colors with his name on it.

"Surprise!" they said in unison.

He swallowed his question and tried to look pleased.

"Put it on," Paula urged.

"Right now? Right here?"

"Why not? Come on. We'll see if it fits."

He shrugged. Why not, indeed? He was here for the year and he might as well make the best of it. Fitting in with the crowd was part of that, he supposed. So instead of getting his exercise racing after bad guys in the jungle, he was going to get on machines, was he? Oh well. Yanking off his tie, he began working on the buttons of his shirt.

Darcy had developed the habit of spending most of her lunch hour on the treadmill. Not only did she get a good workout, but it also gave her the time and space to set her mind free and think things through. And today she had a lot to think about.

All the other machines were filled with other employees. She paid no attention to them, but when Mitch arrived in the room, somehow she sensed it. Biting her lip, she tried to stay focused and ignore him. But finally she had to turn her head, just in time to see him begin to pull off his crisp white shirt. She held her breath, and when she realized what she was doing, she closed her eyes for a moment, cursing softly.

When she opened them again, she saw that beautiful body and steeled herself. And then she saw something else. There across his chest was a jagged line of scarring that she knew hadn't been there when she'd known him. It looked fiery and painful and she gasped so loud, heads turned all up and down the room. He looked up and her gaze locked with his, but only for seconds.

She stumbled on the treadmill, losing her pace and almost losing her balance, her heart beating wildly. That beautiful body and that ugly scar. His skin had been smooth and flawless when she'd last seen it, touched it. What on earth had happened to him?

She drew a deep breath, reminding herself she wasn't going to let emotions tangle up her life again. Whatever had happened to him was none of her business. She had two babies to raise and protect and that was enough for her to deal with.

Turning up the mileage on the treadmill, she worked harder, hoping to blot out his presence on the other side of the room. But she was beginning to wonder if she was ever going to be free of him again. And suddenly her mind was full of what it had been like two years before, right after Mitch had left for South America.

She'd been walking on air. Of course he'd told her

he wasn't in the market for a lasting relationship, and she'd accepted that at the time. But something deep inside had whispered lies of wishful thinking to her. Those two days had been magic. She'd never known a man like Mitch, never felt the crazy excitement, the overwhelming affection, the deep and undeniable need she'd felt with him. They had been so good together. She knew he felt the same way. She knew he was just as reluctant to leave her as she had been to let him go. She'd been so sure he would contact her again, despite everything he'd said. How could two people fall madly into love for a weekend and then walk away without a backward glance? It just didn't seem possible.

One week went by. Then another. She was still so sure that she would hear from him soon. With Jimmy totally wrapped up in his racing, spending every free moment at the track, and things at work more difficult than she'd ever expected, she felt very much alone. And then came the horrible afternoon when Jimmy's Formula One car crashed during a practice run. He was rushed to the hospital and died later that night. Darcy had been the one to call his mother with the news—the one to accompany his body back to Texas, the one who supported his mother at the funeral. For days that was all she could think about.

And then she realized she was pregnant.

By then Mitch had seemed very far away. And

when she couldn't find him or get in touch with him, she began to resent him—as though he'd done this to her and then run out on his responsibilities. Again, it was like something out of a book or a movie, only now it had turned from romance to dark drama. A character study in male dependability.

She'd had her babies. She'd gone through it all alone. It wasn't easy, but she was managing. And suddenly, he'd turned up again.

It was all wrong. Things weren't happening in the right order. If only she'd been able to get hold of him right when she realized the babies were on the way. She knew he had no interest in being a father. He'd told her as much that night in Paris— and by the time she knew she was pregnant, she was ready to believe what he'd said was the last word after all. She wouldn't have asked all that much of him. But at least he would have been moral support. She wouldn't have had to make all the decisions on her own. There would have been someone to share things with, even if just in letters or phone calls.

Okay, she was starting to sound whiny now, even to herself. Enough. This was a situation, but she could handle it. She'd toughened a lot over the last two years. She'd handled everything up to now pretty well, hadn't she? And she could do this, too.

Turning off the machine, she grabbed a towel, wiped her face, then threw it around her shoulders, turning to step off. And there was Mitch, waiting for her.

Her eyes widened, but she didn't stop.

"Are you stalking me?" she asked, brushing past him and trying to ignore the lovely bulging muscles his company tank top revealed.

"I'd only be doing that if you were avoiding me," he pointed out. "Are you?"

Turning back, she looked at him. Her first thought was that he had some nerve accusing *her* of being ellusive. He was the original Houdini in her life. But as her gaze met his, she felt her resentment melting. It was those huge blue eyes with those gorgeous dark lashes. She was a sucker for that look—always had been.

"No, of course not," she said. And silently, she raged at herself. *"Wimp!"*

"Good. Because I think we need to talk. Why don't you meet me in my office in half an hour?"

She nodded. This was it. Her heart was pounding. "Okay," she said, then turned and marched toward the women's locker room.

He was right. They did need to talk, about so many things. The question was, should she tell him now? *Could* she tell him now?

"We'll play it by ear," she told herself reassuringly as she slipped into her work clothes. But that was no good. She knew she was just giving herself an out that way. With a sigh, she rejected that and got back to business. There had to be a hundred different ways to broach the subject and get it over with. Why was it that she couldn't think of any?

Focus! she ordered herself as she started walking back to her desk. Think! And once she started trying a little harder, ideas began to come to her. Not that any of them were any good. Still, she'd started the juices flowing.

There really were so many options. There was the blunt method. She could walk into his office, plunk a picture of the almost-fifteen-month-old twins down on the desk in front of him and say, "Look at these. See any resemblance?"

Dropping down into her chair, she made a face. A bit crass, perhaps. But it was a start. Leaning on her elbows, she frowned, deep in thought.

How about writing him a memo—make it businesslike? "Attention Mr. Carver: This memorandum is meant to inform you that you are the father of twins. Please deal with this situation immediately."

She wrinkled her nose.

Well then, how about using the office loudspeaker? "Attention employees. All fathers of twins please meet with Darcy Connors in the conference room right away. Mitch Carver, this means you."

A more subtle approach? "Uh, Mitch, you know when you left me in Paris? You didn't just leave me. In fact, you left behind a legacy, and it's been growing ever since."

Too obscure. He would think she meant the Parisian waitresses were still talking about him. And they just might be, but that wasn't the issue here.

She glanced at the clock and her heart jumped. She didn't have much time left. She had to think of some way to do this, fast, and do it right. Closing her eyes, she tried to concentrate. Her twins deserved a father who didn't completely reject them. And it was up to her to provide that for them. The way she approached this might make all the difference.

A few minutes later she was walking into his office and she still didn't have a plan. She did have a rough idea of what she might say, but she didn't get a chance to say it. Mitch rose from behind his desk to greet her, taking her hand in his and staring down into her eyes in a way that reminded her of how he'd looked in that Parisian doorway, blasting all thought right out of her mind and leaving only a thrilling electricity running through her veins and a bittersweet yearning in her heart.

"I've got to tell you right up-front, Darcy," he said, not releasing her hand. "I've talked to a few people and there's no chance to get your assignment changed. The only way we're going to avoid working with each other is if one of us quits."

She nodded numbly. She'd pretty much accepted that already. But he was still holding her hand and as long as he was doing that, her mind wasn't going to work very well. She gave a tug, but he wasn't letting go.

"I think I understand why you don't think we should be working together," he was saying earnestly. "But that's just it—I agree. You don't have anything to worry about. I swear, I'll make sure everything stays on a businesslike level. We'll work as colleagues and that will be it."

"Good," she said thickly. "Now can I have my hand back?"

He looked down and actually seemed startled to realize he was still holding it. "Oh. Sure. Sorry."

He let go and she took a step back to get a bit of distance from him and settle her emotions. If just having her hand in his was going to send her into a tailspin, she was in big trouble. She had to get control of herself.

Taking a deep breath, she stared at his tie and tried to get it together. Now was the time. They had the privacy she needed. There was a pause in the conversation. It was the perfect opportunity. She ought to launch into a speech that would prepare him for the revelation. She tried to make herself do it. Looking up into his face, she searched for the words.

If not now, when? she prodded herself silently. Come on. Get it out there.

CHAPTER THREE

DARCY opened her mouth. Her lips actually formed a word. But as she gazed up into his clear blue eyes, she just couldn't go through with it. The right words weren't there yet. They weren't coming to her.

"So what do you think?" Mitch asked, looking at her in the deep, probing way he had, that way that gave her the false feeling he saw only her, cared about only her, and would treasure her forever. "Can you work with me?"

"I…I don't know," she said, her voice sounding scratchy from the effort to speak at all. It was that intimate look that made her so crazy. She realized that now. She had to avoid his gaze at all costs. "That all depends. There's something…"

"We'll give it a try," he said when she faltered. "I'm sure we can do it. And it's only for one year."

One year! In one year, the twins would be talking. Talking? They would be writing novels! They would be learning to catch a ball. They would be giving wet baby kisses to the ones who loved them. Would that include Mitch?

"One year?" she repeated numbly.

He nodded. "That's all I've committed to. One year. And then I'm going back overseas."

"I see."

Well, wasn't that just typical? Full commitment wasn't his thing, was it? Resentment rose in her again.

"I…I guess I'm just surprised to see you working back here at all," she noted distractedly. "The last I heard you were smuggling arms into Nepal or something."

Amusement flashed across his handsome face. "Who told you that?"

"Someone at Jimmy's funeral, I think."

He shrugged, his gaze suddenly hooded. "He didn't get it quite right. It wasn't Nepal, and it wasn't arms."

"What was it?"

He paused just long enough to make her think whatever he said was going to be something he probably made up.

"It was rock concert T-shirts, into a country which shall remain nameless," he said at last. "I do still have my Fifth Amendment rights."

She barely restrained herself from rolling her eyes. "That you do, but you're the only person I've ever known who actually feels he needs to use them," she said a bit caustically.

"Actually we were just importing the shirts." He paused, and then added softly, "And then 'exporting' a few political refugees."

"I see." She knew he was involved in dangerous things overseas. He'd told her a few hair-raising tales that night in Paris. And she was pretty sure the story behind that new ugly scar across his chest was going to fit right into one of those scenarios. "I guess you were just born to be a businessman, weren't you?" she added wryly.

He laughed softly. "Of a sort."

She bit her lip. Now *that* was something to keep in mind: Don't make the man laugh. He looks too good doing it.

"So is that why you're back?" she asked quickly. "Are you on the lam?" Where had that phrase come from? She didn't know, but she kind of liked it. It fit. "Is Interpol after you? I guess you got tired of being shot at and decided to come home for a rest, huh?"

He groaned, sagging down into a leather chair and stretching his long legs out before him. "You watch too much television."

"Then why *did* you come back?"

He looked up at her and smiled sweetly. "My mother asked me to."

She stared at him. *Because his mother asked him*

to? That didn't fit in with the always-a-rebel, devil-may-care, to-hell-with-convention image she had of him. And now here he sat in a suit and tie—looking like he was ready to take the business world by storm. It seemed his mother had a bigger influence on him than she'd thought.

Mitch's parents had been another dilemma for her. Her impulse had been to tell them about the twins soon after she'd known she was pregnant. The fact that Mitch was so adamant about wanting nothing to do with them was what had made her hesitate in the beginning.

And the more she thought about it, the more she wondered if she really wanted them getting involved in how she raised her children. Without knowing how things really stood with their son, did she dare let that happen? If there had been a different attitude, she might have told them.

But at first, she kept thinking Mitch would show up in one way or another. Or at least, that she would find a contact point. And that once she'd settled things with him, he should be the one to tell his parents.

She actually tried to talk to his mother at the company memorial service held for Jimmy. The woman had been gracious in a distant way, but when Darcy had tried to ask where Mitch was, she turned frosty fast.

"I'm sorry. I haven't talked to my oldest son for

a long time," she said. "You'll have to find some other way to get in touch with him."

After that, she realized that if she went directly to the Carvers and told them about her pregnancy, they would immediately assume she was after money. She had to admit, a little financial aid would have come in very handy at that time. But once she'd thought things through, she knew it was just too dangerous. Money bought influence and got lawyers involved. It was much safer to take care of things herself.

That meant, sadly, that the Carvers were deprived of their grandchildren, and the twins were cheated out of grandparents, but she couldn't see a way around that at the time.

"So there's actually something you respect," she said slowly. "Your mother. That's sort of touching."

She'd meant it as a barb, but once the words were out of her mouth, she realized it was true.

"You're damn right I respect my mother. Have you met her?"

"Yes. She's a lovely woman."

"That she is."

She frowned, thinking back on the things he had told her almost two years before. "It was really your father you had the quarrel with, wasn't it?"

His face hardened. "That's something I'm not going to discuss."

Yes, she remembered now. All the bad feeling in

the family revolved around some sort of feud with his father. And it obviously still burned deeply in him.

"You know, Darcy," he said, leaning back in his chair, "I didn't find out about what happened to Jimmy until just a few weeks ago." He frowned and muttered, "I really ought to go by and pay my respects to his mother. I always liked her."

Darcy nodded. Mimi was great. In fact, it was Mimi, Jimmy's mother, who had taken her in when she had the twins. She was living with her right now. Mimi had health problems and Darcy had two little babies who required looking after. They needed each other and they seemed to have the perfect fit, for now.

"You really have been out of touch, haven't you?" she noted. "How did your mother manage to find you?"

"She hired a private investigator."

So he hadn't even contacted the mother he claimed to be so close to. She frowned. This lack of family feeling did not bode well for his having any interest in the boys. But she'd known that all along.

"So all those things you said when we knew each other in…" She had force herself to say the name of the city. "In Paris…"

"Ah. You remember Paris, do you?" He pretended to be surprised.

She frowned, looking away. "Of course, I remember Paris."

"But you'd like to forget," he said softly, then grimaced. "Why do I get the feeling that what happened in Paris is looming over us like…like this giant vulture ready to pick apart the bones of our relationship?"

"Relationship?" she responded tartly. "Do we have a relationship? I thought that was one of those things you vowed never to have."

He sighed. "Tell you what, Darcy. I'll make you a deal."

Folding her arms, she looked at him sideways. "What sort of deal?"

"Look. Facing reality, we're probably going to be working together. It would be best if we could fix things so that's possible. So why don't we just put Paris behind us? That was then. This is now. We've both changed. Circumstances have certainly changed. A lot of water under the bridge." He shrugged. "Let's start over again. Completely new."

He rose and stuck out his hand. "Hi. I'm Mitch Carver. And I'm very pleased to meet you, Darcy Connors. I'm sure we'll work well together."

She stared at him and found her hand enveloped in his once again, but she couldn't join in the general good cheer he was trying to promote. Act as though Paris never happened? Sorry. There were two little impediments waiting for her at home that made all this impossible.

Still, his touch had power. She felt his energy, his inner strength, and especially, his raw, masculine appeal, just in the warmth of his hand. Her pulse began to race, as though something exciting was about to happen. Startled, she pulled her hand out of his.

"You are so arrogant," she told him gently, wishing she could will away his attractive presence. "You think you can wipe out the past, just by deciding to."

"Of course. Why not?"

She shook her head. "I think you still have a lot to learn," she said, regarding him narrowly.

Okay, she finally had a plan. She would think things over tonight, develop a method of attack, and give it to him in the morning. It would probably be best to do that somewhere outside of work. After all, she had no idea how he was going to react, but she did have a feeling it was going to be messy.

"Tell you what," she said, turning to go. "Meet me tomorrow morning at The Jumpin' Bean. You remember where that is, don't you? Seven-thirty. There's something I need to talk to you about."

He frowned, rising to see her out, his gaze suddenly alert. "What is it?"

She shook her head. "Tomorrow," she said. "Will you meet me?"

He shrugged. "Of course."

She nodded. "Okay. See you tomorrow."

And she left his office feeling a little better about the future. At least she had a plan.

"Look at that, boys," Mimi Foster announced in her slow Texas drawl. "Your mama's home!"

Darcy swept her two toddlers up in her arms, laughing as they babbled at her happily and Sparky, Mimi's little white fluffy dog, danced around her, barking noisily.

"Oh hush, Sparky," she said, and to her babies, "My little ducks, I'm so glad to see you." She cooed, kissing one and then the other and holding both tightly. "Have you been good for Mimi today?"

"They've been perfect angels, both of them," Mimi lied kindly. A tall, slender woman, she favored exotic caftans and chandelier earrings.

"Right. I'll just bet they have." Darcy sighed as she put them back down in the playpen. Looking around the tidy front room of the modest Spanish-style house she'd been sharing with Jimmy's mother since she'd come back to Terra Dulce in the San Antonio area, she shook her head. "Oh, Mimi, I don't know what I'd do without you."

"Darcy, darlin'," the older woman said, rising and giving her friend a hug. "You know the three of you are my family now. Without y'all I would just wither up and blow away."

Mimi and her mother had been best friends, and

though they lived in cities hundreds of miles apart, there had been plenty of visits and vacations spent together. For years her mother and Mimi had planned and plotted, trying to conjure up a romance between Darcy and Jimmy that just never quite panned out. Jimmy had always been more interested in cars than he had in girls. And Darcy…well, Darcy had seen Mitch.

The first time she'd noticed him, she must have been about eleven. He was probably fourteen and full of teenage swagger. He'd stopped by the Foster house to help Jimmy work on an old car Jimmy's dad had in the driveway. Darcy's family had been there on their usual summer visit and she'd watched from the window. She thought most boys were "icky" at that point in her life. But Mitch was different. She couldn't take her eyes off him. From then on, Mitch was her standard for male excellence.

And now he was here and she was finally going to have to tell Mimi that he was the father of her children. She knew Mimi had hoped that Jimmy was their father at first. She'd let her know that wasn't the case, but she hadn't gone any further than that and Mimi hadn't tried to pry it out of her. The rest of the world, especially those she worked with, assumed Jimmy had been the father, and she hadn't done anything to counter that. When you came right down to it, she hadn't told anyone the full truth. And now, she had to find a way to tell Mitch.

She spent the next hour playing with her children and thinking about Mitch. Tonight she would take a long bath and work up a good way to present the facts to him. She had to phrase it just right. She had to let him know that she expected him to be a factor in their lives.

A part of her wished she could just grab her kids and make a run for it, start over somewhere fresh without all these problems. But she knew running just brought up new problems. And then the old ones came along and found you anyway.

Besides, it didn't seem likely she could get away in time, especially as, looking out the picture window, she saw Mitch coming up the front walk at this very moment. In seconds he would be knocking on the front door.

Sheer panic shot through her veins. Without thinking twice, she snatched up both babies, kicked the playpen behind the couch and whisked them into their bedroom before the doorbell rang. Her only hope was to move up naptime by an hour. Would these two little mop-heads cooperate?

"Mitch Carver! You darlin'!"

Mimi had answered the door and Darcy knew she was throwing her arms around the man who had been her son's childhood friend. Darcy listened intently as she put her babies down in their beds, hoping against hope they might take a nice nap. Maybe this could be quick. Maybe Mitch would just pay his respects and be on his way. Maybe Mimi would forget to mention that Darcy was living here with her.

Maybe.

"Mama," Sammy was saying sleepily, giving her a toothless smile. "Mama, Mama, Mama."

"Shush! Go to sleep, you little rascal," she whispered to him, love pouring out of her heart as she looked down at him.

Sean was already drifting off, his little thumb sneaking up into his mouth. No matter what, her total agenda was protecting these two adorable children from harm. She would do whatever she had to do.

She looked around the room and sighed. It was small for two cribs, one dresser and an ancient changing table, not to mention a shelf system that was beginning to pull away from the wall. This was not exactly what she'd dreamed of for her little ones. Hopefully, if she got the raise she was expecting next month…

"I wanted you to know how sorry I am about Jimmy," she could hear Mitch saying from the next room.

"His death was a tragedy," Mimi responded sadly. "You were always such a good friend to him. He idolized you, you know. He missed you so when you went off and joined the Army."

They chatted a bit more, but Darcy couldn't make out the words. Darcy bit her lip. So far, so good. Maybe he would just leave now, without ever hearing that she was just a few steps away.

"I don't know if you ever knew Darcy Connors," she heard Mimi mentioning, loud and clear.

"Darcy Connors?" Mitch sounded surprised. "Sure, I know Darcy."

Her shoulders sagged. Oh well. So much for that hope. Nothing was ever easy, was it? The boys were dozing. At least she was getting a little luck there. Very quietly, she crept out into the hall, ready to leap out and stop Mimi from bringing up the children if she possibly could.

"I was so happy when she got the assignment in France," Mimi was saying. "She and Jimmy became quite close while they were working together over there."

"I… yes, I guess I knew that," Mitch replied a bit stiffly.

Mimi was chattering on. Darcy crossed her fingers, hoping she would forget to mention the twins.

"Yes, she came to live with me right after she got transferred from the Atlanta office. And now she and her two—"

Time to make her move.

"Hello there," Darcy interrupted, bursting onto the scene with a bright smile before Mimi could get the rest of that sentence out. "I thought I recognized your voice," she said, nodding to Mitch.

He was firmly ensconced on the couch, unfortunately. She wasn't going to be able to shoo him out the door any time soon. Flopping down into a chair across from him, she kept on smiling.

He gave her a puzzled look and she knew he was wondering why she hadn't told him she was living with Jimmy's mom. *It just didn't come up,* she tried to convey with a subtle shrug.

Mimi was laughing about the past. "All those long summer days with you and Jimmy playing in the canyon out back, and me driving you to Little League games and buying you hamburgers at Merle's drive-in."

"Merle's Mammoth Mouthfuls." Mitch grinned. "I remember it all. Some of the happiest days of my life were spent right here in your backyard."

"You and Jimmy, what a pair." She sighed. "I'm glad he had you in his life. And Darcy, too," she added with a smile. "I hope you two get to know each other."

Darcy and Mitch exchanged a quick, furtive glance.

"I haven't told Mimi yet," she said quickly.

"Told me what?" Mimi asked.

Mitch was staring at her, his eyes wide, as though

he couldn't believe his ears, and she suddenly realized what he might think she was talking about.

"That we're going to be working together," she re-assured him quickly. She turned to look at the older woman. "Yes, we're going to be working together, Mitch and I. He's come back and he's working for ACW. Isn't that nice?"

"Well, yes," Mimi said. "I'm so glad, Mitch. I know your mama must be pleased as punch. I haven't talked to her for years but she always seemed like a gracious lady."

Mitch looked as though he was still reeling from his brief misapprehension. How he had thought she was going to bring up the Paris incident she couldn't imagine. But it was pretty obvious he'd thought so, for just a moment there.

"Uh…yes, she is," he managed to get out.

Mimi smiled at them both. "So where did you two meet? How do you know each other so well?"

"I wouldn't say we know each other well," Mitch said hastily.

"No, not at all," Darcy echoed quickly.

"Well, what was it? You didn't just meet today, did you?"

Darcy smiled nervously. "Oh, no. We've met before."

She hesitated, glancing at Mitch and reading the wariness in his eyes. *Don't worry,* she wanted to tell him. *I'm not going to bring up Paris.* In fact, she was going to go back a lot further than that.

"Remember that summer, the first time my mother was sick and you invited me to come and stay with you?" she said to Mimi.

"You were still in high school."

"Yes. It was in August. You wanted to get my mind off my mother and all that. So I came to stay for a couple of weeks. You tried hard to get Jimmy to pay some attention to me, to take me out to where the teenagers gathered, but all he wanted to do was work on that souped-up car he loved so much."

"Of course! I remember." She smiled fondly. "I was so mad at him! He would barely give you the time of day. I guess it was a coming-of-age sort of thing with him."

No. It was the fact that he loved cars better than people. But that wasn't something she was going to point out to his mother.

"Anyway, you felt sorry for me, so one day you sent me off to the rodeo with a bunch of kids. Friends of Jimmy's."

"Did I?"

"Yes. I think that's the first time I really met Mitch." She glanced at him. He had the look of a man trying to remember details.

"I'd forgotten all about that," he said. "Was that really you?"

Their gazes met and something flashed between them, but Darcy ignored it as best she could. "That was me. I was the one who got charged by the bull that got out of the pen."

He grinned as the picture cleared for him.

"I remember that," he said as though enjoying the memory.

"And you pulled me out of his path at the very last second," she added. "My hero." She tried for a mocking tone but somehow it came out sounding almost sincere.

"I do my best," he said, managing to hit just the right note of irony, coming off modest and noble at the same time.

She shook her head, but she could have told him more. She could have told him that he really had become her hero that day. She could have recalled everything he was wearing, from the backward baseball cap to the tight muscle T-shirt and the ragged jeans. She might have recited everything he said to her, from, "Hey, watch it kid," to, "So you turned sweet sixteen yesterday, huh? I hope Jimmy kissed you. No? Well then, I guess I'll have to do it."

Even now, the memory of that silly little kiss could curl her toes. But there was no way she would ever tell him that.

Oh, he remembered all right. She'd said something about it when they first met again in Paris and he'd acted like he didn't remember then. But she could see it in his eyes—he remembered now. The scene played out like a holograph between them— the two of them waiting for the others behind the stadium, the sounds and smells of the rodeo, the August evening heat, the way he'd grinned and tilted her chin up with a curved finger, then bent slowly to touch his warm lips to hers, the way the world had melted around them.

And then the others had come charging around the corner and they'd pulled apart. Mitch was quickly talking and laughing with his friends. But Darcy was in a dream, and she stayed there all the way home.

"So I suppose you'll both be working on the Heartland Project we've been reading so much about in the papers?"

Darcy's mind snapped back to the present. She and Mitch would be working on finishing up the Bermuda Woods assignment, but she knew it was possible it could flow seamlessly into this new project. She hadn't considered that before.

Mitch was looking at Mimi questioningly. "The Heartland Project? What's that?"

"You haven't heard of it? It's going to be huge. A planned community out in the Sargosa Hills. The whole town is buzzing about it."

Mitch raised an eyebrow as he looked at Darcy. She nodded. "We're bidding on a portion of it. But I don't think Mitch and I will be working on it, except in a peripheral way. I'm sure the old-timers have dibs on it. People like Ned Varner," she added for emphasis, naming the senior vice president of the firm.

Mitch looked thoughtful and Darcy wondered what he was thinking. It would indeed be interesting if he decided he wanted to get in on the biggest project ACW had ever been involved in. If they did win the bid.

"Let me get you something to drink," Mimi was saying, rising expectantly. "Some nice iced tea? Some lemonade?"

Realizing what Mimi had said, Darcy's heart sank. If he accepted refreshment, he'd be here forever. But Mitch quickly revived her hope as he started rising from the couch.

"Oh, no. I'd really better get going. I just wanted to stop by and say 'hi'. And to let you know I'm around if you need anything."

Mimi reached out and warmly took his hand. "I hope you'll come by and see us often."

His smile to her was just as warm. "I will."

Darcy sprang up. Inside, she was exalting. He was going! Great. All she needed was some time to get her thoughts together. Tomorrow he would know the truth.

"Yes, well, it's been awfully nice seeing you."

She pulled open the door and smiled, waiting for

him to make his way out onto the porch, mentally urging him forward.

And for just a moment, it looked like she was going to get her wish. He started toward the door. As he came even with where she was standing, he looked at her sideways. She gave him a tiny shrug and he shook his head just enough for her to see. She wanted to reach out and plant the palm of her hand between his shoulder blades and push him out the door, but she resisted, gritting her teeth with the effort. He was almost gone.

And then Mimi spoiled it all.

"Well, wait a minute," she said, frowning. "You can't go yet. You haven't even met the babies."

CHAPTER FOUR

DARCY froze, holding her breath.

"Babies?" Mitch was saying, just the way she'd imagined he would. "What babies?" He looked thunderstruck.

"Darcy's two little ones, of course," Mimi said. "The twins. Didn't you know?"

He turned back into the room. His gaze met hers.

"You've got babies?" He said it as though he was sure there had to be some sensible answer to this puzzle, hopefully one he could accept.

"Bring them out, Darcy," Mimi was urging. "Let Mitch see them."

She licked her dry lips. This was not the right way to do it. "Uh, they're sleeping."

"Already?" Mimi looked skeptical. "You just put them in there. How did you get them to sleep so fast?"

"Magic powers?" she quipped, still hanging on to her last shred of hope.

The sound of a crash came from the bedroom, and hope was gone.

"Noisy sleepers," Mitch said dryly, his steel-colored eyes penetrating. "I'm guessing your powers aren't quite what you thought they were."

Darcy managed a tremulous smile, then turned on her heel and headed for the bedroom to see what had happened. Mimi and Mitch were close behind her. There was no way to stop this now. He was going to see the boys. And what was he going to see when he looked into their blue eyes, so like his own? Was he going to recognize parts of himself staring back at him? And if he did, what was he going to do about it? Apprehension shivered through her.

She opened the bedroom door to reveal a scene of minor chaos. Somehow, Sammy had gotten out of the crib and made his way to the changing table, which he had tried to climb, knocking down the baby powder, which landed on his head. There he sat on the floor, covered with powder and grinning broadly, very pleased with himself. Meanwhile Sean sat in his own crib, looking through the bars at his brother and laughing with a silly hiccuping sound. Sammy tried to clap his hands. He missed, but he did manage to send up a cloud of baby powder, making Sean laugh even harder.

"He climbed out!" Darcy cried, looking at the extra-high bars she'd paid extra for. "How did he do that?"

"Oh my," Mimi said, shaking her head. "How could one little boy do so much damage in such a short time?"

It took a few moments and Mimi's help to get things back in order. Darcy murmured a few stern words, then a few more soft reassurances to Sammy as she cleaned him up and then safely installed him back in bed. In the meantime she'd forgotten all about Mitch standing there, watching it all, until she turned and saw him leaning against the doorjamb.

Meeting his gaze, she tried to read what he was thinking from the look in his eyes, but his gaze was hard, hooded. She deliberately lifted her chin. She was proud of these little guys and she wanted to show that.

"Mitch, this is Sammy and this is Sean. My boys." She made a flourish and waited to see what he would say.

Mitch was numb. This changed everything. Darcy had children. Twin boys. And they looked way too familiar for comfort.

His first thought was that these must be Jimmy's children. After all, Darcy was living here with Jimmy's mother. It seemed logical. But there was a problem with that theory. He couldn't remember exactly what color eyes Jimmy had, but he was pretty sure they weren't blue. Darcy had eyes that flashed almost ebony. And these little boys had the bluest eyes he'd ever seen—outside of his own baby pictures. In fact, these babies could have been stand-ins for him and his brother.

He turned and looked at Darcy. She looked at him. There was an air of defiance in her face. He felt like he couldn't pull a breath in all the way.

"We need to talk," he said softly.

She nodded.

"Why didn't you want me to know?" he asked her bluntly as soon as they were far enough away from the house to speak freely.

Biting her lip she kept her head down. They were walking between two houses, heading for the open area of scrub pine that lined the canyon that ran just north of the neighborhood. Mimi had agreed to watch the babies for a while, to give them time to take a walk.

"I was going to tell you tomorrow, when we went for coffee," she said, wishing it didn't sound like an excuse.

He shook his head, rejecting her statement. "I don't know, Darcy. You weren't acting like someone who wanted to come clean." There was a real flash of anger in his voice. "You don't contact me for two years. You move to the place you know I've sworn I'll never go to again. When I show up, you act cagey." He turned to face her. His eyes were troubled and the muscles of his neck stood out like cords. "I don't buy it. You didn't want me to know."

She stopped and stared up at him, mouth open with astonishment. "What are you talking about? You're the one who stepped out into a crowd in Paris and never looked back. You might as well have stepped off the face of the earth. You certainly disappeared from my life without a second thought. I...I tried for months to find you."

She paused to steady her voice. She wasn't going to let emotions take over and the last thing in the world she wanted to do was cry.

"That had to be a very deliberate disappearing act to let you vanish so completely," she pointed out.

"You knew where I was going."

"Oh sure. Brazil." She threw up her hands and started walking again, mostly so she wouldn't have to look into his eyes. "It's a big country. But I suppose I could have called up the Brazilian phone company and asked to be connected to that tall, handsome American who went by various names but might have entered the country as Mitch Carver." She flashed a scathing look over her shoulder. "I'm sure they would have found you right away."

He sighed, shoving his hands down into his pockets. "Okay, I guess I wasn't the easiest person to find at the time," he admitted gruffly, his long stride keeping pace with her quick steps. "But you knew the kind of work I do. You knew I was going to be melting into other cultures. I told you what my life was like."

"You did. And that's fine. I can understand that."

She could understand it on a certain level. But she couldn't forgive the fact that he hadn't felt the need to contact her in any way. Had he forgotten her the moment he'd stepped on the plane? Had the time they spent together, time that had changed her life for good, been so meaningless to him? Was she just another woman in a string of affairs? Her heart cracked when she thought that way.

"I understand that you can't be tied down," she was saying. "I never really expected that of you. Not while I was sane, at any rate," she added, letting a note of sarcasm creep into her tone. "And I don't expect it now."

He swore softly, shaking his head. "What I don't get is, what made you so sure…?"

"That they're yours?" She swung around to face him, her eyes glittering. "I can't believe you could ask such a thing!"

He stared at her. "Darcy, I didn't ask it. I can see they're mine. You don't have to prove anything to me."

"Oh. Well, good." Her cheeks filled with color and heat, but the relief that also filled her blotted out any embarrassment. She hadn't really let herself formulate the fear, but now she knew she'd been dreading that he would want explanations and promises. And if he had demanded those things, she was ready to hate him.

As if that were possible.

Well, anyway, she'd been planning to be really, really angry. Only now, she didn't have to be. That left her with an empty space inside, but it quickly filled up with more yearning. She just couldn't help it. Even when she was angry with him, she couldn't turn off the feelings that surged in her when she looked at him.

They reached the edge of the canyon and both stopped, looking down at the sharp drop off into wild brush. Mitch's mind went back for a moment to when he and Jimmy had spent hours in all that wilderness as boys, losing themselves in adventure fantasies. He hadn't realized at the time that he would grow up to live some of those playacting scenes out in real life. He kicked at a rock and listened as it skittered down the side of the canyon, until it got lost in the underbrush.

"I guess we weren't as careful as we should have been, were we?" he mused, remembering that for the short amount of time they'd spent together, there had been an awful lot of chances to forget to be careful. Once they'd begun, they'd both been insatiable— probably because they knew they had so little time. What else could have made them so crazy?

"So what now?" he asked gruffly. "Do we get married, or what?"

"Oh!"

She let the small word out with so much outrage, he looked up in surprise. He was only trying to figure out what was expected in situations like this. He'd never been here before. Was he supposed to know everything?

"I wouldn't marry you if you were…" She clamped her lips shut, cutting off the cliché, but they both knew it by heart. She took a deep breath. "Let me put it this way," she said more carefully. "There are men who are fathers, and there are men who are biological donors." She glared at him. "We'll just put you into the latter category, okay? You've made your most important contribution. Now all we need from you is health information and maybe an occasional financial donation. And that, only when absolutely necessary."

He frowned. He didn't like the way she was putting things, but right now, he hadn't thought the situation through well enough to know what he wanted to say in rebuttal. Still, he did know he didn't want to shirk his duty in any way.

"Listen, Darcy, I agree that a marriage between you and me just wouldn't work out, but I definitely want to help you in any way I can. We need to figure how much money you'll need and I'll set up a monthly fund."

"No!"

She was cringing inside. How was it that he didn't understand that his offer was so hurtful she could hardly bear it—that it was even worse than his half-hearted mention of marriage that seemed so easy to brush away? That it was so obvious he just wanted to get the hell out of here. She closed her eyes, but only for a few seconds. She couldn't let herself weaken.

"I will take some help because I'm going to need it," she said, her voice rough as she tried to rein in her emotions. "But only enough to make sure the twins are okay." She drew in a deep breath. "But help is one thing. Taking over my life is another."

"Who said anything about taking over your life?"

She stared down into the canyon. "Those who give money always end up seeking control. It's human nature."

And then she wanted to bite her tongue. Why was she being so testy? This bristling edginess between them seemed so strange. They'd never been this way with each other before. In the old days, when he'd hardly glanced her way, she'd watched from afar, thinking he was the most wonderful thing in the world.

And then there had been Paris. The attraction between them had been immediate and explosive— a match being struck and igniting into instant flame. The joy of being together in that beautiful city, the ecstasy of the love they'd made in that narrow bed in his tiny hotel room, walking together down the wide boulevard and watching the dawn arrive over the spires and treetops of the sleeping city—it had all been a magical fantasy that she would cherish forever.

But that was then. This was reality, where they were giving each other scathing looks and tight-lipped smiles and acting as though they could barely stand to look at each other. What had happened? Was it just because of the babies?

She tried to imagine what it would have been like if there were no children, if he'd come back and found her much the way he'd left her. But no, it wouldn't be very different. Even without the babies, there was still the fact that he'd walked off and forgotten all about her in a few short moments after that weekend. And she'd been able to think about nothing else—until Jimmy's accident took center stage in her life. After all, when their eyes had first met in that washroom, there had been no spontaneous burst of joy between them. To the contrary, there had been an instant antagonism, an instant wariness—and it hadn't been just her.

Face facts, Darcy, she told herself bitterly. He's a love 'em and leave 'em guy who doesn't particularly care to find the ones he's left turning up on his doorstep. That much is obvious.

"Who knows about this?" he was asking.

"That you are their father? Nobody." She shrugged. "Nobody but you and me. And I think Mimi is probably figuring it out as we speak."

He nodded. "Okay. Do you want to leave it that way?"

No, of course she didn't. But what else could she say? She turned so that he couldn't see her face.

"I guess so. Especially since we're going to be working together. I think it would be best, don't you?"

He nodded again.

She looked back at him. "You might want to tell your parents."

His handsome face registered surprise. "Why would I do a thing like that?"

"They're grandparents and don't even know it. Don't you think they have a right to know?"

Slowly he shook his head. "They have nothing to do with my private life."

"Oh." She searched his face, puzzled by his attitude. His tone was so bitter. "I've met your father. I think he's a very nice man."

"Most people do."

She rolled her eyes, just a little. "I see. Those who don't know him like you do."

"You've got that right."

She frowned, shaking her head and searching his face for clues. "What did he do to you, Mitch?" she asked gently.

Something hard flashed in his gaze and he grimaced. "We're off topic," he said. "We were talking about the fact that you had two kids who are part mine and you didn't tell me about it."

She lifted her chin. "No. We're talking about the fact that I had two kids who are part yours and you wish I hadn't."

He stared down at her. How could he deny what she'd just said? It was true. She'd dropped a bombshell on him and he hadn't recovered from the impact yet. He really wasn't sure what he thought.

But one thing he knew for sure—babies or not, life-changing news or not, antagonism or not—he still wanted her like he'd never wanted any other woman. Every time he looked at her he felt that same pull, an attraction so strong, so deep, that it seemed almost physical. She drew him like a magnet. He longed for her, ached to hold her, hungered to feel that open, unrestrained response she'd given him in Paris. And yet, that seemed to be more and more impossible every moment. He could almost see the gulf widening between them. He hated that, but he had no idea how to stop it.

He'd been in a state of denial. He realized now that he'd felt this way for a long time. He'd dreamed about her on cold, empty nights in the Himalayas, seen her face in the reflective glass of windows on the streets of Brasilia, thought about her when he was alone and when he was in crowds. She'd been haunting him for two years. No wonder he'd finally had to come back.

But that didn't make any sense. He hadn't known she'd be here. He shook his head, rejecting that random thought. And yet...

Now, suddenly, the woman who obsessed him was the mother of his children. That brought him up short. What was he supposed to do with that? Emotions were churning inside him but he needed to sort them out. He wasn't sure what he thought, what he felt. He needed a little time to think it all over.

"Listen, Darcy," he said, turning to head back toward the house. "This has really knocked me for a loop. I can't seem to put together a coherent thought right now. I need some time."

She nodded. They walked back in silence, the crunching of the rocks beneath their feet the only sound. A cool breeze was kicking up, slapping her blond hair against her face. She shivered and drew her arms in close. As they came back in front of the house, she turned to him. Despite everything, she longed to have him love the boys the way she did. Maybe, if he got to know them...

"Do you want to come in?"

"No."

She drew back, startled at his abrupt tone of voice.

"No," he repeated, deliberately sounding gentler this time. "I think I'd better go. I've got to think about this."

She nodded, but her heart sank. He seemed to read her disappointment in her face, because he hesitated and added, "Darcy, you know I'm not used to this yet. You've had two years to get used to it. I'm just starting down that road."

"Sure," she said. "I understand."

He raked fingers through his hair and looked at her with a half smile. "Do you? That's good. Because I sure don't."

She could have used a sharp retort against him but she didn't. Something in the lost, bewildered look in his eyes stopped her. He really had been sent into a tailspin and needed to right himself before they talked more. She could see that. So she nodded when he said, "Goodbye."

"See you tomorrow," she said simply.

She watched him get into his car and start down the driveway. She stood where she was until he was out of sight.

"Why me?" she whispered to whatever power in the universe might be listening. "Surely there are others who deserve to be tortured much more than I do."

This was all so disturbing, but she thought she understood him to a point. Yes, she understood his need for time to think, but there was something she didn't understand. Or, maybe she understood it too well and just didn't like it. He didn't want to come in and see the babies again. Maybe he would never want to see them. That thought was like a knife through her heart. How could he turn his back on those two sweet babies?

And yet, what did she expect him to do? Oh sure, he could write a check and pretend that took care of everything. But what else did she want from him? It wasn't even clear to her yet. Something was bruised deep inside her and she tried to figure out just exactly why. She was hurt and disappointed that Mitch was acting like he didn't want the babies, but this was more. This had to do with his reaction to *her*.

Maybe it was for all she'd lost. She wasn't that girl anymore, that open and loving woman who'd clung to him and made love to him so freely, so full of joy. That girl was gone forever. She could no longer do things just because she wanted to. She had two little babies to care for. She had to take them into account before she did anything at all.

So maybe that was it—a sense of mourning for the lost Darcy of old.

"Whatever," she muttered to herself. "Good riddance, anyway."

But her eyes brimmed with tears.

* * *

"Has he gone?" Mimi asked as she came back into the house.

"Yes," Darcy answered. "Thanks for taking the babies for me. Are they down?"

"Yes indeed, and sleeping soundly. They were all worn out from their escapade."

Darcy smiled.

"Mitch is such a nice fellow," Mimi went on, bending to pick up a toy lodged halfway under the couch. "He was always one of my favorites of Jimmy's friends. Even with that mother of his."

"His mother? Do you know her well?"

"Not well, but of course we had to deal with each other over the years, our sons being friends and all." She stopped and considered, head to the side. "I always had the feeling that she wished Mitch would find someone else to spend his time with, someone from the wealthy neighborhood they lived in. But that could have been my imagination, I suppose."

Darcy nodded. "I had a similar feeling the day I tried to talk to her about getting in touch with Mitch."

"Oh. I see."

She saw everything and knew everything. Darcy shook her head, half laughing. "Oh, Mimi, the answer is yes, Mitch is the father of my babies."

Mimi shook her head, looking bemused. "Well, come on into the kitchen and have a cup of tea with me," she said, "and tell me all about it. This is a story that's been a long time coming, so it better be good."

Darcy laughed lovingly as she turned to follow her friend. She knew Mimi was still disappointed that she and Jimmy hadn't clicked romantically, but she was bighearted enough to want the best for Darcy anyway. And for the babies.

"It's a fairly short story," she warned. "But I'll see what I can do to embellish it for you."

"You do that," Mimi said approvingly. "And I'll brew the tea."

CHAPTER FIVE

IT HAD been three long days since Mitch had returned. He and Darcy had been working together for two of them, and he hadn't said a word about the twins. She'd started out on pins and needles, jumping every time he came near, waiting for him to bring up her babies and get things settled between them. But he was acting for all the world as though that afternoon at Mimi's had never happened. And she was rapidly losing patience with him.

"Why didn't you want me to know?" he'd said to her accusingly.

Well, Mitch, maybe this was why. Maybe it was because I knew you wouldn't react the way I wanted you to react. Maybe it was because you're just a big jerk.

Not really. After all, how could she criticize him for acting right in line with the way he'd warned her. He didn't want kids, didn't want to be tied to one woman, or tied down in Texas. So what did she expect?

Still, she came into work resolved on the fourth day. This was the day. It was time. She was going to confront him, get everything out in the open, make sure they each knew where they stood. She'd pumped herself up. She was ready to make him deal with the situation.

Sitting down at her desk, she was a model of fierce determination, drumming her fingers on the heavy wood and waiting for him to show his face.

And then she heard the laughter in the hallway. Turning, she beheld the spectacle of Mitch being escorted into the office suite by a bevy of the building's most attractive young women, all seemingly in a party mood. They giggled and called out teasing suggestions as they left him, and he looked very pleased with himself as he waved them off.

As the elevator doors closed on the last of them, he turned back to favor Darcy with a crooked grin. His tie was pulled open, as was the neck of his crisp white shirt. There were lipstick marks on his cheek and neck. His blue eyes were dancing with pure male happiness.

"Good morning," he said.

She couldn't respond. Something was choking her.

"Uh…sorry I'm a little late," he added, shrugging with boyish helplessness. "Some of the girls asked me to come in early for a meeting. I didn't realize they were planning a little surprise 'welcome back' party for me."

"I see," she managed to get out, and darned frostily, too.

But it was no use pretending. All her confidence was draining away, as though someone had pulled the plug on her reservoir. She didn't need to be reminded of what an attractive man he was. Women responded to him the way flowers turned toward the sun. It was a natural phenomenon she couldn't have stopped if she'd wanted to. She knew he had a thousand other options besides dealing with her and her twin boys.

So where was this confrontation she'd been planning? He walked on into his inner office, whistling tunelessly, and she closed her eyes. No confrontation, no settling of things. What was she trying to prove, anyway? If he wanted to be a part of her life, he would have said so by now. If he had any interest in the babies, he would have asked about them, or come by to see them. She couldn't make him care. If it wasn't there, it just wasn't going to be and she might as well face it.

Hurt and anger simmered inside her, but she tamped them down. She had work to do, and luckily, a reason to get out of the office and leave all this behind for most of the day. She had a few loose ends to attend to and then she was off on a field trip—and as far away from Mitch as she could get in one business day. The trick would be to avoid him and get out of here before he knew she was going.

Working quickly, she spent the next hour clearing up the work left over from the day before. She was almost ready to leave when she heard him coming back out of his office and she started typing furiously, concentrating like a laser beam on her work. Maybe he would notice how busy she was and go on by. She could always hope.

"Ah, Darcy," he said, almost as though he hadn't already seen her that morning. "There you are."

She sighed. Oh well. Looking up, she threw him a glance with the hint of a glare.

"You're right," she said tartly. "Here I am. Just like always. On time and with my wits about me." She stacked a few folders as though that was a very important thing to do right now.

He stood right over her and she didn't have to look up to know he was smiling. She knew he actually enjoyed it when she didn't play the docile employee. Why did she keep providing him with red meat this way? She couldn't seem to help herself.

Though they'd been working together for days now, she'd managed to avoid too much direct contact. Luckily he'd been spending a lot of time in meetings. Even luckier, the requirements of her job kept her out of the office a lot of the day. She was planning to do as much fieldwork as possible from now on.

"I'll agree you've got a strange sense of humor about you," he was saying. "But wits? We'll see."

He was trying to make a joke, trying to lighten the mood between them. But she didn't want it lightened. She made another careful pile of folders.

"I'm busy," she said without looking up.

"As usual," he noted. "But maybe you can spare me a minute or two."

She finally raised her head and reluctantly met his gaze. She'd been right. He was silently laughing at her.

"What can I do for you?" she asked with as much regal chill as she could manage.

"You can type up these meeting notes for me." He waved pages of yellow paper with a lot of things scribbled on them in her direction. "Okay?"

She looked at them. Her impulse was to grab them and start typing away. After all, it wouldn't really take all that long. But she stopped herself. She had to guard against letting him put her into a role she didn't deserve. So instead of accommodating him, she flashed him a look and shook her head.

"No, actually, I can't. Give them to Paula."

"She's out this morning."

"She'll be back."

"Maybe."

He still stood there, waving the papers at her.

She glared at him. "I guess I need to remind you again. I'm not a typist."

He frowned as though he didn't understand the word. "You're not a what?"

"A typist." She rose and opened a drawer, pulling out her little molded purse. It was obvious he thought she was being silly, but she didn't care. She'd worked hard to achieve her position and she wasn't going to let him discount it.

"I'm also not a secretary. I'm not even an administrative assistant. In fact, if you think about it really hard, I'm sure you'll recall that I'm a property acquisitions agent."

She tucked the purse under her arm and started toward the elevator, looking back at him over her shoulder.

"And I'm off to do some acquiring work right now. In fact, I'm late for a meeting with a contractor on the Pearson Development. So if you'll excuse me…"

He was following her, looking interested. "You're meeting with him right now?"

"Yes. I'm going out to Shadow Ridge."

"Great. I'll go with you."

Stopping dead, she swung around to face him. "What?"

He shrugged, looking remarkably handsome and civilized now that he'd wiped off the lipstick and straightened out his dark blue suit and the silver-blue tie. "Why not? I've got to get to know more about this business. You can show me the ropes."

She sagged. The last thing she needed was to spend the day carting him around and feeling resentful while doing it. "But Mitch…"

He was taking no arguments. "Look, Darcy. I'm like someone who's been dropped out of the sky here. I mean, I know I used to work here part-time when I was in high school and college, but I never paid much attention. I only wanted to get out of this town as soon as I could. On the whole, you know a lot more about this business right now than I do. If I'm going to do a decent job, I've got to learn. You can teach me."

She was supposed to teach him all she knew? Hah! That would be the day. She'd come by her knowledge the hard way, and he could do the same. Still, she couldn't deny him a seat in her car. If only there was some way she could talk him out of coming with her.

"You're going to miss lunch," she warned him hopefully.

"Lunch." He narrowed his eyes speculatively. "Are you talking about those cardboard slices of bread with some kind of fish substance slathered between them that they sell in the break room vending machine? Hmmm. Yes, that is a lot to give up just so that I can ride out into the warm sunny day to a rural area and listen to builders talk building. But sacrifices must be made." He gave her a lopsided grin that was, unfortunately, totally endearing. "Besides, we can grab something on the road. A hamburger maybe."

Folding her arms over her chest, she frowned, feeling sulky. "I don't 'grab things on the road.'"

He smiled, leaning across her to press the button for the elevator. "Don't worry. There's nothing to it. I'll show you how."

"Oh brother!"

"Besides," he said, his smile fading and eyes darkening seriously as he leaned close to say it softly, "we have some things to talk about. This will give us a chance to do that."

Her heart began to thump in her chest. So he wasn't going to ignore their situation after all. Well, good. Maybe. But just the fact that he thought they could discuss things on the fly given an odd moment or two didn't bode well. You just didn't make life commitments that way, did you?

As they hit the highway and left city traffic behind them, her anxiety began to melt away. How could she stay tense when that big ole Texas sky was shockingly blue and almost cloudless above them? There was something irresistible about an open road. She relaxed, her hands loose on the wheel.

Mitch had been quiet since they'd left the parking

garage. Glancing at him sideways, she wondered what he was thinking. Was he preparing what he wanted to say to her? Or was he still mulling things over? Why didn't he just go ahead and get it over with? She had a feeling it must be really bad if he couldn't just spit it out on the spot.

Now she was getting tense again. This was no good.

"What kind of music do you like?" she asked, suddenly wanting something to fill the silence between them.

"You choose."

She hesitated. "Well, are you still Texan enough to take in a little country and western? Or have you become too cosmopolitan and sophisticated for us hayseeds?"

"Am I still Texan?" He turned toward her, appalled by the question. "Is the Pope Catholic?"

She refused to give him a smile. "Last time I looked."

"There's your answer." He snorted. "Am I Texan?" he repeated, and for good measure, he sang her a few lines from a popular song, finally coaxing a smile from her.

"Not bad," she had to admit. "You're a man of many talents, aren't you?"

He laughed softly. "Darcy, I have only just begun to reveal myself to you."

She shook her head but she knew he was still

feeling a bit full of himself after the way all those women had treated him that morning. He stretched out his long legs as best he could in the confinement of the car, and suddenly she was very much aware of him as a man—a man with a hard, gorgeous body, which she remembered only too well. She caught her breath as memories flooded her for a moment, pictures of his golden form stretched out on white sheets in lamplight.

Oh my. She hadn't thought of that for ages—and she really should block those things out of her mind, if she possibly could. She started to reach to turn up the air-conditioning, then caught herself just in time. But she couldn't stop the heat from flooding her cheeks, and she was only glad he seemed too occupied with the passing landscape to notice.

"You know, Darcy, you've got a few surprising facets to your persona as well," he said a few minutes later, turning toward her again. "It was a real shock to find out you had… the twins." His voice deepened. "I have to admit, though I thought of you often over the last two years, I never pictured you as a mother."

Well, that was just downright annoying. Sure, she was a mother. But that very fact made him a father. He seemed to be forgetting that part.

"I never thought of you as a Texas businessman," she shot back. "So we're even."

He frowned. "I'm not a Texas businessman," he protested.

"No?"

"Not really. Only temporarily."

"Well, cleaned up like you are, you could pass for one."

"Gee, thanks."

"Don't mention it."

They were silent for a moment, then he spoke again.

"So what *did* you think of me as?" he asked curiously.

She raised an eyebrow. "Fishing for compliments?"

"Not at all. Just curious."

She hesitated. What had she thought that day when she'd opened the door to Jimmy's pied-à-terre and found the hunky hero from her teenage years standing there in the Paris rain? He was exactly what any woman would have conjured up for herself if she'd had a magic wand. But what had come to mind at the time?

"An adventurer I guess." That wasn't exactly it, but the best she could come up with on short notice.

"An adventurer." He said the word as though that startled him, as though he wasn't sure he liked it.

"That's not the way you see yourself?"

He shook his head, looking distracted. "No. Actually I see myself more as a human rights worker."

She looked at him in astonishment, then had to

swerve back into her lane. A human rights worker? And here she'd thought he was some sort of modern day mercenary. Maybe they had different ways of defining that term.

"You're kidding. Right?"

He sighed. "Never mind. For now, I guess I'm a businessman."

"So that's for sure, is it?" she asked, turning onto a smaller two-lane road. "You're saying that this return to your home town isn't permanent? That it's just something temporary in order to make your mother happy for a while?"

That seemed to offend him. "Leave my mother out of this," he said gruffly.

She looked at him in surprise. After all, he was the one who had originally brought the subject up. She hadn't realized it was out of bounds.

But he seemed to recognize what she was thinking.

"Sorry," he said. "I'm sort of defensive about my mother right now. I'm feeling a little protective."

Mitch protective toward his mother. She'd thought rebelling against his family situation had been the whole point. That was the impression she'd had from what he'd told her in Paris. Obviously she didn't have a handle on the full picture.

She pulled the car into the parking lot at the construction site. The twin mobile trailers, which served as the administration and engineering offices, sat in front of where they'd parked. Switching off the engine, she turned to look at the man beside her.

"I'm not sure why you came back," she told him candidly, "but since you did, we need to settle the business about the twins. We can't leave it up in the air the way it is now. Just what is your role going to be in their lives?"

He didn't answer right away, but he was studying her face, his gaze sliding over her lips, her nose line, her smooth skin, then tucking into the protected area around her ear. When his gaze finally rose to meet hers, she saw a sort of storminess there. But only for a moment.

"We'll talk," he promised. "Later today. Right now, we've got work to do." He turned away and reached to open the door. "Let's get this show on the road."

She followed more slowly, wondering what she was going to do with this man who wanted her to "show him the ropes." She should resent him, but somehow she just couldn't do that. Still, she had to be careful. "Give him an inch and he'll take a mile," she whispered to herself, shaking her head. That was just it. Keep track of your inches!

It was over an hour later when they emerged from the trailers. Darcy was feeling a bit shell-shocked. The meeting had started as usual. She and the contractor had gone over some figures and discussed a timetable. She'd brought up a few minor issues she'd had problems with and he tried to smooth over her concerns. All the while, Mitch had watched silently. And then he asked a question about the Heartland Project.

It was like he'd lit a fuse. The contractor seemed to take his question as a challenge, and before Darcy knew what was happening, the two men were shouting at each other and arguing about things she thought were pointless. She tried to intervene, but they didn't seem to hear her. They argued sharply, then came to an agreement about something. What it was she couldn't have said.

Then, as quickly as it had started, the firestorm was over. The two men had found a point in common and were talking like—well, maybe not old friends, but old acquaintances, at least. And as they left the trailer, the contractor shook her hand warmly and told her he would take care of all her little items, no problem.

"Thanks, Darcy," Mitch was saying as they walked back toward the car. "I learned a lot." He grinned. "I especially learned that I'd better leave the talking to you whenever possible."

"On that point," she said, sliding in behind the wheel, "I think I agree."

He glanced over as she started the engine. In truth, he'd been impressed by the way she'd handled herself. She was good at what she did, good at talking to contractors, good at holding her own when the going got tough. Funny how that opened a whole new side of her to him, a side he'd never thought about during that weekend in Paris.

But it didn't change anything. It didn't help him to get over this weird fascination. He still wanted her with a deep, throbbing ache that wouldn't go away, no matter how much he tried to ignore it.

He'd spent the last two days trying to figure out a way this was going to work. At first he'd thought maybe he would get used to having her around all day. After all, there were plenty of other beautiful women at ACW. Just that morning he'd flirted with a lot of them. Unfortunately, as pleasurable as it had been to be lionized by a group of lovely ladies, he'd found himself looking at his watch and wondering whether Darcy had come in to work yet long before his welcome party was over.

Which just went to prove that this situation was impossible. He couldn't work with her. It was slow torture to see her and not be able to touch her. He looked at her now as she turned onto the highway. She was wearing a short, tailored skirt that rode up enough to display a nice view of her gorgeous legs. Just watching the interplay of muscles as she worked the accelerator made his blood begin to race a little faster.

It was a bittersweet reaction that came up all the

time. A part of him reveled in his instant response to this woman, and another part rejected it, trying to turn it back before it caused him to make another mistake.

But it still happened every time she walked past him and he caught a hint of her fresh, sweet scent, every time she spoke to someone else in the outer office and he sat with his eyes closed listening to her cool, rich voice, every time she got up from her desk and he watched surreptitiously as she walked away toward the elevator, her silky hair rippling sensually, her round little bottom swaying impertinently, while sweet desire surged in his body, and cold, hard reproach stirred in his brain. No other woman had ever played with both his mental and physical response the way Darcy Connors did. He loved it and hated it at the same time.

And that was why he should be working to get her out of his daily life.

"How close are we to the perimeter of the Heartland Project?" he asked suddenly, realizing they must be passing near it.

She looked at him sideways. "There's a pullout at that hill ahead that gives a pretty good overview of the eastern boundary," she said. "I've got a pair of binoculars in the glove compartment."

"Great. Let's stop and take a look."

"Sure."

She pulled off the highway at the viewing area, rolling up to the thick guardrails.

"Here we are," she noted.

"Great," he said. "I really want to get a good look at this." He gazed at her earnestly. "But first I want to talk about our situation for a minute."

She threw him a startled look, but she did as he suggested, turning off the engine and turning toward him in the car. She didn't say a word, waiting for him to take the lead.

"Okay, here's the deal," he said firmly, determined not to show how mixed his feelings were about her. "We can't deny that we made two children together. And of course that it's as much my problem as yours."

She reacted as though he'd attacked her. "My babies are not a *problem*!"

He frowned, regretting his wording. "Darcy, relax. I didn't mean it that way exactly."

She was glaring at him. "Obviously they are a problem for you."

He sighed, not sure how they'd gotten off to such a bad start so quickly. "That's really not fair, Darcy. You knew from the beginning that my life was going to be nomadic. That I never expected to have a wife or kids because I couldn't be fair to them. I never pretended otherwise."

She took a deep breath and nodded. "I know," she said softly, her tone almost as good as an apology.

"Okay. Listen, first of all I want to commend you for having the babies. I know that's easy for me to say, not being with you or even knowing it was happening at the time. You went through it all by yourself for nine months. I can't tell you how sorry I am. And how much I admire you for it."

"It was a beautiful period of my life," she said somewhat defensively. There had been plenty of not-so-beautiful things about it, of course, but she wasn't going to whine about them.

"That may be," he said. "But I know it was hard."

She bit her lip. If he kept being so nice about things, she would start to cry. Her eyes were already stinging and she knew what that meant, but she refused to let it happen. She would not cry in front of him! If tears came she was going to jump out of the car and throw herself over the edge and into the canyon.

Well, not really. But thinking that gave her the strength to hold back the emotions that tried to overwhelm her.

"So, tell me this," he went on, staring out at the plains stretching out away from their position instead of looking her in the eye. "Why didn't you put them up for adoption?"

A sense of shock, very near horror, shot through her. Anger came tumbling behind it, but she pushed it back. She was going to stay calm if it killed her.

"I guess I'm just too selfish," she said gently.

He nodded. "You did consider it?"

"Of course. I went for counseling about it. I met some wonderful couples looking for babies, people who would have given my boys a great life, probably better than anything I can give them. But in the end…" She shook her head. "I just couldn't do it. I wanted them so much."

He nodded again. "Okay. And you're holding to that decision?"

She stared at him. Just the fact that he could ask a question like that showed how little he understood what parenthood was all about.

"Are you asking me to consider giving them up now? Are you insane?"

He held up a hand. "Okay, okay. I just wanted to make sure. I want to get things perfectly clear between us." He shifted uncomfortably in his seat. "I think we need to establish a base so that we can figure out how we're going to do this. I want to provide for them in an equitable way so that the burden isn't entirely on you."

She stared at him, vaguely aware that he was still talking, going on about monthly payments and trust funds and clothing allowances. He hadn't said a thing about the boys themselves. He wanted to start writing checks to remove himself from the entire mess. He just didn't get it, did he? The anger that had been simmering bubbled up.

"Stop," she said firmly. "I don't want to hear it. It's not money that I need from you."

He looked surprised. "If you're talking about… well, commitments, Darcy, you know I can't…"

She looked away, avoiding his eyes. "I know that. I'm not asking you to completely change your life around."

"So what exactly are you asking from me, Darcy?" he asked softly.

She closed her eyes. It was a darn good question. What she wanted in her heart of hearts was something impossible and she didn't even bother bringing it up. Opening her eyes again, she turned and met his gaze. This was so important. If only she could find the right words to make him understand how very important it really was.

"I've tried to think this through and define what's best for the boys," she said. "They need a dad. You're the first choice. You don't have to marry me to be their dad, you know. If you could imagine just being a presence in their lives…"

Her voice choked and she stopped. He made a move toward her, but she pulled back.

"If you don't think you can do that," she went on in a rush, "I wish you'd tell me right away. Because I'll have to find someone else to be their father-figure."

His blue eyes registered shock at that. "What do you mean?"

She straightened her shoulders, regaining her strength. "I think that was pretty clear. I'll need to marry someone. Someone else," she added hastily.

"Someone else? Who?"

She shook her head, feeling stronger all the time. "Oh, I don't know. There are a few candidates."

"Kevin?" he asked, a hint of scorn in his tone.

She shrugged. "He's a possibility. But actually, I was thinking more along the lines of…" She hesitated, wondering if she really wanted to say this, then rushed ahead. "Bert Lensen in accounting."

"Bert Lensen?" He frowned. "Isn't he that short, chubby, balding guy?"

"Yes. Very nice man. Not married. Seems to like me. Always asks about the twins."

"Uh-huh" He shook his head, looking skeptical. He was beginning to suspect he was being snowed. "I don't know, Darcy. I just don't see you with a man like that."

"No?" Her eyes flashed. "Well, think again. He's perfect, actually."

"Perfect! You're not serious."

"Sure. I'm not looking for a weekend fling," she said pointedly. "I'm looking for a 'slow and steady wins the race' sort of guy. I need a real father for my children. I need someone reliable."

"Unlike me."

She drew breath deep down into her lungs. She

could read a deep sense of injury in his gaze. She hadn't meant to hurt him, just make him think a little.

"That's not what I said."

"But it's what you meant." He turned away. "Face it, Darcy. Using your criteria, I'm not good enough to be the father of my own children."

"Mitch! I never said that!"

"You didn't have to say it. It's obvious." He raked his fingers through his hair. "And damn it all," he said gruffly, shifting back to look at her, "you might be right."

She was not going to make a comment. And this had all the signs of a conversation going nowhere. Maybe they needed to take a break from it.

"We ought to get going," she said, staring hard into his blue eyes.

"Sure," he responded, holding her gaze with his own.

Something sizzled in the air between them. The air was suddenly thick and hot and she felt as though she couldn't breathe.

"Why don't you grab those binoculars and let's go take a look at the landscape," she said, reaching for the door handle and making her escape.

He stayed where he was for a moment, watching her get out of the car and walk over to the railing. This was just plain nuts. He'd never felt so out of control.

He'd always prided himself on being able to stay detached from the women he had relationships with. He was up-front about what could be expected. No one he'd ever dated had cause to complain—and he'd never stayed in one place or with one woman long enough to build up any sort of commitment expectations.

But everything had gone out of whack with Darcy. From the moment their gazes had met in the rainy doorway, it had been as though something were drawing them together. He'd never felt this way before. And now, when she started talking about marrying Bert Lenson… The first thing he'd felt was an ugly urge to go beat the poor guy to a pulp. The thought of another man touching her was like a knife in his gut. He couldn't stand it. But as of this moment, he had no real claim to her.

Nothing was making any sense.

Swearing softly to himself, he took the binoculars from the glove compartment and left the car to join her at the railing.

CHAPTER SIX

"Look," Darcy said, making a wide sweep with her arm. "Texas in the noonday sun. Isn't she beautiful?"

Mitch heard the emotion in her voice and started to smile, but then he looked at what she was presenting to him and he frowned instead. He gazed at the rolling hills, the scattered stands of pecan and live oak, the rocky creek bottoms. A red-tailed hawk was circling a water hole and he thought he caught sight of a white-tailed deer flashing into a thicket.

It suddenly occurred to him that she was right. Why was it he had never noticed before? Texas *was* beautiful.

He'd spent most of the last few years in countries where deep green jungles and jagged mountains and turquoise water defined beautiful landscape. This was a different type of beauty and it resonated deeply with something in his inner core—his heart and soul.

Texas was home. It had been a long time since he'd thought of it that way.

He turned and looked at Darcy. She was trying to figure out just where the borders of the Heartland Project stood and she took the binoculars from him to check. He watched the breeze ruffle her hair, exposing her tiny ear. It curled like a pink shell against her head. He wanted to touch it, run a finger around its curve. He moved closer and she looked up from the binoculars, startled to find him so near.

"Uh…I think we can see the border better from that ledge just through those bushes," she said, gesturing toward another vantage point. "I'll go take a look."

She turned and went quickly, as much to flee from the look she'd seen in his eyes as anything else. Her heart was thumping in her chest. She pushed her way through the brush, looking back to see that he was following. And then a branch tangled with her hair.

"Ouch!" She stopped, caught by the bramble, yanking at it and only making matters worse.

"I'll get it," he said, reaching into her hair and prying the tangle loose.

She closed her eyes. He was much too close. She couldn't breathe. He was going to touch her. She knew it without being told.

And there it was. His fingers were still wrapped in her hair, but his lips were on her neck.

"Oh!" she cried, trying without a lot of success to pull away. She swung around to look at him. "Don't."

He held her face in his hands. "Darcy, I can't…"

Can't what? she wondered a bit hysterically, but she knew. He couldn't stop this. Well, neither could she. So who was going to do it?

When his mouth covered hers, she whimpered, as though he were fulfilling a need she'd held back too long, and she opened to him greedily. His hand on her face, his body so close, his mouth on hers. All felt so good, she was afraid she would sink into this ecstasy and never come up for air.

She had to pull away. She had to break this off. She couldn't let this go on for another minute.

Well, maybe just a minute. Or two. For just a little while, could she let herself touch heaven again?

No! She had to be strong. She had to think of her twins.

That did it. She finally pulled away from him, breathless and angry with herself.

"Oh, Mitch!" She wiped her mouth with the back of her hand while staring into his clouded eyes. "Promise me you won't ever do that again."

"I can't," he said very softly, his gaze never leaving hers.

Shaking her head, she tore away from him and hurried back to the car. He caught up with her before she reached it, grabbing her elbow and pulling her around to face him. The moment she looked into his eyes, she was relieved. He looked like a different person.

"You're right, Darcy," he said calmly, dropping her arm when he could see she wasn't going to run. "Of course you're right. And I'm sorry."

She nodded. "Me, too," she said.

He took a deep breath. "We've got too much emotional baggage between us. We've got to deal with it. We didn't settle things about the twins."

She nodded again. "No, we didn't, did we?"

He grimaced. "We got sidetracked with you talking about marrying Bert Lenson."

She rolled her eyes. "I'm not marrying Bert Lenson."

"Then why did you throw his bald-headed hat into the ring?"

I was only trying to scare you. She couldn't say that out loud, but it was the truth—though she didn't even want to admit it to herself.

"I was just using him as an example of the kind of man my boys need in their lives. I just wanted you to understand the reality of the situation. You should know what's going on."

He shrugged. "You know, I'm a little surprised you even think I should have any say in the matter."

She hesitated. "Look, Mitch. I know you can't be

the sort of father I would want for them. But you are their biological father. We have to go from there."

He nodded, searching her eyes. "Just by saying that, you give up a certain amount of control. You understand that, don't you?"

She nodded. "Yes. I know."

He shook his head, studying her as though he could hardly believe what he saw. "I have to admire your integrity for that. It takes guts to take that sort of risk."

She quickly dampened her dry lips with her tongue. "You know, in a funny way, I trust you. I know you'll do the right thing, whatever we decide that will be."

They stared at each other for a long, long moment.

"Okay," he said, taking her hand to lead her back to the car. "We haven't decided what to do, but we've decided to trust each other. That's a step in the right direction."

She nodded. It really was.

They were back on the road in minutes, pulling out onto the two-lane route, heading back toward the city. Mitch stretched and let out a deep breath. "We need to get something to eat," he said brightly.

"Speak for yourself," she responded tartly.

He looked at her, bemused. "Okay, I will. I could eat a horse."

She almost smiled. "That's a dangerous thing to threaten out here in horse country."

She could see his slow grin out of the edge of her vision. "I'll make do with a burger," he said. He sat up straighter in his seat. "And I know just where we can get one."

"Where?" she asked skeptically. They were out in the middle of nowhere. She hadn't seen a gas station for miles, much less a hamburger stand.

"Turn right on the Sorrel Highway." He pointed out the sign just ahead. "It's been years, but I think it'll still be there."

She turned where he'd indicated, but the land looked empty in that limitless way that didn't bode well for hamburgers. How many miles would he want to go before giving it up as a lost cause?

"It's got to be out this way," he reassured her. "I remember it well. My grandfather had a cattle ranch in the Sargosa Hills and I used to go out and help him work the place sometimes on summer vacations. There was this old recluse of a guy—think of your ultimate stereotype of the old prospector with a pickax on his shoulder and a mule by his side. His name was Ry Tanner."

He scanned the horizon, then pointed as a ramshackle building came into view. "There it is! See that bed and breakfast? That's got to be the place. Stop there."

Darcy frowned doubtfully as they pulled up in front of the ancient building. A two-story frame in a rustic Victorian style, standing out alone on the treeless plain, it looked like a survivor of another age. The sign said, Tree Stump Bed And Breakfast. Another sign, hanging by a tattered rope, said, Café. And there were a few tables and chairs set out on the browning grass of the front yard, in the shade of a small stand of cottonwood trees.

"Mitch, are you sure?" she began.

"Absolutely," he said, getting out of the car. "We can get some lunch here. Come on."

She followed him but she wasn't too keen on this. The place almost looked abandoned.

"I don't know," she murmured, frowning.

But Mitch was cupping his hands and calling toward the entry to the building. "Hello! Anybody here?"

There was a dusty silence for a moment, but just as Darcy was starting to turn away, a gruff voice came from the house.

"Go away. We're closed."

Mitch grinned, giving Darcy a wink. "It's him," he said before stepping closer. "Ry Tanner, ya ole re-probate. Is that you?"

There was a pause, then the voice sounded again. "We're closed, I tell you."

But Mitch had mounted the steps to the front door

and was peering in through the milky glass. "Ry Tanner, come on out here."

"Who's that?" the voice demanded.

"Mitch Carver." He spread out his arms. "Don't you remember me?"

The door opened a crack and a grizzled head appeared. "Mitch Carver! Is that you?"

"It's me, all right."

The door opened a bit more and the old man stood in the light. "What are you doin' here? I ain't seen you for years." His gnarled face turned and his beady black eyes took in Darcy, too. "And you got yourself a pretty girl. Poor thing. I never thought you'd find one would put up with ya."

Mitch laughed. "She doesn't. But that's another story."

The man shuffled out onto the porch and nodded toward the tables on the grass. "Come on over and set a spell," he said. "Out here in the cool breeze."

"We came to get some food," Mitch said as they followed him to the table.

He shook his gray head. "We're closed."

"A little snack will do. That's all we need."

Dropping down into a chair, Ry Tanner frowned at his company. "I told you, we're closed."

"No, we ain't." A plump, pretty woman who looked to be in her forties came out of the house.

"Don't listen to him," she said, smiling at them all. "He's just playin' hermit. You're old friends of his? Y'all sit down. I'll get you some food."

Ry grumbled, but it was becoming apparent that his grumbling didn't mean much. Darcy and Mitch sat down across from him and the woman, whose name was Betty, took their order and hurried into the house to prepare their food.

"You two married yet?" Ry demanded, glaring at Darcy.

"No!" they both said at once.

He nodded, looking at Mitch. "Good." He leaned closer, confiding. "But you watch out. Here's a life lesson, son. They try to trap you."

"Trap?" Darcy knew he was just an old man but she couldn't hide her outrage. "Why would I want to trap anyone?"

He glanced at her, then back at Mitch. "Marriage. That's all any woman wants, you know. She wants to pluck you off the vine and plunk you down into her own little teacup."

Darcy blinked at the strangely mixed metaphor.

"I have never tried to trap anyone into anything, much less marriage. And you know what? I'll tell you a secret." She leaned toward him conspiratorially. "I wouldn't marry him if he asked me to."

"See?" He waved a finger in the air. "That's the first trick they use. Playin' hard to get." He nodded knowingly, narrowing his eyes as he looked at her sideways. "Watch out for that one, my friend."

She shook her head. Mitch was silently laughing, his blue eyes dancing. She glared at him. He was having too much fun with this.

"The male ego never ceases to amaze me," she muttered.

Ry seemed to take offense. "Well then, what are you coming by here bothering people fer?"

Darcy's jaw dropped. This crazy old man! "We don't mean to bother you. Mitch just thought…"

He looked triumphant. "Ya see there?" He nodded to Mitch. "There she goes, takin' your side, letting you think she's defending you. That's number two on the roster. Write these down, son. You need to keep a list about you at all times. Ya gotta be prepared to counter their attacks."

Mitch was laughing, Darcy was confused between reluctant amusement and annoyance, and Ry Tanner seemed to be in his element now.

But Betty had her own advice. "Don't listen to him," she suggested as she put a pair of huge hamburgers, with fries, out in front of them. "He just likes to hear himself talk. Don't you, Pops?"

Ry grumbled, but the hamburgers were good and Darcy was famished. She had to admit the old man was like a piece of old Texas. He should be in a museum somewhere. But she couldn't say he was much of a lunch companion. Mitch seemed to have a strange affection for this old man, but she didn't think she could share it.

"So, Ry Tanner," Mitch was saying casually. "What do you know about the Heartland Project? I hear it's going in right next to you here, isn't it?"

Ry nodded. "Yes, that's true. They even wanted to buy out my land. But I'm hangin' tough." He shook his head. "We'll see."

Darcy's eyes widened and she stared at Mitch. The two men went on talking about the project, about what was being planned and how Ry's land might enter into the deal, but she hardly listened. So this was what Mitch had come along with her for, this was what had been his reason for hunting down Ry Tanner.

And here, a part of her had been thinking he might just have wanted to be with her. And that part of her had been reveling in that hope, hadn't it?

What a fool she was! In the first place, for wanting him to want to be with her. And in the second place, for wanting that despite the danger it posed. Was she crazy? So it seemed. That did it. She was going to have to be much tougher on herself from now on. After all, she'd fallen for this man's charm before. She had a record to live down. She had to be doubly careful.

Mitch had a devilish look in his eyes as they walked back to the car. She glanced at him suspiciously. "What?" she asked him.

He leaned against the car door and his gaze rose slowly to meet hers. "The Heartland Project," he said softly. "I want it."

She stared at him, mouth agape. "You're crazy!"

"Pipe down," he warned, laughing at her. "Get in the car. Let's not advertise it."

"There is no way you can get that project," she went on as she slipped into the driver's seat. "You know that, don't you? There are plenty of big boys after it. Ned Varner, for one."

"Ned Varner has been my family's nemesis for years, you know," he told her casually. "He makes moves every time he thinks my father's hold on the company is weak. Fear of what he was up to was the very reason my mother got me to come home."

"Oh. Well, I'm sure she was thinking defensively, not for you to try a suicidal move like trying for the Heartland Project."

His head rose and he had a steely look. "I'm going after it."

She was astonished at his crazy naive attitude. "What are you talking about? You don't have the experience, the background. You don't know what you're doing!"

"I could do it." His blue eyes were intense as they held hers. "You and me together. You can teach me the ropes. I'm a quick study."

Her breath caught in her throat. "Wait a minute.

Why would I be teaching you the ropes?" She threw her hands up. "If I know so much, why aren't I heading the project?"

"Because you don't have the credentials." Reaching out, he cupped her cheek in his hand and looked deeply into her eyes. "Let's face it, Darcy. They won't let you. But you and me together—we could do it."

His touch was something between fire and silk, and she knew it could act on her like a drug. She pulled away, shaking her head. "You're nuts," she said, starting the car.

She was fuming and he was making jokes. He wanted the Heartland Project, and he wanted to use her to help get it. Now wasn't that just special! If she wasn't careful she would get roped into having even more of her life taken over by this man. Who did he think he was, anyway?

But she knew the answer to that, didn't she? Oh! She wanted to scream.

Still, she managed to control herself and she was quiet most of the way back into town. So was Mitch.

Probably thinking over ways to get her to pull in the Heartland Project for him. That was not going to happen!

But how was she going to avoid it, working for him in that office every day? She'd known this was going to be a problem from the beginning.

"It's Friday night," he said suddenly, as they entered the city limits. "Date night. Have you got a date?"

"Yes, as a matter of fact, I do," she said, tossing her hair back and looking at him sideways.

"Oh." That surprised him. "So who's the lucky guy? Bert Lenson?"

Was that sarcasm she heard? Had to be.

"There are two of them, actually," she told him. "A couple of very special guys. We're planning to paint the town. If things really get hot, I might even let them stay up past their bedtime."

He'd realized what she was doing long before she wrapped it up and he waited, a twisted smile on his face. "The joys of motherhood," he said dryly.

That put her back up but she held back the sharp comment that came to mind. "I suppose you've got plenty of old girlfriends you could look up," she said instead.

He laughed. "Oh sure. There are old girlfriends of mine scattered all over the San Antonio area. Terra Dulce is crawling with them."

"I would have thought so."

He turned in his seat, shaking his head. "Are you crazy? Look how old I am, Darcy. All my old girlfriends are too busy organizing car pools for their kids to give me the time of day. Arguably some of them will be divorced, but still…"

"Ah, it's the kids that turn you off, is it?"

"I didn't say that."

She pulled onto the local freeway. They were almost back at work. "What do you have against kids?"

"I don't have anything against them," he said, though he sounded a bit too defensive. "I've dealt with kids before. Last year I hid out with a woman who had two kids and I spent a lot of time helping her take care of them. I can give bottles. I can even change a diaper if I have to. I don't want to. But I can. I'm not totally clueless."

But Darcy was still hung up on what he'd said at that beginning of that monologue. "'Hid out'?"

He sighed, hesitated, then shook his head. "It's a long story. Forget it for now. Someday I'll tell you all about it."

She could tell by the finality in his voice that these were his last words on the subject—for now, at least. She turned into the ACW parking lot and pulled into her space.

"Well, that was fun," she murmured, turning off the engine and starting to gather her things to get out of the car. And then she noticed he was still sitting there, making no move to exit. He had the look on his face that she was beginning to realize meant he had something he wanted to say. So she settled back into her seat and sighed.

"Okay. Out with it."

"Darcy, I've been thinking."

Here it came. He had big plans for things she could do to help him win that darn project.

"Yes?" she said.

He was quiet for a moment, then turned and looked into her face.

"Okay, here's the deal. I think we should get married."

"What?" She couldn't have been more surprised.

"I was thinking that maybe we should reconsider this marriage thing."

She was struggling for breath.

"Why?"

"If you look at it objectively, it's only fair. This whole situation is as much my fault as it is yours."

The man had experienced an epiphany. "Oh, you think so?"

He was frowning thoughtfully. "I realize I've taken too long to come to this decision, but you've got to admit, the twins threw me way off kilter. You had nine months to get used to the idea of having kids before they even got here. I didn't get that luxury."

"But Mitch…"

"It won't be a normal marriage," he added quickly. "I'll be gone most of the time. But at least we'll be married."

She stared at him. This was one spectacular turn-around—only a few hours ago he'd been staunchly declaring he would never marry. Or had she heard that wrong? Whatever it was, she didn't think she had better rely on it. Besides, he still hadn't mentioned the babies.

"Let me get this straight. We'll be married, but you'll be gone most of the time."

He nodded, his eyes bright with confidence. "That's about the size of it."

"I see." She gave him a wry smile. "So you want to tie me down while you are free to go off and do whatever strikes your fancy."

His look darkened a little. "Well, kind of. Though that isn't exactly the way I was thinking of it. You're putting it a bit unfairly."

She looked at him and laughed. She knew that a part of her would always be bound to him no matter what they did. But she had to stay hardened against him. He still hadn't made one gesture toward the boys. If he didn't feel anything for the twins, the rest of this was moot. She didn't even want him in her life.

"Darcy, think about it," he was saying, trying to be convincing. "It could work. There would be advantages. I could check in periodically, sort of like military guys do. If you could live with a part-time husband…"

"No."

"No?" He looked surprised.

Her steady gaze pinned him back. "It sounds like a great idea—for you. You'd be having your cake and eating it, too."

He thought about it for a moment, then shrugged. "What's wrong with that?"

"Mitch…"

"Okay, I'll put it this way." He grabbed her hand and brought it to his lips, then gazed at her over it. "Darcy, will you marry me?"

Something very like a butterfly was flapping around in her stomach. She was very close to being sick. This was so like what she'd dreamed of, and yet, it wasn't good enough. She pulled her hand away from him.

"I can't marry you."

"Why not?"

"You are not marriage material. We knew that from the beginning. Nothing's changed."

He stared at her, his blue eyes turned black as night in the dim light of the parking structure. "That's where you're wrong, Darcy. No matter what we decide here, everything's changed."

CHAPTER SEVEN

"You know," Darcy mused to herself in the mirror two days later. "Just when you least expect it, fate will step in and take control. Happens every time."

She'd been going crazy wondering what she was going to do about Mitch. She was half in love with the man and there were reasons for her to want him in her life. And yet, she knew very well that would lead to nothing but heartbreak in the long run. So it was just too dangerous being around him all the time. If she wasn't careful, he was going to lure her back into his influence and she was going to find herself agreeing to one of his loony ideas—like getting married. And that would be disastrous.

But now, like manna from the heavens, came a reprieve. That very morning, Mimi had announced that she had to go out of town.

"I'm so sorry to do this to you, Darcy. And at such a time. But my sister has fallen and wrenched her back. They might have to operate. She has no family to take care of her, and no money for nursing care, so I have to go."

"Of course you must go," Darcy told her, silently sending up a cheer as she realized the implications. "How long do you think you'll be?"

"Oh, two weeks at least."

"Oh, good."

"What?" Mimi looked puzzled.

Darcy gave her a dazzling smile and amended quickly. "I mean, you're so good—to your sister. She's lucky she has you."

"Well, I hate to leave you in the lurch. I'm going to call around to everyone I know and see if I can find someone to watch the babies."

"No, you're not," Darcy told her sweetly. "I'm going to watch them. I'll take some time off. I'll just have to stay home for a couple of weeks. It'll be perfect."

"Oh, but doesn't Mitch need you?"

Mitch can go pound sand! she thought, with vengeance on her mind. A couple of weeks away from Mitch—nothing could be better at a time like this. This would reaffirm her bond with her children plus she would get away from Mitch's influence. With a little bit of distance, maybe she could think things through more clearly. It was all good.

But aloud, she said, "He'll be fine. There are

plenty of women at ACW who would be happy to take my place, believe me."

She went in to work Monday morning with a spring in her step. She stopped by Human Resources to deal with the paperwork, then breezed into the office almost an hour after the workday had begun. Mitch scowled at her as she stood before him at his desk.

"Where have you been?"

Her bright smile was genuine. "Good morning to you, too."

His grouchy mood melted immediately. "Yeah, well… Hey, I missed you," he said lightly. "It was a long weekend."

Her smile grew a little more forced. He looked very appealing in the morning sunlight that streamed in from the huge windows, especially now that the look in his eyes had warmed. Just looking at him made her heart beat a little faster—which was exactly why she had to go.

"Well, I'm afraid that's something you're going to have to get used to," she said. "I'm not going to be here for a while."

His scowl was back and he rose from his chair. "What are you talking about?"

"I need to take a few days off."

His frown deepened. "Why?"

She wasn't really fond of his tone, so she developed a frown of her own. "I have some personal days coming," she said defensively. "I'm going to take them."

He looked angered and frustrated at the same time. "Why are you taking them now?"

She glared at him. "Do you have to know everything I do?"

"Yes." He hesitated, as though he rather regretted having said that. "After all, you're taking care of my children," he improvised.

"Oh, for heaven's sake." She gaped at him. The nerve of the man! He had the decency to look chagrined—but only for a moment before his natural arrogance reasserted itself.

"Okay," she said quickly. "This is what's happening. Mimi has to go take care of her sister in Dallas, so I'm going to have to stay home with the twins until she gets back."

He shook his head as though he couldn't see what that had to do with anything. "Can't you hire a sitter?"

"Mitch, these are babies. *My* babies. I would hire a stranger if I absolutely had to, but I don't have to. I have the time accrued. And I'm going to take it."

Frowning again, he rubbed a hand through his hair, making it stand up at crazy angles. "But you can't go now. We're wrapping up the Bermuda Woods job. That was your baby before I got here."

She threw out her hands. "You know very well

that is basically signed and sealed and only needs to be delivered. Skylar Mars can handle any loose ends."

"Skylar?"

"I talked to HR and set it up. She's taking my place. You know who she is. She was one of the ladies who had a morning party for you the other day. The redhead."

"Ah." His eyes lit up as he remembered her. And who could blame him? She was quite a beauty. But Darcy had to admit, that look on his face rankled. Still, it didn't last long. Very quickly he was frowning again.

"Well, she may be decorative and know how to present a plan, but does she have any experience with anything like the Heartland Project?"

Darcy hesitated. That was a sore spot. "She can call me for advice any time," she said. "I won't be going anywhere. Except the park." Come to think of it, she did have a few things planned. She began to count them off on her fingers. "And the market. And the doctor's on Wednesday. And the boys' playdate on Thursday. And…"

"Phone calls aren't the same as having first class expertise sitting right here in the office," he interjected impatiently.

Darcy knew that, but Skylar was about as good as he was going to get. "She's done property before," she reassured him. "She'll do everything you need."

He thought that over seriously, but when he met her gaze again he looked a little lost. "But you're what I need," he said, as though it surprised him, too.

Her heart gave a little jog, but she looked at him hard, sure he didn't mean that the way it sounded.

"Sorry," she said quickly. "I've got two weeks coming to me and I'm going to take them."

His face hardened and his tone did, too. Pleading wasn't working. He looked like he'd decided to resort to strong-arm tactics. "You can't. Not now."

She straightened her shoulders. "Yes, I can."

"I'm your boss, Darcy. And I say you can't."

"I've been working here longer than you and have more street clout," she asserted, knowing what she was saying was ridiculous. "More pull with the people who make this company work."

"Oh, yeah?"

"Yeah!"

He glared at her. "I'll have you fired."

Her chin was out a mile. "Great. You do that. That will solve all my problems."

Well, not really. But it would solve one. The big one. The one she was merely avoiding by staying away from him for two weeks. But it was a step in the right direction. Maybe with time, the problem would find its own solution. On the other hand, maybe she was just kicking the can down the road. Either way, she would have two weeks away from this emotional cauldron.

She looked at him, so tall and hard and handsome, and something very much like a lump rose in her throat. He stood silhouetted before his big picture window, looking like a big tycoon. He was the boss and he looked the part. No more romantic renegade. He was a man of corporate power now.

But he wasn't going to fire her and she knew it. She turned to go. He blocked her way, taking hold of her upper arms and staring down into her face.

"Please don't do this, Darcy," he said, his voice soft but hiding a core of steel. "I need you here."

She looked up into his eyes and began to melt. Those gorgeous blue eyes, those thick dark lashes, that flash of excitement—she could hardly breathe. Everything in her yearned toward him. Closing her eyes, she thought of her babies and gathered strength.

"I have to go," she told him, pulling away. "See you in two weeks."

She walked quickly toward the elevator, sure that he would follow her, take her into his arms, make her stay. That scared her. But when it didn't happen, there was suddenly a big empty hole in her sense of well-being. It should have been a relief, but instead, she wanted to cry.

Mitch was in a very bad mood. Office life without Darcy was a whole different animal—an animal he wasn't very fond of. Skylar was definitely beautiful.

Very easy on the eyes. Oh, yes. But there was one problem. Skylar never shut up.

It wasn't so much that she talked to Mitch all the time. He could handle that. A couple of sharp comments and a raised eyebrow had pretty much nipped most of that in the bud. But she talked to everyone else—incessantly. Everyone who walked by her desk, everyone who emerged from the elevator, everyone who called on the phone, got at least a ten-minute conversation. Even when he shut the door to his inner office, her laughter penetrated. That sound could probably bend steel. It certainly raised the hair on the back of his neck, and not in a good way. It also set his teeth on edge. And most of all, it made him think longingly of Darcy.

It had been a long time since he'd worked in an office environment and he hadn't realized how much Darcy had helped transition him back into the groove until she wasn't there to help him anymore. He needed her here.

He needed her here for purely selfish reasons, but that wasn't all. He'd thought that they would talk more about his idea. He'd had this feeling from the first that marriage was the only way to solve their problems, and he'd resisted because it went against everything he'd planned for his life. But the more he'd thought about it, the more he'd realized it might be an answer for them both.

He'd seen men out in the field who had cracked up over time. The work he did out there was stressful, to say the least. It wouldn't hurt to have an anchor at home, something to help keep him on an even keel. He'd never known a woman he could even remotely imagine marrying. But Darcy—well, she was different. Maybe…maybe it would work with her.

He hadn't taken her vehement rejection of his idea too seriously. She hadn't had time to think it over yet. If she were here, they could talk it over and find a way to make it work. If she wasn't here, they couldn't do a thing about it. He needed her here.

That laugh again. He shuddered. Turning to his computer screen, he did a search on "Noise canceling headphones." Hmm. It was a possibility.

"Mitch?"

Skylar came in, looking coy. "I hate to bother you, but the manager out at Bermuda Woods just called and he says there's a document missing from the final packet."

Mitch shrugged. "So find it and get it out to him," he said dismissively.

She hesitated, then smiled flirtatiously. "He told me a bunch of stuff but I can't figure out what he's talking about. I thought maybe we could work on it together. I could really use your help." She looked hopeful.

Mitch frowned. "I'm not up to speed on that

project, either." He sighed resignedly. "Okay, we'd better call her."

Skylar blinked. "Call who?"

"Darcy Connors, of course. She knows everything about this stuff."

"Oh." Skylar didn't look enthusiastic.

"Dial her up." He waved her toward the phone. "Let's get her input."

Skylar sighed big. "Okay."

She looked up Darcy's number and pushed the numbers on the phone.

"Oh darn, it's her machine," she told Mitch, waving the receiver in the air.

"Well, leave a message," he said impatiently.

"Oh. Okay." She put the receiver to her ear. "Hi, Darcy, honey. It's Skylar—at the office? Mr. Carver—Mitch—he would like to talk to you about—um—the Bermuda Woods development. He has some loose ends he wants to discuss. Please call us back. Okay? Thanks. See you soon, honey."

Mitch scowled and glanced at his watch. "If she doesn't call in half an hour, call her again," he ordered gruffly.

Skylar tossed back her fire-engine-red hair, looked like she was going to launch into a diatribe, then stopped herself when she caught the expression on his face. "Whatever," she said, rolling her eyes and flouncing out of the office.

Mitch's teeth were on edge again.

"Whatever," he echoed dully, staring out his window at the growing storm clouds. "Whatever it takes," he added more softly, his gaze sharpening. He needed a plan. He was a man of action, wasn't he? All right then. He would come up with a plan. How hard could that be?

Darcy sat in Mimi's kitchen listening to the message as Skylar gave it. There was no way she was picking up the phone to take the call. She was going to stay strong, even though she knew Mitch was right there, just seconds away. She'd promised she would take calls and help when needed. And she planned to be available by the end of the week. But not now. It was too soon. She and Mitch both needed to get used to the reality of her not being in the office. She couldn't think of anything that couldn't wait a few days. So she was standing pat.

She hadn't realized it would be this hard. She'd managed to remove Mitch from her daily life physically, but there didn't seem to be any way to push him out of her mind.

Still, she was having fun with the twins. Tonight she was making pizza and had games and songs ready. Tomorrow she was taking them to the park. If only she wasn't haunted every step by thoughts of how much Mitch would like these little guys—if he ever let himself.

That night it rained hard for a while. A little thunder. A little lightning. After checking on her babies who were sleeping through the turmoil, Darcy snuggled under her covers and listened to the storm. Was Mitch awake, too? Was he lying there, just a few miles away, staring at the ceiling of his room and thinking of her? For just a moment she could imagine reaching out and making a magical connection. She shivered delightfully, then closed her eyes and dreamed of him.

The next day she ignored another phone message from Skylar—the third one, and packed the boys into the car, taking off for the park. They had a wonderful, if tiring couple of hours, stopped for ice-cream cones on the way home, which turned the inside of her car into a sticky zone, then headed for home.

She knew something was wrong right away. For one thing, Mitch's car was standing out in front of her house. But even more ominous, a moving truck was coming out of her driveway and taking off just as she drove up. She looked back. The two boys were sound asleep in their car seats. She debated leaving them there for a few minutes, then decided against it. You just couldn't be too careful where these young lives were concerned.

That meant she had to take time lugging both car seats into the house. The boys didn't wake up, so at least she got a break there. She left them on the floor of their room with their seats tilted back into sleeping position, and hurried back into the living room to see what the heck was going on.

She could see his car still parked at the curb, but there was no sign of him outside. So that meant he was probably inside somewhere, but where? The garage was her next target, but it was standing empty. She frowned. Maybe the converted sunporch on the side of the house. She hurried to it and opened the wide French doors that led onto the porch. And there he was.

"Hi," he said, leaning back in his desk chair. "I've been waiting for you. Where've you been?"

She gaped at him in consternation, then went down the three steps to his level. He was looking like the cat that ate the canary, very bright-eyed and full of himself, and he was surrounded by an instant office that he must have set up in the short space of time she'd spent out with the boys.

"What in the world…?" she muttered, in shock as she looked at the sparkling glass desk, equipped with a trendy slender notebook computer, printer, fax and copy machine—even his trademark big jar of jelly beans. A huge metal file cabinet sat beside the desk. All the comforts of the office gleaming attractively.

"How did you get in here?" she demanded.

He raised one eyebrow. "Please, Darcy. It's a basic requirement of my profession to know how to get into locked places."

Of course. She knew that. But…but… he wasn't supposed to get into *her* locked places!

"You couldn't wait until I got home?"

"No. The moving van was on a tight schedule."

"Moving van…" She could hardly talk. In her wildest dreams she had never expected this. "But why?"

"Would you believe that my parents kicked me out? Just like high school."

She shook her head, unable to compute what he'd just said. "Kicked you out of what? It's the middle of the day."

He shrugged. "I was only kidding. Actually I left voluntarily. I couldn't take another day in that house."

It was only then that she noticed a large cot had been added to the wicker decor of the room. She stared at it for a moment, taking in the big fluffy comforter and the pillow with teddy bears parading across its case. She turned back to look at him. He hadn't just moved in his work-a-day operation, he'd moved in his entire life.

"You've completely moved in?" she cried, reeling from the implications.

He nodded casually, as though this were nothing outrageous. "I had to go somewhere."

She glared at him and waved one arm in the air. "Then set up a bed at the office. Your *real* office."

He shook his head firmly, as though she just didn't understand the circumstances and would agree if only she did. "I also couldn't stand another day at that office. Not while Skylar walks those echoing marble halls."

She blinked, confused. "Skylar? What's wrong with Skylar?"

He grimaced painfully. "Have you ever tried to work with her? If you had, you wouldn't need to ask."

"She…she…" Somehow she couldn't go any further than that one word.

But he took up the slack without missing a beat. "I was in a quandary. I couldn't work, I couldn't think, I couldn't sleep. So I decided the best plan of action was a direct trek to your house. I brought all the stuff I need to work. And I figure I'll camp out here for the duration."

"No." She was shaking her head. This was impossible. *He* was impossible. Life, at the moment, was impossible. "Oh, no, you won't."

He sighed as though her lack of a charitable response pained him deeply. "I won't be in your hair constantly. I promise. I'll be over here, out of the way. But when I need you for something, I can call you over and—"

"This is just typical of you, isn't it?" she demanded with fury, leaning toward him across the desk. "You see everything through the same prism— what would be best for *you*. Did it ever occur to you that I might have other priorities right now?"

He looked puzzled. "No, actually. I thought maybe you'd be glad for the company. Time can really drag when you're required to talk nothing but baby gibberish all day."

"How would you know?"

He half laughed. "Darcy, I keep trying to make you understand that I've got a broad experience with the ways of the world. I know a lot. About everything."

"Even children."

"Well, probably not as much as you."

"Oh my goodness, what an admission," she said sarcastically. "Well, you're guaranteed to learn a lot more about children than you've ever wanted to know if you think you're staying here," she warned.

He actually looked surprised. "Not if you keep them in their play area. This is a work area."

She stared at him. Was he for real? "I'm warning you, Mitch. The kids will not be kept out of your way. The kids are center stage in this house. If you want a pure work environment, go back to work."

He took a deep breath and obviously decided not to say what first came trippingly to his tongue. "It's good that we're discussing this," he said unconvincingly. "This way we can work to establish the parameters of our working relationship."

She couldn't believe he could be such a dunderhead. "Mitch, get a clue! There's no working relationship. I'm here mothering and you're intruding."

"Darcy, calm down. This is all for the best, believe me."

That did it. She'd never been so furious. Reaching out she grabbed his newly installed phone and began punching buttons.

"What are you doing?" he asked pleasantly, still leaning back in the desk chair as though all was well with his world and her anger was just a minor passing squall.

She glared at him. "I'm calling the police. I've got an intruder in the house."

"Oh. Good idea." He smiled at her. "Did I get a chance to tell you my cousin Daniel just made captain of the Terra Dulce Police Force? Oh, and Justin Cabrera, my best friend from kindergarten is on the day desk these days. You'll probably talk to him first. Tell him 'hi' for me, okay?"

She stared at him for a moment as she digested this news, then slammed down the phone. "What—does your family own this town?"

He grinned. "Let's just say the Carvers have

impact in Terra Dulce. Always have. Funny, I hated that when I was growing up. Now I'm finding it can come in quite handy."

She wanted to wring his neck. She looked at it, imagining her fingers there, slowly tightening. But that proved self-defeating. Touching his neck would quickly turn into something sensual. There was just no escaping the fact that the man turned her on.

"You're impossible."

"That's probably true." His face softened. "Aw, come on, Darcy. Grin and bear it. It won't be so bad." He waited a moment and when he didn't see any relenting on her part, he sighed. "Okay, I should have called first. I should have warned you what I was planning. But you would have marshaled your forces against me, wouldn't you?"

She gave him the barest of assenting nods.

"I have no idea how many muscular bruiser guys you could have invited over to take a whack at me. I didn't think it was worth risking, when I'm so sure you're going to be glad I move in when all is said and done."

"Really?"

"You wait and see." He tried to coax a smile from her. "I had to do this. I wasn't getting anything done without you. And if I'd been locked up with Skylar much longer, I would probably have to start pricing cement shoes."

The thought almost made her smile, but she managed to control it. "For her or for you?" she asked.

He grinned and she could see that he thought she was weakening. And darn it all—he was probably right. After all, he was so…installed. She didn't have a clue how she could pry him loose. And she heard the boys beginning to stir.

And, truth to tell, there was a little place down deep in her heart that was glad he was here. That just showed that she was losing it.

"Just for one night," she warned him as she left to take care of her babies.

"We'll see," he said, cocky as ever. "Maybe having me around will grow on you."

"Yeah, right," she said dryly. But she was already out of earshot by then. And she had a silly smile on her face. This was just plain hopeless.

CHAPTER EIGHT

THE funny thing was, despite everything, Mitch was getting more work done here than he had at the office. He could hear Darcy in the other room, talking to her babies, doing housework, playing a CD and singing in that great bluesy voice for the children. It was… sort of nice. Something about being this close to Darcy seemed to put his mind at rest in a strange way.

But maybe he was making too much of it. Probably it was just that he no longer had to waste time wondering how he was going to get her back at work. Now he'd taken work to her. So that problem was solved.

He worked through the afternoon. Darcy stopped by while the babies were down for a nap. He looked up to see her standing behind the French doors and he motioned for her to come on in.

"How's it coming?" she asked him. She looked a

bit edgy, as though she couldn't get used to his being here in her house. That seemed so different from the reaction he was having, he had to smile, but it did make him a little sad. If only she could accept his good intentions, things would go more smoothly.

"Great. I'm going gangbusters here. But I could use a little feedback from you."

She hesitated. "All right," she conceded, dropping into a chair across the desk from him. He got her to help composing a letter, then made her run through some options on a real estate campaign he'd been asked to give some input on. She responded willingly enough, then looked at all his equipment in wonder.

"How *did* you get all this stuff in here so quickly?" she asked him.

He smiled. "I hire good people. That's why I need you."

She made a face at him. "Too much flattery and I'll stop believing it," she warned.

He laughed. "That's what I like about you, Darcy. You're about the most honest person I know."

A small smile trembled on her lips. "So I've got you fooled, at least," she murmured.

He grinned, leaning forward. "Listen, I want to get started on the Heartland submission. You know the right people. You know what has to be done to win the competition for the job. I'd like you to start working up an outline of our game plan."

Her gaze was hooded and it was a moment before she answered him. "What makes you so sure I want you to win?" she asked.

That set him back on his heels. It had never occurred to him that she wouldn't be in his corner. He frowned, studying her face.

"Why wouldn't you want me to win?"

She licked her lips. "This development is going to take years. You don't plan to be here that long."

He nodded slowly. She had him there. "You're right. I don't."

A spark of something that looked very much like outrage flashed in her eyes. "Then why on earth are you so intent on winning it?"

He drew in a deep breath. He couldn't tell her that. He couldn't even articulate his reasons in words to himself. He knew the feelings involved. Oh brother, did he ever know them. But that wasn't something he could communicate to her. He wouldn't know where to begin.

He knew it had something to do with proving himself to his father. And it had a lot to do with wanting to make sure Ned Varner didn't get the contract. But there was more there. Maybe someday he'd be able to articulate it.

"My reasons don't matter," he said at last, trying to sound crisp and logical. "What I want to do is prove I can do it if I put my mind to it."

"And then you'll walk off and leave the rest of us to pick up the pieces?"

"No." He frowned, realizing she was dealing with much more than what she was actually expressing in words. There was too much emotion in her voice for this just to be about the Heartland Project. "I'll set up a team and give it a vision. I would never abandon a project like that. The groundwork will be laid. I'll do it right."

There were bright red spots on her cheeks. She rose stiffly. "Talk to me again when you're serious," she said.

"I'm very serious," he responded. But she walked away.

He frowned, somewhat baffled by her behavior. She was upset and he wasn't completely sure why. Oh, he had some idea that it had something to do with him and her lack of faith in his staying power. But that fear wasn't based on anything real. She would see that soon, and her misgivings would pass. He really did need her for this project.

Pushing that concern away, he went back to work on some other things he'd been assigned, and a few items he'd taken up on his own. After all, if he was to make an impression in this job, he had to go way beyond the bottom line expectations. Way beyond. Otherwise, what was he here for?

An hour later he was agonizing over a flow chart

when he felt something. The hair prickled on the back of his neck. He definitely had the sense of being watched. Maybe Darcy had undergone a change of heart and was hesitating just outside the room.

Turning quickly, he looked up at the wide French doors, expecting to see her there. Instead he found two sets of blue eyes gazing down at him, plus the dark brown eyes of the dog.

"Hi guys," he said, waving at them.

The only one who responded was the dog, who wagged his tail enthusiastically. The boys didn't move a muscle. He stopped waving. Par for the course. Dogs always did like him. He seemed to be striking out with little boys however.

Suddenly Darcy appeared. He stopped dead and stared at her. She was wearing tight blue jeans and a black V-neck shirt that plunged to reveal a lot of nice cleavage. Her hair was loose and flying about her face. She looked deliciously sexy. Staring at her, he felt an odd quivering inside. As though she'd read his mind, she threw him a glance so piercing, it might have turned a lesser man to stone. Then she herded the boys and dog away from the window. He watched for a few more minutes, but only the dog came back.

Suddenly he felt a little lonely. It was almost time to call it a day. He contemplated throwing in the towel for now and going in to the main house to join them, but then he remembered that he hadn't been invited to do that. It might be prudent to wait until he was asked. So he got back to work. He had to do something to pass the time, after all.

Half an hour later he looked up and the boys were at the door again. That made him smile, even though their faces were still stuck on deadpan. They were obviously checking him out. And good for them. He had to admit, they were a pair of darn fine-looking kids—even if he did say so himself.

"Good genes," he muttered to himself proudly. He waved at them. They stared. He sighed.

"Where's the dog?" he called to them.

But they didn't answer. And when he looked up again, they were gone.

It was almost an hour later when Darcy came to ask him if he would like to join her for something to eat.

"I've put the boys to bed," she told him. "So they won't bother you."

"They don't bother me." He gazed at her steadily. "Darcy, I like kids. Don't pretend I'm a monster."

She finally smiled. "Good," she said. "Now come on before the stroganoff gets cold."

He loved stroganoff. She'd set places at the kitchen table. Red napkins. Blue plates. He was gratified when she brought out a bottle of white wine and poured two glasses. At least she was going to let this seem like a real meal and not a grudge feeding of necessity. She was still wearing the tight pants and the low-cut shirt and he was feeling definitely warm and toasty all around. He raised his glass.

"To women who brighten our lives," he said.

"To men who bully and manipulate," she countered, clinking before he had a chance to draw away.

"That was sneaky," he protested, but he didn't pursue it. Things seemed to be going well right now. No reason to rock the boat.

The food was great, from the creamy stroganoff on pasta to the leafy green salad and the cherry cobbler for dessert. They chatted inconsequentially, falling back into the pattern of banter threaded through more serious conversation they had developed in Paris. By the end of the meal, Darcy was laughing and looking as relaxed and happy as he'd ever seen her. And he was burning to take her in his arms.

But he couldn't do that. Not only would it complicate matters, it would probably result in her kicking him out on his ear, and he didn't relish sleeping in his car tonight.

He stayed in the kitchen and helped her with the dishes and they talked about ACW, and then about what he'd been doing all these years, staying so far away from Texas.

"Tell me about your work overseas these last few

years," she said, handing him a stack of plates to put away in an upper cabinet.

"What about it?" He reached high and confidently slid the plates into place for her.

She leaned against the counter, watching him. "What is it that draws you so strongly to it? How did you get this way?"

He put away his drying towel, then leaned against the counter facing her. "You know that I joined the Army after my freshman year of college," he said.

She frowned. "I thought you had a degree."

"I got that later with the Army's help," he said. "I was in Special Forces for eight years. By then I was ready for a change, so I got out and joined a firm that does security work all over the world."

She nodded. "Okay, I knew that. My impression is that you were doing pretty much the same thing you'd done in the Army, only getting paid better."

He grinned. "That was just about it."

"So would you call what you do being a mercenary?" she asked tentatively, as though she was afraid he might take offense at the term. And in truth, he did.

"A mercenary?" he repeated, distorting the word a bit. "No. Being a mercenary has ugly connotations, like being a gun for hire. That isn't what we do at all. We're more like…" He thought for a moment, then went on. "Well, like a civilian rescue service. In many countries there is a huge gulf between the very rich and the rest of the population. There are all kinds of outlaws who think the rich are like fat, vulnerable piggy banks, and kidnapping is the way to open the vaults. It's practically a major industry in some countries. Family members are always being kidnapped and held for ransom." He gave her his quirky smile. "We specialize in getting them back."

"Really?"

He nodded. "Without paying the ransom, if possible."

"Oh."

"That's the major part of our mandate. We also do other things. We find lost cargo shipments. Get political refugees out of dangerous situations. Things like that."

"I see," she said, her gaze sliding over the open neck of his shirt, then turning back up to meet his eyes. "I didn't really understand that. I have to tell you, that makes me feel a little better about it."

He moved closer, taking in the scent of her hair. "About what kind of work I do?"

"Yes. I was sort of stuck on the outlaw element. Now I see that was wrong and that you could characterize it as humanitarian."

He touched her cheek, brushing off a crumb that had landed there. Her skin was luminous. She was so beautiful, it made his heart feel full of wonder. "You prefer to think of me as one of the good guys, huh?" he said huskily, leaning closer still.

"Of course."

She looked down but she didn't move away. He could see the pulse throbbing at the base of her throat. She wanted him to kiss her. There was no way he was going to be able to resist when it was so obvious she wanted his touch as much as he wanted hers.

"Darcy."

"Yes?"

She looked up. He dropped a soft kiss on her lips, light as a feather, then drew back.

"You'd better go," she whispered, her eyes dark as shadows.

He nodded. "I know," he said.

But he didn't go. He kissed her instead. He took her into his arms, sliding his body against hers. She sighed and when his mouth covered hers, her tongue was there to meet his. She felt hot and smooth and as the kiss deepened, she arched her body into his, pressing hard with her breasts, as though she needed to feel his strength against her most sensitive places. Rational thought slipped away and all he could think of was heat and moisture and his mouth on her nipples. When she cried out, at first he was sure she was giving him an invitation, but pretty quickly, even his libido-drugged mind understood she was trying to get him to stop.

They pulled apart, panting and still clinging, but no longer pressed so tightly together. Darcy was the first to manage a coherent sentence.

"Mitch, this is exactly why you shouldn't be here," she said breathlessly.

"I know." He kissed the tender area in front of her ear.

"Then what are you doing?" she cried, trying ineffectually to pull away.

He snuggled into the curve of her neck. "I think we should explore all the possibilities so we know what to guard against," he murmured.

She laughed softly, but that didn't change anything. Taking a deep breath, she forced him away.

"Look, we've already proven that you can seduce me at will," she said in a sort of mild despair. "It doesn't take much."

He touched her cheek, the side of his hand sliding gently down the length of her face while he smiled at her. "You know why that is, don't you?"

"No. Tell me."

He shrugged. "We're so damn compatible, you and me." He cupped her chin in his hand, studying her full, gorgeous lips. "That's why we ought to get married."

She closed her eyes and this time she managed to

pull completely out of his reach. "Yeah. Right." She went into the hall and toward the sun porch, as though to lure him there and out of her hair. Looking back to see if he'd followed, she said firmly, "You know very well that I can't marry anyone who is not willing to be a father to my children."

He shook his head, frowning as he walked behind her. "What are you talking about? I'm a father. I know it happened while I wasn't paying attention, but you can't deny the biology of the situation."

She turned back to face him, looking sad in a way that made him crazy. "Biology isn't enough."

He reached for her but she dodged him. "Look, Darcy," he said. "I like them just fine. They're cute little kids."

She nodded. "You like them, but you don't love them."

He searched her gaze. "How do you know?"

"It's obvious. A vague sense of affection won't do it. I need a man who is prepared to go all the way." She flattened her hand over her chest. "I need a man who feels it right here. In the heart."

In the heart. He could do that. Couldn't he? Why not. "Darcy," he began, not sure what he was going to say but determined to defend himself.

"Good night, Mitch," she said, leaving him at the door to the porch. "Breakfast is at seven. See you then."

He watched her go. Everything about her appealed to his senses, but also to his mind and heart. She was the whole package as far as he was concerned. The only problem was, he wasn't in the market for what she offered. Could he change his life around in order to accept delivery? He couldn't make promises like that. Not yet. Maybe never.

The light, airy feeling of joy and buoyancy he'd felt with her was gone. Sadness and uncertainty was back. He wasn't sure this story was going to get its happy ending.

It was earlier than seven when Mitch woke up in his cot on the sunporch. He knew right away that he wasn't alone. He felt something move on one side, and then someone was sitting on his arm on the other. He looked up and found a pair of bright blue eyes staring right down at him. Looking to the right, he met another pair of eyes. It was the twins, both making odd gurgling noises. He blinked at them sleepily, not sure if he was pleased that they'd come for an early morning visit or annoyed that they had interrupted his sleep.

His first impulse was to call for Darcy to come and get these little monsters off him but he stopped himself. After all, these were his kids, too. He ought to get to know them a little better. So he managed a lopsided grin at the two of them. They were sure cute. He was going to have to learn which was which so he could call them by name.

But he began to notice something strange. He hadn't remembered them with such round faces before. Their cheeks seemed awfully chubby. Then he realized they were both chewing on something, and a stream of shiny blue drool began to drip down one small chin.

"Hey," he said. "What's in your mouth. What have you got in there?"

The drooler opened his mouth obediently, revealing a large mush of multicolored jell. His brother immediately did the same.

"Oh my God!"

Mitch craned his neck to look at his desk. Sure enough, his large jar of jelly beans was standing empty.

"Darcy!"

He jumped out of bed and grabbed one boy, trying to pry his jaws back open. The boy began to yell and Darcy burst into the room and cried, "What are you doing?"

He looked up, his hand full of a sickeningly sticky mass. "I'm trying to prevent a jelly bean poisoning incident," he told her crossly, holding out his hand and gazing at it in horror. "You'd better get the other one," he added, as twin number two toddled quickly from the room. "He's got a mouthful of them, too."

Darcy dashed after him, but he could hear her laughing. That reassured him a bit. He'd been afraid that this might have actually done real damage, but if Darcy was taking it lightly, maybe he could relax. He picked up his charge and carried him into the house until he found Darcy at the kitchen sink, rinsing out number two's mouth.

"Which one is he?" he asked.

She glanced up and took in his lack of attire, her eyes widening. Quickly she turned away. "Uh, you've got Sean. I've got Sammy," she said, doing an exchange and starting on the next boy. In a few minutes they were both cleaned up and had been set on their feet and had run for cover, both whimpering a bit. Losing those jelly beans seemed to be a major tragedy in their young eyes.

"They hate me now, don't they?" he said ruefully.

"No." She shook her head, bending to clean up the sink. Anything to keep from looking at that beautiful naked torso. "They don't hate you."

"But they don't understand. They probably just think I'm a mean old guy who won't let them touch his jelly beans."

She bit her lip and willed him to turn and walk away before she had to face him. But it seemed he wasn't going anywhere. Taking a deep breath, she was the one who turned. She gazed into his blue eyes and tried to keep from noticing anything else. But that was like ignoring the elephant in the room.

"You're not dressed," she said.

He looked down as though this was the first he'd

known of it. "I've got on pajama bottoms," he said defensively.

That he did—lightweight, flimsy things, barely hanging onto the hard bones of his hips and slumping down precariously between them. It didn't take much imagination to see him as though he didn't have on anything at all. One glance down and she felt as faint as a nineteenth century Southern belle before she'd found her smelling salts.

"Listen," she said, suddenly breathless. "Go get dressed and come on back and we'll have breakfast."

He grinned. He knew she was in jitters over this. "Why don't I just come on into the kitchen and help you?" he teased.

She jabbed him in his chest with her forefinger. "You go get your clothes on," she ordered.

"Okay, I will," he said reluctantly, smiling into her eyes. "If you kiss me."

"What? No, it's too early in the morning."

He hovered close. "Kiss me and I promise I'll be good for…oh, at least an hour."

She couldn't resist an answering smile. "Three hours," she countered.

"An hour and a half."

"Deal."

His lips touched hers and she closed her eyes, savoring the sweetness of his token of affection.

When she opened them, he was still there, looking down at her with a bemused smile on his face. She glanced at his chest, then reached out to touch the fiery scar.

"How did that happen?" she asked him.

"A knife fight in a bar," he said dismissively. "Nothing to worry about."

She frowned, searching his eyes. She didn't believe him. Someday she was going to get him to tell her the truth.

He kissed her again. She kissed him back. This time he drew away and left the room, but she couldn't open her eyes. She stood there for a long, long moment, letting the glow of him wash over her. And when she finally regained her sanity, she was smiling. What was that warm feeling inside? Ah yes, she remembered it now. It was something very close to happiness.

Mitch wasn't sure how he was going to like having breakfast with the twins, but in the end, he had a great time. The boys were little barbarians and Darcy definitely had her hands full with them. He was surprised to find that a word of warning in his deeper voice could stop them in their tracks where Darcy's pleadings went unheeded. But all in all they were good kids, if a bit rambunctious.

He enjoyed watching them, especially when Sean

began laughing uproariously because Sammy had somehow figured out how to make milk shoot out of his nose. Darcy put her head in her hands in despair, but Mitch laughed right along with the boys. He looked from one to the other and couldn't stop grinning.

Something was clanging deep down in his memory file. This scene seemed so familiar. He couldn't pin down the specifics, but he was sure he and his brother had been there, done that. These were great little boys, really. Great little rowdy boys. How could he not like them? How could he not feel an affinity to them and their pranks?

"Hey guys," he said, gazing at them both. "What else have you got planned to drive your mother crazy with today?"

Sammy stuck his spoon to his nose and Sean began dropping bits of cereal over the side of his high chair tray, leaning over to watch as the kernels jumped and scattered. Mitch looked at Darcy and she looked at him and they both started to laugh in a helpless fashion. Funny, in all that mess and confusion, the thought came to him that life was good.

CHAPTER NINE

BY LATE in the morning, Darcy had developed enough confidence in Mitch's relationship with the boys to leave them with him while she went to the store. It should have been a quick trip. She just needed bread and enough milk to make up for the supply Sammy had wasted at breakfast with his nose-spewing antics. But it seemed like she ran into people she knew down every aisle and everyone wanted to hear how Mimi was and where she was and how her sister was doing. So it was a bit later than she'd expected when she got back and she hurried from the car, feeling anxious.

"Hello," she called, coming into the house with her arms full. "Where is everybody?"

No answer. Her heart began to beat just a little faster. She stowed the bags onto the kitchen counter and began a search. One room after another turned up empty and they weren't out back. The garage was cold and silent. By now she was beginning to feel a bit frantic. Mitch's car was still out front. Where could they be? She ran out into the street and looked up and down. What now? Should she call the police? She turned back toward the house, and at the same moment, she heard a dog bark.

"Sparky?"

She ran toward the sound, realizing it was coming from the path between the houses that led to the canyon. And there they were, coming back through the weeds, Mitch carrying a boy in each arm. Tears of relief popped into her eyes and she ran to meet them. Sparky barked and danced around them as she took Sean from Mitch.

"I'm glad you showed up," Mitch said, looking tired. "These guys are heavy."

"What were you thinking?" she demanded. "They're too young to go to the canyon."

"I guess you're right," he said ruefully. "They pooped out about half way there."

She shook her head. They barely knew how to walk and he had them hiking to the canyon? It was obvious he didn't know much about little boys this age. But then, how could he? At least he'd wanted to do something with them instead of planting them in front of the television or putting them in a playpen.

"Oh good, you put on their little tennis shoes," she noted as Sean snuggled close, his eyelids drooping.

She saw the burrs in their socks and shook her head. He'd actually had them walking through the weeds. Suddenly she was chuckling.

"Oh, Mitch, you're a peach," she said, gazing at him with blatant affection.

"And you're the apple of my eye," he countered, pretending to look sultry. "So I guess that makes us even. Sort of."

"Sort of," she agreed, leading the way into the house.

They put the babies down for their naps and she went into the kitchen to put away the groceries. He followed her there.

"Oh, by the way. Your friend Kevin called while you were out."

"He did?" She looked up in surprise. "What did he want?"

"I don't know." Mitch grinned. "He was quite amazed when I answered the phone."

She grinned back. "I'll bet he was."

He smirked, raising one eyebrow significantly. "I don't think he'll be calling again."

"Mitch! What did you say to him?"

"Nothing. I just let him know he didn't have a chance with you now that I'm back in town."

"What?" She pretended to be outraged, but she really couldn't muster the emotion for it. After all, he was right. Now that Mitch was here, no other man had a chance of catching her attention. The only thing was, who knew how long he would stay?

Just after lunch, Darcy went out to the street to get the mail from Mimi's mailbox. She pulled out a magazine, some bills and a postcard from an old college friend, and as she was reading the note on the back, a long, low Cadillac pulled up alongside her. She turned and looked curiously as Mitch's mother leaned across the seat and sent the window down.

"Miss Connors, may I speak to you for a moment?" she asked.

Darcy was surprised, but she recovered quickly. "Of course. It's nice to see you, Mrs. Carver."

The woman motioned for her to get into the car and she did so, sliding into the passenger's seat and turning to face the older woman. Mrs. June Carver was expensively dressed and coiffured and it was quite evident she'd once been a very beautiful woman. Diamonds sparkled on her fingers, gold chains accented her dress.

"I understand my son is staying here with you," she said, turning off the engine and settling back to talk.

Darcy studied the woman, noting the tragedy shadowing her eyes. Her natural reserve melted. She felt nothing but compassion for Mrs. Carver at the moment, despite the coolness the woman had exhibited toward her in the past.

"Yes, he is."

June Carver sighed. "He's very angry with me. I know that. I want to get beyond that, though. And I'm hoping you'll help me."

Darcy shook her head. "I don't know how I can do that," she said. "He hasn't really talked about his disagreement with his family," she added quickly. "I don't know much about it."

Mrs. Carver drew a breath deeply into her lungs and began to explain. "I'm afraid I exaggerated his father's condition in order to lure him home under somewhat false pretenses. Once he found out the truth, he was furious."

Darcy shook her head. "I'm afraid I still don't understand."

The woman stared at her for a long moment as though trying to decide how much to tell her. Finally she went on.

"Both of my sons became estranged from their father years ago, and that meant that I hardly ever see either one of them. I wonder if you can understand the pain a mother feels in such a situation. I love my boys deeply. Having no contact was torture for me." Her hands tightened on the wheel. "I finally found Mitch and told him his father had suffered a heart attack and we needed him home to help keep the company from falling into the hands of certain rival factions who have always borne us ill will."

"Ned Varner," Darcy guessed softly.

Mrs. Carver nodded. "Yes, Ned has always tried to wrestle control of the company away from my husband. I knew Mitch's competitive spirit would respond to that appeal. He promised to come home for one year to make sure that the worst didn't happen."

Darcy shook her head, studying the woman. "Was it all a lie?"

"Not really." She sighed. "But it wasn't the whole truth, either. Robert does have a heart condition and he could have an attack at any time. And he was in the hospital, but for a minor angioplasty, not a full-fledged heart attack."

"So Mitch found that out."

"Yes."

Darcy frowned, thinking about things he'd said. "But he hasn't threatened to leave, has he?"

She hesitated. "No. Actually he seems to be tied up in some sort of competition for a contract that he doesn't want to lose." She half smiled. "As I said, his competitive spirit seems stronger than ever. So he may stay for that full year after all."

"But if you don't see him…"

"Exactly. I'm right back where I started. And that's where you come in."

"Me?"

"Yes. Please, Miss Connors…"

"Call me Darcy."

"Darcy, then. If you care for my son at all, I'm sure you would want him to have good relations with his family."

She looked pathetic and Darcy was sure it was very difficult for a woman with her pride to let herself come this close to being seen as a miserable beggar for the kindness of strangers.

"If you could convince him to come back and just talk to us…to his father…that would be wonderful."

Reaching out, she covered Darcy's hand with her own. "I'm not asking you to make a commitment. Just think it over and do what you think is best. But please understand how much we love him." Her eyes were brimming with tears. "And how much we want him back on speaking terms with us both."

On impulse, Darcy covered the woman's hand with her own. "Mrs. Carver, I happen to think that family relations are among the most precious possessions we are blessed with. And sometimes the hardest to maintain. I will do what I can. You can count on me. But whether anything I say will have any weight with your son is another story. I can't promise that."

Mrs. Carver closed her eyes for a moment and her tears slipped down her powdered cheeks. "Thank you. Darcy, you don't know how grateful I am."

Darcy smiled. "I'd better go in," she said. "If you'd like to see Mitch…"

She shook her head. "No. Not right now. But I do appreciate this, Darcy. I'll be in touch."

Darcy walked into the house slowly. Detouring past the French doors, she looked in at where Mitch was working. He looked up and smiled, and she waved, but she didn't go in. She had to think over what his mother had told her. She knew instinctively that his relationship with his parents was directly related to what his relationship with her and her boys would be. She wanted to do this right.

Darcy was getting the boys up from their nap when Mitch came looking for her.

"Here you are," he said, coming into the boys' room and grinning at their sleepy faces. "Listen, have you given any thought to how we should attack the Heartland Project?"

"No," she said a bit testily. Dealing with two toddlers at one time did tend to put her nerves on edge at times. "I'm a little busy right now."

"So I see. Here, I'll take Sammy."

She handed him over gratefully, then stopped and looked at the picture Mitch made with the little blond head on his shoulder. Her heart skipped a beat. Father and son—it was just too perfect.

Taking Sean out of his crib, she put him on the

changing table and reached for the baby powder on the shelf above it. Unfortunately she jostled the shelf and the whole thing tipped, spilling the contents to the ground.

"Oh, this stupid shelf system," Darcy cried, leaning down to pick up the baby powder, along with two stuffed animals that had slid off the shelf as well. "We're going to have to try to find a local handyman to fix this thing before it comes down on top of us all."

Mitch gazed around at the room. "Actually there's quite a bit you could do here to fix this up," he mused. "The boys should have a better room. Something decorated to their tastes and better equipped for their needs."

She glanced at him sideways. "I've got neither the time nor the money to do much renovating."

He nodded, thinking as he gazed about. "I could fix this shelf system."

She turned, astonished. "You?"

"Sure, me. Why not?"

A slow grin crept over her face. "I didn't know you were handy. In that around-the-house way, I mean."

"Sure. All you need is a couple of screws in the right places. A hammer. Some nails. Hey, I'll take care of it this afternoon."

Darcy shot him a quizzical look, but he hardly noticed. He was in a state of shock himself. After all, what was he saying? He knew about as much about using a power saw as he knew about using a lacrosse bat. He was pretty darn handy at making his way over guarded borders and hacking his way through jungles, but he'd never learned how to do normal household maintenance. It had only been in the last few weeks or so that he'd even lived in a normal house again. His father had never been one to bond over teaching his son manly activities—and he'd never had much reason or interest in learning how to do basic carpentry on his own. And now he was going to strap on a tool belt and come to the rescue? Was this really going to work?

Oh well. No real problem. After a couple of seconds of apprehension, he settled down. He was pretty sure he could figure out how to use a hammer and a screwdriver. One thing he had learned in his precarious way of living was how to use the resources he found around him. He would probably do okay once he got into it.

"You know," Darcy was saying, "Kevin is an amateur carpenter. He does very nice woodworking. Maybe we should call him to come over and give us a hand."

That would be the day. He heard the slightly teasing tone in her voice and knew she was goading him. But he didn't take the bait. He was going to figure out how to do this on his own, just like the man of the house would do. He smiled to himself, feeling good about it. This was something he probably should have learned how to do years ago. Better late than never. He gave the little boy in his arms a hug, feeling the wonder of such vibrant life so near. He wanted to do something for these kids. After all, who knew how long he would be around to watch them grow?

He helped Darcy finish cleaning up the boys and put them into the playpen for a bit of playtime before a planned trip to the park. He was wondering where he was going to find the tools to do what he'd promised when Darcy gestured from the kitchen.

"Mitch, we need to talk," she said.

"Oh. Sure thing."

He followed her into the kitchen. She'd set out tall glasses of iced tea and they both sat down at the kitchen table to sip on them. It wasn't until he took his seat that he noticed the look on her face and began to feel a quiver of apprehension.

"What's up, Darcy?" he asked.

Her gaze was clear and direct. "I saw your mother today."

He stiffened. "Where?"

"Out in front of the house. She was looking for you."

He digested that and nodded. "Why didn't she come in?"

"She wanted to talk to me. She asked me to give you a message."

"Great." His mouth twisted. "So she didn't have

the nerve to meet me face-to-face? She has to send me messages now?" His anger was growing and he tried to leash it in. Getting angry usually meant you were going to do something stupid, and he didn't want that. "So what did she say?"

Darcy licked her lips. "She wants you to come by the house and speak to your father."

He snorted. "Cold day in hell," he muttered.

She winced. "I think you should go."

He looked at her as though he couldn't understand how she could say such a thing. "Darcy this has nothing to do with you."

"I know. But your mother…she looked so sad." Darcy shook her head wishing she knew the words that would persuade him. She had a feeling this was important, that he really should do this. But she knew "feelings" weren't going to change his mind.

"You don't know the background, Darcy. Our family is like those families they make movies about, where there are secrets tearing people apart. I know that sounds melodramatic, but in a way, it's true. There's a past here you don't understand. You can't fix things."

"That's probably true—that I don't understand. But Mitch…" She gazed at him earnestly. "Nothing is ever beyond repair. If you could see your mother. This is obviously tearing her apart. And maybe you *can* fix things if you just—"

"No." He rose from the chair, threw her an angry glance and turned on his heel. "Just stay out of this, Darcy. I won't go to see my father. Forget it."

Darcy sat and watched him stalk off. A warning her own mother used to make kept echoing in her head. *One thing you should always remember, Darcy. You watch how a boy treats his parents. That's the same way he'll treat you someday. Take a lesson from it.*

How he would treat *her* wasn't so important. How he treated the babies—that was the crux of the matter.

The rest of the week seemed to fly by. Their routine very quickly fell into patterns that fit both their life-styles very well. Mitch spent most of the day working. Darcy spent most of the day with the children. The four of them came together for break-fast and lunch, but Darcy put the boys to bed before dinner, which she and Mitch had alone.

They had daily telephone calls from Mimi who was thinking she might be able to get home sooner than she'd thought when she left. Mitch and Darcy looked at each other when they heard the news. Neither of them said anything, but neither of them wanted this idyll to be over just yet. This time together seemed special, an oasis from the real world. And part of it, he had to admit, was being with the children. They would never be this age again. This little family would never be quite the same again, no matter what happened in their individual lives. This time was to enjoy.

Mitch worked on the shelf system in the boys' bedroom for two days before he began to get the hang of it, but now he was spending a lot of time at it, repairing things and building shelves everywhere he could find a need. He loved it and was proud of his work. Darcy was proud of it, too, but she was beginning to worry he was going to overrenovate if she didn't hold him back.

"We've got to do something with the walls in this bedroom," he said when he finished the shelving. "It needs something."

"A fresh coat of paint?" she suggested.

"More than that. It needs murals."

"Mitch, you're not an artist," she said quickly, alarmed.

"No. I'm not. But I know one."

"Who?"

"Ginger Hiro. I went to school with her. She works in Graphics at ACW nowadays. I'll bet she'd do it for us."

"That might be nice." Darcy mused, looking the area over. "I could see bunnies on the wall."

"Bunnies?" he said with scorn. "Are you kidding? It's gotta be monkeys."

She frowned. "I don't know. Bunnies are sweet. Monkeys might encourage bad behavior."

"Monkeys," he insisted. "No wimpy little bunnies for my boys."

He went on as though he hadn't noticed what he'd said and the way he'd said it. But she had, and she stared at him. She had to admit, there had been a sea change in the way he treated the children. He obviously liked them a lot and they adored him. It made her heart swell just to watch them together. Was it enough? She wasn't sure. And it was his relationship—or lack of it—with his parents that gave her the most trouble now.

That same afternoon he asked how she was coming on plans for the Heartland Project and she finally had to come clean. She hadn't done a thing to help him, because she'd decided she wasn't going to do anything to help promote his chances.

He was stunned when she told him. He couldn't understand her reasoning.

"Okay, Mitch," she said at last, knowing this could very well drive an immutable wedge between them. She didn't know how to avoid that. She had to be honest with him. There was no point in pretending things were okay when they weren't.

"Okay, here's the deal. I'll only help you on one condition—that you make a pledge that if you win the contract, you'll stay and guide it all the way. That you'll see it out, make a commitment to complete what you've started. If you can't do that, I don't think you deserve to get the contract and I won't help you."

He stared at her, his gaze clouded. "You're talking about making a promise to stay for years."

Her chin rose defiantly. "Yes, I guess I am."

He shook his head as though he couldn't believe what he was hearing. "Basically you want me to promise to put down permanent roots. To pledge not to leave for a very long time, no matter what."

She looked into his eyes and was chilled by the hard, cold look she saw there. He was not taking this well. But she couldn't let herself crumble.

"That's about it," she said firmly, though she was quivering inside.

His eyes narrowed. "You know I can't do that."

A wave of desolation swept over her. "Can't you?"

"No. Of course not. And I'm surprised that you would even suggest it."

She closed her eyes and turned away. "That's that, then."

He stared at her, anger simmering deep in his bones. He couldn't believe she was asking this of him. She knew better. She'd known from the beginning that he would have to go.

And so she thought she might be able to force him to do things her way by denying him the help he needed. That was what made him angry. He felt betrayed. He'd counted on her and now she'd turned on him. He would show her. He would win the damn contract without her help. He'd been depending too much on her as it was.

But he knew he was only blustering. As the first flush of his anger faded and he let it ebb and flow, he began to think it over a little more sanely. He knew she had her reasons, and that those reasons were valid by her lights. He also knew very well that her concern about the Heartland Project was nothing but a metaphor for her concern about him becoming a permanent part of the life of her family—someone who was around. And that she was losing hope.

That hurt. Didn't she know he was in love with her? That he'd loved her since that night in Paris? That he was crazy about the twins, too?

Yes, she knew. But she was letting *him* know that it wasn't enough. And maybe she was right. Maybe the pull of that other world he lived in was just too strong for him to ignore. He wasn't sure yet. He just didn't know.

That night he decided to tell her about his fight with his father. Maybe that would help her to understand him a little more. He waited until the boys were asleep and their dinner was finished and the dishes washed. Darcy made them each a cup of hot cocoa and they sat side by side at the kitchen table while he explained how it had happened—the betrayal that had shaped his life.

"It was the summer after my freshman year in college. I was pretty full of myself. I came home to work at ACW for the summer and I brought my girl-friend with me. Kristi was from Baton Rouge. She was so pretty, with that sort of late teenage bloom. Not very bright, but the sort of girl a dumb kid of nineteen thinks is just terrific. I was pretty crazy about her. I got my father to give her a job in the typing pool. We had a great summer planned."

"Sounds like a pretty typical summer during the college years," Darcy said, trying not to feel a ridiculous flash of jealousy.

"Sure. But I was the boss's son, heir to the throne and all that. I thought I was hot stuff and I thought that Kristi thought so, too."

Darcy smiled at the picture he was painting, though she knew the way he was presenting it meant he was setting himself up for some sort of fall.

"I got assigned to go out to the Panhandle for a few days, to meet with some farmers, look at some land, make some evaluations. The whole time I was out there, I was thinking about getting back to Kristi. I got a chance to hitch a ride and got back early. I went straight into work, even though it was the lunch hour, and went to leave my paperwork on my father's desk." He shook his head ruefully. "Only Kristi had gotten there before me. She and my father were doing some extracurricular work right there in his office."

"Oh, Mitch." Darcy had known it would be bad but she hadn't quite expected this. It hit her like a sock in the stomach.

"I always had a suspicion that my father played around a bit. I hoped that my mother didn't know. I was always a bit too protective of her from the time I was a little boy. It always seemed like she was good and my father was not quite good enough." He shook his head again. "But to find him doing my girl-friend was a bit much. Like a fool, I raced home to get my mother to pack up her things and let me take her away from the cad she was married to." He laughed shortly. "She told me to mind my own business and pick a better girl next time." He winced, hurt by that even now. "I felt like my world had fallen off its axis."

She pulled her arms in tightly, wanting to give him a hug but not sure he wanted her to. "So you took off."

"Exactly. I did just what I knew they would hate the most—quit college, joined the Army and went to see the world. I didn't want to see either one of them ever again."

"I can understand that."

"Can you?" He looked up at her, his gaze intent. "Can you really, Darcy? Can you understand how deep that break in trust was? How much it hurt? How I can't forgive, even today?"

The pain was plain in his eyes. Reaching out,

she covered his hands with hers. "I'm so sorry," she murmured.

He seemed to shake himself. "Yeah, well, that was a long time ago. A lot of water under the bridge." He cleared his throat.

She nodded. "You know you've got to forgive him," she said softly, knowing he would reject that out of hand, but needing to say it.

"What?" He looked at her like she was crazy.

"Has your mother forgiven him?"

"I suppose so, but…"

"Then you can, too." Her fingers tightened around his hands. She stared into his eyes, trying hard to convey just how serious she was about this. "I'm not saying this for him. I'm saying it for you. Mitch, you're the one I care about."

He was shaking his head, but he was also searching her eyes, looking for answers in the dark depths of them. "Why do you care about me?" he asked her huskily.

She blinked and straightened slightly. "Why do you think? You're the father of my children."

He turned his hands so that they were holding hers. "And?"

"That's enough."

He started to smile. "Liar," he whispered. He pulled her closer. "Tell me the truth."

She half laughed, captured by him. "Which truth

are you talking about?" she teased evasively, even as she turned her face up to him. She was just glad he wasn't angry with her. If they could keep from arguing, they might have a chance to find common ground.

"This one," he said, beginning to drop nipping kisses on her full lips. "Tell me how much you like me, Darcy Connors."

"I like you lots, Mitch Carver," she said earnestly, succumbing to his kisses without making any effort to fight them. "Lots and lots."

"Lots better than any other guy?"

She snuggled against him. "Lots better," she agreed with a happy sigh.

"Good." He buried his face in her hair, holding her close. "I like you lots and lots, too."

Darcy closed her eyes. It was heaven being here with him this way. But why couldn't either one of them mention the 'l' word out loud? Was admitting there was love between them going a step too far? Did it create a commitment neither one of them dared make? Were they scared? Or just too cautious?

Funny—they managed to get the silly playfulness of lovers down pat. But the spirituality completely eluded them.

CHAPTER TEN

THE next morning Mitch awoke to an attack from the twins. They were taking turns climbing up on his desk chair and jumping off onto his stomach as he lay on the cot, laughing maniacally all the while.

"Darcy!" he called pitifully. "Help!"

That made the twins laugh even harder and by the time Darcy came running in, they were lying on either side of him, convulsed in hiccups and he had a hard time convincing her of what they'd been doing.

"They never did that," she insisted. "Even if they could climb up on the chair, how did they manage to jump? They can't jump. They're babies."

"They're baby monsters," he grumbled sleepily, but not too sleepily to notice Darcy was still in her robe, and that the boys had jumped off the cot and were headed back into the house as fast as their chubby little legs could take them. "The spawn of their monster mom."

"Oh, and I suppose their monster dad had nothing to do with it?" she countered, standing over where he lay, pretending to be stern.

"Come here, monster Mom," he muttered, grabbing her when she bent too close and pulling her down onto the cot with him. She came with a shriek and they wrestled for a moment, laughing. Mitch took the opportunity to pull her soft body close. Her unbound breasts felt so soft he almost groaned aloud when he touched them. She pulled away quickly, and just as she did, the front doorbell rang.

She looked at him. He was suddenly alert.

"Who could this be?" she wondered, tying her robe tightly and hurrying toward the front of the house.

Before Mitch had fully pulled on his own robe, she was back. "It's your mother," she said, her cheeks flushed.

June Carver was right behind her.

"Mitch," she said, going directly to him and taking his hands. "Your father has had a heart attack."

A tiny tremor of shock went through him, but he managed to hide it. "No kidding?" he said, his voice dripping with sarcasm. "I think I've heard that one before."

Mrs. Carver slapped her son, shocking him and stunning Darcy.

"Mitchell Carver, you have been acting like a snotty brat ever since you came back from overseas. It's time to grow up. Your father is not a perfect man. Neither are you. We all have our problems. Get over it."

She was shaking with emotion. Darcy could see that her state was affecting Mitch even more than her slap had.

"Your father has done many wonderful things for you in the past. You've blotted them all out in order to keep your anger churning against him. It's time you gave that up." Her eyes filled with tears and her voice shook. "Your father loves you. He thinks the world of you. It's been a horrible burden for him all these years to have a beloved son hate him so."

"That's pretty much his own fault," Mitch responded, ignoring the imprint of her hand on his face. Darcy noticed the sarcasm was gone and his look had lost its hardness.

"Yes. It is. And he knows that." She wavered, shaking her head, and her voice took on a more pleading tone. "He's a different person now, Mitch. He's in the hospital. He needs to see you. If you would only give him a chance…"

"I'm not a pushover like you are, Mom." He pulled the tie of his robe more tightly. "But I will come and see him. If it makes you happy."

Darcy closed her eyes and sighed with relief.

"Have you found Dylan?" Mitch said, speaking of his brother who was missing the same way Mitch had been.

"No. No, Mitch, it's just you and me to take care of your father." She lifted her head and stared at her son. "If you have the guts to do it."

Darcy left the room. The emotion between mother and son was too raw to include outsiders, and that was definitely what she was. She was sorry Mr. Carver was ill, but she was so glad Mitch was willing to make an effort to see him. If he could find a way to repair his family, maybe... Well, she didn't dare think things like that. Not yet.

Mitch went to see this father that morning, and in the afternoon, he went again, and Darcy went with him. They took the boys. Mitch had decided, with his father hovering near danger, it was time to introduce him to his grandchildren.

The twins were a hit. June Carver cried. Mr. Carver didn't cry, but he couldn't speak for quite a while. They both watched the babies and fell in love.

Darcy was overwhelmed with emotion. It was a joy to see these people admire the twins as much as she did. She laughed and encouraged the boys to show off and enjoyed the entire experience. But when she looked into Mitch's face, she saw shadows there. He wasn't completely won over to this new close family situation she was hoping to build. And that gave her chills.

That night they spent some time talking things over and she told him how glad she was he was opening to his family, even if just a crack.

"We all have things in our lives we're ashamed of," she reminded him. "Look at us. We shouldn't have done what we did in Paris. But we did it. It's over. And now we have these beautiful children."

"We redeemed ourselves," he said wryly. He grabbed her hand in his. "Only you did all the hard lifting," he acknowledged. "Darcy, have I told you lately how much I appreciate you?"

Appreciation was nice. Love would be better. She bit her lip and smiled a bit sadly.

The next day the medical news was good. Mitch's father was out of immediate danger. But Mitch came back from the hospital as full of anger as he'd ever been. Darcy didn't know what his parents had said or done to set him off, but he was fuming when he walked in the door.

"You see, Darcy, this is exactly why I have to get out of here," he said, pacing the floor. "They drive me crazy. I *am* getting out of here. I'm going back overseas where I belong."

He stopped and took her shoulders in his hands, looking down into her eyes with all the passion she wished could be channeled into love instead of anger. "But, Darcy, this time you and the boys are coming with me."

She stood very still, staring past him and out the window. It was a step. He was admitting how much he needed her and the babies. But she knew his scenario wasn't realistic. It just wasn't going to happen. It couldn't happen.

"What about the Heartland Project?" she asked him as he returned to pacing.

He hesitated, then shook his head. "The funny thing is I think I've got that one in the bag, if I want it," he told her, looking rueful.

She turned to look at him. "What makes you say that?"

"Ry Tanner got in touch with me the other day. I went out there this morning before I went to the hospital. He'll sell, but only to me."

Oh my. That was huge.

"But instead of taking advantage of that tremendous opportunity, you want to chuck it all and run overseas?" she asked, incredulous.

His gaze was rock hard. "You got it."

She shook her head, incredulous. Didn't he see how nuts this was?

"So you're going to throw out everything just so you can do it again—hurt your parents. Make them pay for not being who you wish they were. You'll wave the Heartland Project in front of them, show them what could have been, and smash it all to bits while you run off to play soldier games in foreign countries."

Darcy was angry. She was more angry than she'd ever been in her life. Finally she felt she was seeing things as they really were. And trying to make him see them, too.

He stopped and looked at her, his eyes narrowed. "You don't approve."

"That is putting it mildly. I think it stinks."

He ran a hand through his hair, looking tortured. "Why am I getting the sense that you have no intention of going with me?" he said softly.

"You got that right. You want me to pack up the boys and rip out our roots and follow you to God knows where, just so you can run again?" She shook her head firmly. "No. That's not going to happen."

He stood staring at her. "Darcy, listen," he began.

But she shook her head even more vehemently. "No, Mitch. You listen. You can't keep running away from your problems." She grabbed him by the lapels and forced him to look down at her. "I'm begging you, please don't do it. Stay here and learn to deal with things. Learn to forgive and to ask for forgiveness. Give the rest of the world a little slack. I'll stand by you forever if you do that." Letting go of his lapels, she took a step back, away from him. "But I won't run with you."

He stared at her for a long moment, then turned on his heel and left the house. She felt the tears coming and this time she let them fall. Was she really going to lose him again?

Mitch was preparing to leave. Mentally, emotionally, he was ready for it. He stopped by a packing shop to pick up a couple of cardboard boxes and headed for Mimi's house. It was time to get this show on the road.

He slipped into the house and went straight to the sunporch, ready to pack up his things and get out of there. He could hear Darcy vacuuming the boys' bedroom. He hesitated only a moment. No, it would be better to avoid seeing her again. He stepped down onto the sunporch and found his sleeping cot was filled with something he hadn't expected.

All tangled in the comforter were Sean and Sammy and Sparky, and all three were sound asleep. He stood looking down at them, a lump in his throat. Something about the faces of these beautiful, innocent children struck directly into his soul. He slowly sank into a chair that sat beside the cot. Watching the babies, his heart filled with such raw, deep emotion, he choked. Funny, just a couple of weeks before, he hadn't even known Sean and Sammy existed. Now they were very near to being the most important people in his life. Could he really go off and leave them behind, not see those rascally smiles, those bright blue eyes filled with mischief, not watch them grow and change and become boys?

Had two boys ever been so loveable, so endearing? How could he turn his back on these beautiful children? How could he shut his family out of his life? Was he crazy?

He thought of the work he did overseas as humanitarian. Here he was planning to go off and do that sort of thing again. He'd spent the last decade of his life working around the world for anonymous people thinking he was doing good. It suddenly came clear to him that he just might want to rethink a thing or two about that. Why wasn't he focused on doing good for his own children? What about a woman that he cared about? What about his own family, the people he loved? Maybe it was time to clean up some messes and take care of his own.

He stared down at the boys and such love welled up in his heart, he could hardly breathe. Maybe this was what was really important right now.

"They've been waiting for you," Darcy said from the doorway where she'd been watching for a few minutes. "I guess they fell asleep."

He looked up at her and she could see the trouble in his eyes. She looked at the packing boxes strewn on the floor. If she let him leave again without saying a word, how could she face their children? She wasn't very good at begging but this was something she had to do. She couldn't let him walk out without one last try to change his mind.

"Mitch," she said, trying hard to keep the quaver out of her voice as she walked to where he was sitting and dropped to the floor in front of him. "Please don't go. Don't leave us." Resting her elbows on his legs, she looked up into his face and added softly, "I love you so much."

Her eyes were shining like stars. He took her face in his hands and looked down at her and even with tears filling her eyes, she could see the affection there.

"I love you, too, Darcy," he said huskily. "And I love Sean and Sammy." He smiled. "And I'm just beginning to realize there is no way I can leave you. You're a part of me, all three of you. There's nothing I can do about that. It just is."

Her smile radiated joy. "Oh, Mitch!"

"I belong with you, Darcy. And we all belong in Texas."

"Oh, Mitch, I'm so glad you see that. ACW will be glad, too. And everyone involved in the Heartland Project."

"It's going to be a fight," he warned her.

She nodded. "I'll be at your side, fighting next to you all the way," she promised.

"Great."

He drew her up and into his lap and kissed her, hard.

"Okay, we really need to get this done." He touched her chin and frowned. "Will you marry me?"

He asked as though it was a hard question, as though he had no idea what her answer might be. And that was only fair. She had been turning him down all month, after all.

She began to laugh. Will you marry me? he'd asked. She threw her arms around him.

"With bells on," she cried, suddenly exuberant.

He bent to kiss her again. The boys were stirring and that meant he had to get any lovemaking in fast. Once the twins were awake, the action would really begin around here.

That made him laugh, deep in his throat. He'd just signed on for a very bumpy ride, but one that was going to be full of thrills as well as spills. And he'd be with Darcy, all the way.

And that was just how it ought to be.

TWINS FOR
A CHRISTMAS BRIDE

BY
JOSIE METCALFE

Josie Metcalfe lives in Cornwall with her long-suffering husband. They have four children. When she was an army brat, frequently on the move, books became the only friends that came with her wherever she went. Now that she writes them herself she is making new friends, and hates saying goodbye at the end of a book—but there are always more characters in her head, clamouring for attention until she can't wait to tell their stories.

CHAPTER ONE

SHE was going to die!

Sara's eyes widened in disbelief as the car headed straight at her in the narrow side street. The headlights almost seemed to pin her in position and she knew in an instant that she would never be able to get out of its path in time.

Instinctively, she took a step back, her foot slipping as it tried to gain purchase on the uneven surface. Her hands flew protectively to her belly to cradle the new life nestling deep inside, a tiny corner of her brain acknowledging the fact that it was far too small to survive even if it were to be delivered by emergency Caesarean.

She heard the car's engine roar suddenly, almost as though its driver had floored the accelerator in direct response to the defensive gesture.

Then, in that final second before the powerful vehicle made contact, it was as if time ceased to exist. She could see everything around her with the pin-sharp clarity of a high-definition photograph—the gleam of the recent rain on the ancient cobbled street; the skinny cat that had been hunting in the gutter for scraps, quickly darting into the safety of the shadows; the harsh glitter of artificial light on expensive automotive paintwork and chrome, and the reflection of her own face in the windscreen where the driver's face should be…her reflection contorted in an expression of rage and… Even as she opened her mouth in a scream of denial the sound was cut off instantly as she was flung aside to land on the unforgiving granite.

She felt a sickening thud as her head struck the kerb with a glancing blow, then the world turned black and disappeared.

'I got the job I was after,' Sara volunteered diffidently into the lull when her vivacious sister finally stopped talking long enough to draw breath.

It was always this way when her shifts allowed her to join the family for a meal. Her mother listened avidly to every scrap of Zara's gossip—about the exotic places she'd been, the fabulous clothes she'd modelled, and the A-list celebrities she'd rubbed shoulders with—obviously believing every word.

Sara had her doubts.

She'd known for many years that every one of her sister's stories was carefully tailored to her audience, regardless of the truth. Even as she listened to yet another tale of her sister's glamorous life her fingertips were taking a well-worn path, absently tracing the line of scarring at her temple that had become the only way she and her twin could be distinguished from each other as children.

The rest of the world had believed Zara's tearful tale of

a childish prank gone wrong. Sara knew better; she had always known that her twin resented the fact that they'd been born identical and that Zara was the younger. The very idea that the injury might have been deliberate was unthinkable and had sickened her, but it had only taken one glimpse of the satisfied expression on her sister's perfect face, when she'd returned home from the accident department with a prominent row of stitches marching all the way from her shaven eyebrow into her uneven hairline, to know the truth.

From that day on, although she'd still loved her sister dearly, she'd never totally trusted her.

'I started the job a couple of months ago...in the accident and emergency department,' she added into the next pause, although no one had been interested enough by her announcement to ask her for further details. Even the father she adored was dazzled by the show his glamorous younger daughter put on for him.

Then a sudden imp of mischief tempted Sara into one of those rare attempts at competition with her sister. Would she never grow out of the childish urge?

'By the way, Zara, there are several rather gorgeous doctors in the department...one in particular is every bit as tall, dark and handsome as that actor who was chasing you a while back.'

The blank expression on her sister's face was enough to confirm Sara's suspicion that Zara couldn't even remember the story she'd told them after her last visit to the United States. In all probability, the rather famously married star hadn't done anything more than smile vaguely in her sister's direction at a crowded party. Then she saw her twin's expression change suddenly into a horribly familiar calculating look and instantly felt sick.

What on earth had made her draw Zara's attention to Daniel's existence? she berated herself the next day when her beautiful sister just happened to arrive at the end of her shift to be introduced to Sara's new colleagues. The last thing she needed was for Zara to turn up flaunting her perfection, especially when Sara was looking her exhausted worst at the end of a gruelling shift.

She and her handsome new colleague had quickly discovered that they worked well together, but as for their personal relationship, that was still in the fragile early stages, barely beyond the point where she and Dan had admitted that they enjoyed each other's company outside work, too, and wanted to see whether it could develop into something lasting.

Well, that had been as much as Dan had been willing to admit, so far. On her part, she'd known from their first meeting that he was special; that he could very well be the man she'd been waiting for her whole life. There had been something about the gentleness and compassion with which he treated his patients allied with the aura of strength and dependability that surrounded him...to say nothing of the fact that he was probably the sexiest man she'd ever met...

Those weeks of tentatively getting to know each other might just as well not have existed the day Zara walked into the department wafting her signature perfume and demanding to be introduced to all her sister's dedicated colleagues.

'Of course, the whole family is so proud of Sara for taking all those exams,' she gushed with a wide smile. 'I certainly couldn't do her job...all that blood and pus and...' She shook her head so that her artfully dishevelled locks tumbled over one shoulder and shuddered delicately.

Sara could have predicted exactly how the ensuing scene would play. From the day that puberty had given her sister that spectacular set of curves, she'd seen it so often before. She didn't need to watch to know that every male in the vicinity was about to make a complete fool of himself as they all vied for one of Zara's smiles, or, better yet, one of the sultry come-hither looks she sent them from under impossibly long dark lashes.

'You didn't tell me you were a twin,' Dan complained as he distractedly delivered the mug of coffee he'd been making for her before Zara's arrival. His eyes were flicking from one to the other and Sara suppressed a wince, knowing just how badly she would come out in the comparison. There was no way that she could compare with such a polished image of perfection while she stood there in crumpled scrubs without a scrap of make-up on her face, especially with her hair dragged back into an elastic band with only a few straggly tendrils to camouflage the worst of the puckered scar that drew her eyebrow into a permanently quizzical arch.

'Hard to believe, isn't it?' she said with a tired smile. 'Have you met her yet?'

She needn't have bothered offering, knowing deep inside that this introduction was the sole reason why her sister was here. In fact, Zara was already undulating her *way across the room towards them in her best catwalk strut, her slender legs seeming endless atop heels high enough to induce vertigo. Sara felt sick when she saw the intense way her sister's eyes focused on Dan as she drew nearer, almost devouring him piece by piece from his slightly tousled dark hair and broad shoulders to his lithe hips and long powerful legs.*

'So, this is the handsomest man in the department, is it?' she purred, all but rubbing herself against him and blinking coquettishly as she gazed up into his amazing green eyes. 'Sara was telling me I just had to come and meet you.'

It was far too late to wish that she'd kept her mouth shut.

What can't be cured must be endured, her grandmother's voice said inside her head, and Sara felt an almost physical wrench as any lasting relationship she might have had with Dan was torn out of her reach for ever. She shut the pain away with all the rest she kept in the box in a dark corner of her soul, and summoned up the appropriate words.

'Daniel, this is my sister, Zara,' she said formally, unable to conjure up even a pretence of a smile. 'Zara, this is Daniel Lomax. He's one of the senior…' She fell silent, realising that she may as well have saved her breath because neither of them was listening to her.

'Hi, Danny,' Zara breathed, and Sara winced, knowing that he hated that diminutive…only this time there was no automatic correction. Well, why would he object now that her sister had both hands wrapped around his arm, blatantly testing his muscles?

She knew how those muscles felt, the taut resilience overlaid with warm skin and silky dark hair. She'd been holding that arm on the way out of the hospital just last night at the end of their shift, delighting in the way his free hand had covered hers to reinforce the fact that he had been enjoying the contact, too.

'If you'll excuse me, I'll go and have a shower and change out of these scrubs,' Sara said, abandoning her untasted coffee as she made a strategic retreat, unable to bear the thought that he might give Zara's hands that same warm caress.

The last glance she threw over her shoulder as she reached the door left her certain that neither of them had even noticed that she'd gone.

Sara woke to a world of pain and noise and eye-searingly bright light. Slamming her lids shut against the unbearable glare, she groaned, unable to decide which part of her hurt the most.

Her hip was agony, but so was her shoulder…and as for her head…

What on earth had happened to her? Had she fallen out of bed in the night? With nothing more than polished floorboards around the new divan it would certainly account for the feeling that she was bruised from head to foot.

'Sara?' said an urgent female voice right beside her ear, but she tried hard to ignore it. It wasn't until she felt the familiar sensation of disposable gloves against her skin as a gentle hand awkwardly stroked the side of her face that she realised that she had an oxygen mask covering her mouth and nose. She tried to turn her head towards the voice but discovered that she was unable to move because of the padded blocks positioned on either side.

She had seen the situation far too many times not to recognise what those sensations meant. She was strapped to a backboard with her head and neck restrained because of the fear of exacerbating a spinal injury.

'Sara, can you hear me?' the voice said over the cacophony of bleeping monitors and voices snapping out orders. 'Sara, love, you've had a bit of an accident and you're in the hospital…' And with those few words terror gripped her. Suddenly she remembered everything that had happened to her in excruciating detail.

The car appearing in the narrow road just as she started to cross it on her way back to her flat…the brightness of the headlights as it came straight towards her…as it hit her and sent her tumbling to the ground…deliberately?

Then she remembered something even more important.

'My baby…!' she keened, her voice muffled behind the oxygen mask, panicking when she was unable to move her hand to her belly, so desperate to know by the familiar feel of the gentle swell that it was still safely inside her.

Then she heard the echo of what she'd said and guilt hit her hard. 'The baby,' she said, deliberately damping the forbidden emotions the way she'd been forced to right from the first day she'd had the pregnancy confirmed. 'Is it all right? Has anything happened to the baby?'

'Stay still, Sara,' ordered the familiar voice of the senior orthopaedic consultant. 'You know better than to move until we've taken spinal X-rays and checked them.'

'No! No X-rays!' she gasped, feeling almost as if she was trapped in a terrifying nightmare. 'I'm pregnant! No X-rays!'

'Hush, sweetheart,' said a softly accented voice, just another of those voices that she'd only recognised in the guise of colleagues before. Everything was so very different now that she was the helpless patient; they were her doctors and nurses and they would decide what treatment was best for her. 'You just lie there and trust Sean O'Malley to know how to take an X-ray without harming your child,' he said, coming to stand in exactly the right place so that she could see his familiar freckled face and carroty curls and the sincerity in his bright blue eyes. 'I promise you on my word as an Irishman that the wee angel won't come out glowing in the dark.'

Sara gave a hiccup that was part laughter, part sob and somehow found a smile. 'I trust you, Sean O'Malley,' she whispered, knowing absolutely that a man who delighted in every one of his four rambunctious red-headed sons would never do anything to risk anyone's child, let alone a colleague's.

The one voice she didn't hear, even though it seemed as if every last member of the A and E department was crammed into the resus room around her, was Daniel's.

What sort of irony was that? she mused silently, a tear tracking from the corner of her eye into her hair and stinging as it reached the place where her head had come into contact with the granite kerbstone. The one person she wanted beside her as she tried to cope with the terror, the one colleague who had the most to lose if anything happened to the child she was carrying—and he wasn't there for her.

'You're late, Sara,' her mother scolded, almost dragging her into the house as soon as she set foot on the doorstep. 'You could at least have tried to get here on time for your sister's big announcement.'

'Sorry, Mum,' she apologised automatically as she shrugged out of her voluminous jacket. 'Where's Zara going this time? Or is it a contract with one of the really big fashion shows?'

'Oh, Sara! You're not wearing that old thing again! You could at least have made an effort.' This time there was a sharper edge to her mother's voice as she saw what her daughter was wearing. 'I really don't understand why you always look such a dowdy mess. No one would ever believe that the two of you were identical twins.' She flung up her hands in despair as Sara glanced down at her favourite black trousers teamed with the soft ivory blouse that she usually wore with it. It had always been enough for a family supper before, so what was different tonight?

Then her mother opened the door into the lounge and she heard the buzz of conversation that could only be made by several dozen voices and froze.

'Mum? Is there a party or something?' she demanded, hanging back. She was suddenly horribly conscious that she hadn't bothered putting any make-up on after her shower and had done nothing other than run a brush through her hair either.

'Sara, you know very well that your sister and Danny

are making their big announcement this evening,' her mother snapped as she beckoned her with an insistent hand. 'She rang you up and told you all about it more than a week ago and everyone else has been here for hours. We've only been waiting for you to arrive.'

'Dan…?' Sara felt her eyes widen as the implication hit her with the force of a wrecking ball.

Zara and Dan?

A big announcement that her sister had told her about?

For just a moment she thought she was going to be sick, but with her mother's hand now firmly clamped around her elbow she had no choice but to enter the room beside her as she pushed the door wide.

The room seemed to be crammed with people, every one of them dressed to the nines in their most elegant finery, but the glittering butterfly in their midst, effortlessly outshining them all, was Zara.

So why was it that the first pair of eyes she met were the luminous green ones that belonged to Dan…eyes that only had to glance in her direction to double her pulse rate and send her blood pressure into orbit no matter how serious the medical emergency they were working on.

Hastily, she dragged her gaze away, knowing that she couldn't afford for anyone to guess just how much it was costing her to keep herself together while her world fell apart around her.

This was the first time that she'd seen her sister since the day that she'd turned up in A and E to be introduced to Dan, and when she'd heard nothing more, Sara had dared to breathe a sigh of relief. Even if they had gone out together, Zara's attention span was notoriously short and she was certain her fickle sister would soon tire of an escort who would never be at her beck and call.

She was so confident that the two of them hadn't hit it off together after all that she'd actually been contemplating screwing up her courage to ask Dan out for a drink later in the week, hoping that the two of them could continue the relationship they'd embarked on when she'd joined the department, longing to see where it would lead them.

The last thing she'd expected was that he and Zara had been carrying on a whirlwind courtship that would result in an engagement. Zara hadn't dropped a single hint...and she certainly hadn't phoned her a week ago to invite her to their engagement party.

It was a good job that she'd had years of practice at hiding her feelings from her manipulative sister. Even so, she needed a moment or two to compose herself, grateful for the time it took for her mother to walk across the room to join her father. Then he tapped the edge of his glass to attract everyone's attention. He beckoned Zara and Daniel to join the two of them in front of the fireplace before he cleared his throat portentously.

'Friends,' he began.

'Romans and countrymen,' added one of Zara's modelling friends with an inebriated giggle, only to be hushed by one of the older, more sober guests.

'Friends, as you all know, this is a very special occasion,' Frank Walker began again as Zara finally met Sara's gaze and she saw that, oh, so familiar smug expression followed by a cuttingly dismissive glance from head to toe that told Sara as clearly as anything that her sister had deliberately neglected to tell her about the purpose of this evening's gathering for exactly this reason.

If ever there had been a moment that demonstrated how different the two of them were it was this one, with Zara…flawless, beautiful Zara…the centre of everyone's admiring gaze while she was purposely relegated into the background, not even afforded the courtesy call that would have allowed her to look her best. No one would be left in any doubt why Dan would choose Zara over her dowdy, less-than-perfect twin.

'Audrey and I are delighted to welcome you all this evening to celebrate the engagement of our beautiful daughter Zara to this handsome chap here.' There was a muted cheer and happy laughter from a small group who could only be Dan's family—not that she'd ever had the chance of meeting them before. 'In case you haven't heard all about him yet, he's Dr Daniel Lomax, and I have no doubt at all that he'll soon be a consultant in emergency medicine at one of the top hospitals in the country. So, I'd like you all to raise your glasses to wish them both every happiness. To Zara and Danny!'

With all the glasses being raised and the voices echoing her father's words, the fact that she hadn't been given a glass shouldn't have been noticed, neither should the small detail that she was totally unable to utter a word, her eyes burning with the threat of tears. But Zara noticed, and once more smiled like the proverbial cat that had got the cream.

Then Daniel noticed too, his slightly dazzled expression replaced by a puzzled frown when he caught sight of her standing alone just inside the door with her hands hanging heavily by her sides.

Then Zara noticed the focus of her new fiancé's attention and put an immediate end to it, reaching up to cup his cheek with a hand that glittered with a million points of fire as the light caught her engagement ring, then she leaned possessively against him to give him a prolonged kiss that had the room hooting encouragement and left him branded with her scarlet lipstick.

This time when her gaze met Sara's from the circle of Daniel's arms her expression screamed just one word— mine.

'Relax. The baby's fine,' soothed the technician as she slid the probe through the gel on the pale curve of Sara's exposed belly. How few weeks ago it had been that she'd celebrated the fact that she was actually beginning to look pregnant. 'Look, Sara, you can see the heart beating for yourself and there is absolutely no sign of an abruption or any other sort of a bleed in there. Now, did you want me to print an extra copy for you? I might even be able to get a shot that tells you whether you're having a—' Her cheerful patter halted abruptly as she leant forward to take a closer look at the screen then moved the probe to change the angle of the view. 'What on earth…?' she muttered under her breath.

'What? Rosalie, what's wrong with the baby?' Sara demanded, the pain in her head intensifying with her fear for the life of the child. 'Is it something to do with the accident? Was the baby injured or…?'

'Not at all! There is absolutely nothing wrong with your baby,' the young woman announced as she turned with a wide grin on her face. 'In fact, there's nothing wrong with either of them. Look, Sara…it's twins! There are two heart-beats!'

Suddenly, Sara didn't know whether to laugh hysterically or cry. As if her life wasn't in enough of a tangle already. Now she was going to have to tell everyone that it wasn't just one baby she was carrying but two. Both sets of future grandparents would be ecstatic, without a doubt, but Dan would be the only other one in the family who would understand just how much more perilous this pregnancy had become.

As if thinking his name had finally conjured him up, there he was, standing in the doorway with an expression Sara had longed to see on his face for so long…concern for her welfare. Or was it, as ever, concern for the pregnancy?

'What on earth have you done?' he demanded as he strode in, grabbing her case notes as if he had every right to examine them, and she realised that nothing had changed. Any concern he felt was obviously for his precious offspring.

Disappointment made her headache even fiercer and lent an acid edge to her tongue.

'Don't worry, *Danny*, the baby's fine. In fact, you could even say you're getting a genuine bargain—buy one, get one free.'

'What on earth are you talking about?' he snapped, and turned towards the startled woman standing in front of the high-tech control panel. 'Has she been concussed?'

'No, I'm not concussed,' Sara insisted before Rosalie could even draw a breath to answer, completely ignoring the fact that she'd apparently been unconscious among a stack of soggy cardboard boxes for the better part of half an hour before anyone had found her after the accident. 'In fact, according to everybody, I've been extremely lucky. My foot slipped on the wet cobbles as I tried to turn away from the impact to protect the baby, so I only sustained a glancing blow from the car.' She ticked her injuries off on her fingers, a slightly difficult feat with one arm strapped across her body.

'I've had a couple of stitches and got a goose egg on my forehead and I'll probably end up with one or even two black eyes; I dislocated my shoulder, but that's been put back where it belongs—hence the strapping; my hip is black and blue where it hit the granite cobbles, but even without X-rays of the region the orthopaedic consultant's almost certain I didn't break anything there and he says the cracked fibula should heal without any complications. Oh, and apart from that, I feel as if I've lost several yards of skin from various portions of my anatomy.'

She'd been glaring at him throughout her recitation and couldn't help feeling a little remorse when she saw the colour swiftly drain from his face. Not that she intended letting him off the hook. After all, it wasn't Sara, the person, that he was worried about, it was Sara, the person who had been systematically browbeaten by her family into agreeing to carry a surrogate baby for Dan and her inexplicably infertile sister.

'So, let's get to the really good news,' she continued bitterly, with a gesture towards the image frozen on the screen between them. 'Exhibit A is the scan that not only confirms that there is no evidence of injury to the brood mare's procreative organs, but also the fact that she's carrying not one but two babies. Congratulations, Danny-boy! You hit the jackpot first time!'

And even though it brought tears of agony to her eyes to force herself to turn away from him, she made herself to do it, unable to bear looking at those heart-stopping green eyes any longer.

'Are you sure you don't want to change your mind about the pain relief?' Rosalie murmured, startling Sara into the realisation that the young woman was still standing there. She'd been so focused on her acrimonious conversation with Dan that for a moment she'd completely forgotten that there was anyone else in the room with them. Not only had the technician heard her swiftly muffled groan of pain when she'd turned away from the man but she'd had a ringside seat for every word that had gone before it. Now, the fact that she was pregnant by her sister's husband would be food for gossip right around the hospital.

'Hasn't anyone given her any analgesia yet?' Daniel exploded, confirming her suspicion that he was still standing behind her…still gloating over the image of his children, no doubt.

'I don't want any unnecessary drugs,' she snapped. 'I

used the Entonox while they put my shoulder back and stitched me, knowing that was safe for the baby…oh, excuse me, *babies*. I'm quite capable of deciding for myself if I want or need anything else. Now, please, go away and leave me alone. Shouldn't you be off duty by now? Zara will be waiting for you,' she added pointedly.

That thought caused a different pain altogether and was nearly enough to persuade her to accept the drugs on offer. The idea of wiping all the agony away with a swift injection was growing more attractive by the moment. After all, if she was unconscious, she wouldn't be able to think… wouldn't have to try to unscramble the images inside her head, the impossible images that were trying to tell her that it had been her own sister who had tried to run her down in that narrow side street.

CHAPTER TWO

'SARA! How could you be so clumsy? Your dress is ruined!' her mother exclaimed in horror as she followed her into her hotel bedroom.

Sara hid a grim smile of satisfaction as she unceremoniously stripped the torn dress off and kicked the revolting garment towards the bin in the corner of the room. Even in a crumpled heap in the shadows the colour was offensive and from the first horrified moment she'd seen it she'd realised exactly why her sister had chosen it, and had been determined to thwart her plan. Even if today was her sister's wedding, she had no intention of being made a laughing-stock in front of all their friends and family...and especially, she admitted guiltily, in front of Dan.

'I'll just have to step down from being a bridesmaid,' she said logically, putting Plan A into action even as her mother hurried across to retrieve the expensive dress to examine the extent of the damage. It wouldn't be nearly so hard to stand in the background while she tried to hide her emotions from everyone else; to hide the fact that she desperately longed to be the one standing beside Dan—the *man she loved—exchanging their vows. Zara was the twin accustomed to standing in the limelight and putting on the face that the rest of the world expected to see. 'It won't take me long to put my smart suit on,' she continued, refusing to think about anything beyond the immediate situation. 'I'll catch up with the rest of you downstairs before the ceremony starts.'*

'You can't!' her mother wailed, wringing her hands. 'You've got to be Zara's bridesmaid. You're her only sister…her twin! What would everybody think?'

'Does it really matter what they think?' Sara asked with her head in the wardrobe, already reaching for the black silk suit she'd chosen as an elegant alternative to the burnt-orange meringue her sister would have had her wear.

The thing that had amazed her was that her mother had apparently been oblivious to what had been going on right under her nose while the attendant's clothes had been chosen for the wedding party. She'd commented approvingly about the clever idea of a colour theme graduating from the creamy ivory of the bride's dress through various shades of gold and topaz for the dresses her wraith-thin modelling friends would wear, but how could she not have seen that both the colour and the style Zara had decreed for Sara's dress were an abomination that did absolutely nothing for her second daughter's colouring or more rounded shape?

And as for the hairstyle… Sara's eyes flicked towards the mirror, her glance taking in the simple severity of the swept-back style that would have complemented the fine lines of her face if it hadn't also revealed the imperfection of the scar her sister had inflicted on her so long ago.

The fact that her mother was oblivious to everything but that things should be exactly as her beautiful daughter wanted was an old hurt that was unlikely to go away any time soon.

There's none so blind as them that will not see, she could hear her grandmother say darkly, and Sara smiled, remembering that the indomitable old woman she'd adored had been one of the few who had seen straight through Zara. Granny Walker had been the person who had always known when her younger granddaughter had been practising her wiles and had taken no nonsense, especially when Sara had been the butt of Zara's machinations.

'You're not wearing black to your sister's wedding,' her mother pronounced as she whipped the hanger out of Sara's hand and angrily flung the contents onto the bed. 'There must be something we can do with your dress. It's a designer original. The man did it specially…as a favour to Zara because she's his favourite model.'

Sara knew without question that there was no way she was ever going to be able to wear that dreadful dress again. She'd made certain of that when she'd decided exactly what damage she was going to do to it. As far as she was concerned, everything about the dress was proof that the designer must have detested her sister…maybe even the whole female half of the world's population.

'How about this?' she suggested as she switched to Plan B and took out the dress that had been hanging in the wardrobe just waiting for the right moment. 'I was going to change into this after the photos. Do you remember it?

It was an evening dress of your mother's, from before Nana married Granddad. I thought that if I wore it for part of the day, it would be almost as if she were here, too.'

The dress was simplicity itself and while the fluid silk looked nothing special draped over a hanger, once she was wearing it, the rich honey-coloured fabric was so supple that it looked as if it had been poured over her curves with a delicate hand.

'Oh, darling...' As she'd hoped, her mother caught her breath at the sentimental idea and when she reached out a tentative hand to stroke the fabric, Sara knew that she had won the first skirmish.

'Shall we see if it fits me well enough?' she suggested, already knowing what the answer was going to be—the dress fitted her as if it had been made for her. This battle plan had been worked out in every detail, knowing that it was the only way she was going to outwit her spiteful sister. 'I remember you told me once that my hair is exactly the same colour as Nana's was.' Unlike Zara's, which had been lightened season by season until it was now at least half a dozen shades paler than Sara's dark blonde.

Her mother was quite misty-eyed as she helped Sara into the substitute dress, trying not to disturb either her hair or her make-up, and when she stood beside her in front of the mirror and had to resort to biting her lip so that she wouldn't cry and ruin her own mascara, Sara knew that the battle was won. There was just the matter of teasing out a few 'accidental' tendrils of hair to camouflage the twisted line of scarring that pulled her eyebrow up at an angle...

'*Whatever you do, don't catch this one on the doorhandle,*' *her mother warned with a sniff into her lacy handkerchief as she bustled towards the door.* '*I'll just go and make sure that everyone else is ready. Zara's hairdresser was just putting the finishing touches once her veil went on when you had your accident. We don't want to keep dear Danny waiting any longer.*'

With those few words, the taste of victory over what she would wear was ashes in Sara's mouth. What did it matter how much better she looked in her grandmother's dress, or that her ugly scar was hidden? Dan probably wouldn't even notice she was there; he wouldn't have eyes for anyone other than his beautiful bride.

Zara looked like a flawless life-sized porcelain doll, Dan thought as he pushed open the bedroom door and found her lying on their bed.

It was hardly surprising that she'd fallen asleep. He was hours later than usual tonight, but he just hadn't been able to make himself leave any sooner. The thought that Sara might be stubborn enough to insist on going home, even after such a potentially fatal encounter, had found him hanging around until he'd made certain that she had agreed to spend the night in hospital and was settled into a side ward.

He smiled wryly when he saw how perfectly Zara was posed. It was as if she was expecting her favourite photographer to start clicking away, her hair spread artistically over the pillow and one hand draped elegantly over the edge of the bed. It would almost have been a relief to find her curled up in an untidy ball with creases on her face from the pillow. As it was, sometimes it felt as if he was married to a mannequin, with her face always perfectly made up and never a hair out of place, even on the increasingly rare occasions that they made love.

The heavy sigh took him by surprise and the weight of regret that accompanied it made him feel very guilty.

He'd realised almost as soon as he'd placed the ring on Zara's finger that he'd made a dreadful mistake, but by then there had been no way out.

Even if he *had* divorced his new wife, he'd known that there was no way that Sara would have stepped straight into her sister's shoes…what woman would, especially after the way he'd treated her?

He might only have met Sara a few months earlier, but they'd already admitted to a mutual attraction and had been exploring the possibility of a long-term relationship. For the first time in his life, he'd even found himself wondering about the possibility of marriage in the not-too-distant future.

Then he'd met Zara and discovered the meaning of the words 'whirlwind courtship', his feet hardly seeming to touch the ground before he'd found himself engaged and caught up in the planning of an uncomfortably high-profile wedding.

Up to that point, their relationship had been conducted largely in secret—at Zara's insistence that she didn't want to chance the media intruding—so he hadn't really noticed that she was such a favourite with her parents. It had only been after their marriage that he'd noticed just how little her family regarded Sara, in spite of the fact that she was now a qualified and highly proficient doctor in a busy A and E department. All their pride was definitely focused on their glamorous, vivacious, younger daughter.

In a strange way, he could even understand it, to a certain extent. He'd certainly been blinded by Zara's lively attractions when she'd set out to captivate him. What man wouldn't have been flattered to have such a stunning woman hanging on his every word in such an ego-stroking way?

How could he not have realised that she was all outward show with very little substance beneath it? Why had it taken him so long to recognise that Sara was worth a dozen of her self-centred twin?

Well, there was nothing he could do about it now. He was married, and even though he knew it had been one of the worst decisions of his life, he was not a man who broke a promise, so he certainly wouldn't go back on a solemn vow. He would just have to be content with the fact that Sara had agreed to carry a child for the two of them…two children, in fact, he recalled with a sudden surge of the same incredulous delight that had swamped him when he'd learned of it. Although how Zara would respond when he told her that she would shortly be learning to cope with being a mother to not one but two newborn babies…

'Zara?' he called softly, stifling a sigh of resignation. His wife was not going to be in a happy mood when she saw how late it was, even though it had been her sister's welfare and that of the babies she carried that had caused the delay. She was almost fanatical about preserving her looks with adequate sleep and certainly didn't like eating at this hour. 'I'm sorry I'm late, but it was unavoidable. Your sister had a rather...' He broke off with a puzzled frown.

She hadn't so much as stirred, even when he'd lowered himself wearily to the edge of the bed. Something rustled as it slid to the floor between the side of the bed and the cabinet—a letter she'd been reading before she'd fallen asleep? Perhaps it was a glamorous new contract she'd wanted to gloat over while she'd waited for him to come home?

He reached out and touched her hand...her curiously lifeless hand.

Suddenly, he switched into doctor mode as all the hairs went up on the back of his neck in a warning that something was seriously wrong.

'Zara!' he called sharply as he leant forward to take a closer look at the silent figure. He'd been standing in the doorway wool-gathering for several minutes and only now was he noticing that she was so completely still that she didn't even seem to be breathing.

'Zara, wake up!' he ordered harshly, his fingers automatically searching her wrist to find a pulse. 'Zara!' He heard the panic bouncing back at him from the expensively decorated bedroom walls when there was no sign of any rhythm under his fingertips. Was that because his ordinarily rock-steady hands hadn't stopped shaking from the moment he'd heard that Sara had been knocked down? Frantically, he probed her slender neck and breathed a sigh of relief when he felt the reassuring throb of the artery under his fingertips.

It was slower than it should be…much slower…and her skin felt cold and clammy. It was no wonder that he hadn't been able to see her breathing because her respiration was so shallow as to be almost imperceptible.

But at least she *was* breathing and her heart *was* beating, so that gave him precious time to try to make a diagnosis so that he could help her survive whatever had happened to her.

But first…

'Emergency. Which service do you require?' said a crisp voice in his ear as he continued to make his examination, trapping the phone in position with one shoulder.

'Ambulance,' he said tersely. 'My wife has had some sort of collapse. Her pulse and respiration are both depressed and her pupils are fixed and dilated.' He managed to give the operator his address even as he reeled with horror at the possibility that Zara was imminently going into cardiac arrest.

Without some secure means of administering oxygen and the supplies to set up an IV line he had no way of improving her tidal volume or boosting her systolic pressure above 80. At the moment it must hovering around 70 because her femoral pulse was barely perceptible. If it dropped below 60 the carotid pulse would disappear, too, and she would be just minutes away from irreversible brain damage and death…

'Come on! Come on!' he urged as he transferred her swiftly to the floor and began carefully controlled cardiac compressions to boost the volume of blood going to her brain, desperate to hear the sound of a siren drawing closer.

The weight of his guilt was almost crushing as he kept automatic count inside his head. If he'd come home when he'd said he would, rather than hovering over Sara and waiting till she was settled in her room, would he have arrived in time for Zara to tell him that she was feeling ill?

Would he have been able to prevent her collapsing in the first place?

A sudden hammering on the front door made him realise that he'd completely forgotten to release the catch for the ambulancemen to get into the flat.

'She's in here,' he directed as he quickly led the way back to the bedroom and dropped to his knees beside her again. 'Her systolic must have been close to 70 when I found her because her femoral pulse was barely palpable and her pupils were fixed and dilated.' He glanced across at the man who dropped to his knees on the other side of the body to begin his primary survey, and they came face to face for the first time.

'Dr Lomax!' the paramedic exclaimed, clearly shocked to see him, but he immediately became the consummate professional. 'Do you know what happened to her, sir?' the paramedic asked as he bent over the ominously still figure between them to check her pulse and respiration rates for himself.

As he did so, Dan heard the man's foot strike something to send it skittering under the bed but no one even bothered to glance at it. At the moment nothing mattered more than giving Zara a chance to continue her vibrant life.

Out of the corner of his eye Dan saw the man's colleague depositing an oxygen cylinder on the carpet and he reached out for it, leaving him free to set up the defibrillator with the swift ease of much practice.

He was ashamed to see how badly his own hands were trembling as he fumbled to tighten the mask against her face, blocking out the heart-stopping thought that Zara might already be in need of the defibrillator's violent charge to reset her heart rhythm. It was several horrified seconds before he remembered that it could also be used as a valuable monitoring and diagnostic tool.

'I've no idea what happened to her,' he said, dragging his thoughts back to the question he'd been asked, frustrated when he saw that the man was having trouble finding a vein. But, then, with her blood pressure so low, it was hardly surprising. Still, he had to fight the urge to take over and do the job himself. They needed to get the IV started and the lactated Ringer's running into her veins as soon as possible to get her blood pressure up. If she'd had some sort of spontaneous bleed that had caused a catastrophic drop in her blood pressure…

'I came home from work to find her lying on the bed,' he continued, forcing himself not to waste any time second-guessing, even as the need to do *something* urged him to continue CPR. 'At first, I thought she was sleeping, but when I tried to wake her…' he shook his head in disbelief. 'That's when I realised how ill she was.'

'Do you know if she'd had any alcohol to drink before you found her?' he asked, and Dan almost smiled.

'It's unlikely. She never drinks anything stronger than a white wine spritzer…too many calories,' he added.

'Do you know if she's taken any drugs, sir?' the young

man asked as he peeled the gel pads from their protective backing and positioned them swiftly on Zara's chest, and even though Dan knew that the questions were necessary for him to do his job, the suggestion shocked him.

'No!' he exclaimed immediately, horrified at even the thought that this bright beautiful woman might have wanted to kill herself. Then he remembered a conversation he'd overheard at one of the parties she'd dragged him to earlier on in their marriage. He'd been shocked to learn just how many of her fellow models resorted to chemical assistance to maintain their almost skeletal slenderness.

'Oh, God,' he muttered, praying that Zara hadn't been tempted down that route. In a profession that valued the freshness of youth above almost everything else, her age was already counting against her. Had she been that desperate to extend her modelling career that she would use drugs to help her compete with all those younger wannabes?

'I don't know,' he admitted finally. 'I've never seen her taking anything, but…'

'Could you go and have a look in the bathroom, please, sir,' the paramedic asked firmly, as he gestured to his colleague to take his hands off their patient while he activated the machine to monitor the state of her heart. 'We'll take over here now.'

'Stand clear. Analysing now,' said the disembodied voice programmed into the machine as he strode into the *en suite* bathroom, almost grateful for an excuse not to watch if they were going to have to make her beautiful body convulse with the brutality of a shock.

It took precious seconds to search through a mirror-fronted cabinet crammed full of beauty products of every shape and size, but the only tablets he could find were those in a half-full plastic bottle of over-the-counter painkillers.

'No shock required,' the voice was advising as he came back into the room, and his heart lifted briefly at the thought that at least Zara hadn't gone into ventricular fibrillation or cardiac arrest.

'Did you find anything, sir?' prompted the paramedic as he rejoined them and he saw that in his absence they'd intubated Zara to secure her airway, rather than relying on the face mask, and had connected her to their portable oxygen cylinder. The monitor clipped to her finger was already starting to record an improvement in the saturation level in her blood.

'No drugs, other than some generic analgesics,' he said, disorientated by the fact that he was little more than a bystander in a situation where he was usually the one in charge. But this was completely different to working in A and E. There, he could work fast and effectively, treating any number of cardiac arrest patients in a single day with his brain working swiftly and clearly and every possible piece of equipment readily to hand.

Here, it felt as if his thoughts were travelling through treacle as he saw the paramedic's gloved fingers sort through the pre-loaded syringes in his kit. Somehow, he just couldn't get his brain to tell him what the man should be looking for, or why.

'They were paracetamol and the bottle was half-full,' he added, before the man could ask.

'What about the bedside cabinet?' prompted the other man, and Dan dragged his gaze away from what the two of them were doing to stride across and pull the drawer completely out. He upended it over the bed and several items fell off the edge of the mattress and hit his foot to land out of sight under the bed.

'Some herbal sleeping tablets and…a bubble pack of contraceptive pills,' he added in disbelief, suddenly wondering just how many kinds of a fool he'd been. So much for Zara's grief that she couldn't give him a child! If she'd been taking contraceptives to prevent herself getting pregnant, had anything about his marriage been real?

He reached under the bed to retrieve the items that had fallen, his first sweep revealing nothing more than a couple of pens and the locked diary that Zara had written in each night.

His second sweep shocked him to the core.

'*Barbiturates!*' he exclaimed when the empty bottle rolled into view and he caught sight of the name of the contents printed on the label. 'Where did she get barbiturates from?'

There was an awful silence in the room, with only the soft sibilance of the oxygen to break it, all three of them gazing at the slender beauty with varying degrees of disbelief, incomprehension and pity. They all knew that the incidence of barbiturate overdose had dropped considerably with the introduction of newer, safer sleeping tablets, but if the label on the bottle was genuine, the dangerously addictive drugs were clearly still readily available in other parts of the world to globe-trotters such as models.

Although why *Zara* would feel the need to take…

'We need to get her to hospital quickly, sir,' the paramedic said briskly, as he selected several syringes. 'Do you know your wife's approximate weight so I can give her the first dose of sodium bicarbonate?'

Thank goodness he'd found the prescription bottle, he thought, realising wryly that he was probably one of very few husbands who would know almost to the ounce what his wife weighed, the result of Zara's obsessive morning ritual had been a cause for alternating delight or despair for every single day of their marriage.

At least they now knew precisely which barbiturate she'd taken and that it was one that bicarbonate would promote more rapid urinary excretion—anything to get the drug out of her system before it could do any more damage. Zara was already deeply comatose and if he'd arrived home any later…

He shook his head, deliberately shutting that thought away as he followed every move that the two-man crew made with critical eyes. Not that he doubted their competence. From the moment they'd entered the flat they hadn't made a false move.

His colleague had already piled everything else back into their packs and as soon as it was closed he straightened up. 'I'll get the stretcher,' he announced and took off out of the flat.

'Do you want to travel with her, sir, or—?'

'I'll follow you,' Dan interrupted, and understood the look of relief that briefly crossed the man's face. He didn't know many paramedics who would be entirely comfortable about doing their job under the eagle eyes of an A and E doctor, especially when the patient was a member of that doctor's family.

Apart from anything else, he and his colleague were probably wondering at the situation between Zara and himself that could have led her to make such a desperate gesture.

He sighed heavily with the realisation that there was no way this would remain a secret, no matter how strict the rules were over patient confidentiality.

'The last thing any of us needs is speculation and gossip,' he groaned under his breath as he followed the stretcher out of the flat and paused just long enough to make sure the front door had locked behind him. It was going to be hard enough to tell Zara's family that she had made an attempt at taking her own life without the whole hospital speculating what went on behind closed doors.

If that was what it had been, he continued agonising as he followed the flashing lights through the busy traffic, the urgent scream of the siren an audible reminder that the outcome of the situation was far from certain.

Suicide? Zara? It still seemed impossible. Had she just intended to give him a scare? Had it only been the fact that he had been late that had made this such a serious situation, the extra hours giving the drugs so much more time to do their damage.

And if she…*when* she survived? He hastily altered the words inside his head, feeling a renewed stab of guilt that he could even contemplate the alternative.

Anyway, he thought heavily, as far as her health was

concerned, no one could predict how well or how badly she would recover. Only time would tell how much permanent damage the drugs had done to her system.

The fact that she was his wife was another matter entirely. Zara wasn't anywhere near as important a model as she pretended to be, but any speculation that it might somehow be *his* fault that she'd come so close to death could start a media feeding frenzy that would ruin all their lives, to say nothing of his career. The lower end of the tabloid market would have the whole situation blown out of all proportion the minute they heard that she'd taken an overdose, especially if they unearthed the fact that the two of them had resorted to a surrogate pregnancy.

He followed the flashing lights all the way to the emergency entrance, his brain rerunning everything that had been done to try to stabilise Zara's condition. He was so preoccupied that he only just remembered in time to pull into the designated staff parking area rather than cluttering up the area around the emergency entrance.

As his feet pounded across the tarmac towards the emergency doors, the lights cast long shadows that made it seem as if the doors never got any closer, but finally they slid silently open in front of him.

'Dan? What on earth are you doing back here?' demanded his opposite number on the night shift, but he didn't even slow his pace, his long strides taking him unerringly through to the resuscitation rooms at the other end of the department.

'Dan! Come in,' called the consultant already standing the other side of Zara's ominously still body, his face creased in concern as he beckoned him into the room.

For a moment, as he shouldered his way through the doors, Dan was filled with dread. Had things got worse during the ambulance journey from his flat to the hospital? Zara's condition had been so serious that he was hardly likely to look across the clinically stark room and find her sitting up and preening herself in front of any males in her audience, but if the bottle of barbiturates she'd taken had been in her body too long, it was all too likely that she might never come out of the coma.

As he stared across at her, she looked even more like a porcelain doll under the unforgiving fluorescent lights, with an almost waxy sheen to her skin.

He slumped back against the wall and watched in awful fascination as his superior did everything *he* would have done if she were one of his patients, from aspirating her stomach contents to remove any tablets still undigested, to trying to neutralise any drug-laden fluids with activated charcoal before they could be absorbed by her body.

This just couldn't be happening, he thought, his helplessness making him feel sick to his stomach.

Zara had so much to live for, and before this he would have sworn that she was far too self-centred and conceited to ever think of suicide. Why on earth would she do something so...so...?

'I'm sorry, Dan,' the consultant apologised, and Dan knew that he was going to confirm his worst fears...*life extinct*.

Just the thought of those solemn words was enough to change the way he saw the woman who was his wife. Somehow her slenderness became mere gauntness without the aura of her vivacity, her expert make-up smudged into a caricature of its usual perfection and her shimmering blonde hair artificial and brassy.

He closed his eyes to try to block out the images, unable to look at her any more.

How *was* he going to break this latest news to her family? It had been bad enough when he'd been contemplating the best way to tell them that Sara had been knocked down, but *this*…

'We're going to have to put her on IPPV,' the consultant warned when a monitor suddenly shrilled a warning that her oxygen saturation was falling dangerously low in spite of the mask. Dan's eyes flew open and he blinked in disbelief. How had he managed to convince himself that Zara was dead when the room was filled with the sound of all those monitors?

'Her respiratory effort is so badly depressed by the drugs…' his superior continued, almost apologetically.

'It's OK,' Dan reassured the man, immeasurably relieved that all was not yet lost. 'Just do what you have to do. You don't have to talk me through every step. I trust you.'

More than he would trust himself at the moment, he admitted silently. The whole scene seemed totally unreal, especially coming so soon after Sara's narrow escape. How many disasters could one family cope with in a single evening?

At least he'd given in to Sara's request not to inform her parents what had happened to her. He'd been reluctant, knowing how excited they were about the pregnancy, but

Sara had promised that she would go straight to them when she was released in the morning, confident that hearing about the accident would be far less traumatic if they could see with their own eyes that she was perfectly all right.

Well, more or less, he temporised, imagining just how badly bruised she must be after such an event. Her pale skin would soon be all the colours of the rainbow, and as for the pain…that must be considerable, especially as she'd refused any further analgesia.

His respect for his sister-in-law couldn't have been any higher, as a colleague, as a person and as the temporary mother of his children. Sara might not always get along with her twin—an understandable case of sibling rivalry, perhaps?—but she'd certainly proved how much she loved her sister by putting herself through the traumas of a surrogate pregnancy.

Behind his closed lids he saw a flash of another image—that of two tiny hearts beating side by side. And he could picture equally clearly the fiercely protective emotions in Sara's eyes. It had been obvious just how much it had meant to her to see the babies for the first time and to know that her accident had apparently left them untouched.

A secret regret hit him afresh, one that he'd been living with for several years now.

He knew that he'd behaved stupidly when Zara had set out to entice him, had already realised, even then, that Sara had been more than halfway in love with him. He'd probably been heading in the same direction until her sister had started her determined pursuit.

And he'd been stupid enough to be flattered and intrigued by the prospect of being desired by a woman so confident in the power of her beauty. Had it been the fact that she was the twin of someone to whom he was already attracted that had made him believe he had been in love with her?

Enough!

Enough rationalisation! Enough excuses! Whatever the truth had been then, now was a different matter entirely.

He straightened his shoulders and deliberately opened his eyes to gaze directly at the woman he'd married, confronting his blame head on.

It had been his responsibility to protect her, and he'd obviously failed if she hadn't felt able to come to him with her problem—be it depression or a dependency on drugs. He had no idea when it had started or how long it had been going on…no idea whether her brush with death had been an accidental overdose or a deliberate one.

No doubt the police would have to be involved and would doubtless grill him at length about the state of his marriage.

How much worse would it have been if she'd died while he'd been hovering around Sara until she had been settled on the ward?

As it was, even if she did recover fully, it would be some time before Zara was in any fit state to answer questions. He certainly had no idea what had made her take this drastic action, so if the police needed to know why she'd done it, they would probably have to interview Zara's friends and colleagues as well.

'She's stable now, so we're transferring her up to ICU,' the consultant said, and Dan suddenly realised just how much time had elapsed while he'd been lost in his thoughts.

His superior patted his shoulder reassuringly, but there was something else entirely in the expression in his eyes, something that didn't need to be put into words. They both knew that there was no guarantee of a happy outcome.

'I've sent samples up to the lab, just to confirm what she'd taken to make sure we've done all the right things,' he said quietly, then added, 'Give them half an hour or so to get her settled up there,' exactly the way *he* would have done had she been one of *his* patients.

'How long before we know…? How badly is she…?' He couldn't finish a single question, knowing there were no real answers.

'I'd love to be able to tell you that she's going to be all right,' the consultant said, patting Dan's shoulder again. 'But you know as well as I do that only time will tell. Shall I leave it to you to contact the other members of her family, or would it be better coming from me?'

'I'll do that now,' Dan said, his voice sounding almost rusty as it emerged from a throat tight with too much emotion.

How *was* he going to break the news to Zara's doting parents?

CHAPTER THREE

SARA heard the all-too-familiar swoosh and creak of the door to her room as someone pushed it open, and barely managed to stifle a groan.

Not *another* member of staff preventing her from sleeping! There couldn't possibly be an inch of her body that hadn't been examined, poked and prodded...or had a needle stuck in it.

When nothing happened after several seconds of silence, she opened cautious eyes, wondering what was going on. Seeing Dan standing beside the bed, gazing down at her, immediately doubled her pulse rate, then she realised that the oversized gown she'd been given had slipped right off one shoulder. She had to stifle a groan of agony when she tried to hike it back into a more modest position with the wrong hand.

'Dan?' she croaked, trying for impatient but only managing to sound pathetic. 'I thought you were going home. You don't need to keep checking up on me, too. There's an army of nurses doing that every two minutes and...' She had to bite her tongue to stop herself delivering another tirade when she still owed him a massive apology for the first one. He'd come to see her just after she'd had her ultrasound scan to see if she and the babies were all right and she'd jumped right down his throat. It just wasn't fair that she was taking all her fear for the babies out on him.

'I didn't come to check up on you,' he said quietly, one hand going out to the chair beside her bed, then pausing.

It was almost as if he wasn't sure whether to stand or sit, and if it was sit, whether it should be on the chair or on the side of her bed. The whole incident took no more than a few seconds but it was totally uncharacteristic of a man who was usually decisiveness personified.

Finally, he perched uneasily on the edge of the bed, his lean hip nudging against her bruised thigh…not that she would say a word. Secretly, she still revelled in every occasion that he was close to her…close enough to smell the clean soapy scent of his skin and see the tracks where his fingers had raked through his hair. Close enough to see the lines of strain that had grown deeper still since she'd seen him just an hour or two ago.

'Dan? Is something wrong?' Panic struck her and her hand flew to cover the precious duo nestling deep inside her. 'Is it something to do with the babies? Has something shown up on one of the tests?'

'No!' he exclaimed, clearly startled. 'I'm sorry, Sara, I didn't mean to frighten you. As far as I know, everything's still fine.'

'So, what's wrong?' she demanded. 'I can tell you've got something serious on your mind and… Is it Mum and

Dad? I *told* you not to tell them about my accident. I was
going to go and visit them as soon as I'm set free in the
morning, so that they could *see* that I'm not—'

'It's not your parents,' he interrupted, then sighed
heavily and shook his head. 'Sara, I'm sorry but there's
only one way to tell you this. When I got home this
evening, I found Zara unconscious. She'd taken an
overdose of barbiturates.'

'Barbiturates?' she gasped, reeling. 'No! Not Zara. She
wouldn't.' It was her turn to shake her head at the impos-
sibility of what he was suggesting. Her sister might be
selfish and egotistical but she wasn't anyone's fool. She'd
seen far too many of her fellow models slide down the
slippery slope of drug addiction, hooked when the desire
for impossible slenderness came with an intoxicating high.
With a few high-profile exceptions she'd seen it ultimately
ruin their careers as model agencies and advertisers alike
crossed them off their books.

Anyway, barbiturates were usually prescribed for
people having difficulty sleeping, so they wouldn't be any
use to someone wanting to get high. Deliberate overdoses
were usually confined to people who were depressed and
that definitely didn't sound like her vivacious sister.

'There was no name on the bottle and the drug name
was generic…possibly bought abroad or over the internet…and the bottle was empty when I found it on the floor
beside her,' he said quietly, and she could see from his expression that he was already blaming himself.

'How long ago…?' she began, only to halt in mid-
sentence as a sudden thought struck her. If Zara had been

at home, taking an overdose, then her crazy suspicion that it had been her own sister driving the car that had run her down this evening must have been just that…crazy. Unless she'd gone home after she'd done it and taken the drugs in her remorse…but, no, that didn't make sense either. Nothing made sense. Not the fact that she'd been absolutely certain that it had been Zara behind the wheel of the car that had deliberately aimed at her, or the fact that she would have access to barbiturates or would deliberately take an overdose.

'She was in a pretty bad way when I found her,' he said, answering the question she would have asked if her brain had been working well enough to formulate it. 'She was already comatose, her breathing and pulse rate both depressed, but when her stomach was pumped, there were a fair number of undigested tablets, so she must have taken them some time this evening.'

Sara's relief that her sister couldn't have been responsible for her accident faded with the realisation that there would still have been plenty of time for her to have returned home and swallowed the drugs before Dan had found her. But that begged the question: why would Zara do it, especially when Sara was expecting the child… *children*…that she'd begged Sara to carry for her?

'Have you told my parents?' Sara could only imagine the state her mother must be in, knowing that her beautiful perfect daughter had…

'Not yet. I had to come and tell you first,' he said simply.

Pleasure that he'd wanted to break the news to her *before* notifying his in-laws flowered inside her, only to wither to dust when he added, 'I didn't want you to get a garbled version if the news reached you through the hospital grapevine.'

That was more like the Dan she'd been working with for the last couple of years—logical and practical. Of course there hadn't been a personal reason why he would have wanted to give her the news in person. When was she going to stop searching for traces of the connection they'd made when they'd first met? When was she going to come to terms with the fact that any feelings he'd had towards her had vanished the instant he'd met Zara?

'Where is she? What treatment is she receiving? When can I visit her?' she demanded briskly, forcing herself to be equally logical and practical. She tried to push herself up in the bed and fell back with a groan when every muscle and joint complained.

'You're in no fit state to go anywhere yet,' he growled as he carefully slid one arm under her shoulders and effortlessly lifted her up, supporting her while he positioned the pillows behind her.

Sara shivered. Every tiny hair had suddenly stood up in reaction to the warmth of his arm surrounding her. Not that her hospital room was cold. If anything, it was far too hot. But somehow it was different when it was Dan's body heat in a wide swathe across her back where his strong arm held her, and as for the soft wash of his breath stirring her hair against her face and neck…

'But…' It was hard to get her thoughts in order when he was so close. Thank goodness they never did any more than brush against each other when they worked together, or she'd never be able to do her job properly. Still, she didn't dare to take a full breath until he laid her gently back against the pillows and released her to step back a little from the bed. The last thing she needed was another lungful of that familiar mixture of soap and musk to contend with.

'Sara, I'll let you know as soon as they say she's stable enough for visitors,' he promised, his green eyes darkly serious. 'At the moment she's so deeply unconscious that she wouldn't even know that you were there, and you wouldn't be doing yourself any good either. You need to give your body time to heal.'

'But you're going to have to tell Mum and Dad tonight, aren't you…about Zara, I mean?'

'And that means I'll have to tell them about what happened to you, too,' he pointed out.

'No! *I'll* tell them, when I—'

'Sara, think about it,' he interrupted. 'They're going to want to see you…they'll be *expecting* to see you when they arrive at the hospital, waiting outside ICU until Zara's consultant allows you in to see her.'

'But…' She closed her eyes in defeat. He was right, of course. And she wasn't in any fit state to be sitting around in the little relatives' room all night.

'Which would you rather—that they knew that you'd been involved in an accident or that they thought you couldn't be bothered to be with them when they need you?' he challenged, and she slumped back against the pillows, knowing that she couldn't argue against that sort of logic.

'You will tell them that the babies are OK, won't you…?

Oh!' she exclaimed with a shadow of her usual smile. 'They don't know that it's twins yet!' She groaned as she tried to reach into the bedside locker for the precious picture of the scan. 'Could you get the photo for me, so you can show it to them?'

'Actually…' He paused a second and she was startled to see a soft wash of colour sweep across the lean planes of his cheeks as he reached into his pocket to take his wallet out. 'I hope you don't mind, but I asked the technician to print an extra copy.'

For Zara. Of course.

'I should have thought of that…to get one for the two of you. After all, they're going to be *your* babies, so you actually have *more* right to a picture than I do.'

'Sara, don't,' he said swiftly, and startled her by trapping her hand in the warmth of his, the green of his eyes darkening as they gazed intently down into hers. 'I can't imagine how difficult the whole process is for you, but you have every right to a picture of the babies that are developing inside you. I'll never be able to thank you enough for what you're doing. An extra picture of an ultrasound scan is nothing in comparison.'

His sincerity was obvious and actually managed to soothe some of the ache that had been filling her heart ever since she'd been persuaded along this path. The last thing she'd wanted to do was carry the children of the man she loved, only to have to give them away. The fact that he genuinely seemed to appreciate the sacrifice she was making was like balm to her soul. All she had to do was make sure that he never had any idea of her true feelings towards him.

* * *

It had been every bit as dreadful as he'd thought it would be, Dan thought wearily as he propped himself against the wall of the ICU waiting room several hours later.

Unfortunately, it had been his mother-in-law who had answered the door of their smart suburban home, and when she'd realised that Zara hadn't been with him, something in his face must have told her that he was the bearer of bad news.

'She's had an accident, hasn't she?' she wailed. 'I *knew* something must have happened. I just knew it! I've been waiting all evening for Zara to call to let me know she'd returned home safely. I told her she should have asked you to drop her car off at the garage.'

As he ushered her through to her smartly decorated lounge, trying vainly to calm her down, a small corner of Dan's brain registered the odd snippet of information. What had been wrong with Zara's car that it had needed the attention of a mechanic? Both their vehicles had only recently been serviced.

'What's the matter? What's going on?' his father-in-law demanded gruffly from his favourite seat at one end of the settee. He fought to fold the newspaper that had spread itself across his lap and tried not to look as if he'd fallen asleep in front of the television.

'Our Zara's had an accident!' his wife keened. 'I told her she shouldn't be driving in London traffic. Danny should have looked after her. *He* should have taken her car to the garage if there was something wrong with it.'

'Is that true, lad? Is she hurt? How bad is it?' Frank might not be so openly emotional as his wife but it was plain that he was immediately worried about his precious daughter.

'Can we sit down?' Dan suggested, still uncertain just how much he should tell them. The results hadn't come back from the lab by the time he'd left the hospital, so he still wasn't certain what level of concentration the drugs had reached in Zara's body and what that would mean for her prognosis. If they had depressed her respiration and starved her brain of essential oxygen long enough to cause permanent…

'She's *dead*! My baby's *dead*!' Audrey cried hysterically, and for a moment he almost relished the idea that he might need to slap some sense into the woman.

'No! She's *not* dead!' he contradicted firmly, hoping that he sounded more confident than he felt. He took hold of both her shoulders and guided her until the backs of her knees met the edge of the settee and she collapsed next to her husband. 'Neither of your daughters is dead,' he said firmly, desperately praying that he was telling the truth.

'You mean, something's happened to *Sara*?' Frank demanded. 'But I thought… I'm confused. Did Zara ask you to come and tell us? Why didn't she come herself, or is she staying with Sara?'

'Is it something to do with the baby?' his wife demanded sharply. 'Zara will be *so* disappointed if anything's wrong with…'

Between the two of them he was having a hard time getting a word in edgeways. It looked as if he was going to have to abandon any idea of breaking things to them gently.

'Sara was knocked down by a car this evening as she

was walking home from work,' he announced bluntly. Too bluntly? he wondered when it looked as if the pair had stopped breathing.

'No!' He should have known that their mother would recover the power of speech first. 'Oh, Danny…how? Oh, tell me she hasn't lost Zara's precious baby.'

'She was knocked unconscious, her leg was broken and she's badly bruised, but she had a scan to see if she had any internal injuries—'

'She didn't have any X-rays, did she?' Audrey demanded sharply. 'I don't want my first grandchild being born deformed because it had X-rays.'

Not a word of concern about the injuries *Sara* had suffered, Dan noted, even as he had to stifle a smile when he remembered Sean O'Malley telling him just how fiercely Sara had objected to having X-rays. He could just imagine that she'd been the very picture of a lioness defending her cub.

'Actually,' he said, sidestepping the issue of X-rays entirely to focus on the news that still sent his spirits soaring, in spite of all the trauma of the last few hours, 'the scan showed us something we weren't expecting to see— that Sara's carrying twins.'

The momentary silence had a completely different feel this time, but even as they began exclaiming in delight he despised himself for his cowardice. He should be telling them about the much more urgent situation confronting their younger daughter.

His reprieve was all too brief.

'What did Zara say when you told her?' his father-in-law demanded with a beam. 'I bet she was delighted.'

'Well, I was very late getting home, after making sure that Sara and the babies were going to be all right,' he began, even as a voice inside his head jeered at him for trying to assuage his guilt for arriving home so much later than he'd intended. The outcome would have been very different. 'I thought she was asleep, but when I went to tell her the news, I couldn't wake her and had to call an ambulance to take her to hospital.'

'Hospital?' his mother-in law shrieked in disbelief. 'Zara's in hospital, too? Why? What's the matter with her?' She began to struggle to her feet, slapping viciously at her husband's hand when he tried to stop her. 'I've got to go to her straight away. *You'll* have to take me,' she declared with a glare at Dan.

'Why wouldn't she wake up? What's the matter with her? Do you know?' Frank demanded, clearly dumbfounded by the news.

'It looks as if she's taken an overdose of drugs…barbiturates,' he said, and was nearly deafened by the howl of denial.

'*Drugs!* That's a lie! My Zara wouldn't touch the filthy things.' Audrey was sobbing with rage now. 'Why would you say such a dreadful thing about your own wife? You should know she's the most beautiful, most perfect—'

He ignored the start of the familiar litany, interrupting bluntly. 'The bottle was found beside her, and some of the drugs were found still in her stomach when we got her to the hospital and pumped her out.'

'But—' Frank began, but as ever his wife's voice overrode his tentative attempt.

'Then you got them all out and she's going to be all right?' she demanded shrilly, in spite of the fact that her certainty about her daughter's convictions had been summarily destroyed. 'Did she tell you why she took them? It must have been a mistake…a…a…'

'They pumped out as many as they could, but she'd already absorbed enough to send her…' At the last moment he paused, wondering if the mention of the word 'coma' would be the final straw. Instantly, he knew that his mother-in-law would definitely have hysterics if he so much as mentioned the possibility, and sidestepped the prospect by choosing a less emotive word.

'Zara's deeply unconscious, so she's been taken into Intensive Care where she'll be monitored constantly until the drugs wear off and she wakes up.'

He hoped they were too shocked to notice the guilt he was trying to hide, but no way was he mentioning the very real chance that the drugs might have already caused significant damage. He knew that, as her parents, they had a right to information about their daughter, but he was hoping that he wouldn't have to be the one to tell them. It was bad enough that *he* knew that Zara might never wake up again, at least not in any meaningful way.

It might be cowardly, but he was intending to leave it to the consultant to tell them that, even when the effect of the drugs she'd taken did wear off, the daughter that the two of them idolised might already be lost to them for ever.

Sara was a different matter. There was no way he could

have left her to find out what her sister had done, not after the shock her system had already sustained this evening.

He stifled a weary sigh as he assisted his sobbing mother-in-law into his car, knowing that there would be very little chance that he would be seeing his bed tonight.

Hoping that his silence could be taken as the result of navigating the busy streets, he tried to get his thoughts in order.

He would definitely have to contact Human Resources as soon as possible to notify them that he wouldn't be in for his shift the next day…or for the foreseeable future, at least until the drugs had left Zara's system and he had some idea what sort of prognosis they were looking at.

He would also have to see if there was a relatives' room free for the Walkers to use. He couldn't imagine that anyone would be able to persuade Audrey and Frank to leave the hospital until their daughter was out of danger, but they might be persuaded to rest in between the short visits they would be permitted by her side.

Then there was Sara.

Bruised, bloodied and broken her body might be, but her spirit appeared even stronger than ever if the way she'd confronted him was any gauge.

He found himself stifling a grin when he remembered the way she'd turned on him like a spitting cat. It was the closest she'd ever come to telling him exactly what she thought of him, although he had a pretty good idea.

He'd barely admitted to himself how much of his time had been spent thinking about her, even in those first few weeks. Then he'd been stupid enough to allow himself to be snowballed into marriage with her sister, committing the oldest blunder in the book when he'd allowed his hormones to overrule his heart.

Then, when he and Zara had been unable to conceive, he'd been amazed and delighted when his in-laws had told him that Sara had volunteered to act as a surrogate mother for them.

How stupid could he have been? He should have known that her parents' desire to give Zara everything she ever wanted would have made them resort to any means to persuade her soft-hearted sister to agree.

No wonder she had so little time for him, even when he was concerned about her welfare. No wonder she'd been convinced that his only interest was that his child had been unharmed.

Children, he reminded himself with a surge of mingled joy and terror.

He'd been amazed and delighted to see not one but two hearts beating strongly on the ultrasound screen, evidence that they were both still snugly ensconced in their rightful environment and supremely unaware of their narrow escape. One side of him was ecstatic to see the evidence that his precious children weren't just a dream but a miraculous reality. It was the other side—the doctor side of him—that knew enough to be afraid; the doctor half of his brain that knew just how much more dangerous the existence of that second baby was, both to the pregnancy and to Sara herself.

Bearing a child was already one of the most dangerous things a woman could put herself through, and to carry twins…

He shook his head when he realised that he was already planning a session on the computer to access all the relevant statistics, irrespective of the fact that knowing the figures would worry him even more.

'What's the matter?' Audrey demanded in a panicky voice as she entered the relatives' room at exactly the wrong moment. 'Why did you shake your head? Did the doctor say something to you while we were in with Zara? She's not going to…? Oh, no! Please! She can't die. Not my beautiful girl!'

Dan swore silently as her voice rose shrilly with every word, his head thumping unmercifully.

'No one's told me anything,' he said firmly as he took her by the shoulders and leant down to force her to meet his gaze. 'Audrey, the only time I've spoken to Zara's consultant was when you were with me. The situation hasn't changed. We've just got to wait and see how her body copes with whatever it is she's taken. We've just got to be patient.'

'How *can* I be patient?' she demanded angrily, shrugging his hands off and whirling away. 'I'm her *mother*! You have no idea how dreadful it is not being able to do anything. Just waiting…'

'You could visit Sara,' he suggested. 'She must be wondering what's happening down here, worrying about—'

'If she were that worried she'd be here with us,' Audrey interrupted sharply. 'I can't believe how selfish that girl is, to be lying in bed when she should be down here with her sister…with us…'

'Sara's in no fit state to go anywhere,' Dan snapped,

rapidly reaching the end of his tether. It was unbelievable that parents could be so concerned about one of their daughters and so dismissive of the other. They seemed to care so little for Sara and were so unappreciative of her and everything she'd achieved that it bordered on emotional abuse.

It certainly wasn't something that he would ever do to *his* children. His heart missed a beat when he visualised the flickering evidence of those two tiny beings that would one day look up to him and call him Daddy. It was an awesome responsibility and he would make certain that they both knew that their father loved each of them as much as the other.

'Mum? Dad?' said a hesitant voice from the doorway, and Dan spun on his heel, his eyes widening with disbelief when he saw the shaky figure sitting in the wheelchair.

The bruises on her face looked livid and angry already, especially against the stark white of the dressing covering her stitches. He could only guess how many other injuries were hidden under the back-to-front gown she wore as a wrap, but nothing could hide the ungainly cast stabilising her broken leg.

'Sara!' He strode towards her when he saw her struggling one-handed to propel herself further into the room, her face so pale it seemed almost bloodless. He didn't know whether to be angry with her for being crazy enough to make the journey when every inch of the distance between her room and ICU must have been agony for her, or proud that her determination was enough to bring her here in case her parents needed her support.

All he knew was that he was suddenly filled with an overwhelming need to protect this valiant woman from anything that might cause her any more pain.

CHAPTER FOUR

DAN was still seething when he finally took half an hour to race home for a shower and a change of clothes.

'Those parents of hers are unbelievable!' he growled as he leaned wearily against his front door, almost too tired to make his way to the bathroom.

He was sure his mouth must have gaped when there hadn't been any evidence of sympathy at the shocking extent of Sara's injuries, not a single word of concern that she must have escaped death by the merest whisker, to say nothing of the possible loss of their grandchild…grand-*children*, he corrected himself and felt that crazy grin creep over his face again, banishing his bad mood at a stroke.

He reached for his wallet and extracted the precious image printed from Sara's first scan and awe joined his feeling of delight. Not one but two tiny beings were still growing safely inside her womb, in spite of their close brush with death. He could still feel that first surge of emotion when he'd seen the image of their minuscule hearts, the beats so rapid that they'd almost seemed to flicker on the screen.

'My babies,' he whispered as he outlined their precious images with a visibly trembling fingertip and was shocked to feel the hot press of tears behind his eyes.

This…*these*…were the one good thing that had happened in such a very long time. These two tiny beings made everything worthwhile.

Even the knowledge that your wife is lying dangerously ill in ICU? asked a disapproving voice inside his head. That brought him up short for a moment and guilt struck him hard that he was feeling such delight while Zara's health—her very life—hung in the balance.

His shoulders slumped still further when he realised that even though her situation was serious, with no guarantee for a happy outcome, he found it strangely hard to care any more than he would if Zara were just another patient brought into A and E in the course of his working day.

'That certainly took the smile off your face,' he muttered as he strode across the lounge towards the bathroom with the weight of a very long day pressing down on his shoulders again. At the last moment he veered towards the mantelpiece to prop the precious image in full view, torn between the desire to replace it in his wallet to keep it close to him and the equally strong need to keep it safe.

His first step inside the bedroom was like a punch to the gut. He and Zara were both reasonably tidy people so it was a real shock to be confronted with the shambles that remained from his efforts to keep her body functioning until the paramedics arrived.

The bedclothes straggling onto the floor were mute testimony to the way he'd hastily pulled her down onto the firmer surface, and there certainly hadn't been time to straighten anything up before he'd leapt in his car to follow the ambulance to the hospital.

He stepped forward and reached out to gather up the bedding then let it fall again, unable to find the energy to care that the bed needed making or, more to the point, the inclination to sleep in it at all when he thought about what had so nearly happened there.

He needed sleep. In fact, if he was honest with himself, he was nearly out on his feet with exhaustion, both with the stresses of a long hard shift and then the double shocks of first Sara's and then Zara's admission to hospital. Even so, he couldn't face the thought of climbing into that bed, not when he didn't know whether its last occupant was going to survive.

He nearly fell asleep standing under the shower, the fierce pummelling of the water jets on the back of his neck and across his shoulders almost as blissful as a massage.

Not that he'd had the time or inclination for massages recently. In fact, not since the last time Sara had taken pity on him in the very early days of their fledgling relationship.

'Don't go there!' he groaned aloud, but that did nothing to stop the images playing through his head.

It had been a rough shift, not unlike the last twelve hours, and he'd made the mistake of sitting down at the table in the staffroom rather than going straight home. The next thing he'd known had been Sara's voice in his ear, calling his name and waking him to the realisation that he could barely move his neck for the crick in it.

'Can I see if I can get rid of that stiffness for you?' she'd offered, and for a moment he hadn't been certain which stiffness she'd been talking about. Waking up with her soft voice and the warmth of her breath in his ear had matched perfectly with the dream he'd been having, and both had had a predictable effect on his body.

Her fingers on his neck and shoulders, alternately stroking then firmly kneading only helped his neck and shoulders. His other reaction he'd had to keep to himself until he'd returned to his bachelor digs with images of persuading Sara to join him there as soon as possible playing in his head.

Had there been a hormonal overload in his system at the time, because it had been just days later that he'd met Zara and been completely bowled over by her blatant interest in him...so different to Sara's more reserved manner and so flattering to the male ego.

The steam followed him out of the shower as he padded through to the wardrobe with nothing more than a towel wrapped around the back of his neck.

He was operating on auto pilot now, knowing that he needed clean clothes and to put something in his stomach and knowing that his duty was to support his in-laws while they waited impatiently for the scant five minutes in each hour that they were allowed to spend at their daughter's bedside. It was so wearing to sit with them knowing that they were pinning their hopes on finding a dramatic improvement each time they went in.

He was already running on his reserves and knew he needed to sleep, and sleep soon, but somehow...somehow he couldn't think about sleeping while Zara's condition was unresolved and especially while Sara was valiantly sitting with her parents, waiting for better news. She had worked just the same killer hours as he had and had then suffered the trauma of being run over.

The clean shirt made him feel a bit less ragged and he was just reaching for some bread to toast to fill the gaping hole where his stomach should be when his pager shrilled.

'Daniel Lomax,' he said, his heart in his mouth by the time the phone was answered in ICU and he was switched through to the consultant's office. He wasn't on duty but had told the ICU staff he was taking his pager home with him if they needed to contact him.

'Daniel, I thought you'd like to know that we've had another set of results back from the lab and—'

'I'm on my way, sir,' Dan interrupted, when he heard the strange note in the consultant's voice. Suddenly he knew that something was wrong, and a surge of adrenaline instantly banished his exhaustion. 'I'll be there in about eight minutes,' he promised, already halfway out of the door as he ended the conversation.

By the time he reached the street he'd fought his way into his jacket and had his keys and phone safely in his pocket. The rain was still lashing down and for a moment he considered going round the back of the flats for his car, then shook his head. The flat had been chosen because of its proximity to the hospital but the security system protecting the cars from opportunist thieves would take longer to get through than if he ran. Nothing was going to interfere with getting to ICU as quickly as possible.

He was soaked to the skin and so wound up that he was shaking by the time he made it up the last flight of stairs.

'What's happened?' he gasped as he reached the interview room, one of the nurses having pointed the way as soon as she'd seen him.

'It's good news!' Audrey exclaimed with tears in her eyes. 'They've found out that Zara *hadn't* taken an overdose of barbiturates after all. I *told* you she wouldn't. She's not into all that drugs nonsense.'

'Not barbiturates?' Dan said with a frown, turning towards Mr Shah. 'But the bottle was on the bed beside her when I found her. I don't understand.'

'It's possible that it was some sort of…' he hesitated a second and threw a glance in Audrey and Frank's direction. 'A decoy of some sort, to make you think she'd taken something else.'

'Well, it worked,' Dan said flatly, hating the thought that even in something as serious as an overdose of drugs Zara was playing stupid games. 'So what *had* she taken?'

'The lab results say that the majority of the tablets were paracetamol but there was definitely some phenobarbitone, too.'

'See!' Audrey exulted, obviously completely oblivious to the serious expression on the man's face. 'It was nothing more than some over-the-counter tablets. We'll soon have her home again, good as new.'

'We knew in A and E that there was something wrong when her stomach was pumped,' Dan said, remembering his shock when he'd seen just how many tablets there'd been. It had looked like handfuls of them still largely undissolved, to say nothing of the ones that must have already dissolved and entered her system. 'The label on the bottle meant it should have been capsules but they were bringing up plain white tablets.'

'Well, it looks as if she thought she was taking just enough phenobarbitone to send her to sleep, and miscalculated. She's still comatose.'

And that wasn't the worst of it, Dan knew with a sinking feeling, already working out for himself what Mr Shah was going to tell them next.

'She was given activated charcoal when she was brought into A and E after her stomach was pumped,' he recalled with a feeling of dread.

'Unfortunately, not long after the IV was set up, she had an adverse reaction to the antidote we were giving her,' the consultant said, obviously trying to keep things simple for Frank and Audrey. 'We've given her antihistamine to dampen the reaction but, because she's had the charcoal, methionine won't be an effective alternative.'

To say nothing of the fact that she was still unconscious and would be unable to swallow the methionine tablets, Dan added silently. He'd been horribly right in what he'd feared. 'That means you're going to have to start the same IV again at the lowest possible infusion rate so you don't trigger the reaction for a second time.' And *that* meant it would take that much longer before the drug in her body was rendered harmless—time in which it could be doing untold damage to her liver and kidneys, especially to someone who was borderline for malnourishment, the way so many fashion models were.

'So, how long will it be before she wakes up?' prompted Audrey eagerly. 'How long before we can bring our little girl home?'

The consultant sent Dan a wry look, sharing the knowledge that here was yet another set of parents who were only hearing what they wanted to hear.

'We're giving her medication to mop up the drugs still in her system, but everything else is largely up to her own body. She won't wake up until the sleeping pills she took have worn off, and we have no idea how long that will take. It's just a case of waiting,' he explained kindly, and Dan knew that the man had recognised that neither of his in-laws was capable of taking in the possibility of any other outcome. As far as they were concerned, Zara would wake up as quickly and easily as though she'd fallen asleep in front of the television the way she sometimes did after a long flight.

'Excuse us,' Frank said suddenly, getting out of his seat after a quick glance at his watch. 'It's our time to go and sit with Zara. We wouldn't want to miss it.'

'By all means,' the consultant said, getting up courteously to open the door for them. He glanced back at Dan as though asking whether he wanted to leave, too, but he didn't move. There were so many more questions he needed to ask, particularly about the lab results and the level of concentration of the paracetamol that had been found in Zara's blood.

At the last moment, just as the door swung closed, he caught sight of a slight cotton-clad figure in a wheelchair out in the corridor.

'Just a moment, sir,' he requested, and hurried across to open the door again, to find Sara making her laborious way towards her sister. Her parents must have passed her just seconds ago but had clearly left her struggling on her own.

'Sara,' he called gently to attract her attention, and stifled a wince when he saw how gingerly she turned her head towards him. She shouldn't be wheeling herself about when she was so badly bruised. She should be lying in bed, giving her body time to heal.

'Did you want to have a word about Zara?' he invited. 'The latest lab results are in.' He glanced over his shoulder to find that the consultant hadn't been quite so quick to mask his reaction to Sara's injuries. 'Do you have any objection if she joins us, sir? Zara is her twin, but Sara is a doctor on the staff here, down in A and E.'

'I've no objections at all. Come in, my dear. Let me hold the door for you.' He hurried to hold the door wide while Dan strode out to take hold of the handles and provide the propulsion she needed. 'My word, your family *is* in the wars. What on earth happened to you?' he asked as he gently shook her hand as though afraid she would shatter.

'A hit-and-run accident on my way home from work,' she said, as she used her hand to shift her cast to a more comfortable position, the wry smile that she sent him doing nothing to lift the evidence of pain from her face.

Dan ached for her, wishing there was something he could do, but there was no one on earth who would be able to persuade her to take painkillers if she'd decided against them.

'How bad were the results?' Sara asked quietly, as ever

going straight to the point. 'How much damage has she done to herself? I suppose she got the barbiturates on one of her foreign trips.'

'Actually, my dear, it's not the barbiturates that are causing the biggest problem,' Mr Shah explained. 'The majority of the drugs your sister took were paracetamol.'

Dan wouldn't have believed that Sara could have gone any paler until he saw it happen. Her lips were almost colourless and she had to lick them with a flick of her tongue before she could speak.

'So, she's on IV N-acetylcysteine? What concentration has the paracetamol reached? Is it still rising or is it on the way down now?'

'It's not rising any more, but it hasn't started dropping yet,' the consultant said apologetically. 'As you say, we put her on IV NAC, but she quickly developed side effects. We've had to administer antihistamine and drop the dosage of the drip right down.'

The small frown pleating her forehead told Dan that she had worked out for herself the reasons why they couldn't use the alternative antidote, and admired the fact that her brain was still working just as fast as usual in spite of everything that had happened over the last day.

'Also,' Mr Shah continued inexorably, 'we have no way of knowing how long the drugs have been in her system. If it is only a short time—less than eight hours—then it will not be such a big problem, but we cannot assume anything.'

Dan was watching Sara's face as the consultant was speaking, so he saw the sudden widening of her eyes and the deepening of her frown. The expression must have pulled her stitches if the wince and the protective hand that came up to cover the dressing was any indication.

For a moment it was obvious that she was conducting some sort of internal debate and the way her hazel eyes darkened told him it wasn't a pleasant one. Then her hand dropped to the curve of her belly in a protective gesture as old as time and panic roared through him. Was she in pain? Was she suffering a delayed reaction to her accident? Was she miscarrying?

'Sara,' he began, fighting for self-control when all he could think of was the precious picture propped on his mantelpiece, 'is everything all right? Are you feeling—?'

The sudden sound of a hasty knock at the door cut him off as the consultant excused himself before calling, 'Enter.'

'Mr Shah, Zara Walker seems to be waking up. Did you want to—?'

'Thank you. We will come now,' he said swiftly, already pushing back his chair. 'Do you want to follow me?' he threw over his shoulder, but didn't wait for a reply as he hurried out into the corridor.

'Here, let me. It'll be quicker,' Dan said as he took over the propulsion of her wheelchair, leaving Sara to slump back into the seat.

She must be really close to the end of her tether, he realised when he saw the slump of her shoulders. Zara might be the professional model but Sara had an innate elegance and style of her own and poor posture wasn't a part of it.

'Are you sure you're all right?' he asked, taking advantage of the fact that there simply wasn't enough space for the wheelchair in Zara's room—there were just too many people in there at the moment. 'For a moment, back in the interview room, you looked…worried. Is it the baby? You're not having contractions, are you?'

'*Babies,*' she corrected softly. 'And, no, I'm not having contractions, thank goodness. I was just…' She paused for a moment, then shook her head. 'No. It's nothing.'

'Are you sure?' Some sixth sense was telling him to press her. 'If it was something that could possibly help Zara…'

There it was again, a look of indecision, as though she couldn't bring herself to say something…detrimental about her twin. He had no right to insist that she speak to him and was still trying to find a way to persuade her to trust him with…well, with whatever it was putting that frown on her face when an all-too-familiar voice called his name.

'Danny?' it quavered, but whether the weakness was real or feigned he wouldn't like to hazard a guess. It could just as easily be either, knowing Zara. 'Is Danny there?' There was a plaintive note this time and he had to stifle a wry smile. Now certainly wasn't the right time to question Sara, but he was definitely going to make a point of it before he left the hospital this time.

'I'm here, Zara,' he confirmed lightly, straightening up so that she could see him above the general mêlée of medical staff and her parents. Her vital signs had already been checked and if he wasn't mistaken, there was more blood being drawn for another lot of tests to track the progress of the antidote.

'Come closer, Danny,' invited Audrey, beaming widely and beckoning with the arm not wrapped around her precious daughter's shoulders. 'Look! Isn't it wonderful? Our Zara's back with us as good as new. Isn't she beautiful?'

Zara had been born beautiful, Dan thought dismissively. It was all on the surface, not something she'd had to work for…unlike Sara's medical qualifications.

Zara's initial expression when her mother drew her attention to him was one of open delight, then her wide hazel eyes drifted to one side as though she was trying to see what had attracted his attention away from her at such an important moment.

He took a step aside so that she could see her sister sitting in the wheelchair beside him. He was totally shocked when, instead of an expression of concern or, at the very least, an equally welcoming smile for her sister, her look was one of…what? It was definitely more than horror at the fact that she'd suffered such injuries, it was almost revulsion, or even…hatred?

Impossible. He must be more exhausted than he'd thought if he could imagine such a thing. Twins were closer than almost any other people, and in their case, with Sara putting herself through pregnancy on her sister's behalf, they were bound to be closer than most.

Then, without a single question about how Sara came to be so injured, Zara held out a hand towards him in a blatantly theatrical plea.

'Oh, Danny, I'm so sorry for putting you through this but…' She bit her lip and peered up at him. 'I just couldn't cope with it any more. It was all just too much.'

'Couldn't bear what?' he asked, not buying her panto-mime for a minute, although there must be something serious behind her actions. Someone as self-centred as Zara didn't do anything without planning it down to the last step, like her plan to seduce him.

'Well, didn't you read my note?' she demanded crossly. She was clearly wrong-footed by the fact that he didn't know what she was talking about, but he had no doubt he would be hearing all about it in exhaustive detail.

'I didn't see any note. When did you write it? Where did you put it?' he demanded. It certainly hadn't been on the mantelpiece when he'd put the picture of the scan there, although he hadn't really been looking at anything other than those two indeterminate dark blobs with the bright flashes where their hearts were beating.

'Oh, Danny,' she cried, and accepted the pretty hand-kerchief her mother offered, actually managing to squeeze out a tear or two. 'I poured my heart out to you…told you how insecure I was feeling…how afraid that… Oh, what's the use?' she said petulantly, and turned her back on him.

'She's overwrought,' Audrey said in a stage whisper. 'She'll feel better when she's had a good night's sleep in her own bed.' She turned her attention to Mr Shah. 'When can we take her home? Do we have to fill in any papers?'

'Oh, my dear Mrs…Mrs Walker,' he said after a quick glance at Zara's notes to refresh his memory. 'Your daughter is perfectly within her rights to sign her self out of hospital, but I certainly wouldn't advise it.'

'Why on earth not?' challenged Frank. 'We've all been waiting for her to wake up and now she has. Surely that's an end to the whole miserable episode.'

'I wish it were, sir, believe me,' the consultant said with a shake of his head. 'Unfortunately, the fact that your daughter has woken doesn't mean that all the drugs have left her body, and until the drip has neutralised the paracetamol, the drug could still be doing damage to her liver.'

'But…' Audrey looked almost comically disappointed.

'It really would be better if she stayed until we can give her a clean bill of health. She probably still feels rather shaky and tired and would rather not make a journey before she's absolutely ready.'

Dan smothered a grin when he recognised the way the ICU consultant had got the measure of the Walker family. To suggest, obliquely, that Zara needed specialist attention for a little longer was the one strategy that her parents wouldn't want to argue with.

After that, it wasn't very long before the senior sister had used a similar technique for persuading Audrey and Frank that it would be in everybody's best interests if they went home and had a good night's sleep.

Sleep! It had been so long since he'd done it that he felt quite punch-drunk, but something still wouldn't let him leave until he'd gone to check that Sara was finally getting some rest. After Zara's little pout he'd turned to say something to her, but neither the wheelchair nor its occupant had been anywhere in sight.

'What do you think you're doing?' he growled when he found her clothed in a set of baggy blue scrubs and trying to work out how she could use a pair of crutches with one shoulder taped up after a dislocation. 'Are you completely crazy? You should be in bed, allowing your injuries to start healing.'

'And that's exactly where I'll be as soon as I get home,' she countered with a stubborn lift of her chin.

'And exactly how were you intending getting there?' he asked, wondering what it would do to his credibility as a doctor if he stood in the middle of the corridor and screamed out his frustration. Why wouldn't the wretched woman see that he was trying to take care of her?

'Well, as walking is plainly out of the question until I'm a little more proficient, I would have thought that the obvious alternative is a taxi,' she snapped in frustration, standing on one leg and clearly in danger of losing her balance and falling over as she tried to put her coat on.

'And when you get home?' he persisted. 'How were you going to get up all those stairs to your little eyrie?'

He almost felt sorry when he saw her shoulders slump in defeat.

'I can't stay in here, Dan,' she said turning those golden hazel eyes on him in mute appeal. 'Won't you help me?'

'If you're really adamant about leaving, you've got two choices. Either I can drop you off at you parents' house—'

'No way!' she exclaimed with a shudder. 'I haven't spent a night there since I left for medical school and I don't intend changing that. What's the other alternative?'

'That I take you home to my flat.'

'*Your* flat?'

Her expression was so shocked that he hurried to continue. 'I—*we*—do have a spare room, Sara, and I'm sure that your sister would be delighted to know you're somewhere safe.'

Under her breath she muttered something that sounded very much like, 'I doubt it.' He almost asked her to explain but as she was conceding defeat over donning her coat it looked as if he'd at least won that round, even if was only to get her to stay here for the few hours left till morning.

'I'll give you a lift after morning rounds if the orthopod gives you the all-clear, and see what we can do to make you comfortable and safe…all three of you,' he added quickly when she bristled again at the suggestion that she couldn't take care of herself. He wasn't above using her pregnancy as a weapon if it got her to take care of herself. 'The last thing you need is to have a fall down the stairs. You might not be so lucky a second time.'

CHAPTER FIVE

SARA felt as if she'd been tricked into staying in hospital for the last few hours.

It had taken her some time to recognise the way Dan had played on her concern for the two tiny beings residing inside her to persuade her to agree, and she'd even had to smile at his astuteness, but she had no intention of staying any longer. Now was the perfect time to make good her escape, while the staff were all too busy elsewhere to notice her going. What did it matter that she would now be leaving in daylight in a pair of oversized scrubs that looked like a clown's baggy pyjamas and a coat that looked as if someone had rolled in the gutter in it—which she had.

'Maybe the dry-cleaners will be able to do something with it,' she muttered as she awkwardly balanced her borrowed crutches across the arms of the wheelchair to reach for the button to call for the lift. If the coat wasn't salvageable…well, it was easy come, easy go. It had been one of the items Zara had been throwing out because she'd needed to make room for more up-to-the-minute items, ir-respective of the fact that it was made of some horrendously expensive fabric like cashmere or vicuna. All Sara knew was that it was the most deliciously warm coat she'd ever worn and she'd be loath to lose it. She certainly wouldn't be able to replace it with anything as good.

'Making your escape?' said a deep voice behind her, and she jumped so high she had to scrabble to hold onto the crutches.

'Dan! Don't do that!' she snapped as her heart gave its familiar leap in response to his closeness.

'I had a feeling you wouldn't be waiting about this morning,' he said wryly. 'It's nice to be proved right.'

'Actually, I was just going to call in to ICU to see what Zara's latest results are. Have you already been? Do you know?'

The lift gave a quiet ding and the doors slid open to disgorge half a dozen assorted staff and visitors. 'Let's find out together,' he suggested as he took charge and wheeled her into the lift. Then the doors slid closed and the two of them were trapped in the enclosed space, isolated and alone in a way she'd been careful to avoid ever since the day Zara had turned up to be introduced to her tall, dark and handsome doctor friend.

'Sara, are you really well enough to be leaving so soon?' he asked quietly, and her heart gave a stupid extra beat when she saw the caring expression in his eyes.

He's a doctor. Caring's what he does, she reminded herself firmly, just in case she got the idea that it was her as a person that he cared about.

'I'll cope,' she said firmly. 'I'm a fit, healthy person, so I'll soon be on the mend. You don't have to worry about me.'

Her timing was perfect as the doors slid open just as she
finished speaking, and the people waiting to board the lift
prevented Dan from saying anything more.

'Ah, Daniel. Good. I'm glad you're here,' Mr Shah said,
almost as soon as they'd set foot in the unit.

'Problems?' Sara heard the edge in his voice that told
her he'd been expecting this conversation.

'More problems than I'd like,' the consultant admitted
as he showed them into his office. 'Your wife's liver
enzymes are raised and rising but time is critical. If only
we knew exactly how long it was since she took the
overdose. We'd have some idea how much further they
might go.'

Sara felt sick as she took in the information. She knew
that the raised enzyme levels were evidence of liver
damage but she also knew that the number of hours
between overdose and the start of treatment was very important. If a patient received the antidote within eight hours
there was a far better chance of saving the liver from permanent, if not fatal, damage.

In her mind's eye she replayed the split second before
she'd been struck by that car, the instant when she'd been
looking straight towards whoever was driving it and had
seen her own face looking back at her.

Had it been her own face, reflected back at her from the
windscreen, or had the person behind the wheel been the
only other person in the world with a face exactly like
hers?

She didn't want to know, couldn't bear to know if it had
been Zara, because whoever it had been, there was abso-

lutely no doubt in her mind that they had aimed the car at her deliberately, that they had intended to kill her and the babies inside her.

But…logic told her that knowing might be essential for Zara's health. If she *had* been the driver, that would mean that she probably hadn't taken the paracetamol until she'd returned home. That would give Mr Shah the timeline he needed to gauge how much more aggressive his treatment needed to be if he was to be able to rescue Zara's liver.

She was still conducting her silent debate when one of the nurses ushered her parents into the office to join them.

'I'm afraid Zara won't be going home today,' the consultant stated firmly as soon as the pleasantries were over.

'But I've got everything ready for—' Audrey protested.

'She's not well enough to leave today,' he said. 'Her latest results are showing us a problem with her liver and she needs to stay here until we know she's stable.'

'Her liver? What's wrong with her liver?' Frank demanded with a look of disbelief. 'She's never been a big drinker, not like some of these girls who go out and get drunk all the time.'

'Partly she's having the problem because she's underweight,' Mr Shah explained patiently. 'Her liver didn't have enough reserves, so when her body started to break down the paracetamol, it began damaging the tissues of the liver.'

'So, how bad is it?' Frank was suddenly very subdued, as though the severity of the situation was only now coming home to him. 'And is it going to get any worse?'

'The damage means that her liver will develop areas of

necrosis—that means the tissue dies,' he explained hastily when he saw their puzzled expressions. 'We don't know yet whether it's going to get any worse. It's just a case of wait and see.'

'How long will we have to wait? Weeks? Months?' Audrey asked tearfully, clutching her husband's hand like a lifeline.

'Not as long as that. Usually, it's no more than a few days before we can tell whether the liver is damaged beyond repair.'

'What happens then?' Audrey was pale and shaky but clearly intent on fighting for her precious daughter. 'What are you going to do to make her well again? Will she need medication or dialysis or what?'

'Dialysis isn't an option—it can only be used for kidney failure—but some patients with quite severe liver damage can recover with the right diet and support. For the rest, there are surgical options, but we won't go into that unless it becomes necessary.'

The meeting broke up then, with her parents hurrying off to spend time with Zara while Sara was left trying to manoeuvre wheelchair and crutches out of the office without taking a chunk out of the door.

'Let me,' Dan said, and took over the propulsion again. And even though being this close to him caused every nerve in her body to tense up, she wasn't about to refuse the loan of some muscle power to get her to the lift.

'Thank you,' she murmured, careful not to look in his direction while they waited for the lift to arrive. She was grateful they weren't the only ones in it this time—the more people sharing the space the better if she wasn't to risk making a complete fool of herself. How long would it take before he realised that she'd never got over him, even though he'd abandoned her in favour of marrying her sister?

She could have groaned when he insisted on pushing her across the expanse of the main reception hall and out of the electronically controlled doors.

'Where do you want to go?' he asked, absent-mindedly flicking the keys in his hand against his leg.

'I can get a taxi,' she pointed out with a glance towards the couple already waiting outside the front of the hospital, their drivers chatting to each other with the ease of long acquaintance.

'Ah, but will it be driven by someone willing to stay long enough to make sure you get up your stairs safely? Are you willing to risk falling down and breaking something else—or injuring the babies?'

He didn't play fair, Sara grumbled silently as she tried to make herself comfortable on the plush grey upholstery. If he hadn't mentioned the babies, she would have stuck to her guns, she told herself as she tried to get her cast into the footwell, grateful that he'd thought to slide the passenger seat back as far as possible to accommodate her lack of mobility.

She breathed a sigh of relief when she was finally able to click the seat belt into position then regretted it when she drew in that tantalising mixture of soap and man that would forever signify Dan.

Think of something to talk about, she told herself sternly as he pulled out of the car park, but the only topic that came to mind was Zara. Still, it did prompt an idea.

'Nice car,' she commented blandly. 'What sort is Zara driving these days?'

'I didn't think you were into cars.' There was a hint of laughter in his voice, the laughter that she'd loved to share with him when she'd believed they'd had a future together. 'You don't even own one, do you?'

'I didn't see the point of buying one for the sake of it,' she said stiffly, fighting off the memories. 'I live within walking distance of the hospital and the shops, and if I need to go further afield, there's always a taxi or the train.'

'So, why the interest in Zara's vehicle?'

'Just wondering if you ever let her drive yours.' That was bound to get her the information she wanted. She knew how much he loved his bad-boy black BMW with its pale grey interior, had been with him the day he'd taken delivery of it, the first new car he'd ever owned.

'No way!' he exclaimed fervently. 'But she insisted that she needed to be able to get about and wanted something equally sporty, so…'

'His and hers? Matching cars?' she teased and held her breath.

'Well, yes,' he admitted uncomfortably, then added, 'Except hers is metallic silver with black upholstery.'

'Big difference!' she teased again, although how she found the words she didn't know. A silver car with dark upholstery. That was an image that would be imprinted in her memory for the rest of her life.

But there must be thousands of silver BMWs. It could

have been any one of them, said the corner of her brain that didn't want to believe that her sister could have done that to her. Except, she argued with herself as her fingers crept up to trace the scar on her forehead, you know what she was capable of when she was just a little girl. She's grown up now, but has she grown out of such tendencies or has the scale of them grown with her?

'I hope you won't mind if I stop off at my flat first,' he said, and she was so relieved that he was interrupting the darkening spiral of her thoughts that she would have agreed to almost anything. 'It shouldn't take me long, but you can come up and wait for me if you like.'

'And have to go through all that effort of posting myself back into the car? No, thank you,' she said. 'If you park in the underground car park, I'll be quite safe while I wait for you.'

He tried to change her mind but she was adamant, a new plan already fully formed in her head.

As soon as he disappeared from view she opened the passenger door and began the time-consuming struggle to extricate herself from the car. All the while her pulse was racing, afraid that she wouldn't have time to achieve what she wanted to before he came back.

'A silver BMW with a black interior,' she muttered aloud, having had to admit defeat with the crutches when her recently dislocated shoulder refused to take the pressure. Anyway the pain was too great and she didn't dare to do it any more damage or it could be a problem for the rest of her life.

So it was her eyes rather than her feet that set off along

the row of cars while she leant against Dan's, her eyebrows lifting a little more with each expensive model she recognised, but in spite of the fact that there were two other BMWs, neither was silver with a black interior.

'So much for my idea of seeing whether there was any damage on her car,' she grumbled as she made her halting way back to Dan's vehicle. But if it wasn't here, where could it be? Zara certainly hadn't driven herself to the hospital in it.

'Sara, what's the matter? Why did you get out of the car?' She hadn't even heard the lift coming down but there was Dan hurrying towards her across the oil-stained concrete.

'Um…I had a touch of cramp and needed to get out to move about a bit,' she invented clumsily, hating not to tell the truth, but how could she make such an accusation without a single shred of proof?

'Are you ready to get back in or would you rather change your mind?' he offered. 'It wouldn't take me five minutes to put clean sheets on the bed.'

Dan and bed in the same sentence weren't the ideal combination to ensure she had a good sleep. 'I'd rather go where I'm surrounded by my own things,' she said, while her brain was trying to find a way to get the answers she needed.

Finally, there was only one way.

'I couldn't see Zara's car in the garage,' she said, hoping it sounded like idle conversation while he steered them out of the garage and back onto the street.

'You wouldn't. It's usually parked in the slot next to

mine, but apparently she had an argument with a bollard the other day and dropped it off at the garage to have some scratches repaired…not for the first time, I might tell you,' he added with a chuckle.

'So, when did she take it to the garage?' Sara asked, and the frowning glance he threw her way told her that she'd pushed too far.

'Sara, what's all this about?' he asked as he drew up in front of the converted Victorian house she lived in. He turned to face her. 'Why so many questions about Zara's car? What do you *really* want to know?'

Sara swallowed hard when she met his gaze, knowing the frightening level of intelligence contained behind those green eyes. There would be no point insulting that intelligence with a half-baked invention.

'I wanted to know because…' She swallowed again, afraid that this was going to be the moment when she lost all semblance of friendship with the man she'd never stopped loving. 'Because the car that ran me down was a silver BMW with dark-coloured upholstery and I'm almost certain that it was driven by a woman with long blonde hair.'

To say he looked shocked by the implied accusation was an understatement, and the longer she looked at those eyes and the way they widened and darkened endlessly with the repercussions had her hurrying into speech again.

'I can't believe that *anyone* would want to do such a thing deliberately, least of all Zara, but…but I needed to know…about her car, and about the damage she did to it. Then I'll have the proof that it *wasn't* my sister who tried to…to…' She choked on the press of tears and couldn't say another word but, then, she'd already said more than enough if his expression was anything to go by.

There was an agonisingly long silence in the car while she tried to concentrate on keeping the tears back. Crying was one of Zara's favourite weapons and all her life Sara had consciously fought against them for just that reason.

'Well, then, there's only one thing to do, isn't there?' Dan said suddenly as he released his seat belt. His voice was so frighteningly devoid of any emotion that Sara felt sick.

'W-what?' she stammered as he threw his door open and prepared to slide out. 'What *are* you going to do, Dan?'

He didn't answer until he reached her side of the car and pulled the passenger door wide. 'Find some answers, of course,' he said briskly. 'Now, leave your crutches in the car because they're no use to you till your shoulder's a good deal less painful, and let me give you a hand out of there. You need to get some proper clothes on if you want to travel in my car again.'

Her startled grin must have been the reason he'd added that last proviso, and it had worked. In fact, it had worked so well that she didn't even think of objecting when he virtually carried her up the four flights of stairs that led to her little flat up under the eaves.

'Hop to it,' he joked as she did just that with one hand against the wall on her way to her minuscule bedroom. 'Give me a shout if you need any help.'

'As if,' she growled as she unwrapped herself from the grubby coat and shed the hospital scrubs in short order.

Clothing for her upper half wasn't a problem, barring the twinges from multiple bruises and pulling scabs while she put them on. All she had to remember was to put her injured arm in first because the strapping didn't allow for very much mobility.

Unfortunately, her underwear didn't come with a tie waist and the cast wouldn't fit through the appropriate hole when she did manage to get her foot through it and pull it up with her other toes, even though it was a pair designed for halfway-through-pregnancy mums.

'Damn, damn, damn,' she muttered as she pushed the stretchy fabric off with the other foot and heaved herself up off the end of the bed for another trawl through her underwear drawer.

'Sara, I'm not being funny but… You must be very stiff and sore this morning and I can imagine that it's almost impossible to manoeuvre things over that cast,' Dan said at the very moment that she unearthed the black lacy thong that she'd bought to cheer herself up shortly after Zara had made that fateful visit to A and E. It was testament to how well it had worked that it still sported a dangling price tag.

Well, she thought with a fatalistic shrug as she tugged the tag off and flicked it towards the bin in the corner, it was probably the only underwear she possessed that would work. As for outer clothes, the only ones to hand that were wide enough to encompass the cast without having to resort to splitting a seam was a pair of heavy silk loose-fitting palazzo pants with a drawstring waist, not unlike the scrubs she'd just taken off, now that she came to think about it.

'I could keep my eyes closed and take directions if you need a hand,' he offered, and the suggestion was so sensible, so helpful, so considerate, so *Daniel* that she felt the threat of tears again. And he wouldn't even have to see her bruises, scabs and bulges if he kept his eyes shut.

'You promise to keep your eyes shut?' she demanded as a strange thrill of excitement shot through her that he would offer to do such an intimate thing for her.

'I promise,' he said firmly. 'Now, is it safe to come in?'

'No! Wait!' she shrieked as she saw the door start to swing open, and grabbed for the nearest thing to cover her naked lower half. 'Now it's safe,' she announced, all too conscious of the slight quiver in her voice and hoping like mad that Dan couldn't hear it.

'So, what do you want me to do?' he offered, and suddenly a whole X-rated scenario leapt into her head and she could feel the heat of a deep crimson blush move up her throat and over her face. 'Which bit do you want to do first and how do you want to play it?'

Her imagination leapt into overdrive and it was only the patient expression on his face and the interrogative eyebrow sending creases over his forehead that reminded her he was waiting for an answer.

'Um, if I put my…my underwear on the floor and step into it, could you pull it up for me—just as far as my knees?' she added hastily, and was treated to one of Dan's most devastating grins.

'Spoilsport!' he complained with a long-suffering air. 'OK, where is this…underwear?' She knew his hesitation was a deliberate copy of her own but was determined to ignore it. It was enough that she had to sort out which way the thong needed to be placed on the floor without having to cope with the soft wolf-whistle Dan gave when he caught sight of them.

'Well, well, well!' he murmured as he bent to position the scrap of fabric at her feet. 'Who would have thought it?'

'And why shouldn't I wear something pretty?' she demanded, stung by his reaction.

'These aren't just pretty,' he said, his voice sounding strangely husky as he began to slide them up past her ankles and on towards her knees, every inch a sensual torment as her eyes followed them all the way. 'Pretty is lace and flowers and pink and white. *This* scrap of nothingness is something else entirely!'

'That's far enough,' she said hurriedly, embarrassed all over again when her voice ended on a squeak. 'I can manage from there,' she assured him, and he gave another sigh and shook his head.

'What's next, then?' he asked, nearly catching her settling the slender elastic straps over her hips.

'Those trousers, please.' She pointed at the silky pile on the corner of the bed. 'You might need to feed them up my legs a little way before I can stand up without treading on the bottoms of them.'

'Hey,' he said brightly as he got the job right the first time. 'I've just realised that this is good practice for when I'm helping those children in there to learn how to dress.'

And that was just the reminder she'd needed, she told herself when she was sitting in his car a few minutes later.

It had been absolute agony to try to keep some distance between them on the way down the stairs when she had needed his help every step of the way, but that was what she'd *had* to do. It had been so wonderful to slip into the light-hearted banter that had been so much a part of their relationship, even in those early days, but that was all in the past.

She couldn't believe what the two of them had been doing up in her room. They'd almost been flirting with each other and there was no excuse for that. Dan was a married man and he was married to her sister. To allow anything to happen between them would be the worst sort of betrayal and she just couldn't be a part of it.

The trouble was, her love for him hadn't died when he'd married Zara, no matter how much she'd prayed that it would. Yes, he was the father of the babies she carried and, yes, she would love nothing better than that he would be at her side as together they guided them through childhood and into adulthood, but it wasn't going to happen.

'Because he's married,' she whispered fiercely as he circled the front of the car. 'He's married to your sister and the only thing he wants of you is what you're carrying in your womb—the babies that Zara can't give him.'

Something in her expression must have told him that her mood had changed because the atmosphere in the car that could have been too cosy and intimate was all business as he put the key into the ignition.

'So, what *do* you remember of your accident?' he asked as he joined the stream of traffic heading back into town.

Too much, was the first thought that came into her head,

but she knew he needed a logical answer from her. She was just overwhelmingly grateful that he hadn't angrily brushed her suggestion off as the ravings of someone who'd had an unfortunate random accident. He could have accused her of using the incident to get some sort of petty revenge against Zara or…

'Sara?' She'd almost forgotten he was waiting for an answer, so lost had she become in her thoughts.

'I always walk home the same way…out of the back of the hospital and past that little parade of shops, just in case I need to pick anything up on the way.' She glanced across briefly and saw the tiny frown pulling his dark brows together, the way they always did when he was concentrating. Afraid she'd lose her train of thought if she looked any longer, she stared straight ahead and continued.

'I'd gone over the crossroads and was just crossing one of those little turnings that seem to lead round to the back of the shops, for deliveries or something…not a real residential road, if you know what I mean?'

Out of the corner of her eye she saw his brief nod but he didn't say a word to distract her—she could manage to distract herself without any help.

'I heard a car coming and glanced towards it and I remember thinking that it wasn't the sort of vehicle I expected to see coming out of there, then I realised that it didn't seem to be slowing down and I realised that I was too far away from the kerb to get to safety and when I tried to turn away so that the impact wouldn't hurt the baby, my foot slipped on the wet cobbles and then the car hit me and I went down and my head hit the kerb and…and I woke up in A and E.'

'So, what made you think it might have been Zara?' he asked, his white knuckles clenched around the steering-wheel testament to the fact that he wasn't nearly as calm as he sounded. 'It sounds as if it all happened pretty quickly...too quickly to have seen anything much.'

Sara knew he was right, but she also knew what she'd seen. 'Well, I can now tell you from firsthand experience that when it looks as if you're going to die, there is a split second that's imprinted indelibly in your mind. It's so clear that if I were any sort of an artist, I'd be able to draw it for you with the accuracy of a photograph.'

'Tell me,' he prompted softly. 'What do you see in the photo in your mind?'

'The cobbles are wet and shiny, and there's a skinny cat running towards the shadows of a pile of cardboard boxes and his fur's all wet from the rain, and the light is gleaming off the car as it comes towards me...off the paintwork and the chrome and the windscreen as it's getting closer... And when I realised that it was going to hit me, I realised that it might hurt the baby...this was before I knew there were two of them,' she interjected in a crazy non sequitur. 'But when I put my hand over my bump—as if that would protect it from half a ton of car—the person in the car pressed their foot down on the accelerator and I heard the engine roar in response.'

Dan muttered something under his breath but the scene inside her head and the emotions she'd been feeling at the time were so strong that she paid him no heed.

'I was staring at it in disbelief, so sure that the person would put the brakes on, but she was staring straight ahead—straight at me—and her hair was long and blonde and down over her shoulders and her face… At first I thought it was *my* face reflected back at me and that could *still* be what I saw but…' She drew in a shaky breath and continued, 'Her hands were gripped round the steering-wheel…up at the top of the wheel so that her thumbs were nearly touching…and I have the impression that her nails were really long and painted with a dark varnish, but I can't be sure what colour…' She closed her eyes for a moment in the hope that it would help her to focus, but it didn't get any clearer so she went back to her narrative, to the part that still made her feel guilty that it had happened at all.

'Dan, I really did try to get out of its path,' she assured him fervently, desperate that he should believe that she'd done her best to protect his child, 'but it was coming at me far too fast and then my foot slipped but the car still hit my leg and I spun round… Actually at the time I thought it was the streetlight that was spinning round me…but I was falling and falling and I couldn't stop myself and then my head hit the ground and everything went black.'

He was silent for so long that she wondered if he was ever going to speak to her again. What was he thinking? That she was crazy? That he'd made a monumental mistake in asking her to carry his children in case she passed her craziness on to his innocent offspring?

'So, what part of the car would have hit you?' he asked, his voice sounding more like a rough growl until he cleared his throat, and tears threatened when she realised that his question meant he hadn't dismissed what she'd told him out of hand. 'Would it have been the front, the wing or both?'

CHAPTER SIX

DAN and Sara stared down at the broken light on the passenger side of the BMW while the mechanic wiped his hands on a rag so black and oily that it couldn't possibly be doing any good.

'It's not the first time she's brought it in but, then, that's women drivers for you,' he added with blatant chauvinism and a knowing wink for Dan.

Sara didn't have the breath to argue this slur on her half of mankind. She was still devastated by the evident damage to her sister's car.

'You say she's brought it in for repairs before?' Dan questioned, and from the tone of his voice that fact was news to him.

'Oops! Sorry if I'm dumping you in it, love,' he said to Sara, 'but last time it was the back bumper. She said she'd managed to reverse it into a bollard somewhere up near the London Eye.'

'And what did she tell you about this?' Dan pointed to the recent damage.

His uncomfortable look in her direction, not quite

meeting her eye, made Sara suddenly realise that he thought *she* was Zara, being taken to task by a far-too-calm husband. He probably thought her rapidly developing black eye and the dressing on her forehead were signs of wife abuse, she realized with a crazy urge to laugh.

'Actually, she didn't say anything because she didn't drop it off until after the garage closed. And last night, that was six o'clock because we were waiting for a customer to come and pick his vehicle up and settle his bill—you don't mind staying open a bit longer when it's for a good customer bringing you money, do you?'

His attempt at comradeship fell flat as Dan leant forward to take a closer look at the damaged light, reaching out to fiddle with the shattered remains for a second before he straightened up again.

'Well, thank you for your time,' he said politely. 'Let me know when the vehicle's ready for collection, won't you?' He wrapped a supportive arm around Sara's waist and helped her to hop the couple of steps to his car.

'So, it could have been any number of things that caused the damage, if she's in the habit of bumping into things,' Sara said almost before he'd closed his door, trying to find a logical reason why the damage they'd seen had nothing to do with her injuries.

She hated the thought that her sister might have wished her ill, although that long-ago episode with the piece of wood and the 'accident' that hadn't been accidental at all. Still, she was desperately afraid that she'd set something in motion that couldn't be stopped.

But, then, did she want it stopped? If her sister *had* tried to hurt her by driving that car straight at her then it was important to find out why or she might never be safe. And what if it had been the pregnancy that had been Zara's target? Sara couldn't bear the thought that her precious babies might be put at risk if she handed them over to her sister.

Had Zara been taking some of the more exotic designer drugs that her colleagues brought back from their foreign photo shoots? If so, they could have disturbed the balance of her mind and caused her to do such an outrageous thing.

But there hadn't been any evidence of strange chemicals in any of her blood tests—at least, nothing beyond the sleeping tablets and paracetamol that they already knew about.

She shook her head, at a loss to know what to think. It was already aching enough with out this mental stress, but that was probably because she'd been on her feet far too much already today. It certainly wasn't what she would want a patient of hers to do after such an incident.

Into the silence of the car came the unmistakable sound of Dan's pager and he cursed softly under his breath as he tried to find a break in the busy traffic to pull over to the side of the road.

Once there, it only took seconds before he'd used his mobile phone to call the unit and Sara suddenly realised that it was the first time she'd heard him speak since they'd left the garage.

What had he been thinking while her brain had been strangled by conflicting ideas? Had he dismissed her claim that she'd recognised Zara as her assailant now that he'd seen that there was no real evidence or was he, too, worried about the ramifications for the children she was carrying if their mother-to-be had really tried to injure them?

'That was your mother,' he announced as he ended the call and pulled back out into the traffic. 'She says that we need to go back to the hospital straight away. Zara's next set of tests results have come in.'

'Is she worse?' Sara demanded anxiously, because, no matter what she'd done, Zara was her twin and she loved her.

'Your mother didn't say. All she told me was that we had to go straight to the hospital, so…' He shrugged, his eyes never leaving the road as he navigated the quickest route.

'Mum. Dad. What's happened? What's the problem with the latest results?' Sara asked as soon as Dan pushed her into the unit in a hastily purloined wheelchair and found her parents just inside the doors, as though they'd been waiting impatiently for them to arrive.

'What took you so long?' her mother demanded, whirling to hurry up the corridor. 'Mr Shah has got the results in his office and he needs to have a word with us.'

Sara suspected that the consultant was waiting to have a word with Dan rather than her parents. After all, as her husband he was legally Zara's next of kin.

'Daniel, come in, come in,' the dapper gentleman invited, but it was Audrey who pushed in ahead of the wheelchair and took one of the two available chairs, closely followed by her husband. Daniel was left to prop himself up on the wall beside Sara to wait for Mr Shah to open Zara's file sitting on his desk.

'The nurse said you've had some more results, and I want to know when we're going to be able to take our daughter home,' Audrey said with the air of a general firing the opening salvo in a war she fully intended winning.

An expression of annoyance slid briefly across the consultant's face, probably at the knowledge that a nurse had been giving out more information than she should have. Sara could imagine that before the shift was over her superior would be having a sharply worded conversation with whoever was responsible.

In the meantime, the man's face had settled into the sort of bland expression that always preceded less-than-welcome news.

'Unfortunately, the news isn't good enough for us to be able to give you that sort of information,' he said quietly. 'Her liver function tests are giving us more cause for concern and it looks as if there may be more necrosis than we'd expected.'

'Necrosis?' Audrey pounced on the word. 'What's necrosis?'

'It means that sections of her liver have been damaged and are dying, so they are no longer able to perform their proper function.'

'So it's the same as what you found on the last tests,' she summarised for herself.

'Yes and no,' he prevaricated. 'Yes, it's the same condition but, no, it's not the same as before because the condition has worsened.'

'So, what are you going to do about it?' Frank asked, and Sara wasn't surprised to see how pale he was looking at the thought that his precious daughter's health wasn't improving the way they'd hoped.

'I'm afraid we can't do much more than we're already doing as far as infusing the antidote into her system and supporting her and keeping an eye on the concentration of various components in her blood. It's still very much a case of wait and see, but I thought you would want to be informed of the results so that you would know to prepare yourselves in case—'

'Would a transplant cure it?' Audrey interrupted, clearly unwilling to hear that particular eventuality even as a theory.

'Well, yes, we can do liver transplants in some conditions—for example, in people with cirrhosis or hepatitis and also in some cases where the patient has had medication toxic to the liver—but the success rate is not as good as for kidney transplantation and there's still the problem of finding a compatible liver donor while there's still time to do the operation.'

'Well, that's not a problem, then...not for Zara,' her mother announced with a beaming smile. 'Sara will give her one of hers. I've seen it on television and they said that identical twins are a perfect match. Once you operate, Zara will be as good as new.'

'No,' Sara said sharply, and her mother turned on her with a look of utter disbelief on her face.

'What do you mean, *no*? Sara, you *can't* refuse to help your sister if she needs one of yours.'

'Mother, I've only *got* one liver, so I can't give it to her. The operation would mean chopping a chunk of mine away and that's major surgery. Anyway, I doubt if you'd find a surgeon willing to do it because I'm pregnant and it wouldn't be good for the babies.'

'Well, then, you'll have to get rid of the babies,' her mother announced with a breathtaking lack of feeling for the unborn lives nestling inside her. 'You can't refuse to help save your sister's life. She could die.'

'But you would be quite happy for me to murder *my* babies to save *your* baby?' Sara couldn't believe the pain that thought caused, her heart clenching inside her chest as though every drop of blood had been wrung out of it.

Ever since she'd seen those two hearts on the ultrasound screen, beating so valiantly in spite of the recent trauma, it had brought the reality of her pregnancy home to her the way no amount of reading pregnancy books had done. She felt so connected to those tiny beings, so protective, that the thought of deliberately scouring them out of her womb and flushing them away was anathema.

'So.' She lifted her chin and stared her mother right in the eye. 'What if I refuse to do it?'

'You *can't* refuse because they're not *your* babies, they're Zara's, and if she needs them to die so that she can live—'

It was Sara's turn to interrupt and she did so without a qualm.

'They might be babies I'm *carrying* for Zara, but they're growing in *my* body and from *my* eggs…and what's more, it's *my* liver you're talking about and *no one* can have it if I don't want to give it.'

Her mother broke into noisy sobs and no matter what her father said she wouldn't be consoled.

Sara felt dreadful.

She now knew firsthand just how fiercely a mother would defend her child and couldn't really blame her own mother for wanting to do everything she could to give her daughter a chance of being well again.

But she was a mother, too—at least while those two helpless innocents were still inside her—and she was going to fight every bit as hard for their survival.

Poor Mr Shah didn't seem to know what to do for the best. Her parents were clearly beyond listening to anything he said, even though he repeatedly tried to reassure them that Zara's condition hadn't yet reached the point of no return.

While Dan…

Suddenly, Sara realised that the one person with the most to lose in this whole disastrous situation was the only one who hadn't said a single word.

A single glance in his direction was enough to tell her that he'd retreated behind what she'd privately dubbed his 'stone' face. There wasn't a single emotion visible, until she happened to see the way his hands were clenched into tight fists inside his trouser pockets.

As if her mother had sensed that her attention had wandered she turned a tear-ravaged face to her son-in-law. 'Danny, do something,' she pleaded. 'You have to tell Sara to save my precious girl… You must *make* her give Zara a new liver!'

'No,' he said quietly with a reinforcing shake of his head. 'It's not time for that discussion, Audrey. Listen to what Mr Shah's been trying to tell you. Eighty per cent of

patients with even severe liver damage eventually recover
on their own, so it's just a case of waiting to see if Zara's
liver is going to do the same.'

'But the transplant,' she persisted. 'Because they're
identical twins it would be a perfect match and—'

'And it might only give her another year of life,' Dan
finished brutally, and literally robbed her of the breath to
argue any further, her mouth and eyes open like a gasping
fish. 'That's the average survival rate for liver transplants
at the moment,' he told her with an air of finality.

Sara knew from reading medical journals that some
patients had survived considerably longer. It was probably
the poor survival rate of liver cancer transplant patients that
brought the overall rate down, but it wasn't accurate statistics that she cared about, it was the fact that he had
managed to take her completely out of the firing line…for
the moment at least.

'Now,' said Mr Shah, looking unusually flustered by the
open warfare he'd just had to witness, 'I think it would be
best if you were all to go home and have some rest.'

'Oh, but we haven't seen—' Audrey began, but was
totally ignored as he continued inexorably, drawing a line
in the sand.

'You may come back at visiting time this evening, but
no more than two of you may visit at a time. That will
ensure that my patient will have what remains of the day
to rest and hopefully give her body a chance to start to
recover.'

It was beautifully done, Sara acknowledged wryly as
they filed silently out of the consultant's office, but it had

left all of them in no doubt who was wielding the power in *his* unit.

'Would you like a lift?' Dan offered quietly, when they'd watched her parents scurry out of the unit before he began to push her in the same direction.

'Don't you have to go to work today?' she asked, desperate to spend what time she could with him but knowing it wasn't a sensible idea. 'You don't have time to keep ferrying me about.'

'Actually, I've got all the time in the world, having just been banned from visiting until evening visiting hours,' he contradicted her as he pushed the button for the lift that was just taking the Walkers down to the main reception area.

All Sara hoped was that it would deliver the two of them to the ground floor before it returned for Dan and her. She didn't think she could bear to be shut up in such a small space with her parents, even for the short time it would take to travel a couple of floors. Mr Shah's office had been bad enough with all that animosity flying around.

'Anyway…' Dan continued, breaking into her silent replay of the moment when her mother had glibly talked about aborting the precious pair already making their presence felt under her protective hand, the curve of her belly already noticeably bigger than it would have been for a single baby at the same number of weeks. 'As I'm on compassionate leave until we know what the situation is with Zara, you can just name your destination.'

'You're going to regret that offer when you find out where I need to go,' she warned, suddenly immeasurably grateful that the rest of the day didn't stretch out in front of her like an arid desert.

'Don't tell me!' Dan said with a groan as he pushed the chair into the waiting lift. 'You need to go shopping!'

'All right, I won't tell you…but that doesn't mean that I don't need to go.'

'All right,' he said with an air of long-suffering that caused several smiles on the faces of the people sharing the lift. 'I offered so I'll take you. Just tell me where you need to go and let's get it over with.'

'What is it with men that they don't like shopping? Is it a genetic thing?' Sara mused aloud, drawing a few smiles of her own, then relented. 'It shouldn't take very long because I only need to do some grocery shopping while I've got someone to carry the bags for me,' she added with a grin, then another thought struck her.

She hesitated for a moment, wondering if there was some other way she could achieve what she wanted and feeling the increased warmth in her cheeks that told her she still hadn't grown out of the habit of blushing. 'I'm sorry but I'll also need to do a bit of clothes shopping.'

He groaned as he waited for their companions to exit first then pushed the wheelchair out into the spacious reception area, thronged as ever by a constantly changing stream of visitors going in and out of the hospital. 'My absolute favourite occupation…not!' he complained in tones of disgust. 'If you're anything like your sister, that will take the rest of the day.'

His assumption stung her more than she had a right to feel and loosened the leash on her tongue. 'Apart from the obvious physical resemblance, over which I have *no* control, I am absolutely *nothing* like my sister!' she snapped. 'And furthermore, far from taking the rest of the day, my shopping should take me no more than five minutes because I only need some comfortable underwear that I can pull on over my cast.'

The words almost seemed to echo around the whole reception area—probably right around the whole of the hospital if the gossip grapevine was operating in its usual mysterious way.

'Oh, good grief!' she moaned, and covered her face when she saw just how many inquisitive faces were turned in their direction, *and* how many of them were sporting broad grins. 'Just get me out of here,' she ordered through clenched teeth, hoping that her long curtain of her hair was hiding the furious heat of her blush.

Dan didn't make the situation any better when he leaned forward and murmured in her ear, '*Comfortable* under-wear, Sara? Is that what they call black lace thongs these days?'

'Shut up!' she hissed. 'Just shut up and get me to the car.'

'Ah…in just a second,' he promised as he veered the chair towards the policeman who had just entered the reception area. Then he abandoned her in the middle of the floor to hail the man and the two of them stood talking earnestly for several minutes.

Sara was puzzled when Dan reached into his pocket to pull out a disposable glove, especially when the two of them peered at something inside the glove.

They both had serious expressions on their faces but she was far too far away to hear a single word either of them said, especially with the constant hubbub of passing humanity around her.

'Right! To the car!' Dan announced as he came back to her with the air of a man pleased with a mission accomplished. 'Which would you rather do first—groceries or underwear?' he demanded cheerfully, and the chance to ask what that little episode had been about was lost in the return of her embarrassment.

The grocery shopping was done and they were standing in front of an embarrassing display of female underwear in her favourite high-street shop when Dan's mobile burst into the opening bars of the 1812 Overture.

Grateful for the fact that he wouldn't be looking over her shoulder for a moment, Sara grabbed a packet containing some very definitely non-sexy underwear in a size several larger than her usual one, in the hope that the leg opening would be loose enough to accommodate her cast. But she couldn't resist grabbing another containing a rainbow mix of coloured thongs, telling herself that at least she knew that they were relatively easy to get on. The fact that they were far sexier than the 'old lady' pants in her other hand had absolutely nothing to do with her choice.

There was a frown on his face when he turned back to her.

'That was the hospital,' he began, and her heart leapt into her throat.

'Zara?' she said, immediately feeling guilty that she and Dan were out shopping for her underwear when he should have been waiting for news of his wife. 'Is she worse?'

'No, Sara, no,' he soothed, looking contrite that he hadn't realised that she'd immediately panic. 'It was nothing to do with your sister. It was A and E, asking if I could possibly go in. With the two of us out and two others called in sick—that flu bug that's going around has finally felled Derek when he was only boasting the other day that he never catches anything—they're desperate for another doctor.'

'Desperate? As in…they're building up a logjam of patients and the waiting time's becoming unacceptable?' she asked as she handed over the two packages and had to submit to the indignity of having Dan pay for her underwear, too. He'd already paid for her groceries when she'd belatedly realised that sneaking out of the ward meant that she hadn't collected the purse that had been given into Sister's safekeeping.

'That, and the fact that the traffic lights are on the blink at one of the crossroads and there's been a whole series of prangs as people take the law into their own hands. Pedestrians, cyclists and car-drivers, some more serious than others.'

'Ouch!' She pursed her lips as frustration swept through her. She was certain she would be able to work if she'd only injured her leg. Having a doctor working away in minors, doing the bread-and-butter jobs of stitching and retrieving foreign bodies from various apertures, wouldn't be too taxing as she would probably be able to sit down for much of it, and it would definitely take some of the load off the rest of them. But with her shoulder strapped to prevent her using anywhere near the full range of motion and with the rest of her body complaining whenever she moved a bruised portion, she'd be more of a liability than a help.

'Stop brooding,' he chided as he pushed her back towards his car at a far faster rate than the companionable stroll with which they'd started their outing. 'You're in no fit state to work, so don't even think about it.'

'Hmm! I see you've added mind-reading to your diagnostic skills,' she sniped, uncomfortable that he'd been able to tell what she was thinking. She hadn't realised that she was so transparent and now worried just how many of her other thoughts he'd been privy to. 'Was that the Masters course in Mind-reading or just the Diploma?'

He laughed. 'Nothing so low-brow. I found I was so good at it that I went all the way to PhD.'

He quickly had her settled in the blissful comfort of the passenger seat and they were on their way—at least, they should have been on their way. The journey from the car park to her flat was only a matter of two streets but they weren't even able to join the stream of traffic on the first one because nothing was moving.

'This isn't going to work,' he said aloud as, with a careful look around, he put the car into a swift U-turn and went back the way they'd come. 'I'm sorry, Sara, but if I'm going to arrive at the hospital in time to do any good I'm going to have to drop you off at our place instead.'

She wanted to object because she really didn't want to spend any time at all in the place that her sister shared with the man *she* loved, but logic told her that she didn't have any other option. Even if she were to ring for a taxi, that would still leave her with the insurmountable obstacle of getting herself and her groceries up four flights of stairs with only one leg and one arm in any sort of usable state.

'I'll come back as soon as the panic's over and deliver you and your goods and chattels as promised,' he assured her as he deposited her shopping bags on the pristine work surface in his kitchen. The journey up in the lift had been a breeze in comparison to the struggle it would have been to install her in her own flat.

'Sling your perishables in the fridge so they don't succumb to the central heating,' he ordered briskly, his mind obviously already racing ahead to what he was going to find when he reached A and E.

'And make yourself at home,' he added, almost as an afterthought, with one hand already reaching out to the front door. 'It shouldn't take more than a couple of hours to sort through the worst of it.' And he was gone.

'Make myself at home?' Sara said into the sudden emptiness of Dan's home and knew it would be impossible.

And it wasn't just because this was the home he shared with Zara. It would have been just as bad *whoever* he was sharing it with because she'd hoped that any home he lived in would have been *her* home, too.

It was because she'd started to dream at one time that it would be her future for the two of them to choose the home they were to share together, to decorate it and choose the furniture and accessories together and… She looked around her, able to see into each of the rooms from her position in this compact central hallway. To the kitchen with the clean-lined Scandinavian cupboards trying desperately to soften the over-abundance of cold stainless-steel appliances and work surfaces; to the bathroom with what should have been a stylish art-deco-inspired combination of black and white that had been made overpowering with the excess of black on floors, walls and paintwork; to the bedroom with the oversized four-poster bed that was totally out of place in such a modern setting and whose voluminous floral drapery looked more like something a pre-schooler would prescribe for a fairy-tale princess.

In fact, the only room in which it looked as if Dan had finally put his foot down was the living room. That alone was an oasis of calm understatement with restful neutral colours a backdrop for the stunning views out of the wide uncluttered windows.

The furniture, when she finally made her way to it, was deliciously comfortable, particularly the reclining chair that was in reach of everything she could need, from the remote control for the television and another one for the stereo system to a wall of bookshelves that had everything from Agatha Christie to massive tomes on emergency radiographic diagnosis.

She quickly realised that this was the one place in the whole flat where she might be able to feel at home, but it wasn't until she turned her head and caught a hint of the shampoo that Dan used that she understood why.

'This is *Dan's* chair,' she said, and cringed as she heard

the words coming back to her sounding like the sort of reverential tones of a besotted fan of her favourite idol.

Disgusted with herself for mooning about like this, she forced herself up onto her feet—well, onto her one weight-bearing foot and her single crutch—and struggled her way into the kitchen.

'It's not your home, so don't go criticising it,' she told herself sternly as she sorted through her shopping to put the perishables away in the enormous American-style fridge. 'And don't go getting comfortable in it either…not even in Dan's chair. You're only going to be here for a short time—just until the panic's over in A and E—and then you'll be back in your own place.'

Her own place with the little poky rooms that were too small to have anything bigger than doll's-house furniture and the old draughty windows and iffy heating.

'But it's mine, everything in it is something I've chosen and it suits me,' she said aloud, even as she silently wondered who she was trying to convince.

It was two hours later that Dan phoned her.

Of course, she didn't know that it was Dan until the answering-machine kicked in and she heard his voice projected into the room.

'Sara, pick up the phone…it's Dan,' he announced—as if the sound of his voice wasn't imprinted on every cell in her body.

'Dan?' she said, furious that she sounded so breathless when she'd only had to reach out her hand to pick up the phone. Pathetic!

'Sara, I'm sorry to do this to you, but they really need

me to stay on till the end of the shift. Arne's had to go home
with this wretched flu, too. He was nearly out on his feet
and we could just about fry eggs on his head.'

Sara chuckled at the mental image painted of her colleague. Arne Kørsvold was an enormous gentle Swedish
doctor who disguised the fact that he was rapidly losing
his natural platinum-blond hair by shaving his whole head.

'Anyway, if you're OK with it, I'll stay on and work the
rest of the shift, then call in for an update on Zara. I
promise I'll take you back as soon as I can get away.'

What could she say? A and E's needs were far more
urgent than her own so she resigned herself to several
more hours of sitting on the chair that faced Dan's recliner
and tried not to imagine what it would be like to spend her
evenings sharing this lovely room with him.

Sara had no idea when the television programme finally
lost her attention and she drifted off to sleep but she was
completely out for the count by the time Dan let himself
in.

She didn't know how long he stood in the doorway to
the living room, watching her sleep; didn't see the way he
frowned when he saw the shadows around her eyes that
spoke of her exhaustion or the way his eyes softened as
they traced the swelling curve of her belly.

The first thing she knew was a hazy realisation that
Dan was there and that she was in his arms as he lifted her
off the settee. Then he was laying her gently down again
and she couldn't help giving a little whimper of disappointment when he took his arms away again.

'Shh,' he whispered softly as he stroked a soothing hand

over her head, and as she drifted off to sleep again, comforted by the fact that he was close to her, she imagined that she felt the butterfly brush of his lips on her forehead.

CHAPTER SEVEN

'I'M GOING to go mad if I have to stay here any longer,' Sara told the four walls of her borrowed bedroom.

She was spending yet another day in Dan's spare room…Dan and *Zara's* spare room, she corrected herself, although it was getting harder and harder to make herself remember that fact.

Because of the continuing staff shortages, Dan had returned to work full time. He was, however, being allowed time to go up at intervals to visit Zara.

Each evening, when he returned to the flat, Dan gave Sara a full report on the latest test results, but Zara's body seemed to be struggling to rid itself of the toxic metabolite of the paracetamol she'd taken.

'No doubt it's because her liver had reduced glutathione stores as the result of her years of drastic dieting,' he said soberly.

'But the liver can regenerate itself,' Sara reminded him. 'Surely the paracetamol hasn't done that much damage that it can't be repaired.' She shook her head and pushed her plate away, unable to eat any more even though it was her favourite tagliatelli carbonara.

'Oh, Dan, I'm in such a muddle. Half of me desperately wants her problem to be the result of taking the drugs earlier in the afternoon, which would mean Zara couldn't possibly be the person driving the car that hit me. But the other half wants just as desperately for it to have been her in the car, because that means the drugs hadn't been in her system so long and she's more likely to recover.'

There was a strange shadow in Dan's eyes but he didn't comment on her dilemma, choosing instead to tell her about one of the department regulars who'd turned up again after an absence of several months showing all the usual signs that she'd fallen off the wagon again.

'Somebody hadn't remembered to flag her name, so the new junior registrar went sailing into the cubicle to find dear old Alice lying there with all her worldly goods piled around her on the bed and snoring her head off.'

'Oh, dear! He didn't touch any of her bags, did he?' Sara chuckled. 'And she woke up and yelled the place down?'

'She started shouting "Fire!" then realised it was a male doctor in the cubicle with her and changed it to "Rape!" with all-too-predictable results.'

'Poor chap!' Sara laughed even louder, remembering her own noisy introduction to Alice and her obsession with her bags. 'I bet he got an even bigger shock when it took less than thirty seconds for the cubicle to fill with half the hospital's security personnel.'

'He was shaking and as white as a sheet and looked as

if he couldn't decide whether he was going into cardiac arrest or giving up his medical career on the spot.'

'The trouble is, rules and regulations are so tight these days about what you can write on a patient's notes, it's difficult to leave a message on them saying, "Treat with extreme caution. Liable to explode," or the hospital legal department would go into orbit. I take it you managed to smooth things over?'

'Well, eventually,' he said, and she was intrigued to see a wash of colour travel over his cheekbones.

'What did she do *this* time?'

'Oh, she was just her usual outrageous self,' he said with a self-conscious shrug.

'You may as well tell me,' she pointed out, her imagination in full flight. 'It will only take a single phone call to find someone else willing to spill the beans, and who knows how much bigger the story has grown in the meantime?'

'Don't remind me,' he groaned. 'I was counting on the fact that you're not fit to work at the moment so that particular bit of gossip would pass you by.'

'So?' she prompted, ignoring the comment about her fitness to work in pursuit of the punchline of the story. Her upcoming return to work was a topic she didn't intend to discuss with him. 'Tell me, tell me. What did she do?'

'It wasn't so much what she did as what she said,' he muttered, looking seriously uncomfortable. 'In front of half the damn department and heaven knows how many patients and relatives she told me she loved my green eyes and invited me into the cubicle to give her a damn good... um...bit of passion.'

Sara burst out laughing. 'Knowing Alice, I bet she didn't use such a genteel phrase.'

Those gorgeous green eyes were sparkling now. 'You'd win that bet,' he conceded. 'The trouble is, I'm never going to hear the end of it.'

'Oh, you will,' she reassured him. 'As soon as the next juicy bit of gossip comes up, that little proposition will all be forgotten…by the rest of your colleagues, at least.'

And it was relaxed conversations like that one last night that were making life so difficult for her. It was becoming harder and harder to stop herself from doing or saying something that would reveal her secret…the fact that she was falling deeper and deeper in love with him the longer she shared his flat.

'Well, enough is enough,' she said firmly as she pushed herself up onto her one good foot and reached for a single crutch.

She'd been practising getting around over the last couple of days. There had been so many empty hours while she'd waited for Dan to return that she'd worked out for herself how she could manoeuvre without needing a pair of them because her shoulder was still too sore to take the weight, even with elbow crutches.

It wasn't an elegant way of getting around, more of a stumbling lop-sided lurch, in fact, and definitely required the presence of a nearby wall as a last resort to stop herself losing her balance completely. The one good thing about it was that she'd almost perfected a way of getting around unaided, and that meant she could leave the danger zone of Dan's spacious flat and take herself back to her own far humbler one.

'It will probably take me a couple of hours to go up all four flights of stairs,' she muttered, feeling exhausted just thinking about it. She stuffed her belongings into a carrier bag, resolutely ignoring the fact that the packet of granny knickers hadn't even been opened, tied the handles to her crutch, then phoned for a taxi. By the time it arrived, she was waiting in the entrance with just a short hop across the pavement left to do.

'Hang on a minute, love,' called the cabbie and heaved his considerable bulk out of the driving seat to give her a steadying hand to climb inside. 'You're in a right mess, aren't you?' he commented soothingly, his eyes meeting hers in the rear-view mirror once he was back in his seat. 'Finally decided to get away from him before he does any worse? You've made the right decision, love. I've got no time for men who think it's OK to knock women about. Need someone to give them a bit of their own medicine.'

'Oh, good grief, no!' Sara laughed. 'It was a car that did this. I nearly got run over the other night.'

'That's right, dear. Get a good story ready to tell people so they won't twig what's really going on. Most of them will probably believe you, but me?' he shook his head and drew in a breath through his teeth. 'I've seen too much of the rough end of life and I can tell the difference, but don't you worry—even if he gets the police out looking for you, I'll never tell where I take you.'

He straightened up in his seat and put the engine into gear. 'Right, now, where do you want to go? To one of the refuges?'

'That's very kind of you, and I'm so glad that there are

people like you who will help battered women, but I've been staying with my sister and brother-in-law—' she didn't see the harm in stretching the truth a little, just to put the man's mind at ease '—ever since I came out of hospital. If you could drop me off at my flat, that will be great.' She gave him the address and was certain that he was quite disappointed he wasn't going to be a brave knight coming to the aid of a maiden in distress.

Except when he drew up outside the multi-storey Victorian building, all his protective instincts seemed to re-surrect themselves.

'I hope you're on the ground floor, love,' he said as he lent her a hand again.

'I wish!' she joked, and looked right up towards the very top windows. 'That's me, all the way up there.' And then, no matter how much she tried to reassure him that she could manage, he insisted on keeping her company all the way up all four flights, carrying her bag of belongings in case they unbalanced her and steadying her when her poor overworked leg began to tremble with overuse.

Sara was close to collapse when she finally got the key in the lock and swung the door wide, screwing her nose up at the shut-in smell that seemed to gather even in the space of a couple of days. Then she had a battle to make the man accept the proper fare for bringing her home, and when she tried to add a tip to thank him for spending the time to help her all the way up the stairs he drew himself up with an air of injured dignity.

'I didn't do that for money, love. I did that because you were someone who needed a helping hand. Now, you take this.' He handed her a business card. 'If you need to go anywhere, you ring that number and ask them to send George.'

'Oh, that's just perfect,' she said with a little quiver. 'Just like St George killing the dragon, you came to the aid of a lady in distress.'

He snorted and went a bit pink. 'I don't reckon my missus thinks I'm any sort of saint, but I know what you mean. Now, you take care of yourself.'

He was just about to shut her front door behind him when she remembered what she'd planned to do that evening.

'Oh, George,' she called. 'You don't go off work before seven, do you? Only I'll be needing a taxi to get to the hospital for visiting hours.'

'I told you, love, you need me, I'll be here,' he said with a broad grin. 'Will a quarter to seven be early enough for you?'

'Perfect. I'll see you then.'

It was just after seven o'clock when the lift chimed to announce its arrival on Zara's floor.

This time, thank goodness, she wasn't trying to get about with her single crutch because as soon as she'd arrived in A and E, courtesy of George, she'd been whisked off by a bevy of colleagues and given the loan of a wheel-chair.

'At least my immediate welcome in the department seemed to put his mind at rest,' she mused as she wheeled her awkward one-handed way towards Zara's room, then an alternative suddenly struck her. 'Or perhaps he took it as proof that they know me well because I'm always in here for treatment.'

She was still smiling at that thought when she tapped on Zara's door and began to push it open.

'There she is!' Zara announced, her face twisting into an unattractive scowl. 'And look at that smirk on her face. She just couldn't wait to get her foot in the door, could she? All this time she's resented the fact that Danny chose me and she waited until I'm too ill to do anything about it to move in with him and—'

'Zara!' Dan's voice cracked over her increasingly hysterical rant like a whip. 'That's enough! You're talking nonsense.'

'It's *not* nonsense!' she argued fiercely. 'How could you have let her move into my home after all the trouble she's caused? Didn't you read my note? It's all her fault. Everything is Sara's fault.'

'Ah, yes. The note,' Dan said, and Sara seemed to be the only one who noticed a strange edge to his voice.

'You mentioned it before,' he continued. 'Remind me, when did you write it and where did you put it?'

'I wrote it the afternoon I took the tablets, of course, and I put it on my bedside cabinet, where you'd see it when you came in… And I'm so sorry for doing that to you, but if you'd read the letter you would know how desperate I was…that I just couldn't cope any more with Sara wanting to keep the baby and…'

'Shh, sweetheart,' Audrey soothed, reaching for one of her daughter's flailing arms. 'It can't be good for you to get in such a state. Perhaps it would be better…' She turned with a scowl on her face to send a meaningful glance between Sara and the door.

Sara hadn't known whether to leave so that her sister didn't upset herself any more, but Dan had already drawn the wheelchair fully into the room and shut the door for some semblance of privacy so she was completely trapped when he drew a slightly crumpled piece of paper out of his jacket pocket.

'I take it that this is the letter you're talking about?' he said, and Sara felt sick when she saw the malice in Zara's glance across at her.

'You found it!' she exclaimed. 'So now you know exactly—'

'"My darling Danny,"' he read flatly, interrupting her without an apparent qualm. '"I can't bear it any more. You know how hard we tried to have a baby and what a wrench it was for me to have to have my sister being a surrogate for us. I know that she's always wanted you for herself and I'm just so afraid that she's going to steal our precious baby and there's nothing I can do about it. I just can't bear it any more, Your loving Zara."'

Sara felt the blood drain from her face then flood back in a scalding blush when he read the note for all to hear. Didn't he realise how humiliating it was for her to have her unrequited love spoken about like that? Didn't he realise that, even if she hadn't loved him, she would still have loved the children she was carrying because they were an intrinsic part of her?

And the letter was a complete lie because even though

she desperately wished that she was carrying Dan's babies for the two of them, there was no way that she would have broken her promise to him to give him the family he wanted. He was going to be a wonderful father and Audrey would spoil her grandchildren at every opportunity and provide the feminine touch that Zara would probably be too busy for.

She really didn't need all this extra emotional stress, to say nothing of the embarrassment of having her private feelings paraded for all, not when all the pregnancy books advised calm and serenity for the sake of the baby. After all, she was still recovering from her injuries and had, admittedly voluntarily, just gone through the exertions of moving out of his flat and back into her own.

And going from mind-blowing topics to the merely petty, there was the fact that she wasn't certain her smart-enough-for-work trousers would ever recover from her decision to come all the way down four flights of stairs on her bottom.

'Look at her face!' Zara demanded shrilly, pointing straight at Sara. 'At least she has the honesty to look guilty.'

With everyone's eyes directed at her, Sara had felt the heat of embarrassment flooding into her face. She was unused to being the centre of attention at any time, least of all when she was in the same room as her twin.

She hated what Zara was doing to her but she had known for far too many years that there was no point protesting her innocence. Zara's position as everybody's favourite was unassailable. The thing that hurt worst was the fact that Dan was privy to all Zara's spiteful lies. At least in the past it had been kept within the family.

'You ask her, Danny,' her sister demanded, with every evidence of being on the verge of tears. 'You ask her if she hasn't been thinking about keeping the kid for herself.'

Of course she'd been thinking about it, Sara admitted silently as she reached for the rim of the wheel to turn herself around. She was carrying the babies of the man she loved so it was obvious that she would long for the chance to bring them up with him, and there was no way she was staying in this room to allow her sister to make something shameful about a normal human response.

'Sara, stay,' Dan said in a low voice, his lean fingers resting on her wrist to dissuade her from opening the door. 'Please?'

There was something in those amazing green eyes that told her she could trust him, that he wasn't asking her to stay to have more humiliation heaped on her head. And even though she had no idea where this dreadful conversation was going, she knew that she *could* trust him, implicitly.

She missed the warmth of his touch when he took his hand away, but then he reached into his pocket again and pulled out a plastic bag.

Walking over to the side of Zara's bed, he tipped out a piece of plastic onto her lap.

'Do you know what that is?' he asked in a quiet conversational tone.

Sara almost gave herself away with a gasp of surprise. The last time she'd seen a piece of plastic like that had been in the garage when they'd been asking about the damage to Zara's car.

'Of course I don't know what it is,' she said with a dismissive shrug. 'It's just a bit of scrap plastic.'

'Actually, it's a bit more than that,' he said with a noticeably sharper edge to his voice as he retrieved it and put it back in the bag, without touching it with his fingers. 'It's part of the light from your BMW—the one you broke when you ran your sister down and left her lying in a side street, not caring whether she was alive or dead.'

'That's a lie!' Audrey gasped, clearly shocked out of her unaccustomed bystander's role. 'That's a wicked, wicked lie. Danny, why are you doing this to Zara? She's your wife and she's ill. You should be supporting her, not spouting this ridiculous nonsense that Sara's been feeding you.'

'Audrey—' Dan said forcefully, trying to break into her tirade.

'*I* know why you're doing it,' she continued, condemnation in every stiff inch of her. 'The two of you have got your heads together and made the whole thing up to cover up the fact that you've got a thing going between you. *You're* an adulterer and *she's* no better than a…'

'Mrs Walker,' Dan barked, apparently reverting to formality as nothing else seemed to be getting through. 'If you dare say one derogatory word against Sara, I shall assume you're hysterical and slap you.'

'What?' Her eyes and mouth were wide with shock but she must have seen something in his face that made her believe he would do what he'd threatened because she subsided ungracefully into the chair on the other side of Zara's bed.

'As I was saying,' Dan continued, apparently calm

again, but from her position Sara could tell from the way his veins were distended that his anger must have sent his blood pressure up. She would have to suggest that he have it checked, but for now she was still amazed that he would have sided with her against the rest of her family. No one had ever done that before. 'Unfortunately, it's the truth. I took that piece of plastic from the BMW and gave it to the police because I saw that there were fibres caught in it. Their forensic labs have confirmed that they were strands of top-quality vicuna and that they were an absolute match for the fibres in Sara's coat—the one you gave to her and that she was wearing when you knocked her down.'

There were several seconds of horrified silence at the end of his recitation and Sara almost felt sorry for her parents when she saw the way they were staring at their beloved daughter…almost as if they didn't recognise her any more…as if she'd suddenly grown a second head, or something.

'All right!' Zara snapped. 'So it all went a lot further than I expected, but I *still* didn't get what I wanted, and that was to get rid of the kid.'

It was all too much for her mother to cope with and she burst into noisy tears, unwilling even to be consoled by her husband.

'Why did you have to go poking around? Why couldn't you just leave it alone? After all, bones heal and she's still carrying your precious baby… Oh, I'm sorry, it's *babies*, isn't it? There's two of the ghastly ankle-biters in there, gradually bloating her body until she's going to look like a hippo.'

'Why, Zara?' Frank demanded, obviously completely confused. 'What went wrong? You seemed so happy until you couldn't have children, but then Sara offered—'

'Sara didn't offer,' she interrupted rudely. 'Mum virtually blackmailed her into it because I said I couldn't get pregnant.'

'Well, there was very little likelihood that you'd be able to while you were taking the Pill,' Dan supplied dryly.

Zara blinked, as though surprised that he knew that she'd been lying to him, but he was already moving on. 'What I don't understand is why you went through the whole pantomime in the first place.'

'Typical man!' she scoffed, tossing her head in a well-practised move that sent her hair tumbling over one shoulder. 'It's obvious. It was all a game, just a bit of fun seeing how easy it was to take you away from Sara, especially when I could tell that she had already fallen head over heels for you. *I* didn't love you—never really wanted you, if you want the truth—I certainly never had any real intention of going as far as marriage.'

Her mother gave a little whimper of distress but that only seemed to enrage Zara further and she turned her fury on her parents. 'If you two hadn't been so bloody eager to put on the big flashy fairy-tale wedding, none of this would have happened. I'm a successful model and there's a possibility that I might get a part in a Hollywood film. The last thing I want is to be stuck at home, nothing more than a housewife with two brats.'

'So, let me get this right,' Dan said icily. 'Everything you've done—married me, almost killed your sister because she's pregnant with the child you said you wanted, *and* taken an overdose of drugs—which, by the way, you carefully timed so that, if I hadn't been taking care of Sara, I would have found you before they'd had time to get into your system—*all* of that is somebody else's fault and beautiful Princess Zara is the innocent victim? I think not.'

He took a step closer so that he positively loomed over her and his words had the precision of surgical steel.

'The police are waiting for me to report back before they charge you with the attempted murder of your sister and her unborn children. If you're found guilty…which I hardly think is in doubt…you can expect to be sentenced to a minimum of twelve years in prison, but it's more likely to be eighteen years.'

'Eighteen years!' Audrey wailed, but Zara didn't say a word, at last speechless now that she'd been confronted with the probable consequences of her actions. 'She didn't mean to do it.' Audrey turned pleading eyes on Sara, as ever protective of her favourite daughter. 'You couldn't possibly send your own twin to prison.'

'I really didn't mean to do it,' Zara said suddenly, the subdued tone of her voice and the ghastly pallor of her skin telling Sara that perhaps she really was telling the truth this time. 'I've had a couple of photo shoots on the West Coast—of America,' she added, in case they weren't following. 'And when the possibility of this acting job came up and then became a probability, I suddenly felt trapped because the baby…*babies*,' she corrected herself, 'weren't due until a couple of weeks after filming's due to begin.'

'That still doesn't explain why you would decide to

run your sister over. Why on earth would you want to kill her?'

'Why? Because she's too bloody perfect,' she snarled. 'She got all the brains in the family and just sailed through school and medical training, *and* she got the beauty as well.'

'That's why you did this,' Sara murmured as she traced her original scar, the one Zara had given her so many years ago. 'I thought it was because you wanted people to be able to tell us apart. I never dreamed it was because you hated me.'

'No!' It was the first time that her sister hadn't rushed to claim that it had been an accident and the fact that her first instinct had been to deny that she hated Sara thawed something deep inside her that had been frozen for a very long time. 'Oh, everything just got so muddled in my head, probably because of the tablets one of my friends gave me.'

'Tablets?' Dan demanded instantly. 'What tablets? Where did you get them from?'

'My friend said she got them from America, on the internet. They call them designer drugs. They're gone now,' she added hastily. 'I flushed them when I got back to the flat after I…after…' She shook her head and started to shed what were probably the first genuine tears in years. 'My friend and I were high on them when she said my only option was to get rid of the baby, then I wouldn't have to be stuck in England, and my head was so messed up that it seemed to make perfect sense. Then, when I was driving towards Sara in that lane and her first thought was to save the baby…I was just so angry that she always…always did the *right* thing that I…that I aimed straight at her and… Oh, God, I'm sorry, Sara,' she gasped. 'And I'm just so glad that I didn't…didn't k-kill you…'

One part of Sara's brain must have been registering the changing figures on the electronic monitors because somehow she wasn't in the least surprised when Dan reached for her sister's wrist to feel for himself just how fast her pulse was beating.

'What's wrong?' Audrey demanded. 'What's the matter with Zara?'

'Probably nothing more than too much stress in the last half-hour,' he said soothingly.

'It's not her liver, is it?' her father suggested fearfully. 'It's not packing up completely, is it?'

'It's unlikely that it will pack up.' This time his tone was reassuring. 'That was one of the reasons why I started investigating Sara's accident, because if it had been Zara responsible for running her over, then it meant the drugs probably hadn't been in her system long enough to do serious permanent damage.'

'So, what's the matter now?' That was her mother again, holding onto Zara's hand as though it was a lifeline. 'Why are the monitors peeping and pinging like that?'

That, in far more clinical terms, was Mr Shah's first question when he appeared in the doorway a few seconds later, obviously alerted by the member of staff at the unit's central monitoring station.

'Her pulse and respiration were probably elevated by a family discussion,' Dan said blandly.

'In that case, I think I will have to ask you to leave,'

the consultant said formally. 'There has been a slight improvement in my patient's condition and I don't want anything to reverse it. Please, if you could return at the next visiting hour?'

Her mother obviously knew from the man's quiet air of command that there was no point trying to persuade him to change his mind and she bade her daughter a tearful good bye before leaving the room with her husband's arm supportively around her shoulders.

She was so wrapped up in her misery that she barely glanced in Sara's direction, so nothing had changed there.

'You, too, please,' Mr Shah said to Dan and Sara. 'I know you are both doctors in this hospital so you will know how important proper rest is for a body when it is recuperating.'

'Of course, sir,' Dan said respectfully, and walked round behind Sara to take charge of the handles of her wheelchair.

At the last moment before she left the room, Sara glanced back over her shoulder to meet the golden hazel eyes that were the absolute double of her own.

'The authorities will *not* be informed,' she said cryptically, and saw from the dawning relief on her sister's face that she had understood what Sara was trying to tell her.

'I take that you meant you won't be preferring charges against your sister,' Dan said in a low voice meant for her ears alone.

'I'm presuming that you didn't give those authorities enough information to work out what happened with the car?' she countered.

'So you're just going to let her get away with it?' he asked in a voice that was as unreadable as the face in front of her in the lift.

'As there was no permanent damage done…' she agreed, very conscious that they had a captive audience. 'The penalty seems out of proportion.'

'I wouldn't know,' he admitted with a fleeting glimpse of a grin. 'I made that bit up.'

Sara nearly choked trying to subdue her sudden laughter. 'Remind me not to play poker with you.'

'Shame,' he teased as he pushed her across the reception area. 'I was thinking of suggesting a game after we eat tonight. What do you think?'

What she thought was that she'd completely forgotten to tell him that she'd moved out of his flat today.

'Um… Actually, Dan, I've moved back into my own place, so I won't be—'

'What? When?' he demanded, clearly startled, and just for a moment she tried to persuade herself that he looked disappointed, too. 'And how did you get there?'

'St George rescued me from the dragon,' she said, opting for laughter rather than tears as she suddenly realised that she had absolutely no idea where she stood with him any more.

CHAPTER EIGHT

THERE had been no mistaking the expression on Dan's face that time, Sara thought while he drove her towards her flat in complete silence. That had definitely been more than disappointment on his face, it had been hurt.

'Can you manage by yourself from here?' he asked briskly, and she suddenly realised that he had pulled up outside the front of her house.

She sighed heavily, wondering when she was ever going to get anything right.

'Dan, you saw how difficult it was for me to get into the car once I was out of the wheelchair. There are only two ways of getting up the four flights of stairs once I get in there, and that's either on my bottom the whole way or if someone helps me.'

'So why did you move back here, then?' he demanded impatiently. 'My place is eminently more suitable for someone in your position because it's got a lift.'

Unfortunately, it had far more than a lift. It had Dan living there, too, and she just couldn't cope with staying with him any longer.

'And it's Zara's place, too, and with any luck it won't be too long until she's ready to come home to it.'

'And?' Those green eyes were far too astute. Sometimes she was convinced that he could read her mind.

'And there's no way that Zara and I can live in the same flat, not after what's happened,' Sara said bluntly. 'She said she's sorry and she didn't mean to do it, but she said the same thing about this…' She pulled her hair away from her race to reveal the first scar her twin had inflicted on her so long ago. 'And she's said it over and over again until… Well, let's just say I don't really trust her because the only one who matters to Zara is Zara.'

He reached his hand out towards her and gently laid it over hers where she'd unconsciously splayed it protectively over the hard curve of her pregnancy.

'You don't trust her to be too close to the babies?' he asked, but they both knew it wasn't really a question.

He closed his eyes and drew in a deep breath then opened them again and gave a brisk nod as if he'd just come to some momentous decision.

Rather than telling her about it, he released his seat belt and slid out of the car, leaving her feeling strangely dissatisfied.

'Come on, then, let's get you up those stairs,' he said, and hauled her unceremoniously to her feet.

'All I can say is it's a good job you're not coming into work for a few weeks yet, or you'd have to set off the previous day to get there in time for your shift,' he teased when they finally reached the top floor.

That's what you think, she mused as she lay in bed later

that night and contemplated the prospect of weeks of sitting around, twiddling her thumbs.

'It would drive me completely mad, just staring at the walls when I could be making myself useful at work,' she continued aloud.

She tried to remember a precedent for a member of staff coming in to work a shift while they were sporting a cast and couldn't, but… 'There's that doctor who uses a crutch on that American hospital drama!' she remembered. 'She can get up a fair turn of speed on it and still manages to take care of patients.'

She gave a quiet snort of laughter, trying to imagine herself using an actress in a fictional hospital to argue her case for an early return to work.

'Well, that character may be fiction but I'm not. This is reality and the hospital is chronically short of staff. And even if I have to put up with weeks of being stuck in minors until the cast comes off, that's what I'm going to do.'

An hour later she was still lying there wide awake, her brain going round and round the same scene, even now unable to believe that her sister could have wanted to harm the infant she was carrying. It was hard to drift off to sleep when all she could see in her mind's eye was the harsh glare of the headlights bearing down on her.

'Did I do the right thing in promising not to press charges?' she wondered aloud. 'Should I have made some sort of formal complaint so that, if at some time in the future something should happen to the babies, they'll investigate Zara first?'

That hadn't been the right thing to think about as she

was trying to sleep. She felt sick at the very thought of something or somebody hurting them.

But what would she be able to do about it once they were born and she'd handed them over? On that day she would officially become their aunt rather than their mother and would have no legal say in what happened to them.

A feeling close to panic started to fill her and for several mad moments she imagined herself grabbing her passport and slipping out of the country. There was a whole wide world out there and in almost every country there were people crying out for doctors to treat their sick and injured. Surely she would be able to find a way to support herself and the two precious lives inside her?

Then she imagined how Dan would feel, knowing that somewhere in the world there were two children bearing his genes and he'd never seen them…beyond a fuzzy ultrasound picture.

Just the idea of the man she loved gazing longingly at that image year after year was enough to bring the hot press of tears to her eyes and she knew she couldn't do it to him.

So, what was she going to do?

A strange sensation deep inside drew her attention away from that insoluble conundrum and she pressed her hand over the firm curve, remembering with a smile the way Dan had placed his hand over hers.

Oh, yes, he was going to be such a good father to this little pair. Kind and gentle and endlessly patient and…

What was that?

She froze into complete stillness and concentrated, aware that all the textbooks said it was far too soon but…

'There it is again!' she exclaimed aloud when she felt the faint fluttering, hoping it was something more than gas travelling through her gut.

When she felt it for a third time she was certain and wanted nothing more than to whoop with delight, no matter that it was pitch dark outside and everyone else in the flats was probably fast asleep.

But she couldn't just lie here in the dark and savour it all alone. She had to share the news with someone else or it wouldn't feel as if it was real. She had to speak to…

'Dan? Did I wake you?' she asked apologetically when he answered the phone.

'No. I'm in bed but I haven't gone to sleep yet. What's the problem? Is something wrong?'

'No. Nothing's wrong,' she reassured him quickly. 'It's just that I was lying there and…and…' Suddenly, it felt so wrong to be telling him such momentous news when he was on the other end of the telephone. These were *his* babies, too, and he should have been here with her to feel…

'There *is* something wrong,' he said decisively. 'I can hear you crying.'

There was the sound of a crash on the other end of the line and some muttered words that were probably unprintable, then he was back with her again.

'I'm coming over,' he announced in a don't-argue-with-me voice. 'I'll need you to drop a set of keys down to me out of a window, because you're *not* to come all the way down those stairs again.'

'Drive safely,' she said, worried about his state of mind, but he'd already broken the connection.

Suddenly, she remembered that he didn't live more than a few streets away and in that powerful car of his it would only take minutes to get there.

'Keys. Keys,' she muttered as she heaved herself out of bed, briefly registering that round about the time that she finally had her bulky cast removed it would also be the time when her pregnancy made moving about more difficult.

'So, this is what my life is going to be like for the next few months,' she grumbled, then subdued a shriek of horror when she caught sight of herself in the mirror on the back of the bathroom door.

'Talk about the wreck of the *Hesperus*,' she moaned as she dragged a brush through the tangles put there by her restlessness. At least she wasn't having to do it with her injured arm. If she'd dislocated her right shoulder she would have been strapped up and completely out of action for several weeks yet.

And as for what she was wearing…this old T-shirt hadn't just seen better days, it had seen better years, and was so worn out that it really *was* translucent in places.

Before she could strip it off, she heard the deep purr of one of the more expensive makes of car outside the front of the house and her heart did a crazy little tap-dance at the knowledge that Dan had arrived.

'The keys! What did I do with…? Ah!' She pounced on them and hobbled over to the window, steadying herself against the furniture. 'Catch!' she called in a stage whisper as she lobbed them in a gentle arc towards him, then fastened the window as fast as she could and went back to changing her clothing.

He must have taken all four flights two at a time because he was already at her front door and fitting the key to the lock before she'd pulled a fresh, slightly less disreputable T-shirt on while balancing on one leg.

'Very fetching!' he teased, and she knew he'd caught sight of one of the packet of thongs she'd bought with him the morning after her accident.

'A gentleman wouldn't have looked, and if he accidentally caught sight of something he shouldn't, he certainly wouldn't have mentioned it,' she said sternly.

'Whatever made you think that I was a gentleman?' he said with one of those cheeky grins that never failed to turn her inside out, right from the first time she'd met him.

Oh, how hard it had been, day after day, forcing herself to keep a strict distance between the two of them and making herself treat him the same as all the other A and E staff.

'So, tell me,' he said as he guided her back to the side of her bed, the rumpled covers mute evidence of her lack of sleep. 'What had you so upset that you were crying?'

'I wasn't upset,' she denied, then had to blink as her eyes began to fill with tears again. 'I was lying in bed and I was resting my hand on the bump—'

'You do that a lot,' he interrupted seriously, once more resting his much longer, much broader hand over hers. 'I've seen you doing it around the department, and when you're sitting having a break you sometimes stroke your hand backwards and forwards and round and round.'

For a moment she lost the power of speech. How had he managed to see so much when she hadn't even noticed him looking?

'I'm sorry. I interrupted you,' he said, sliding his fingers between hers so that their sensitive tips were stroking her, too. And even though there was a layer of soft stretchy fabric between them, his fingers were so warm that she could feel each one of them and the tracks they made on her skin as clearly as if she'd been naked under his touch.

'You were saying that that you were lying with your hand on your bump, and…' His voice was deeper and huskier than before, almost as though he was as affected by the contact between them as she was.

'And I felt them move,' she finished in a whisper, and saw his eyes flare wide in response.

'Are you sure?' Now he was staring down at the curve that was still almost small enough to be spanned by fingers as long as his. 'Surely it's still far too early?'

'That's what I told myself,' she agreed, 'but then it happened again, and a third time and…and I thought you would want to know and…'

He drew in a shuddering breath and she was stunned to see the bright sparkle of tears gathering in his eyes.

'Oh, thank you, Sara,' he said, so softly that she almost had to lip-read the words. 'I can't tell you how much…' He shook his head, obviously moved beyond mere conversation.

'I don't know if they're still moving, but do you want to…?' She slid her hand out from under his and lay back across her bed, leaving his much larger hand spread across her.

It was so silent in the room that she could hear the

numbers click over on the radio alarm beside the bed, so silent that both of them seemed to have forgotten to breathe while they waited for something to happen.

'What did it feel like?' he murmured so softly that it was almost as if he was afraid of frightening them, as if those tiny forms were timid wild animals.

She concentrated for a moment, recalling the movement deep inside her.

'It felt like a cross between a flutter and a squiggle,' she said in the end. 'It wasn't quite as delicate as a butterfly's wing—it was slightly too substantial for that. But it wasn't strong enough to be called a—'

'There!' he exclaimed with a look of awe on his face as he stared down at the place covered by his hand. 'Was that what you felt?'

Sara concentrated for several long seconds and was growing worried that they'd reached the end of the performance when she felt the strongest movement yet.

'Yes!' she agreed joyfully, overwhelmed to be sharing this special moment with him. 'That's exactly what I felt. What do you think?'

'What do I think?' he asked seriously, a hint of a frown drawing those straight dark eyebrows together. 'I think it's boys, because that was definitely the sort of kick that will score goals.'

'Idiot.' She chuckled, delighting in his nonsense, but when she thought he would take his hand away again, he didn't, propping himself on one elbow on the bed beside her so that he could leave it just where it was.

'I was being serious,' he said with a deliberately solemn

expression, then asked, 'What do you think they are? Identical or fraternal? Girls or boys?'

'Or one of each?' she suggested. 'I've never understood some people being adamant about the sex they want their baby to be. I've always believed that it's far more important that it arrives as healthy and as safely as possible.'

Their undemanding conversation had drifted from topic to topic, all loosely connected with pregnancy, labour and the care of newborns, and it was some time before Dan realised that Sara had fallen asleep.

For some while he lay there watching her, glad that the room was still warm enough so that he didn't need to cover her with the bedclothes just yet, not while he was enjoying looking at the changes this pregnancy was causing to her body.

She'd never been as artificially slender as Zara and the soft curves of her burgeoning breasts and the full curve of her swelling belly were so naturally sexy that he'd been hard from the moment he'd walked into her flat and caught a glimpse of that skimpy purple thong.

Oh, what a fool he'd been, to be taken in by Zara's spiteful games. How could he not have seen while he'd been reaching for the paste imitation that he'd already had a diamond within his reach? Sara wasn't just a gifted and hard-working doctor, she was also one of the most genuinely good-hearted people he'd ever met. And, unless some sort of miracle happened, he'd lost her for ever.

So you'd better make the best of this special time, then, said a stern voice inside his head, and he took the words to heart. It might be the only opportunity he ever had to spend the night with her and he wasn't going to waste a moment of it.

In the end, exhaustion got the better of him and the next thing he knew he was waking up with Sara's softly curvy form wrapped firmly in his arms as if he was never going to let her go.

'If only,' he mouthed, full of regret, and whispered a kiss over the crown of her head.

A casual glance towards her bedside cabinet brought her clock into focus and he had to stifle an oath when he saw what time it was.

He hated having to do it, but there was no way he could untangle himself from her without disturbing her sleep. Besides, her cast had been resting over one of his ankles and he didn't know whether he was even going to be able to walk on it. It felt as if the weight might have caused permanent damage to his circulation.

'Sara?' he called gently, hoping he might be able to rouse her just far enough to extricate himself. 'Sweetheart, I've got to go,' he said a little more firmly when she just tightened her hold on him. 'I'm going to be late.'

'Late?' she repeated sleepily, and blinked…then blinked again and stared at him in disbelief. 'Dan? What are you doing here?'

'You invited me. Remember?' He only meant to prompt her memory by stroking his hand over the curve of her belly but when he found himself stroking naked skin he pulled his hand away as swiftly as though he'd been burned.

'Sorry,' he muttered, mortified to feel the heat searing his cheeks as he rolled swiftly out of reach and leapt to his feet.

His shoes were scattered on the floor and his keys were…under the edge of her bed, and his brain was definitely lodged south of his belt while she was curled up in the middle of all those crumpled bedclothes like a sleepy cat.

'I'm sorry but I've got to run or I'll be late for my shift,' he apologized, and let himself swiftly out of her flat, then nearly tripped on his way down the stairs when his hormones reminded him that he'd never seen a sleepy cat with such long slender legs…even though one of them was temporarily encumbered with a clumsy cast…or wearing such an outrageous scrap of underwear.

To lessen the danger that his preoccupation might cause an accident in the early-morning traffic, he forced himself to concentrate on the evidence he'd seen of how well her injuries were healing.

It hadn't been many days since she'd cheated death by inches, but already some of the bruises were starting to fade, working their way through the colour progression that marked the body's reabsorption of the various constituents in the blood.

He'd only caught a glimpse of her shoulder and most of the injured area was still covered by the strapping that was providing stability and support while the internal damage to the structures in and around the rotator cuff were repairing.

The grazes on her arm were much better than when he'd last seen them. Then, she'd been with Rosalie, the technician, having an ultrasound to find out if the pregnancy had been compromised, and she'd looked as if she'd been flayed raw almost from wrist to elbow.

It was all scabbed over now, evidence that none of the damage had gone very deep, and within a few more days she would be left with nothing worse than a deep pink mark on her skin that would probably be completely un-detectable in a matter of weeks.

The rest of her skin had looked silky-smooth and perfect and he'd longed to explore every inch of it in great detail and…

Whoa! That sort of thinking wasn't the right way to keep his car safely on the road. For that, he needed to keep his thoughts on the straight and narrow, too, as befitted a married man.

And if *that* reminder wasn't enough to take the shine off a morning that had started so sweetly, with the mother of his unborn children wrapped so trustingly in his arms, then nothing could.

Sara was cross with herself that she hadn't remembered to set her alarm the previous night. This morning she'd intended getting up bright and early so that she could go in to the hospital to negotiate her partial return to work.

By the time she managed to get herself washed and dressed, she was going to arrive hours after the morning shift had started and was going to give the department manager grounds to doubt that she could cope with coming back to work so soon.

Ah, but she couldn't really find it in her to regret the

reason why her plans had become so disrupted. Feeling the babies move for the first time had been amazing, and it had been made even more magical when she'd been able to share it with Dan.

Waking up this morning to find that he was still with her and knowing that his body had been wrapped protectively around hers while she'd slept was a bonus she'd never expected, and she refused to feel guilty about it. To have heard that her sister had deliberately ensnared Dan purely out of spite and, worse, that she hadn't even loved him when she'd married him—the whole situation seemed an utter travesty of everything that a marriage should be.

'If he had married me...' she whispered wistfully, then gave herself a shake. '"If wishes were horses then beggars would ride," Granny Walker used to say, and I'm just wishing for the moon, too.' And nothing could come of those wishes because even though Zara might not have loved Dan, he must have loved her or he would never have proposed to and married her.

'And none of that will get this beggar a ride, but a phone call will,' she declared when she was finally as ready as she could be. She reached for her purse and the business card of her own personal knight on a white charger...or in a black cab if she really wanted to be pedantic.

'Sara! What on earth are you doing here?' called one colleague when he caught sight of her.

'You're supposed to be on sick leave, darlin', taking it easy while the rest of us soldier on,' added Sean O'Malley in his lilting Irish accent. 'Have you just come to gloat?'

Everywhere she looked there was the usual morning chaos, except it seemed even worse than usual—or was that just wishful thinking? If everyone was being rushed off their feet, would that mean that she would be welcomed with open arms or would she be seen as a liability and shown the door?

There was only one way to find out.

'Actually, Sean, I wanted to have a word with the department manager and—'

'Oh. Admin stuff,' he said dismissively. 'Well, while you're in those recently refurbished offices sitting on one of their ultra-expensive chairs, will you remind someone that they still haven't scraped the loose change together to find us any replacement staff, not even part-timers? And we're already two and a half doctors down. It's getting beyond a joke.'

The staff in the human resources office reminded Sara of an ants' nest that had just been given a vigorous stir with a big stick.

Not that any of them seemed to be moving with the same innate sense of purpose that you'd find among ants. In fact, as far as she could tell, there was interminable duplication of effort going on while they seemed to concentrate most of their efforts on finding reasons why things *couldn't* be done.

'Have you found the new staff for A and E yet?' she asked sweetly, then gave the nest a deliberate extra stir. 'I heard a rumour that if you don't find them soon, it may have to be shut down because it's dangerously under-staffed, and all the patients will be diverted to other hospitals. Doesn't the hospital get a massive fine if that happens?'

By the time she was shown in for her 'chat' with one of the more senior members of the department, the rumour she'd started seemed to have taken on a life of its own.

'Have you any idea exactly how long you're going to need to be on sick leave?' the man asked from behind a desk that was laden with piles of paperwork nearly tall enough to hide behind.

'That's what I wanted to talk about,' she said brightly. 'The only thing wrong with me is this cast on my leg.' After all, the strapping on her shoulder was invisible under her clothing. 'And the wheelchair is only for show and to give my arms a rest from using crutches.'

It was such a long way from the truth that she almost expected to feel the searing heat of a thunderbolt from on high, but what she got instead was an administrator almost grovelling at her feet when she offered to pitch in to do an hour or two in minors to help clear the backlog. There was absolutely no mention of health and safety regulations, at least not in relation to her own fitness to work. The poor man seemed far more worried about the national disgrace that would ensue if his accident department was summarily shut down due to lack of staff.

'What on earth are you doing here?' Dan growled when he finally had a moment free to get into minors.

All morning he'd been regaled with one after another of his colleagues telling him how good it was to see Sara looking so well, and what a good job she was doing, and what a clever idea it was to have her ploughing her way through all that time-consuming debriding of wounds and painstaking stitchery, leaving the more mobile staff to do the rest of the work in the department.

'You should be at home, in bed.' And with that one sentence there was only one thing that she could think about, and she hardly needed to see the way those green eyes of his darkened with awareness to know he was thinking exactly the same thing.

'Ah…it's purely a temporary measure,' she finally managed to say. 'Someone said that they might be forced to close the department if they didn't find a few more staff—health and safety or something—and you know what chaos it causes when you have new staff who haven't a clue where anything is or how our system works…'

Enough! she ordered herself. Don't babble! Just because you can't stop thinking about the way his face lit up when he felt the babies move, and how it felt to have his arms wrapped around you…none of that means that you have to develop verbal diarrhoea.

For just a moment the way he looked at her made her think that he was going to say something of a personal nature but then he shook his head and gave a sigh of resignation.

'Don't get overtired,' he said softly, and she knew his concern was genuine.

'Don't worry, I won't do anything to risk the babies,' she reassured him. 'They've had enough trauma already.'

She was tired by the end of the day but it was a good tiredness that came from doing a worthwhile job to the best of her ability, and just before Dan appeared to offer her a lift back to her flat, she was given official permission to turn up the next day, too, so the precedent was set.

'I'm still not sure that you should be doing it,' Dan grumbled as he steered around the road that circled the whole of the hospital grounds and aimed for the exit. 'You're entitled to paid sick leave.'

'I know I am, but I really don't see the point of being paid to go mad when I can make myself useful. Go on, admit it. It worked well today, having me restricted to the needlework department. I already know the system and the staff, and everybody's been willing to help me, doing things like fetching more supplies.'

He stopped arguing after that, obviously deciding that there was little point as she had permission, and she was grateful that he would never know the real reason why she'd wanted so much to come back to work so ridiculously early.

'Because that's the only place where I can legitimately spend time with Dan,' she whispered as she watched from her window while he climbed back into his car and drove away.

She'd only had to see the longing on his face when he'd looked at her belly just a few minutes ago to know that he was yearning to feel the babies move again…probably as much as she did. But their situation as nothing more than the genetic parents of those babies made the relationship between them too strained for such intimacy to take place again.

As for the possibility that Dan would wrap her in his arms again and cradle her all night long, she may as well cry for the moon.

CHAPTER NINE

THE wretched woman was driving him mad.

It wasn't enough that she was back at work long before she should have been, and that the whole of the rest of the department had welcomed her with open arms, or that she'd made herself virtually indispensable as she'd beavered away in minors.

Her bright idea was almost single-handedly responsible for the 'new initiative' that the bean-counters had come up with. This meant allocating one member of the medical team per shift to do exactly what Sara had been doing— clearing the department of the vast numbers of niggling minor injuries that, in the strict rotation of normal triage, would ordinarily clog the place up and ruin the hospital's performance figures.

If he were honest, he would have to admit that the new organisation had certainly raised morale among the A and E staff, with far fewer instances of abuse hurled at them from members of the public who had been forced to wait unacceptable hours before there had been anyone free to sort them out.

Not that their department manager was going to allow medical protocols to be buried by upper-echelon diktats. He was far too experienced a man not to know that there were times when victims brought in with major injuries took absolute priority over everything else, and he wouldn't have it any other way.

No, the thing that was driving him completely off his head was the careful distance that she'd been keeping between the two of them ever since that morning when he'd woken up in her bed.

It felt as if he'd been trying to speak to her for weeks but there was never a moment when she was alone. Each time he'd had a moment to go looking for her she'd either been with a patient or in the staffroom surrounded by other colleagues willingly fetching and carrying drinks or food for her, or asking about the progress of the pregnancy, or, worst of all, putting their hands on the rapidly swelling bump to feel the increasingly visible movement inside it.

Oh, he'd been so jealous of the fact that she was letting them do that, and his only consolation was that he'd been the very first one to feel that miraculous quickening.

Zara had left the hospital now, with Mr Shah's final words—telling her that she'd been far luckier than she deserved after doing something so stupid—still ringing in her ears. She had also packed up a substantial amount of her belongings and returned to the welcoming arms of her parents to complete her convalescence. As far as the rest of the world was concerned, this was because her mother would be available to keep her company, whereas *he* would be out at work for long stretches at a time.

In reality, there was another very different reason and he needed to talk to Sara about it…

Of course he'd thought about turning up at her flat, but all the while she was wearing that cast he'd felt too guilty about the idea of forcing her to climb all those stairs in both directions to let him in. He smiled wryly when he remembered the way she'd tossed her keys out of the window to him. If he'd known then what he knew now he'd have put them in his pocket and kept them. It would have made what he was trying to do so much easier if he could just let himself into the old Victorian house and corner her in her little eyrie. Then she would *have* to listen while he explained, apologised, did whatever he had to while he tried to persuade her to give him a chance to get close to her, because only if he could get close would he be able to judge if there was a possibility she would give him a second chance.

He was very aware that time wasn't on his side as far as her pregnancy was concerned, and he had so much to achieve before that day arrived… And then the brainwave had struck and here he was, standing on her front doorstep and ringing the bell on the ground-floor flat.

'Sorry to disturb you,' he apologised when the elderly lady cautiously opened the door with the safety chain firmly in position, 'but could you let me in so that it saves Sara coming down all those stairs?'

'Why doesn't she drop her keys down to you…like she did before?' the sprightly woman asked with a definite twinkle in her eye, and when she saw his surprise gave a chuckle. 'I don't seem to need as much sleep these days, lad, and it's amazing what I see happening outside my window.'

'I wanted to surprise her,' Dan admitted, knowing that it was nothing less than the truth. Whether Sara would see it as a good surprise he had yet to find out.

'And you brought her flowers,' his inquisitor said with a nod of approval before she released the catch. 'That's always a nice touch.'

'How did you know they were here?' he asked as he brought the bunch of freesias—Sara's favourite flowers—out from behind his back.

'The rest of me might be sagging and crumbling by the minute, but my nose is still working perfectly,' she said wryly, then a look of sad reminiscence crossed her face. 'Besides, they're my favourites and I haven't been given any since my Dermot died.'

While she stepped back and pulled the door wide, it took no more than a couple of seconds to slide several stems out of the large handful he'd brought.

'My name's Dan, not Dermot, but at least it starts with the right letter,' he said with a smile as he presented her with the sweetly scented blooms, hoping that one day Sara would have such lovely memories.

'Oh!' A shaky hand came up to cover her mouth and she blinked rapidly as though fighting back tears. 'Oh, my dear boy… Thank you so much, but you didn't have to…' She bent her silvery head to sniff the perfume before looking back up at him, her eyes misty with memories. 'You tell your Sara from me that she's a lucky young woman.'

'I couldn't possibly do that,' he said, wondering if there was a chance that Sara would ever agree with her. 'It would sound far too much like boasting. I'll leave it up to you to tell her yourself.'

She was still chuckling at his nonsense when he set off up the stairs, the flowers clutched tightly in her hand.

'Dan!' Sara gasped when she opened the door to his knock and saw him standing there, obviously the last person she'd expected to see. His heart sank when he wondered if he might be the last person she *wanted* to see.

'I come bearing gifts,' he said, suddenly remembering the flowers he was in danger of strangling to death.

'Oh, thank you!' she exclaimed, and threw him a smile that seriously weakened his knees before burying her nose in the delicate blossoms.

This time there was only the slightest hesitation before she stepped back and invited him in. 'Would you like a cup of tea? I'm afraid I've only got herbal now. Caffeine-free.'

He pulled a face and she chuckled, the simple spontaneity of the sound like balm to his soul.

'I don't much like it either, but it's better for my blood pressure and therefore better for the babies, so I have to put up with it.' She turned to lead the way into her compact kitchen and he stopped in the doorway, leaning one shoulder against the frame as he watched her bustling about.

Except she didn't bustle any more, not now that her pregnancy was advancing so rapidly. Well, rapidly wasn't quite the right word, as the duration of most pregnancies was the same, give or take a week or two. What he'd meant was that the size of her bump had increased rapidly over the last few weeks, and he hadn't really noticed the extent because she'd been spending so much of her time sitting down, working in minors.

But today had been the day that her cast had finally come off, and the first day in a long time since he'd seen her in anything other than the soft drape of a shapeless uniform dress or in a tunic top that only fitted where it touched.

Since she'd come home from work, no doubt ferried by her own personal taxi driver, she'd obviously had a bath and had donned a pair of stretchy trousers that did absolutely nothing to disguise her shape and size...and she looked wonderful, so ripe and womanly and sexy and...

'Whoa, boy! Down!' he muttered under his breath, grateful that she'd turned her back on him for a moment to give him a reprieve, and he dragged his eyes away from her lest he leap on her and carry her through to her bedroom.

'What did you say?' she asked as she turned to face him again with a steaming mug in each hand.

'I was just thinking how good you're looking, Sara.' Which was at least the polite way of voicing his thoughts as he stepped aside to allow her out of the kitchen and into her cosy little sitting room.

'It's such a relief to be out of that cast, I can't tell you.' She sank gratefully onto the settee and immediately raised her legs up onto the other seat.

He could applaud her sensible decision to rest her legs but there was no way that Dan was going to sit in the chair on the other side of the fireplace. That was much too far away for his purposes.

'Hang on to this for a second,' he directed as he held out his mug to her, and she automatically took hold of the handle. 'I'll just do this…and then settle myself here,' he said as he lifted her feet and slid onto the settee beside her before lowering her feet onto his lap.

'Dan…'

'That raises your feet slightly and improves postural drainage in your legs,' he pointed out quickly, afraid that she was going to object. 'It also means that I can do this,' he added softly, as he chose one foot and began the sort of massage that he'd learned she loved back in those days before he'd been so stupid.

'Oh! Oh…that feels so good it *must* be illegal,' she groaned as he worked on each individual muscle until he'd worked all the knots out of both feet.

'Oh,' she said again when he finally stopped, and this time it was in tones of disappointment. 'It would almost be worth getting married to have my feet massaged like that every night,' she added, and completely stole his breath away.

She'd been so relaxed by the time he'd finished that he was certain she hadn't really been thinking about what she'd said, but it was too good an opportunity to pass up.

'That could be arranged,' he said seriously, his heart beating so hard that it almost felt as if it would burst out of his chest.

He felt the tension return as if he'd flicked a switch, and he regretted that he'd spoiled her moment of rest.

'Dan, that's not funny,' she said stiffly as she started to struggle up out of the settee and he put his hand on her knee to stop her for a moment.

'I didn't mean it as a joke,' he told her, and leaned down to reach into the pocket of the jacket on the floor beside the settee.

He drew a swift breath and sent up a prayer that he'd be able to find the words he needed before he handed her the envelope he'd brought with him.

'That's a decree nisi,' he told her. 'In exactly six weeks and one day after the date on that, I can apply for a decree absolute and my marriage to your sister will be over.'

Wordlessly she stared at him then dragged her eyes down to the papers she'd withdrawn from the envelope.

'So soon!' she whispered, and he knew she'd seen the date.

'After that awful scene in her room at the hospital, I went back and had a long conversation with Zara,' he explained. 'The upshot was that our divorce petition papers had already been filed with the county court before she was discharged.'

'But…I thought you had to wait years, or for one of you to be caught being unfaithful or…' She shrugged, admitting her ignorance of such matters.

'I knew as little as you before I did some research on the internet and found out that there are five criteria but the two that applied to our situation were what they call "unreasonable behaviour"—and I would definitely class trying to murder my babies as unreasonable behaviour or…'

'You didn't tell anybody what Zara did?' she interrupted urgently. 'I promised that I wasn't going to press charges but if you've put it on the divorce papers…'

'Shh! Of course I didn't,' he soothed, taking her free hand in his and lacing their fingers together. 'But that doesn't mean I didn't use the threat of it to get what I wanted—her admission that she'd been carrying on with a man over in America. The one who's going to finance the film she's been offered a part in,' he added, although that was neither here nor there to *their* situation.

'And she admitted it? To adultery?' Her eyes were scanning the papers still clutched in her hand. 'Oh, Lord, I bet Mother wasn't happy about that.'

'I think "incandescent with rage that she wasn't going to be able to hold her head up in the neighbourhood" comes closer to the mark. I went down to see your parents to tell them in person what was going on as Zara's already gone back to the States.'

'What did she say?' There was an awful fascination in the question.

'She began by trying to forbid the two of us to divorce at all. Far too scandalous.' She'd also tried to persuade him to say that *he'd* been the one to commit adultery, but he'd been completely innocent, at least in fact if not in his head and his heart. Besides, he'd wanted to be able to come to Sara with the fewest blemishes on his character possible. He'd ruined things between them once—he didn't want to risk doing it again.

'When I finally left, after convincing her that the divorce was already a done deal, she was muttering, "Adultery!" and "The shame of it!" under her breath and your father was going to pour her a large medicinal brandy.'

'Oh, Dan, I know I shouldn't laugh, but…' Gradually,

her smile faded, to be replaced by a pensive frown, and he knew her thoughts had moved on. It was only moments later that she proved him right by asking, 'So what are you going to do now?'

It was time for another swift prayer for courage.

'My plans are already made,' he said, hoping he didn't sound as nervous as he felt. 'I've got two babies due in a matter of weeks now, and I need to find someone willing to be a mother to them, someone who will protect them as fiercely as any mother lioness defends her cubs and will love them to distraction—in fact, almost as much as she loves me.'

Sara's heart felt as if it stopped completely when she heard those words, and it seemed to take for ever before it stuttered into a proper rhythm again.

Dan was going to go looking for a good mother for his babies? But they were *her* babies, too, and…

This time she didn't let him stop her from getting up. This wasn't the sort of news she could absorb while she was lolling back on her settee with her feet propped on his muscular thigh.

Too furious to stay still, she started striding backwards and forwards in the limited space in her little living room while thoughts whirled around inside her head.

How *dared* he think of finding someone else to love her babies when *she* loved them enough to die for them—had already proved it by protecting them at the risk of her own health when Zara's car had come towards her.

She knew he didn't love her…he couldn't have if he'd

chosen Zara instead…but he'd only stipulated that the woman he wanted should love him to distraction. And she did!

But how could she tell him how she felt?

At this precise moment he was still married to her sister…or at least still legally connected so that he couldn't marry anyone else…

She stopped in her tracks as a sudden thought struck her.

Perhaps that was the problem! Perhaps the fact that he'd been married to her sister was the reason why he wouldn't even consider marrying her.

She stared out of the window into the late autumn darkness, a tiny corner of her brain telling her that she should have closed the curtains to keep the heat in, and had to concede that there would be many people who would think it creepy that he could switch allegiance from one twin to the other, as though they were as easily inter-changeable as a pair of identical socks.

'When, in fact, we're more like a pair of shoes,' she muttered under her breath as she began pacing again. 'Fit perfectly one way and complete agony if you put them on the wrong foot.'

Oh, but she and Dan would have been such a good fit, she mourned as her steps gradually slowed. If only she had been just a little more like her glamorous, confident sister instead of her quiet bookish self, perhaps Dan wouldn't have been so dazzled when Zara had deliberately set out to attract him. It was all too late now, she admitted with a sigh, and her feet were dragging as she started to make her way to the chair on the other side of the fireplace, too downhearted to sit next to Dan again.

'Uh-uh!' Dan shook his head as he caught her hand and pulled her back to his side. 'That's too far away when there's still so much to talk about.'

It wasn't worth fighting about so she gave in and sat down in her corner again, resigned to listening to his plans for the rest of his life then wishing him good luck.

'Are you ready now?' he asked, and used a gentle finger to turn her head to face him.

'Ready?' she repeated listlessly, her last forlorn hopes already faded to nothing.

'Ready to listen to the biggest most grovelling apology I've ever had to make in my life.'

'Apology?' She frowned. 'What have you got to apologise for? It was your marriage and it's your right to end it. It's got nothing to do with me.'

'Oh, but it does if it should have been *you* I married in the first place,' he said softly, the expression in those beautiful green eyes so sincere that her heart did that crazy stuttering thing again.

'I was a stupid, gullible idiot when Zara came on to me like that,' he said bluntly, shocking her with his brutal honesty. 'My only excuse is that she seemed to have tapped into the way I was wishing *you* felt about me—that you enjoyed my company, that you found me sexy, that you desired me—and the fact that it all came in a package that looked identical to the woman I was already attracted to seemed to completely scramble my brains and short-circuit any attempt at rational thought.'

He hesitated a moment before he picked up her hand, as though he was expecting her to refuse to let him hold it, but she couldn't refuse him, not when he wore an expression of such despair.

'I knew I was doing the wrong thing even as I was standing waiting for the ceremony to start,' he admitted in a defeated voice so at odds with the dynamic man she knew him to be. 'I saw you walk in looking like a princess, wearing that beautiful dress—'

'My grandmother's dress,' she interrupted briefly, so glad that at least he'd noticed her when she'd been looking her best. He'd seen all too much of her at the end of gruelling twelve-hour shifts.

'I knew what I was doing was wrong,' he continued, 'but I was convinced that I'd completely burned my boats with you…and, besides, I couldn't just walk out and leave Zara at the altar, so to speak. If *she* hadn't killed me, your parents would.'

'You're right there,' she agreed. 'My mother had moved heaven and earth to get everything organised so quickly. She was convinced that the reason Zara didn't want to wait was because she was pregnant.'

'Hardly!' he scoffed. 'Even when we were supposed to be "trying for a baby" she was on the Pill. Then, so I wouldn't "waste my energy", she started taking the packs consecutively so it seemed as if she never ovulated and I was never invited to go near her.'

'But…she seemed so heart-broken that she couldn't have a child with you.' This was one facet of Zara's deception that she hadn't known about before. If she had, her parents would have had no chance of browbeating her into acting as surrogate for her sister…except…

Except in her heart it had never been Zara's child she'd agreed to carry but Dan's. It had been *his* sadness she'd wanted to banish with her gift.

'Sara, there isn't really a socially acceptable way of bringing this up but…your sister and I haven't…haven't been intimate for a long time… About a year before you became pregnant or even more than that. It certainly wouldn't be as if I were leaping out of one twin's bed and into the other…'

'Leaping into…' Sara felt her eyes grow wide. She seemed to have missed part of the conversation some-where along the line because it had almost sounded as if he was saying…as if he was asking… And to her utter shock he slid off the settee onto one knee in front of her, taking both her hands in his as he looked up into her face.

'Sara, I've had to live with the knowledge that I made an utter mess of everything when we were just starting our relationship…when I was falling in love with you. I'll never be able to forgive myself that I've completely wasted the years between when we could have been married, because it was all my own fault. Can you ever forgive me for being so stupid?'

Sara wasn't certain whether she was laughing or crying…probably both, with her emotions in such turmoil.

'Oh, Dan, if it means the difference between not having you in my life and being married to you and making a family with you…of course I can forgive you.'

She quickly realised that pulling her into his arms really wasn't a possibility with such a large bump getting in the way, but she'd loved him for so long that missing out on any more of his kisses wasn't an option.

'I want to hold you,' he murmured when they came up for air a while later, then smiled at her with that same boyish grin that had always set her pulse somersaulting. 'This settee definitely isn't big enough for the four of us.'

He helped her to her feet, the process taking far longer than it should have, in spite of the fact she no longer sported a cast, because neither of them could resist another kiss.

She was a little uncertain that this was the right time for them—after all, it hadn't been very long ago that she'd believed he was going to hunt for someone else to be a mother for his children. But she was wrapped in his arms and she knew that if she led him through to her bedroom she could trust him to be gentle with her because he loved her.

Then, almost at the foot of her bed, he hesitated, as though having serious second thoughts.

'Um, Sara…would you think me very strange if I said I'd rather we didn't make love yet?'

Disappointment had her heart plummeting to her feet. She'd honestly believed that he was just as aroused as she was, but, then, he was a handsome, fit man while she…she was a vast bulky blimp who would soon need a marquee to cover her enormous belly full of babies—definitely not anyone's idea of an ideal sex partner.

'It's not that I don't want to,' he said hurriedly, and squeezed her hand, apparently only realising that there must be something wrong when she hadn't managed to find the words to tell him she didn't mind the delay. 'You only have to look south to know that's not true.'

Her eyes followed his directions and she couldn't help blushing when she saw the evidence that he definitely found her desirable, despite her advanced pregnancy.

So why was she feeling a strange sense of relief that he wanted to take the decision out of her hands, that he wanted to wait for another time to become intimate with her? But she still had questions.

'So why don't you want to go to bed with me?' she asked, needing to hear him spell out his reasons so that she knew what she was going to have to deal with. If his time married to Zara had given him unreasonable expectations about how slim and elegant his wife was going to be…

'It just doesn't feel right to be together yet,' he explained quietly, and gave a self-deprecating shrug. 'I know it's not really logical and there isn't long to wait before I can apply for the decree absolute and I've been wanting to make love to you for so long that even my *hair* aches with it, but…'

Suddenly she realised exactly what he was saying and that she felt the same way, too.

'You mean, you don't want to make love with me until you're completely free of Zara, so that there's a…a separation between those two parts of your life and a real new start,' she suggested, and felt like the brightest pupil in the class when he smiled at her.

'Exactly,' he said with patent relief. '*Do* you mind?'

'How can I when I've just realised that I feel the same way?' she admitted. 'But I would feel more than disappointed if you were also putting an embargo on kisses and cuddles.'

'There's no embargo on those,' he reassured her as he finally guided her across to the bed and laid her down on it, quickly joining her there. 'You can have as many kisses and cuddles as you want.'

In spite of the fact that the hospital was very busy, due to a combination of increasing numbers of patients with seasonal ailments and the resulting staff shortages, the next weeks simply flew by.

Sara had shared a wry joke with Dan that almost as soon as she'd be signed off as fit to return to full-time work she would be eligible to start her maternity leave.

'And not a minute too soon,' Dan growled, when he saw how exhausted she was at the end of a full shift.

In a move that had become a daily ritual since she'd accepted his proposal, he pushed her gently in the direction of the bathroom and flipped the taps on full before he turned to help her out of her clothes. 'You've got to make allowances for the fact that you're carrying twins,' he scolded gently, his eyes already scanning her from head to foot as he searched for any external signs of problems such as pre-eclampsia.

'Nothing untoward?' she prompted when he'd finished checking, but she could already tell from his face that he'd found nothing new to worry about.

'Grab hold of me,' he directed as he offered her a hand to steady her while she climbed into the bath, but she opted to throw her arms around him and share a heartfelt kiss with him first.

Next in the ritual was a leisurely soak while he made

preparations for their evening meal, then an equally lei-surely foot massage that, more often than not, resulted in Sara falling asleep.

It was such a relaxing routine and so devoid of anything stressful that at times she wondered if she was the only one who was aware of the gradually building level of tension. It was worse when they slept together, curled up on the bed on a day off duty when he managed to persuade her to take a nap, or latterly even in the bed when cramp and backache made her nights misery and it was easier to have her own personal physician close at hand to administer the relevant massage techniques.

Finally came the day that he arrived with an even bigger bunch of freesias and a mysterious parcel that he presented to her with a smile from ear to ear.

CHAPTER TEN

'WHAT'S this?' Sara asked as she took in the fact that the parcel looked rather hastily wrapped...most unlike the meticulous way he'd wrapped the present they'd given to her parents when they'd visited them to announce their intended marriage. 'It's a bit early for a Christmas present. That's nearly a month away.' Although it didn't look very much like it because the paper wasn't in the least bit Christmassy.

'No, it's not for Christmas, but I'm hoping that what's in it will make this the best Christmas ever,' he said, managing to look as excited as a child on Christmas morning. 'And I hope you're not going to take for ever to unwrap it,' he added, clearly impatient for her to see what was inside. 'I can't bear it when people unpick each knot or peel off the tape.'

'Well, then, this is just for you.' She chuckled, infected by his air of excitement, grabbed hold of the wrapping paper in both hands and pulled.

He groaned as the contents of the parcel flew in two directions and he had to retrieve them one by one.

'These first,' he directed. 'I took that packet of ugly harvest festivals back and swapped them for the sexiest ones I could find,' he said with a grin, and waggled his eyebrows when she blinked at just how risqué the delicate lingerie was.

'Harvest festivals?' she repeated with warmth in her cheeks, remembering the vastly oversized knickers she'd bought to fit over her cast and then never worn.

'My grandmother used to call them that,' he said with a laugh. 'She said it was because they were so all-encompassing that they reminded her of that hymn that's always sung at harvest festivals, "All is safely gathered in".'

'Well, if *they* were harvest festivals, what are *these*?' She was almost embarrassed to look at them while he was watching for her reaction. She'd worn that thong out of sheer necessity when she'd first broken her leg, but these definitely had a different purpose if his expression was anything to go by. There was absolutely nothing utilitarian about them.

'Those are definitely Mardi Gras, or even Copacabana,' he suggested, 'and I can't wait to see you modelling them.'

The heat in his eyes was enough to send her temperature and pulse soaring and it wasn't something she was used to from Dan. While they had their agreement to wait until he was finally free of his marriage to Zara, she'd recognised that he'd been walking a torturous tightrope. On the one hand he'd been at great pains to make sure that she knew just how sexy he found her ripening body and how much he desired her while preventing the situation getting out of hand.

This, today, was so out of character that she scarcely…

'And *this* is the other "Happy Christmas" present we're going to share,' he said, more seriously this time, as he handed her the other half of the parcel. It was a bulky envelope and looked quite official…almost like…

'The decree absolute,' she whispered, hardly able to believe what she was seeing when she slid the document out. 'Oh, Dan, you're free.'

'Exactly,' he said with delight, flinging both arms around her. 'And tomorrow morning we're both going to present ourselves with all our relevant documents and information and we're going to book our wedding for twenty-one days later.'

'Twenty-one days?' she repeated, quite shocked that everything suddenly seemed to be moving so fast. 'But that's so close to Christmas and…and… Dan, you've been crossing off the days until you'd be free. Don't you want a little while to get used to the idea that you're not married to Zara before you tie yourself to—?'

'Sara, my love,' he said as he tightened his arms around her and settled her head on his shoulder, where it belonged, 'there's only one reason why I've been counting every last second until I could get this decree in my hand, and that's because I can't wait to be married to you.'

'But…'

He stopped her speaking with a hungry kiss, although that was becoming more difficult without some careful positioning as her bump grew ever larger.

'And don't you start trying to come up with all sorts of ulterior motives, such as "he's only doing it so fast because he wants to be married before the babies arrive to make sure they have his name." I can tell you categorically that, while it *would* cut down on a bit of paperwork, I'd be in just as much of a hurry to marry you if you weren't pregnant at all.'

He gave her another kiss that went a long way to convincing her just how much he desired her, then cupped her face in his hands and drew back, but only far enough for her to focus on green eyes that now blazed with all the love she could ever want. He drew in a noticeably shaky breath then declared fiercely, 'Sara, I just can't wait to be able to tell the world how I feel…that the woman I love to distraction has given me the best Christmas gift in the world and is finally my wife.'

In the end, it hadn't mattered in the least that she'd been feeling as if she was the size of a small house, because Dan had been right—all that mattered *was* that they were married at last, and there wasn't a dry eye.

With so few days to go before Christmas there was evidence everywhere from the beautiful display of scarlet and green poinsettia around the room to the fine streamers of red and green ribbon spiralling down from Sara's bouquet of Christmas roses.

Sara suspected that her mother probably hadn't been able to resist comparing this small gathering in the nearest registry office with Zara's elegant ceremony. No doubt she was regretting that neither she nor Dan had been willing to give her the chance to arrange something similar for them.

This was far more intimate and more meaningful, with just their closest friends in attendance to wish them well; and she didn't have to look much further than Sean O'Malley to guess who had suggested that they should all celebrate the unique time of year by wearing red or green.

But there was no way that even Audrey could miss the loving way Dan had ushered her into the room or the supportive arm that had encircled her throughout the proceedings.

Even the registrar had looked ecstatic when she declared them husband and wife, but that was probably because the poor woman was so relieved that she hadn't had to witness a precipitate delivery all over her brightly polished floor.

'Still, it's a bit of a shame,' Sean teased when he came up to congratulate them. 'It would have been so handy for registering the birth.'

Sara was the only one who didn't laugh.

All morning she had been feeling ominous tightenings and Dan hadn't completely been able to convince her that it was just more Braxton-Hicks' contractions. She'd been horribly certain that she would never get this far before going into labour.

'I told you it would be all right,' he murmured smugly when their little gathering had filed out of the office to make way for the next couple. He stroked a loving hand over her ivory silk-draped bump. 'I had a little word with these two in here and told them we had big plans for today, so they were to stay put just a little bit longer.'

'Dan? Sara?' said a hesitant voice behind them, and

there was Zara, looking almost unrecognisable from the sickly person Sara had last seen in a hospital bed. For just a moment the sight of her sister looking so vibrant and healthy reminded Sara all too forcibly that she must look like a hippo draped in a marquee by comparison, and her hand tightened reflexively on Dan's arm.

It only took one glance from those deep green eyes to restore her confidence that he was finally married to the twin he loved.

Standing beside Zara was a man at least twenty years her senior and not nearly as handsome as Dan, but it was obvious from the way he looked at her sister that he was completely besotted.

'This is Zach,' she said, almost shyly, and this new side to her otherwise confident sister took Sara by surprise.

'I'm the guy who's putting the finance together for Zara's film debut,' he announced in an unmistakable American accent, holding his hand out to each of them in turn. 'When she told me that her sister was getting hitched, I just had to do everything I could to make sure she was here.'

'That's very kind of you,' Sara said weakly, slightly overwhelmed by the man's ebullient personality. 'Have you been to Britain before?'

'Oh, many times,' he said with a broad smile. 'My plane could probably fly here by itself, it's been so often. So don't you worry about your sister missing out on being an aunt to those kids of yours.'

'Oh, that's very—'

'And don't you worry about anything,' he added,

dropping suddenly to a confidential tone, his shoulder turned so that neither Zara nor Dan were privy to what he was saying to her. 'First, I'm going to make sure she's fully recovered, then she's going to get her shot at stardom, but somewhere down the line I'm going to do my best to persuade her that she'd like to marry me and have some kids of her own.'

He stepped back and caught Zara's hand to tuck it in his elbow. 'Now, I know this is only a flying visit, but you just send us the pictures when these two decide to arrive and let us know when the christening is. We'll be back for it.'

Sara's last secret fear—that because she'd agreed to carry these precious babies as a surrogate for her sister, Zara might have a claim on them—had just been completely demolished.

She met Dan's eyes to ask a silent question and his smiling nod gave Sara the answer she needed.

'She'll have to come back for the christening,' she announced softly, knowing her next words would send her sister the signal that all had been forgiven, 'because she's going to be their godmother…if she wants to?'

The hug they shared was awkward but heartfelt and Zara took advantage of the closeness to whisper, 'Oh, Sara, I'm so, so sorry for everything. I was such a blind fool.'

Stepping back, she managed to find a tremulous smile. 'Rather their godmother than their mother,' she joked, but Sara caught the gleam of determination in Zach's eyes.

The next day Dan and Sara had just finished decorating their very first Christmas tree together and were about to settle down to tea when there was a phone call from someone in Human Resources.

'That's ridiculous!' Dan muttered impatiently when the call ended. 'There are some papers I've got to sign…something about insurance cover for you and the babies now we're married…and they want me to come in to do it today.'

'Today?' Sara's heart sank with disappointment. They'd had some rather interesting plans for the rest of the day and some of them involved stoking up the fire in the fireplace and just leaving the lights on the Christmas tree while they… *Later*, she reproached herself, silently. *We've got all the time in the world.*

'Well, I suppose it's good that they're getting everything sorted out now, rather than later,' she conceded. 'It shouldn't take you long, should it? We'll still have the rest of the evening…and night.'

'You needn't think you're staying here, tucked up all cosy and warm. There are some things for you to sign, too, so you'd better get something warmer than that robe on.'

Sara groaned and held her hands out so that he could help her to escape from the embrace of his blissfully comfortable settee. Unfortunately, it had never been designed for an easy exit for a woman heavily pregnant with twins.

They were just walking into Reception when Sean hailed them from the other side, his red hair a beacon in spite of all the tinsel and glitter on the enormous tree beside him.

'Hey, you two! Have you come to say hello to the gang?' he asked as he came across to kiss Sara's cheek.

'Several of them were asking how you were after I saw you at the wedding. They were complaining that haven't seen you since you started your maternity leave.'

'We've actually got to see someone in Human Resources about some paperwork,' Dan said with a grimace. 'Can you believe they phoned us on a Friday afternoon *this* close to Christmas?'

'Ah, sure they can wait a few minutes,' Sean said dismissively, beckoning them in the direction of A and E. 'The department's quite quiet at the moment so you'd better take advantage of it. By the time you've finished with the paper-pushers, we could be rushed off our feet.'

Dan and Sara both knew just how true that was, so they didn't need any more persuading, but they hadn't realised that the whole thing was a complete set-up until they walked into the staffroom to a shower of confetti and a united chorus of 'Surprise!' and found the room packed with waiting colleagues.

'They couldn't be there for the ceremony but they weren't going to miss out on the reception, even if they had to lay it on for themselves,' Sean told them with a broad unrepentant grin. 'Can't have A and E missing out on anything this special!'

'And the appointment with Human Resources?' Dan asked wryly, wondering how they could have been so gullible.

'That was the only ploy we could think of to get you out of your love nest,' Sean said with a teasing wink that had Sara blushing, remembering just what they'd had planned for the rest of the day. 'Now, has anyone got a spare suture trolley somewhere? Because you look as if you need it to carry some of that weight around for you.'

The thought of Sara wheeling her bump around in front of her on one of the department's trolleys... 'Suitably decorated for Christmas, of course,' Sean had added...was enough to have them all laughing.

It wasn't until Sara and Dan had circulated for an hour, greeting each of their colleagues as one after another they managed to snatch five minutes between patients, that they finally felt they could reasonably make their farewells.

'A final toast,' Sean announced, holding up a plastic goblet of something fruity and strictly non-alcoholic that almost exactly matched the carroty colour of his hair, apparently having appointed himself master of ceremonies. 'To paraphrase an old Irish toast—May the road rise up to meet you, the rain fall soft upon your head, the wind be always at your back, and may you get to heaven half an hour before the devil knows you're gone! To the bride and groom!'

'The bride and groom,' the rest chorused amid laughter, saluting them with similarly colourful glasses, but when Sara went to raise her own glass in return, she felt a sharp pain somewhere deep inside and gasped.

'Sara? Are you all right?' Dan asked, and tightened his hand around her shoulders, instantly aware that something had happened.

The sudden cascade of fluid onto the tiled floor told him everything he needed to know.

'They're over two weeks early,' she whimpered as she gingerly sat in a wheelchair that had appeared from nowhere.

'That's par for the course with twins,' Dan said reassuringly, then bent closer to whisper in her ear. 'And it's probably due to our enthusiastically thorough consummation of our marriage. They say that the application of male hormones can set things going. And, anyway, Christmas is the perfect time for the very best gift of all…new life.'

Sara hoped it was that same delightful application of male hormones that had been responsible for an absolutely textbook-perfect delivery, with one healthily squalling little boy following the other out into the world in perfectly normal cephalic deliveries.

'Oh, Dan, look! They're beautiful!' she sobbed as she lay there in the specially subdued lighting of the delivery room with one precious dark-haired baby in each arm. 'They're identical and they look just like you.'

'You're the beautiful one,' he argued as he stroked her joyful tears away with gentle fingers. 'You're amazing, Sara Lomax, and I could never tell you how much I love you in a million years. As for you two,' he said as he turned his attention to two little boys that were so perfect that any man would be proud to be their father.

He leaned a little closer, and under the cover of the activity still going on around them said, 'I need to have a word with the two of you for spoiling things. I had big plans for your mother tonight, involving a certain black lacy thong.'

'You idiot!' Sara laughed, knowing she'd had some similar plans of her own.

She loved Dan all the more for teaching her to have confidence in herself as an attractive woman, confidence that she'd never developed when she'd always felt herself to be in Zara's shadow.

'We'll just have to remember what we had planned and save it up for later,' she suggested, her heart so full of love that it felt as if must be overflowing. 'After all, we've got the rest of our lives to love each other.'

BABY TWINS: PARENTS NEEDED

BY
TERESA CARPENTER

Dear Reader,

My sister has a set of twin girls (along with five more girls), and though double the loving, the twins were also double the trouble. So, what better way to bring two strangers together than to care for two orphaned babies?

Love and duty collide as a small-town loner goes up against a world traveller with an extensive family. The instant parents soon learn that ten-month-olds, like animals, can sense fear. Humour and unity help get them through. The common ground is an unexpected, inconvenient attraction that complicates the question of custody!

I had great fun writing about twins. It was a learning experience, though. When I was plotting my story I asked my sister with the seven girls if she thought it was believable for a parent to leave guardianship of their children without ever advising the guardian. Not only did she agree it was, she grinned evilly and confessed she was glad to hear I felt that way, too. Oh, boy, am I praying for her continued good health!

Best wishes,

Teresa

Teresa Carpenter believes in the power of unconditional love, and that there's no better place to find it than between the pages of a romance novel. Reading is a passion for Teresa—a passion that led to a calling. She began writing more than twenty years ago, and marks the sale of her first book as one of her happiest memories. Teresa gives back to her craft by volunteering her time to Romance Writers of America on a local and national level. A fifth generation Californian, she lives in San Diego, within miles of her extensive family, and knows that with their help she can accomplish anything. She takes particular joy and pride in her nieces and nephews, who are all bright, fit, shining stars of the future. If she's not at a family event you'll usually find her at home, reading, writing, or playing with her adopted Chihuahua, Jefe.

To Jill Limber, critique partner, writing buddy,
and lunch companion,
I'm lucky to have you in my corner.
And to Michelle and Gabrielle, my favorite twins
in the whole wide world.

CHAPTER ONE

RACHEL ADAMS was at war. And the enemy outnumbered her two to one. Hands on her hips she surveyed two plump-cheeked, hazel-eyed cherubs smeared head to foot in baby lotion.

"Cody Anthony Adams," Rachel admonished the unrepentant ten-month-old, "if you can't keep your hands to yourself, I'm going to duct tape them to your diaper during your naps."

The sight of the greasy mess acted like scissors to nerves already frayed thin by exhaustion. Inhaling a calming breath, she reminded herself she was a mother now. That it had happened by default didn't matter. She'd made a vow to provide a home for her orphaned niece and nephew.

But boy did she have a lot to learn.

Already she'd discovered that children, like animals, sensed fear.

God knows she'd had little time to mourn the sister she'd barely known. Instead, Rachel had learned that messes happened. Literally. And repeatedly. And if she didn't keep things far enough out of Cody's reach, creatively. Usually with food, jelly, bananas, potatoes whatever he could get into when she turned her back. He liked to finger paint. And his favorite target was his sister.

Yuck, yuck, yuck.

Armed with rubber gloves and a tub of wet wipes she went on the attack, cleaning bodies, fingers and toes. And hair. Both babies needed a bath to complete the job. She made a mental note to move the crib another six inches from the changing table.

It struck her suddenly; this must be love. When forbearance overshadowed disgust and exasperation, letting affection rule, there could be no other explanation.

Sometime over the last six days she'd fallen in love. And it was huge, bigger than anything she'd ever experienced.

The feeling terrified her.

One thing was for sure, if her co-guardian ever deigned to show his face, she'd fight with everything she had to keep her niece and nephew.

"That's right, kiddos, you're stuck with me. I'm wholeheartedly, irrevocably a goner. And I'm keeping you. I promise that you will always know you are loved. You'll never have to worry about simply being tolerated or that you're here only because of a sense of duty.

"We're a family now," she whispered around the lump in her throat.

Stripping off the rubber gloves, Rachel ran her

fingers through the slick darkness of Cody's hair. She kept looking for signs of her sister in the twins, and caught the occasional expression. But they must have gotten their dark hair and eyes from their father, because Crystal had brown eyes and light brown hair.

Crystal had gotten her coloring from her father. Rachel took after their mother with white-blond hair that she kept short and manageable and eyes that couldn't decide if they were blue or green.

A sudden knock at the front door interrupted her musings.

Rachel tensed. "Who could that be?"

Wearily blowing a strand of hair from her eyes, she looked at the naked babies and considered ignoring the door. Whoever it was couldn't have come at a worse time.

Jolie began to cry. In the week the twins had been in her care, Rachel had learned that Cody liked to be naked but Jolie didn't.

A loner who preferred animals and plants to most people, Rachel didn't usually get visitors; not even her neighbors. But whoever banged on her door meant business, pounding again almost immediately.

Leaving the twins in the safety of the crib, making sure nothing else was within Cody's reach, Rachel made her way to the door reminding herself she wasn't a loner anymore. Through the peephole she saw a man half-turned away from her with hands tucked into the pockets of his dark jacket.

Hmm. Could this be Ford Sullivan, co-guardian of

the twins? A Navy SEAL, his commanding officer had explained that Sullivan, aka Mustang, was out of the country when the twins were orphaned but he would be in touch as soon as he returned from assignment.

As far as she was concerned he could stay away.

She opened the door a few inches.

The man appeared bigger and broader than his image through the peephole. Much bigger. Much broader. Dressed in jeans and leather with dark glasses, biker boots and a five-o'clock shadow as accessories, his stance warned he wasn't someone to mess with. Snow fell from a gray sky, landing in white clusters on wide shoulders and dark hair.

This man bypassed bad and went straight to dangerous.

A sucker for a good action movie, the sight of this tall, dark and menacing man sent unexpected, and unwanted, tingles down the back of Rachel's neck.

She crossed her fingers he was a motorist who'd run out of gas.

"Yes?" she said. She purposely did not ask if she could help him. Or smile. She'd found smiling only encouraged people to linger when most of the time she preferred her own company.

"Rachel Adams?" he asked. His deep baritone slid as smoothly as hot coffee through the icy afternoon air.

And just as smoothly and potently down her spine.

"Yes." She shifted restlessly, thinking in the back of her mind that she needed to put her SUV in the barn.

"Your sister was Crystal Adams?"

So much for him being an anonymous motorist. Her

head went back, and she narrowed her gaze on him. "Ford Sullivan I presume?"

He cocked his head in acknowledgment. "Yes. I've come to collect the twins."

Hackles bristling, Rachel planted her hand dead center of his chest when the military man attempted to cross her threshold.

"Hold it, big guy. I don't know you. And so far, I don't like what I'm hearing."

Sullivan didn't give an inch, but his eyes narrowed and she felt the flex of muscle under her fingers, silent warnings of strength and resolution. He reached inside his jacket and came out with a wallet. He handed her his military ID.

She knew of Navy SEALS. They were elite, Special Forces who were dropped into hot spots all over the world. Granted, her knowledge came from movies and books, but there was no denying it rated as very high security stuff.

After a moment, he plucked his ID from her chilled fingertips. "Lady I've driven a long way, and it's cold out here."

Damn him. She didn't want him in her home, not when he talked about taking the twins away. Not when she wanted to keep the twins herself. But he had legal rights she couldn't ignore.

Reluctantly she stood aside and let him come inside. His commanding officer had said Sullivan was an honorable man. Right. His edges were so rough he practically chafed her skin as he stepped past her.

Blowing out a pent-up breath, she closed the door.

Then clenched her teeth against the sight of him framed by the hearth fire. His big body made her blue and gray living room seem entirely too small.

And more disorderly than she'd realized. The babies came with a lot of clutter, and a lot of demands. Picking up was a luxury that came right after sleeping and showering.

Jolie's cries from the bedroom reminded Rachel where she'd left off. Grim amusement lifted the corner of her mouth. She'd just been thinking she was at war and here stood a warrior.

He wanted the babies? She knew just how he could help.

"I'm so glad you're here." Pretending not to see the disdain with which Sullivan viewed her home, she hooked her arm through his and drew him into the bedroom. "Because the twins need a bath."

To his credit Sullivan didn't flinch. He took off his sunglasses revealing sharp blue, expressionless eyes. He tossed the glasses along with his leather jacket onto the bed.

Jolie immediately stopped crying to stare at Sullivan. Rachel didn't blame her. Soft black cotton defined muscular shoulders and hard pecks. His arms were strong and browned by the sun. He heated the room better than a fireplace.

Something she shouldn't be noticing. Still, she empathized when she cleaned the drool from Jolie's chin.

"What happened?" he asked as he stepped up to the crib.

Rachel took perverse pleasure in explaining Cody's little habit.

He hiked a dark brow. "You might want to check on them more often."

"Wow, why didn't I think of that?" Jerk. She lifted Jolie into her arms. "Grab Cody. The bathroom's through here."

Rachel flinched at the sight of dirty towels and overflowing clothes and wastebaskets. Half the contents of her medicine cabinet littered the sink. And—she cringed—was that a fork?

Ignoring the mess, and the rush of embarrassment, she bent to start the bathwater. Once it ran warm she set the stopper and knelt on a towel still folded next to the tub from the babies' last bath. Then she set Jolie in the warm water.

Sullivan knelt next to her, so close his arm brushed her shoulder as he lowered Cody into the water. Rachel jumped away as if singed by steam.

She shot to her feet. "Watch the babies, I'll grab clean towels."

"Clean would be good," he said, making no attempt to hide the derision.

Stunned she swung around to confront him, but his attention remained on the twins. She waffled for several seconds on whether to appease or challenge him on his concerns regarding the condition of the house.

On the one hand, the house was a mess; on the other, she'd been handling their wards on her own for six days. How dare he judge her?

She'd like to see him do better.

No, she turned away to get the towels, that wasn't true. That would mean he'd have the twins and she needed to care for them, to be there for them, because she hadn't been there for her sister.

If he thought she'd simply step aside and allow him to take them away, he could forget it.

"How did you know Crystal?" she asked as she returned to the tub.

Making sure to leave plenty of room between her and Sullivan, she knelt next to him. She glanced at him, then away, pretending not to notice how the twins' excited play had dampened his T-shirt causing the fabric to cling to his impressive chest.

"Eeey!" Cody shrieked in joy and slapped the water with both hands, splashing everyone. Jolie shied away, the movement causing her to slide sideways. Rachel reached for her, but Sullivan got there first, catching Jolie in his large, competent hands.

He held her with such gentleness, righting her and making her giggle. He appeared so calm despite his obvious frustration with the circumstances.

"It wasn't Crystal I knew." He finally answered her question as he scrubbed Jolie's tummy. "At least not well. Tony Valenti was my friend. We worked together."

"The twins' father?"

"Yeah."

"He was a SEAL, too?"

"Yeah." A short pause. "He saved my life."

"I see." Yeah, she did. And the picture didn't look

good. An honorable man, he'd feel all the more obligated to take the twins because of what he felt he owed his dead friend.

An hour later the babies had been bathed, dressed and fed. Lowering Jolie into the playpen and tossing in a few plastic blocks, Rachel had to admit having an extra pair of hands had made everything easier. And faster. It would have taken her nearly twice as long to complete the tasks on her own.

She turned to where Sullivan sat on the sofa with Cody. The little boy looked up at him and smiled showing two bottom teeth. The man ran a gentle finger down the baby's cheek then bounced him on his knee.

Cody reached up and grabbed a handful of dark hair. Sullivan calmly freed himself.

They'd bonded quickly.

She crossed her arms over her chest, denying that his tenderness toward the baby touched her. She walked to the opposite end of the sofa and began folding the clean clothes mounded in the corner.

"What are your plans for the twins?" she demanded.

He lifted a dark brow at her directness. "I plan to honor my friend's request by taking them back to San Diego to raise them."

Her heart clenched as he confirmed her worst fear. "Right. And what about me?"

"Simple. I plan for you to sign over your custody."

"Simple?" She nearly choked on the word. "How can you hold that baby in your arms and call this simple?"

He frowned, shifting the baby. Cody tipped back his head and looked up at the expanse of black fabric, to the man's face. Silent communication passed between them as once again, Sullivan pulled the baby's fist from his hair.

Sullivan focused his blue gaze on her. "I understand this isn't easy for you. But it's for the best."

"You don't understand anything, Sullivan. I failed my sister once. I'm not going to fail her now. Her dying wish was that I raise her children. And that's what I'm going to do."

He eyed her for a moment before cocking his head in acknowledgment. "Your sister never intended for you to raise her children."

Rachel's head went up and back as if she'd taken a blow to the chin. It couldn't have hurt more if Sullivan had actually hit her.

Old guilt rose up to choke her. Resolutely she shook it off. She and Crystal had put the past behind them when their parents died three years ago and Crystal had come to stay with Rachel. And when Crystal had left for San Diego State University, they'd stayed in touch by phone and e-mail.

Rachel was the only family Crystal had had left in the world. Through all of her uncertainty and exhaustion this last week, Rachel had held on to the fact that her sister had trusted her to take care of Jolie and Cody.

She caught herself rubbing her arms as if to ward off a chill. When she felt Sullivan watching her, she clenched her hands into fists and dropped them to her sides.

"Why would you say something so hateful?" Rachel demanded.

"Look I only know what Tony told me. Crystal didn't like it that Tony made a will naming a guardian for the twins without consulting her. So she made her own will and named you as guardian."

"Which just proves she wanted me to raise her children." Something deep inside her eased.

"No, you were leverage. No offense, but Tony didn't want someone who ran away from life and responsibilities, who couldn't maintain a relationship to raise his kids."

Everything in Rachel screamed a denial of his claim, of this whole situation. But it was here; *he* was here, standing in her living room and not budging by the look of it.

"I don't believe you." Believe? Not likely. "If this is a joke, it's in very poor taste."

"No joke." He hesitated, and she could practically hear the debate going on internally. Being free with information obviously wasn't part of his job description. "That would be cruel. Listen, I have a large, close-knit family that Tony was a part of. He wanted the twins to have that connection."

Sullivan bent to retrieve his jacket and withdraw some papers. He extended them to Rachel. "I have legal documents here for you to sign over custody."

She reluctantly lowered her gaze from him to the folded papers he offered. She didn't want to take them, didn't want to think he spoke the truth about her sister's motives. But she'd learned long ago no good came from lying to herself.

Or from avoiding reality.

He looked around the cluttered room then met her gaze. "Clearly you're out of your depth."

"That's ridiculous." She ignored the proffered papers to pick up a tiny set of overalls, folding them over and over. "I'm not overwhelmed. I just need time to adjust."

He rose and settled Cody next to Jolie in the playpen. "And while you adjust, the twins suffer."

Anger, simmering under the surface since she opened the door to this ungrateful man, rose to a boil. She planted her hands on her hips and glared in outrage.

"How dare you? They have not suffered. So I'm behind in my housekeeping. So what? You caught me on a bad day. I usually pick up when they're in bed, but last night I had to write. I had a deadline."

He gestured to the cluttered room, his blue eyes flashing with impatience. "This is more than one day's filth. Make this easy on both of us. Sign over custody to me and you won't have to adjust and you won't have to pick up after them any longer."

"Okay, that's it!" Rachel had had enough. Filth? Oh, she'd had more than enough.

Stomping into her room she grabbed up the diaper bag. A quick glance inventoried the contents. Going to the changing table she stuffed in more diapers, two sleepers, a pack of wipes, some formula.

"You think you can do better?" She marched by Sullivan on her way to the kitchen.

"I think you need to calm down." Sullivan watched her efforts with an impassive expression that only fueled her anger.

She ripped open the refrigerator door, hissing when her thumbnail caught in the handle and tore. Tears rushed forward, but she blinked them away determined to show no weakness in front of the cold man watching—and judging—her every move.

"Oh, I'm calm." She quickly tore off the broken nail and stuffed her finger in her mouth as she held the door open with her hip and plucked two bottles from the refrigerator adding them to the other items in the red baby bag.

Glaring at her nemesis, she stepped up to him and thrust the overflowing bag into his arms. She half hoped he'd drop it, but he quickly controlled the bag.

"I'm just wonderful."

Adrenaline pumping through her, she brushed past him on her way to the playpen where she swooped Jolie up into her arms. From the edge of the playpen Rachel snagged two blankets. Folding one around Jolie, Rachel tossed the other to Sullivan who now eyed her with sharp-eyed wariness.

"Bring Cody."

"What's happening here, Rachel?"

"I'm doing you a favor." Finding her coat, she pulled her car keys from the pocket and headed for the door.

"You're going to sign the papers?"

A bitter laugh broke free. "Better than that. I'm not signing the papers."

He caught up with her at her Toyota SUV and swung her and Jolie to face him. "Where do you think you're going?"

She shook him off. "I'm not going anywhere. You are." She took the diaper bag from him, opened the front door and tossed it inside. "You wanted the twins? You've got them. For the next twenty-four hours."

"Excuse me?" Now his tone held a bite. "I'm not accustomed to taking orders."

"Yes, you are, you're in the Navy."

Let him argue that.

His expression didn't change; he was too much a warrior to give anything away that easily. But his shoulders went up and back, fighting ready. A clear indication she'd hit a nerve.

She should be ashamed of the satisfaction that gave her, but he threatened her on too many levels.

"You seem to think two babies are so easy to care for." Walking around him, she opened the door, put Jolie in her car seat and began to belt her in. "Right. Fine. You're going to get your chance."

Sullivan had left the door open. Cody didn't care to be left alone in the house, and he made his displeasure heard with loud cries. Flashing Sullivan a disdainful glare, she suggested, "You might want to start by getting Cody."

"Not until I understand what's going on here." Before her eyes he changed from civilian to warrior. His hands lowered to his sides, his chin jutted down and his blue eyes chilled by several degrees.

Climbing from the car, she closed the door with soft emphasis. She instinctively kept her distance, out of reach of his sensual appeal. What was with her that this stranger's dangerous edge affected her so easily?

"The first thing you have to learn is you don't get to take the high road when a baby is crying."

He spiked a hand through his dark hair. "You're right." Turning he loped into the house and came back out a few moments later with his jacket under his arm and Cody wrapped in a blanket.

Okay, so Sullivan got points for common sense.

She reached for Cody, but Sullivan held him fast. She lifted one eyebrow and waited.

"We need to talk first," he stated.

"No, we'll talk after." Facing him, she propped hands on hips. "After you've tried to feed and change two babies. After you've spent a sleepless night trying to get them both to sleep at the same time. After you haven't brushed your teeth before noon and your best shirt's stained beyond repair. Then we'll talk."

The sound of grinding teeth reached her across the two feet separating them. He shook his head. "What's to stop me from taking them and driving on to San Diego?"

She narrowed her eyes at him, and this time when she reached for Cody she refused to be cowed.

"Honor. Integrity. I spoke to your commanding officer. He assured me you have both in spades." She walked around the SUV and set Cody in his car seat. Kissing his dark curls, she tucked the blanket around him.

Bending, she gathered a few scattered toys and handed one to each baby. They immediately tried to take a bite. Her heart turned over. How trusting they were. At ten months old life wasn't that complicated.

"I'm doing this for you guys." She told them. "Have no mercy."

She rounded the SUV to rejoin Sullivan.

"Plus, I haven't signed the papers." She held out her hand, palm up. "Keys."

"I thought you meant for me to take them." None of the tension had left those truly impressive shoulders.

"To your Jeep. You're taking my vehicle, I'll need to keep yours."

Silence stretched while she met those compelling blue eyes head-on. The scowl creasing his brow revealed his displeasure at the situation.

"Look, I'm not giving these babies up without a fight, but I'm exhausted, dirty and hungry. In no shape to have an important discussion. And until you've spent some quality time with the twins, you're in no shape for the discussion, either. So we trade keys and regroup tomorrow."

He hesitated for a heartbeat.

Time slowed. Breath misted on the air. Her nerves jumped.

Finally he handed over his keys and took hers in exchange.

"I hope you realize what you're doing," he said as he climbed inside the vehicle and adjusted the seat. "Honor and integrity don't make me a gentleman." He closed the door and turned over the ignition, rolling down the window a crack. "I'm a SEAL. And we never leave a man behind."

Rachel watched the taillights disappear down the driveway, praying she hadn't just made the biggest mistake of her life.

CHAPTER TWO

FORD pulled into a slot in front of his hotel room, slowly turned the ignition off, eased back in his seat and closed his eyes. Twenty hours after leaving Rachel Adams's house and he was ready to run back to her door with head and tail tucked low.

How humiliating.

Using all the stealth learned over eight years in the SEALS; he risked moving to check on the babies in the back seat. Jolie, as tidy and neat as when he'd strapped her in, slept with her pink beanie on her head and her bottle nestled close. Cody, who'd long ago lost his hat and shoes, had a catsup smear on his cheek and a French fry clutched in his fist.

They'd finally fallen asleep an hour ago.

Ford settled back in his seat. He planned to sit right where he was for as long as they slept.

Time well spent finding an appetizing way to eat crow. Only sheer stubborn will had kept him from running back to Rachel's place hours ago. How had she managed on her own for six days?

A call home netted him lots of advice from Gram, and other family and friends, but the twins were having none of it. Nothing he'd done, or said, or sung—yes he'd sung to them—had done any good. Talk about logistical nightmares, he'd rather plan a two-team infiltration any day than repeat the last twenty hours.

Clearly they wanted Rachel.

Hell, he wanted Rachel, and it had nothing to do with the soft curves hidden under her burp-stained sweater. Okay, that was a lie. No man could look at her trim little figure and remain unaffected. But her sweet butt and perky bosom were beside the point. He'd misjudged her big time. For six days she'd cared for the two babies with patience and devotion.

He knew that because they were clean, well fed and distraught without her.

With one or the other, or both, of the babies awake most of the night; he'd gotten about two hours sleep. And she'd had them for six nights. No wonder her pretty sea-green eyes had dark bruises shadowing them.

She was one feisty woman. A blond wildcat determined to stand between him and her cubs. But for all her attitude, she was a lightweight. Barely five foot five, six at the most, her sweet curves scarcely filled out her jeans or rounded out her gold sweater.

Obviously she'd been ignoring herself to care for the twins. Protective instincts had flared when he should have been thinking of ways to convince her the babies were better off with him.

He'd told her a SEAL never left a man behind, which was nothing less than the truth. He could no more leave Tony's twins in the care of another than he could leave a teammate on the battlefield.

He tensed and turned to the window just before the local sheriff rapped on the glass. He held up a hand and eased from the car.

"Officer." Ford addressed the man who looked like Mr. Clean in a uniform. Sheriff Mitchell according to his badge. "What can I do for you?"

"Sir." The sheriff crossed his arms over his massive chest and nodded toward Rachel's SUV. "Problem?"

"No." Ford made sure to keep his hands in plain view as he leaned against the SUV, not wanting the officer to feel threatened. Had the hotel owner called the law? He'd been to Ford's room twice in response to complaints about the babies' crying. "No problem."

The last thing he had time for was trouble from the local law enforcement.

"This is Rachel Adams's vehicle." Sheriff Mitchell took two steps to the side and looked into the back seat. "Those are her wards."

"Yes." What game was Rachel playing? Did she regret sending him away with the twins? "Has she called with a complaint?"

"Well now—" assessing brown eyes were turned back on Ford "—we don't need a complaint to take an interest in the citizens of Scobey."

"I'm sure your citizens appreciate your diligence." Having grown up in a small town, Ford took the sheriff at his word. Which didn't mean he intended to tell the other man anything.

"What's your business in town?"

"That's between me and Ms. Adams."

"I've heard there have been complaints about the babies crying."

Ford's tolerance for the questioning dried up. He opened the back door next to Cody. He gestured inside. "Look for yourself, they're fine. They're still adjusting to the loss of their parents. They have the right to a few tears."

"I suppose they do." The sheriff hiked his pant legs and crouched to look in at the babies. Satisfied he rose to his standard six one. "Why are you sitting out here?"

Ford frowned to see Cody starting to stir. He quietly closed the door. "They aren't sleeping well, we took a drive to settle them down."

"Right. I'll let you go." Mitchell sounded disappointed he had no reason to detain Ford, and his next words held a clear warning. "Just take heed, Rachel Adams isn't alone here in Scobey."

"It's been snowing here for about an hour." Rachel frowned at the view outside the window. Dark clouds obscured the sun. Snow fell, pushed around by whistling gusts of wind. This weather had better not keep Sullivan from bringing back the twins. Maybe she should call him and tell him to come now.

"I can stop by on my way home." Sam Mitchell offered. "Make sure you're all right." He'd called to warn her an unexpected cold front was moving in fast and heavy.

Uh-huh.

He'd already mentioned running into Ford Sullivan in town. She bet. He'd probably hunted Sullivan down at his hotel.

"Mitch, I'm fine. There's no need to waste a trip out here."

She'd broken things off between them nearly two years ago, but the sheriff continued to take an interest in her affairs. Or lack of them, in the hope of reigniting the ardor between them. For an intelligent man, no one buried his head in the sand better than Mitch.

"I heard they're really missing you over at the clinic."

"Hmm."

"Mrs. Regent's Poopsy nipped a couple of the techs during her clipping."

"Rough."

"Yeah. Poopsy doesn't care for anyone but you. Rumor is Mrs. Regent won't be scheduling Poopsy again until you're back from maternity leave."

"Oh joy."

Rachel opened up a new e-mail, wondering, not for the first time, at the man's ability to basically hold a conversation on his own.

Only half listening, she sent her latest article off as an attachment, then closed down her computer. When she looked up, she spotted her SUV pull past the window.

Her glance immediately went to the clock. Sullivan was early. By almost three hours.

Yes!

"Mitch, I've got to go. Sullivan just pulled up with the babies."

"I still don't like the idea of you dealing with him on your own. You call me if you have any problems."

"He's a SEAL, Mitch. I'm either in great hands, or you'll never find the body."

"That's not funny."

"You're telling me." Not that she feared for her life. No, she feared for her peace of mind. Not only because he'd threatened to take the twins from her, but because she'd dreamed of exactly how great those hands would feel against her skin. Her blood heated with the memory of gentle caresses and not so soft strokes. Oh my.

A knock sounded at the door.

"Mitch, I'll be fine. Gotta go." She disconnected and headed for the door fanning herself en route. No way she wanted Sullivan to know he got her hot and bothered.

She opened the door and leaned against the threshold. Sullivan stood alone on the porch. "Sullivan. You're early."

He ran a hand through already mussed hair. The gesture was the first sign of vulnerability he'd displayed. Behind him snow fell from a gray sky—heavier now than a few minutes ago. White clusters covered wide shoulders and dark hair. It did her heart good to see him disheveled.

Red rose high on his cheeks. Rachel blinked, surprised by the sign of discomfort. But was it temper or embarrassment that lit up his features?

"Call me Ford, or Mustang if you prefer. Let me just get this out right up-front." He met her gaze straight on. "I'm sorry. I made assumptions I shouldn't have. You've done a phenomenal job handling Cody and Jolie alone over the past week. Thank you for being there for them."

Oh, unfair. Here she'd hoped for a moment of weakness and instead he showed his strength with a sincere apology. And he wanted her to call him Mustang? The picture of the beautiful range horses came to mind. Proud and wild, free and reckless, she had no problem seeing how he'd earned the nickname that played off his given name.

No, she'd stick with "Sullivan," much less intimate, more distancing.

"Enough already. In another minute you'll have me weeping." She pushed past him. "Let's get the babies inside out of the snow."

She dashed to the nearest door, freed Jolie from her seat and quickly returned to the house. Teeth chattering, because she hadn't bothered with a jacket, she arrowed straight for the fire.

She spread a blanket in the middle of the floor and set Jolie in the center with a couple of Matchbox cars. Then Rachel stepped back and watched Sullivan lower Cody to the blanket.

Moving away, she curled into the corner of the sofa while Sullivan stood taking in the room.

Nothing to be embarrassed about this time. She'd been busy for the last twenty-one hours. Well, okay, she'd slept for the first part of that time, but the rest had gone toward housework and laundry. Plus she'd gotten a couple of articles written for her syndicated column on animal manners.

"Place looks great."

"You don't." Jolie soon gave up on the toy cars to crawl across the living room carpet straight for Rachel. She lifted the girl into her lap. "How much sleep did you get last night?"

"I've had less." He shrugged away her concern. "It's not the lack of sleep that got to me. It's the helplessness. I'm a man of action, but nothing I did was right."

"That's how it was for me for the first three days, then they finally began to calm down." Okay, this conversation wasn't so bad.

He even made her laugh when he told her how he'd found the cereal in the bottom of the baby bag, but since he didn't have high chairs he'd taken the twins out to their car seats and fed them in the SUV. Smart actually, but she'd had no doubt of his intelligence since the moment she'd first opened the door to him.

"At least they stopped crying long enough to eat." Sullivan bent to pick up Cody who was trying to climb his leg.

"They take comfort from each other." Rachel ran her fingers through Jolie's soft hair.

The look he sent her spoke volumes. "You mean they feed off each other's emotions. One starts crying, and they try to outdo each other."

"You have to remember they're traumatized." She

defended her niece and nephew. "They've lost their parents. That's going to take time to get over."

"Yeah." The fire popped and shifted. Sullivan walked over to tend it, easily handling both Cody and the fire poker. "The sooner they're settled the better. Have you considered signing the papers?"

Disappointment washed through Rachel. Back to square one. But she wouldn't be signing any papers. Now or later.

"I'm thinking you should be the one signing the papers," she challenged.

Before he could respond, the lights flickered. Once. Twice. Then they settled.

"Shoot." Holding Jolie close, Rachel leaped to her feet and headed for the front window. A wall of white fell heavily. Actually it blew sideways, the wind's force strong enough to blow the snow horizontal, confirming her worst fears.

The storm had become a blizzard.

"Looks bad." Sullivan stood behind her.

She smelled the clean scent of him. Musk, starch and man, an intoxicating mix. Almost distracting enough to take her attention from the storm.

But that would be a deadly mistake.

"Yeah. Blizzard. Damn, there was no mention of snow in the weather reports earlier." Obviously she should have paid better attention to Mitch.

"Won't be the first time they've been wrong."

The understated response startled a laugh from Rachel. "You've got that right."

Already her SUV was buried under several inches of snow and ice. It needed to be moved to the garage or the engine would freeze.

The lights flickered again. And again they came back steady.

That wouldn't last.

"Do you have a generator?" he asked.

She nodded. "Fuel is in the barn."

Lord, she hoped she had enough fuel to weather the storm. Living alone, she'd learned to be prepared, but a lightning storm in late September had hit a power tower east of Scobey, knocking her power out. She hadn't had a chance to restock before receiving the news about Crystal. Since then she'd been so busy with the twins, she hadn't thought about restocking her emergency supplies.

"I should leave. The hotel will probably let me back in without the twins."

"You can't drive in this." She handed Jolie to Sullivan and then moved to the closet to yank out her jacket and some boots. "Give me my keys."

"I've driven in worse."

"So you're looking to leave me alone with the babies again?" One boot on, one boot off, she propped her hands on her hips. "Look, I don't want you here any more than you want to stay, but I wouldn't send my worst enemy out in a storm this bad. Oh wait, you are my worst enemy."

He lifted a brow as he rocked the babies, but he only said, "We're only six miles from town."

"Only?" She stomped into her other boot. God save her from ignorant tourists. "Where are you from?"

"Southern California. But I've trained in all forms of extreme weather."

"I've no doubt. But there's no need to go all SEAL on me. Now, hand over the keys."

Sullivan frowned his displeasure as he glanced out of the window. "You can't go out there, either."

"I have to. If the SUV isn't moved, the cold will crack the engine block."

"I'll move it."

She shook her head as she wrapped a scarf around her throat and ears. "I need to get fuel for the generator, too. And bring in some wood."

He stepped into her path. "I can do it."

"Look, you're helping by being here to watch the twins." She pulled on her gloves, waiting for him to step aside. "I know what I'm doing."

Giving in, he juggled the babies to reach the keys in his pants pocket, which he handed to her. "Be careful."

"Always. Candles and matches are in the kitchen cupboard to the left of the sink. In case the lights go out before I get back with fuel for the generator."

Ducking into the closet again, she looped a heavy coil of rope over her shoulder.

"What's that for?" Sullivan demanded.

"Snow line. One end hooks to the front porch post, the other I hook around my waist. It acts as an anchor so I can find my way back to the house."

A grim look settled over his features. "This is ridiculous. I can't let you go out there alone."

"Didn't we just have this conversation? I live alone,

Sullivan. I do what I need to survive. That doesn't change just because your macho self is here." She pulled a second pair of gloves from her coat pocket and donned them over the first pair. "And I don't have time to argue."

Not waiting for a response, she moved to the door, stepped out and quickly pulled it closed behind her.

Ford looked down at the babies in his arms. Their care and safety had to be a priority, but it didn't feel right letting Rachel struggle against the elements on her own.

He carried the twins to the playpen. Both babies immediately crawled to the side and pulled themselves up. He tossed a few of the plastic blocks in to keep them occupied. Neither Cody nor Jolie paid any attention to the blocks.

"Ba da da sa." Cody registered his complaint and lifted his arms to be picked up.

"Maa ga do." Jolie put her two cents in and held her arms up, too.

He itched to go to the window and check on Rachel's progress but moved to the fireplace instead. The fire had died down to mere embers. He tossed on a new log, then began to pace, wearing a path in the dove-gray carpet.

"What do you say, Cody, we're the men here. It's up to us to protect the women. And that's not happening with us in here and her out there."

"Mamama?" Jolie stuck her finger in her mouth.

Ford stopped midstride and stared at Jolie. How odd to hear her call Rachel mama or almost mama, he reasoned. But still, it sounded wrong. Felt wrong. And brought home to him how much life had changed in such a short period of time.

Tony and Crystal were gone, killed in an earthquake while visiting a Mexican resort.

Ford had been shocked to return from assignment to learn he was guardian of Tony's children. Yeah, he'd agreed to take on the responsibility, but he'd never really expected it to be necessary. Certainly not so soon. But prepared or not, Ford owed Tony. He'd saved Ford's life; honor and friendship demanded Ford step up to meet Tony's last request.

Tony had always envied Ford his close family, so much so that he'd arranged for Ford to raise his kids. Which meant the twins went home with Ford. He'd be moving in with Gram, who had agreed to watch the babies for him. He'd also be hiring a full-time nanny.

Ford didn't want to hurt Rachel, but it couldn't be helped.

The storm, however, managed to delay the inevitable.

Rachel really surprised him. Her aquamarine eyes and white-gold hair cut short and sassy hid a depth of passion he'd bet few people saw.

Frustrating as her protectiveness was, he respected her spirit, her willingness to put herself on the line for the children in her care.

He just needed to convince her they'd be better off with him.

After he saved her from the freezing hell outside.

For all her feistiness and lean strength, she had to weigh next to nothing. She'd whip around on the end of that snow line like a kite in a hurricane.

It'd only been five minutes, but he couldn't take this. Gram had taught him better than to sit on his butt while a woman did the hard chores. Forget endangering herself in a storm of this caliber.

Checking on the babies, he found the sleepless night had caught up with them. Curled together they slept peacefully.

"Now that's what I call team players." He tossed a blanket over them. "You hang tight. I'm going to help Rachel."

Cold attacked Rachel from all sides, freezing exposed skin, slowing her down, making each breath cut like ice. Snow and hail pelted the windshield, making it hard to see.

The engine refused to turn over the first few tries. She worried it may be too late to move. Crossing her fingers, she gave it one more try and breathed easier when the engine fired up.

Thank God. She didn't want Sullivan stuck here any longer than necessary. Unfortunately necessary looked like several days at the moment. Just damn.

And to top it off, when the weather cleared Sullivan expected her to hand the twins over to him, never to be seen again. She couldn't even think about that without choking up.

So she wouldn't think about it.

As if.

While she waited for the engine to warm, Rachel rested her head against the steering wheel and worried about what she was going to do if Sullivan fought for custody of the twins.

She lived in a one-bedroom house in Scobey, Montana, population barely topping a thousand. And she worked as a veterinarian technician at a pet clinic because she liked dealing with animals better than dealing with people.

Wind buffeted the car as she worried about what she had to offer the twins besides cramped quarters and nonexistent social skills.

A home. A warm touch in the middle of the night. Someone in the world to belong to. The answers came from deep in her soul where she kept her secret hopes and dreams hidden from the light of day.

Belonging. It was no small thing. Rachel vowed she'd fight to give Cody and Jolie a sense of belonging. Because damn, she never thought she could love this deeply or this quickly.

And no one, not Sullivan, not anyone, was going to take them from her.

Lifting her head, she reached for the gearshift.

Next to her the door suddenly opened. She jumped and screamed.

CHAPTER THREE

SULLIVAN stood framed in the opening of the SUV door.

"Jerk," Rachel shouted. "You scared me. What are you doing out here?"

"I came…help."

The storm stole part of his reply, but she got the gist. She yelled out her own concern. "Babies?"

He leaned down so he spoke directly into her ear. "Playpen. Sleeping. Scoot over so we can get this done and get back inside."

She shook her head. No way was she climbing over the gearshift in the bulky jacket and boots. "Go around."

Surprisingly he did so without argument.

Rachel drove the thirty feet to the old-barn-turned-garage at a crawl. She left the SUV idling while Sullivan braved the storm to open the big barn doors. Inside, she found an old blanket and they covered the vehicle.

"I could have handled this on my own." She advised him resentfully as she tugged on her end of the blanket.

"Pull in your claws, wildcat. This has nothing to do with your abilities." He didn't look up from anchoring his end. "I was raised better than to let you do it on your own."

Damn him for making her sound hysterical. "The babies aren't safe alone inside."

"All the more reason to work together so we can get back to them quickly." He came around from the front of the SUV. He wore her yellow raincoat, which dwarfed her but fit him just right.

He looked strong, calm, confident and a little amused as he grabbed his duffel bag from the back seat.

She moved away from him to where she stored the generator fuel. Her heart sank when she saw she only had enough fuel for a couple of days.

Sullivan crowded close to reach the fuel. "Is this it?"

Rachel bristled. "I don't usually let it get so low. I've been a little distracted since the twins came to live with me."

Her whole world had shifted with the arrival of Cody and Jolie. Luckily the pet clinic had given her maternity leave because she'd been so busy getting them settled, becoming accustomed to their presence and schedule, everything else, including her writing had suffered.

She hadn't taken proper care with her normal chores, which in this case could prove costly.

"Cut yourself some slack. You've had a big adjustment to make." He shook a can. "How long will this last?"

His simple understanding floored her. And deflated her snit.

"A couple of days, more if we're careful. We'll probably loose electricity, but we have plenty of wood and propane. And a well-stocked freezer."

If she had any luck at all, the blizzard would be over before they ran out of fuel.

Of course it would take another day or two for the roads to be cleared after the snow stopped. Extra time with a man hot enough to give Brad Pitt a run for his money and who had an unsettling habit of reacting in the way she least expected. And two babies still fretful after suffering the biggest tragedy of their young lives.

Oh joy.

"So we'll be careful," he said with a confidence that indicated he was used to handling difficult situations. "Do we need anything else from here?"

"Yeah." She opened a cupboard and took down a large flashlight. "This is it."

He took the flashlight from her and led the way outside. She stood shivering while he closed the barn doors.

Turning toward the house, she encountered a moving wall of white.

Teeth chattering, hands shaking, she pulled on the snow line until it grew taut, a chore made more difficult because she could no longer feel her fingers.

Sullivan's hand joined hers on the rope. He surrounded her with his strength and warmth, urging her forward. She started for the house.

The last of the light had gone so Sullivan used the flashlight; even so, she saw little beyond her own hands on the rope.

It was hard going, the exertion exhausting, the cold debilitating. Every step became a battle of will against nature. The protection of his bulk sheltered her from the worst of the storm and helped move them along. By the time she spotted the corner of the porch she was truly grateful for Sullivan's help.

The lights were out. She worried about the babies alone inside. Hopefully enough light would come from the fire that they wouldn't get too frightened.

She stopped and indicated the shed on the side of the house. "We need to fill the wood reservoir," she shouted. "We may not be able to get outside for days."

He spoke next to her ear. "I'll do it. You need to get out of this weather."

"I…help."

"Save the heroics. Your teeth are about to crack from the chattering."

He helped her the rest of the way to the porch and handed her the gasoline and flashlight. She leaned close to instruct him on the location of the reservoir door on the outside of the house.

He nodded his comprehension. "Get inside. Take care of the babies." He turned away.

She caught his arm, stopping him. "The rope." She found the hook at her waist and tried to release it.

"Don't need it. I'll be close to the house."

He started to leave again. But fear clutched her gut and she grabbed his coat. "No. Take the rope."

Rather than argue further, he threaded the rope through the layers of his clothes and clicked the hook to his belt.

Once he was rigged up, he stepped over to her rather than away. He tucked her scarf up around her ears. "Get inside where it's warm. I'll be back."

Half frozen, exhausted, and more worried about him than she cared to admit, Rachel let herself inside the house dragging the fuel and lanterns in with her.

She couldn't stop shivering. Even the marrow in her bones felt frozen.

Below the icy discomfort and the natural concern of being cut off from the rest of the world, she was just plain pissed at the quirk of fate that made her anxious for the safety of the man responsible for tearing her life apart.

But then why should life suddenly start playing fair?

After stripping off her soggy outdoor gear, Rachel breathed on her hands to warm them as she stumbled to the laundry room just off the kitchen. She kept a flashlight and candle on a shelf inside the door. She quickly got the generator going and then went to check on the babies.

Her heart melted when she found them cuddled together sleeping. She swayed in relief. Clutching the cushioned rail, she held on tight. She stood lost in awe at the sheer innocence and resourcefulness of them.

After a while she heard the door, felt an icy draft of air.

"How are they doing?" Sullivan appeared next to her.

Emotions more mixed than ever, she moved her gaze

to him, noted his damp hair and skin still flushed from the cold. She'd never admit it to him, but she'd been really glad to see him out there.

"Fine. They're still sleeping."

"They look so peaceful."

"Yeah," she turned away to hide the tears in her eyes. "Too bad it won't last."

"What's that supposed to mean?"

Temper spun her back around. "I mean if you have your way, the little bit of normalcy they've found since losing their parents will be torn away from them by the very people they should be able to trust."

He scowled. "It's not like that."

"It's exactly like that, but you can forget it. I'm not giving them up."

"Hey, hey." He framed her face, caught an escaped tear on his thumb. "I know this is hard. But my friend and your sister entrusted their children to our care because they knew we'd do right by them. Even when it's hard."

The fight went out of her.

"It's not fair." She pulled away from his touch, from the pity in his eyes.

He easily stalled her attempt to distance herself and folded her into his arms instead.

"No." He agreed. "It's not. But you're not alone. We'll help each other through this."

She wanted to riot against him, to push him away and deny his reasonableness. But it felt too good to lean on someone for a change. Someone with a hard chest and muscular arms, who smelled like a dream and warmed her with the heat of his body. Giving in, she laid her head on his shoulder and closed her eyes so he couldn't see her anguish.

"I don't want to like you."

His chest rumbled under her ear when he laughed, and he stroked her hair like she stroked Cody when she held him. The tender caress both soothed and unnerved.

"Well hold onto that thought, tomorrow is another day. Listen, you're cold, tired and hungry. We'll postpone talk of custody for now. Why don't you go take a shower while I fix some dinner."

The truce, like the shower, sounded like heaven. "We should probably conserve the hot water."

"Not tonight. We need to thaw out. You go first while I check out the kitchen."

"The twins?"

His chest lifted and fell on a heavy sigh. "Let them sleep. They didn't get much rest last night."

"They haven't slept well over the last week." Which, except for last night, equated to the same for her. Maybe that's why she felt like she could sleep just like this, standing up with her head on his shoulder listening to the steady beat of his heart. "They've been through so much."

He gave her a squeeze. "It'll get better with time."

He gave out heat like a furnace, thawing not only the chill from her bones but also the frigid wall around her heart. How long had it been since she'd been comforted by a man like this?

Never. Certainly not by the man she'd called father.

The thought was enough to have her pulling away and backing up. She had no business leaning on any man, least of all this man. So he had a point with his argument that the babies' parents had trusted them to do right by their children. That didn't mean she could trust *him*.

His opinion and hers hadn't gelled yet when it came to the twins.

She debated whether to leave him alone with them but there was little enough he could do. The storm prevented him leaving and he'd proven his gentleness when dealing with them.

"I'll go take that shower." She turned toward the one bedroom. When she reached the door, she glanced back. "Thank you."

He'd been watching her, more accurately he'd been watching her butt. He raised his gaze to meet her eyes; no apology there for being caught enjoying the view, just simple male appreciation. He lifted his chin in a gesture of acknowledgment.

A small thrill warmed her, raising every feminine instinct she kept ruthlessly suppressed.

She closed the door between them, deliberately placing a barrier between her and the dangerous man who awakened feelings she preferred to keep buried.

Time to get a grip. How could she spend even a moment in her enemy's arms? No exaggeration. Anyone wanting to take the twins from her rated as an enemy.

Really she didn't understand why he wanted the twins. As a SEAL and bachelor—his commanding officer had also shared that bit of information—taking on the twins could only be a hardship, even with family to help.

Or maybe he meant for his family to absorb the burden.

Family. Definitely her weak point.

In the bathroom she stripped down and stepped into the shower letting the cascade of hot water soak the cold away.

Her thoughts turned to Crystal. When Rachel had left home, her biggest regret in walking away was in leaving ten year old Crystal behind. But Rachel couldn't stay where she wasn't wanted.

On her seventeenth birthday, she'd learned that the man she'd always known as her dad wasn't her biological father. The news had devastated her, yet explained so much. Like why she'd always felt like an outsider in her own home.

Beginning to thaw out now, she reached for her favorite peach scented soap.

Dan had gotten a raw deal. Rachel had understood that. He'd been lied to, tricked into raising another man's child. Yet he'd fed and clothed her, never beat her. Plenty of other kids had had it worse.

Rachel blamed her mother. She was the one who had lied, who had traded one man's child for another man's pride. Who had traded her child's comfort for her own. Stella Adams could have given Rachel the things

Dan denied her: time, attention, affection. But Stella chose not to rock the boat.

For that Rachel had never forgiven her.

After rinsing, she turned off the water and stepped out of the tub. Wrapped in a large towel, she moved into the bedroom.

Rachel had learned her lesson too well in childhood to easily change now. Rather than chance heartache, she preferred her own company. Sure, she'd had relationships, but they never really went anywhere. Her fault. She wasn't willing to put her heart on the line and risk being rejected by someone she loved.

Not again.

Unfortunately her relationship with her sister had been a casualty of that lesson. But contrary to Sullivan's allegations, they'd forged a new kinship after their parents' death.

Rachel refused to believe Crystal had been faking the rapport they'd shared.

Dressed in thick socks and old sweats, she entered the living room, stopping to check on the still sleeping babies before moving on to the kitchen. She'd expected Sullivan to open a couple of cans of soup, but she'd underestimated him. The scent of garlic and tomatoes made her stomach grumble.

"Smells good."

He looked up from where he was buttering bread. "It is," he said with confidence. "Spaghetti. I thought we needed something hardy."

He'd changed out of his wet clothes while she'd been

in the tub. The jeans and gray T-shirt displayed his mas-
culinity to advantage. The casual clothes should have
minimized his appearance, instead they emphasized his
broad shoulders, muscular thighs, firm butt.

A dark lock of hair fell forward on his forehead. She
fought an uncharacteristic desire to sweep it back, to
feel the tactile softness against her fingers.

Remembering too well how it had felt to be in his
arms, she moved to the refrigerator and pulled out a
head of lettuce. She needed something to keep her
hands, and her thoughts, busy.

"Why don't you grab your shower while the bread
toasts?" She urged him. While she'd been dressing, she'd
come to a decision. The less time she spent in his
company the better. Not an easy chore considering they
were stuck together in a one-bedroom house, but she was
committed to the act of self-preservation. "I'll make a
salad."

He washed and dried his hands. "Sounds like a plan."

Opening the preheated oven, he bent to insert the
garlic bread.

Rachel's hormones, usually under strict control, chose
now to go astray. She wanted nothing more than to walk
over, plunge her hands in his back pockets and squeeze.

Luckily he straightened before she gave in to the
impulse.

She cleared her throat. "I put a towel out for you."

"Thanks." He grabbed his duffel bag and disappeared
into the bathroom.

She breathed a sigh of relief. He took up so much

space in a room. His very presence energized the air. Her recent trip down memory lane served to remind her exactly why she needed to keep him at arm's length. She had everything to lose and nothing to gain.

He came from a different world, here only as long as it would take to shatter her life.

A whimper drew her to the playpen in the living room. Jolie stirred. Rachel tucked a blanket around the little girl and then gently patted her back until she settled down to sleep. Cody didn't stir.

Would they be better off with Sullivan? He'd mentioned a large family, supportive and close-knit. Everything she'd dreamed of as a child.

Yet it seemed a betrayal to the children she'd come to love to even think the question.

Hearing the water go off in the shower spurred her to action. She caught the bread while it was still golden-brown. The salad went together quickly with a course chopping of lettuce and chives and quartered tomatoes.

By the time Sullivan came out of the bathroom, once again dressed in jeans and T-shirt, she had the table set. "Dinner is ready."

"Great." Ford slicked his fingers through damp hair before moving to hold Rachel's chair out for her.

She frowned at the gesture, suspicion alive in those amazing aquamarine eyes. "Who are you trying to impress?" She demanded. "We're not on a date."

Now why did he find her prickliness so appealing? "Blame my upbringing. Gram believes in old-fashioned courtesies."

"Thank you." The words were grudging as she slid into her chair. "You were raised by your grandmother?"

He nodded as he claimed his own seat. "Since I was eight."

"Hmm."

"She raised my five brothers and me after my parents died in an automobile accident."

Her eyes flashed to his then away. "I'm sorry."

Okay, less grudging but still a conversational dead end. He got the feeling she was good at dodging discussion.

Watching the tines of her fork slide through plum-pink lips, Ford fought off the sensual memory of how sweet she'd felt in his arms. Another time and place and he'd be making major moves on her. But he was already guaranteed to bring heartbreak before he left. No sense complicating the situation by acting on the attraction he felt for her.

Which didn't mean he'd allow her to ignore him.

He sent her a chiding glance. "Let me know if I'm boring you."

The cutest thing happened. Her earlobes turned red! And though agitation came and went in her sea-foam eyes, she made an effort to participate in the conversation.

"That must have been a difficult childhood."

"It was tough losing my parents, but Gram loved us and we were able to stay together. That counted for a lot." He leaned forward on his elbows. "You're not very talkative, are you?"

She swallowed a bite of spaghetti. "No."

"Why not?" He speared a tomato.

Silence greeted his question. She obviously didn't want to respond but he waited her out.

With a sigh she finally answered. "Generally because I prefer my own company."

"And in this case?"

"I don't know much about this topic." As if that revealed too much, she added, "And I see no need for us to become all buddy-buddy."

He ignored the dismissal. "What did you mean when you said you'd failed your sister?"

Her eyes flashed. "I'm not talking to you about my sister. You're wrong about her."

What a fake she was. For all her cold facade, she was all heat and passion underneath. And so incredibly vulnerable. Whatever happened in her family, it had left her hurting.

"Crystal said you ran away from home. Why? Family is important."

"Yeah. And I'm all the family the twins have."

Stubborn woman. Yet her relentlessness demonstrated her protective feelings toward the babies. Much as he wanted to exploit her weaknesses, Ford couldn't fault her for that.

"Tell me why you left home," he said.

She cocked her head causing a white-blond lock of hair to fall into her eyes. A quick flick of her hand sent it back into place.

"I know what you're doing, you know."

He hesitated for a heartbeat. "And what is that?"

"Information is power." Rachel drew circles on the table with the condensation from her ice water; a small frown drew her light brown brows together in concentration. "You want me to tell you about my past so you can use it against me to get what you want."

She was right. "I shared my history with you."

"For a purpose." She slanted him a wry glance. "No doubt I'm supposed to believe the twins would benefit from all the male influence tempered by the sweet little grandmother."

"Maybe I'm just making conversation."

She cocked an eyebrow. "Please. All is fair in love and war. And you're a warrior to the bone."

"Very clever." He raised his glass of water in acknowledgment.

"Now why do I feel that surprises you?"

Unabashed, he grinned. "Everything about you surprises me."

"Gee thanks." She clinked her glass against his then sipped. "Considering you think of me as a lazy deadbeat who can't maintain a relationship, I'll take that as a compliment."

He laughed, enjoying the note of humor mixed with the censure.

"I admit I had a few misconceptions. Your courage, patience and dedication were totally unexpected. In my job we put emotion aside to complete the task."

Now *he'd* revealed too much, which hadn't been part of his plan at all. Her quick wit and intelligent eyes made talking to her too easy. And too dangerous. Avoiding her speculative gaze, he stood and carried his dishes to the sink.

She looked as if she wanted to pursue the topic, but thankfully her habitual reticence kicked in.

"I'm beat." Feeling he'd dodged a bullet, he pushed away from the counter. "What do you say we get these dishes done and go to bed?"

CHAPTER FOUR

Go to bed. Go to bed. Go to bed. The words echoed and bounced around the room, bringing to mind images of bare skin, tangled limbs, clinging mouths.

Unnerving to say the least. More so because Rachel was less disturbed imagining him naked than she had any right to be.

Her nipples tightened and her loins clenched around an emptiness she longed to assuage.

Embarrassed by her reaction, because of course he didn't mean they should sleep *together,* she avoided his gaze by clearing the table. Even so, she felt the heat rise in her cheeks, staining them red. Her ire rose, too, because only part of the heightened color came from mortification.

The rest was desire, pure and sinful.

Just because she preferred her own company these days didn't mean she didn't know what to do with a man when she got him in her clutches.

As she neared the counter, she noticed the clock on the oven: 7:03.

"It's only seven o'clock." She pointed out. So much had happened in the last few hours it seemed much later. "A little early for bed."

He checked his watch, then grinned wryly. "Is that all? Must be feeling the effects of yesterday's early start. And did I mention the twins didn't get much sleep last night?"

"You did." She started the water running in the sink, splashed in some soap. She supposed she owed him for her best sleep in days. "Why don't you—"

"Oh." She jumped when she turned and came face-to-face with Sullivan. Instinctively stepping back, she slipped in some water on the floor and she felt herself going down.

"Careful." Lightning fast Sullivan caught her against his hard length. "I've got you."

Startled to find herself in his arms again, she looked up and found only inches separated her from blue eyes filled with stark longing.

She blinked and met a gaze devoid of all emotion.

That fast. Which begged the question if he'd felt anything at all. Or if she'd projected her own longing onto him.

"Sorry," she said, quickly pushing away. He let her go, a little too easily for her ego. Chiding herself for the foolish pang, she hiked up her sleeves and plunged her hands into the sudsy water.

"Did you drive all the way here, or fly?" She latched onto his comment about his trip, determined to maintain a conversation to dispel the awkwardness.

"I drove." Dishcloth in hand, he started drying.

She watched him out of the corner of her eye as they made quick work of the dishes. In her experience men avoided household chores. Likely she had Sullivan's grandmother to thank for his thoughtfulness.

Rachel appreciated his help, if not his proximity.

"Easier that way to pack them into your Jeep and take them home with you." She had no illusions about his strategy.

He lifted one shoulder, let it fall. "That's the plan."

Present tense. So he hadn't changed his mind about the twins even though his impressions of her had improved. Disheartened, she fell silent.

A whimper from the direction of the living room disrupted the moment. The babies were stirring.

"I'll go." Sullivan moved past her into the living room, headed toward the playpen.

Reminded why she kept her own company, she picked up the dishcloth, folded it over the drawer handle and slowly followed.

"Hey, Cody." He lifted the boy into his arms. "How're you doing? Are you hungry? It's time for dinner."

Cody stopped crying and laid his head on Sullivan's shoulder.

Jolie held her arms up for Rachel to lift her, too. Rachel swooped the girl into a big hug. And discovered a desperate need for a diaper change.

The next hour and a half was spent taking care of that problem, feeding the babies and getting them ready for bed.

"There's only the one bedroom. Which is where the crib is." Rachel gave Sullivan the layout. She indicated the slate-blue, ultra-suede sofa. "You can take the couch. I'll get you some blankets."

"This will be fine." He eyed the overstuffed cushions dubiously. With good reason, considering the length fell short of his six-two frame by six inches.

Leaving him to the logistics, she gathered the extra bedding from the hall closet.

Back in the living room, the babies played in the playpen, and Sullivan had the wood closet open as he restocked the oversized basket near the fireplace. A nice blaze burned in the old grate.

The lights in the kitchen had been extinguished, and he'd lit the candles on the credenza behind the couch giving the room a cozy feel.

The whole scene smacked of domestic tranquility. Way too home and hearth for her. It struck her as wrong. Because it felt too right. Sullivan was a stranger, an interloper. They shouldn't be so comfortable with each other, so easy together.

Time for a tactical retreat.

"Here you go." She dropped the bedding on the end of the couch. He was a big boy; he could make his own bed. "I'm beat. And it's past the babies' bedtime. We're for bed."

He closed the door to the wood closet and dusted off his hands. "Thanks. Do you think the storm will be gone by morning?"

"Hard to tell." Did his question mean he felt as antsy

as she did? "We weren't expecting snow, but it was supposed to rain for several days."

"How long before the roads get cleared after a storm like this?"

"Why? You suddenly need to be somewhere?"

"Other than getting the twins home and settled? No." He ran a weary hand through his dark hair. "I was thinking of the fuel levels."

"Right. We need to shut down the generator. That's what we're short on. The heat is on propane, so we're okay there."

"And we have plenty of wood."

Amused, she propped her hands on her hips. "Listen to Mr. California"

He crossed to the couch and started putting his bed together. "We do get snow in California you know." With a flex of biceps the size of ham hocks, he tossed the pillows into the corner. "Paradise Pines is in the mountains east of San Diego. We usually get snow once or twice a year."

Carefully keeping her distance from Sullivan, because she was inordinately tempted to test the strength of those biceps, it took Rachel a minute to process what he'd said.

She blamed her distraction on him. Unused to having strangers in her home, especially tall, muscular he-men intent on taking her cherished wards from her, her normal instincts were off.

She laughed. "And it lasts for what, a day and a half? Please. We lose the refrigerator with the generator. I'll bag up some snow to put inside to keep things cold."

"Okay." He nodded toward the kitchen. "You take care of the snow, I'll get the generator."

Surprised and pleased by his easy acceptance of her opinion, she grabbed a flashlight and headed for the drawer with the extra large plastic bags.

Oh, yeah, he was a mystery. As was the way he made her feel.

Not willing to explore the thought, she made quick work of filling several bags with snow from the back stoop and placing them strategically throughout the refrigerator.

Back in the living room she watched him move his duffel bag from the end of the couch to the head of the couch, then toe off his shoes and place them next to the duffel. He nodded toward the playpen. "Those two are out for the count."

Rachel checked on the twins. Cody and Jolie were once again sleeping curled up together. They looked so peaceful.

"Darn. I hate to disturb them. I know from experience if I wake them just to put them to bed, they'll fight sleep like heavy-weight contenders fight for the belt."

"So let them sleep. I'll be right here if they wake up."

"I'm not sure that's a good idea." No, giving control to this man was definitely not a good idea. What if he took the twins in the middle of the night?

What, her more rational side scoffed, and hike six miles to town in a blizzard?

Not so strange, the mother in her argued, he was a SEAL after all.

Sensing her turmoil, he met her gaze straight-on and

held up his right hand as if making a vow. "I promise, they're safe with me. Come on, Rachel, we all need a good night's sleep."

"All right, but I'll leave my door open to listen for them."

"I'm not going to make off with them, Rachel."

"Excuse me if I'm wary. I just met you." God, was it only yesterday? "What you say and what you do could be two different things."

"No, I'm a man of honor. My C.O. told you so, remember?" His expression said he didn't like being doubted. As a SEAL, she'd think he'd be used to questioning actions and motives and having them questioned in turn.

Was it her? Did he care what she thought of him?

A tingle ran down her spine.

"Oh, yeah. Man of honor. I forgot." She turned her back on the titillating sensation and on him.

At her bedroom door she halted to face him but forgot what she meant to say as the words suffocated for lack of breath.

Sullivan stood folding his T-shirt, firelight danced on his naked skin, his sleek muscles. Boy was he ripped. Dark hair lightly covered his chest narrowing over his six-pack to low riding jeans.

When his hands moved to his zipper, she gasped, inhaling much needed air.

"Good night." Executing an abrupt about-face, she dodged into her room, one thought clear in her mind. She was in serious danger of falling in lust.

* * *

Rachel woke to a gloomy room and the smell of coffee. Under the circumstances, she'd feared she wouldn't be able to sleep, but the last thing she remembered was planning to work on her book à la Abe Lincoln style.

A couple of months ago a publisher, enamored with her syndicated animal antics column, approached her asking for a book on animal manners. She'd been intrigued enough to send out a proposal.

That was before she got the call regarding the children.

Catching sight of the time, eight-thirty, she bounded out of bed. She never slept this late. The babies never slept this late.

Spiking fingers through her tousled hair, she padded in her sweats and socks into the living room. And found the babies where she'd left them last night, sleeping in the playpen. A change of clothes proved they'd been up and about at some point.

Ford was doing double duty. Trying to soften her up by letting her sleep in again. Darn him for being considerate. It wouldn't change her mind.

A rush of love swelled her heart. She bent and ran her hand over Jolie's silky brown hair. More than anything she wanted to do right by Jolie and Cody. She prayed that wouldn't mean giving them up.

Before straightening she traced a finger over Cody's rosy cheek. Whatever happened, the twins were innocents.

A bang in the kitchen spun her in that direction.

Ford stood, arms braced on the granite counter, head

hanging between those amazing biceps. Silhouetted by the window, the violence of the storm outside embodied his internal struggle.

Obviously a private moment.

Rachel back pedaled to give him his privacy. Until he reared back and slammed his fist into the granite, bloodying his knuckles.

Shocked, she stood rooted to the spot. The fierce action exposed a well of anger and grief. *Unresolved* anger and grief. She debated whether to go forward or leave him be.

He drew his arm back for another strike.

"Stop." Rachel lunged forward and grabbed onto his arm with both hands.

Not the smartest move she'd ever made.

Before she'd felt more than the flex of muscle, he'd hooked a foot around her ankle and taken her down to the floor. Blue eyes savage, his body blanketed hers, his forearm pressed hard against her windpipe.

Oh, yeah, he definitely had a dangerous edge.

By rights she should be terrified right about now. But fear wasn't the emotion sending shivers through her body.

He blinked then instantly relaxed his arm.

"Oh God." Unbelievably he lowered his forehead to rest on hers. "I'm sorry."

"Apology accepted." She lay completely still. "You can get off me now."

He didn't move. "I usually have more control."

She bet. "That's good to know."

"It's not smart to grab me."

"I'll remember that." Tentatively she moved her upper body, reminding him he still held her pinned. The movement rubbed her breasts against his chest. Her nipples responded to the contact.

So did his body.

She froze. And looked up into features drawn taut with desire. His gaze locked on her lips, and he began to lower his head.

A baby's cry broke the tension.

Reminded they weren't alone—how could she have forgotten his whole reason for being here? Rachel pushed Ford's shoulders until he rolled off her.

"Don't do that again." On her feet, she straightened her clothes and dusted her butt. And carefully avoided his eyes.

Sure, she felt the attraction between them, saw the want in his eyes. In another time or place, she might be willing to blow off some steam in a no-strings fling. But she had too much to lose with this man in this situation.

No matter how tempted she might be.

He forced her to look at him when he invaded her space. Towering over her, his gaze lingered on her mouth before rising to meet her eyes. "You have my word I won't attack you again."

She scowled at him. "That's not what I was referring to."

He crowded close to gently tuck a wild curl behind her ear. "It's the best you're going to get."

Ruthlessly squashing the thrill the warning gave her,

she pushed past him to check on the babies. Not surprisingly they were awake and wanting to play. To keep them occupied while she dressed, she dumped a handful of toys into the playpen.

She escaped to her room to brush her teeth and change into jeans and a sweater. Mixed feelings kept her company. Such a luxury to go through her morning routine without feeling rushed or worried the twins would wake before she finished. Yet she felt bad for enjoying the indulgence because she loved Jolie and Cody, and they were totally dependent on her.

She both resented and appreciated Ford for giving her these moments of freedom. For allowing her a full night's sleep.

Back in the living room she spread a blanket on the carpet in front of the fireplace and let the babies loose to crawl around. And when they started to wind down, she picked out several of their favorite books then tucked a baby on either side of her on the couch and spent the better part of the next hour reading to them.

Ford spent the time roaming the room. She tried not to think of his big, long-fingered hands touching her things. The sound of the drawer opening and closing in the credenza told her he'd found the broken bit. One side had pulled free of the front of the drawer. It looked like it should notch together but a set of staples prevented the pieces from connecting. She hadn't scraped together two minutes to fix it.

As she read on, he went to the utility closet next to where the generator ran, and retrieved her toolbox. She heard the clunk of it hitting the ground near the credenza behind her.

She finished the story then let the wiggling babies free. They immediately popped up to look over the back of the couch to see what Ford was doing. Rachel moved so she could keep track of the babies, ensuring neither fell backward or climbed over the top.

The new position gave her a premium view of one prime butt as Ford bent to look at the credenza from the bottom up.

Ford? Since when did she start thinking of the enemy by his first name? Maybe since he'd proved he wasn't the enemy by helping her in the snow, cooking her dinner and letting her sleep in.

All signs of a good guy.

Or a clever way to throw her off. Combined with his penchant for touching her at every opportunity and the smoldering glances he constantly sent her way, the strategy was working.

She reminded herself of her plan to keep her distance from him.

"You don't have to do that," she told him.

Sitting back on his haunches, he shrugged, his attention fixed on the screwdriver he wielded. "It's no problem."

"You don't need to be doing things for me." She kept her tone cool. No need for him to know he was getting to her. "I can take care of my own children. Do my own chores."

"I like to keep busy." He eyed her over his shoulder. "It's not a crime to accept a little help sometimes."

"When you live alone, self-sufficiency is important."

"So is making friends of your neighbors."

"Baa da ha." Cody dug his toes into the cushion and pulled himself up.

"Oh?" She ringed Cody's ankle, pulled him gently down. "I've never found that to be the case."

"Ha da ca." Jolie bounced up and down.

Ford's gaze challenged Rachel. "Have you ever tried?"

She stiffened. No doubt his neighbors were nubile young things who brought him casseroles and apple pies.

"Why don't you tell me what the great benefits would be?"

"Well." He fitted the front of the drawer to the sides and tapped them together. "Having neighbors is like being on a team. They look out for each other, help out with big chores, take care of the mail or pets when you have to go somewhere."

"This is Montana," she shot back, this time harnessing Jolie who imitated Cody's stunt in climbing up the back cushion. "Security isn't a huge issue. I can hire someone to help with the big chores. I don't have a pet. And I don't go anywhere for anyone to need to pick up my mail. I don't need a team. They're overrated if you ask me."

"Overrated?" The question held disbelief and a touch of insult. "You're talking to a Navy SEAL. Teamwork means the difference between life and death to me."

She suppressed the urge to squirm. "That's different. That's the military. You have to work together."

"We're an elite team of highly trained officers that go into the hottest spots in the world to save strangers, help governments, retrieve sensitive information."

"You're twisting my words." Giving up fighting the two babies, she set them on the floor and gave them toy trucks to play with, and began pacing in front of the fire. "I respect what you do, but I'm not you. Becoming dependent on others is an invitation to heartache."

Flinching as she heard the revealing comment, she turned her back on the room to hide how much of herself she'd just given away.

She heard the drawer slide neatly into place, the clink of tools being replaced.

"Is that what you want for your niece and nephew? A life of isolation and loneliness?"

She whipped around, chest heaving with fierce emotion. "Don't make this about them. They'll have me. They won't ever be alone."

"Rachel." He came around the end of the couch.

"No." Palm raised she stopped him. "You want to help? Fine. Watch the babies. I'm making lunch."

She escaped to the kitchen, which wasn't much of an escape, but as long as she kept her back to the living room she didn't have to see Ford. Or continue the disastrous conversation.

Damn him for making her defend her lifestyle.

Gathering the makings for sandwiches from the refrigerator, she carried the lettuce to the sink to wash.

Who was he to put her on the defensive? So she kept to herself, what was the big deal? She didn't hurt anyone, and this way they didn't hurt her.

Of course Jolie and Cody would have friends. She knew too well how it felt to be an outsider when you craved to belong.

She plunged her hands under the running water and shivered at the icy temperature. She frowned as she realized there was a definite chill in here away from the warmth of the fire.

Propane fueled the heater and the water heater and ran independent of the electricity. The air in here should be comfortable. Getting a bad feeling, she went to check the thermostat, pushing the slider way up to see if it activated the heater.

Nothing happened.

Dread settled low in her stomach. If they lost the propane—and the heat it provided—her plan to keep her distance from Ford would go with it.

CHAPTER FIVE

"DAMN." Irritation and trepidation sounded in the one word.

Noticing Rachel's agitation as she monitored the thermostat, Ford asked, "What's the problem."

Hands on hips, she waited, as if wishful thinking would kick-start the heater. Finally she conceded. "It looks like something has happened to the propane."

Now he understood her worry. Without the heater they'd be restricted to the fireplace for warmth. A huge gust of wind shook the windows, a timely reminder that the storm still raged outside.

"What makes you think so?" he asked though he didn't truly doubt her take on the situation.

"It's cold in the kitchen, and I haven't heard the heater come on in a while."

"Propane turns to vapor when it freezes." Ford joined her by the thermostat. "It could be nothing more than that. Do you have an above ground or below ground tank?"

"Aboveground, but I've never heard of propane

freezing and I've lived in these frozen wilds for thirteen years."

He lifted a shoulder, let it drop. "It has to be really cold."

She looked from him to the ice-encased window and back again. "Sullivan, I've known really cold, and never lost the propane."

"Then maybe something fell and broke the connection. I'd better check it out." Ford headed for the closet holding the outdoor gear. He took out the yellow slicker. "Where is the tank?"

"What makes you such an expert on propane?" She demanded from behind him.

Ford dug through the closet, finding gloves he thought might fit, and a warm fleece muffler, thankfully in a simple navy. It was cold enough that he'd have worn a froufrou color, but he wouldn't have liked it.

"If something can be used as an explosive, has ever been used as an explosive, or can be mixed with something to form an explosive, it's my job to know about it."

He surfaced from the closet to find her blocking his path. She scowled, something going on behind those sea-green eyes. But whatever brewed in her thoughts she kept to herself as she answered his question.

"The tank is behind the house. You can see it from my bedroom window." Again she eyed the storm out the front window.

He knew exactly what she saw—nothing but swirling white. There'd been no abatement at all in the weather. If anything, the storm had worsened overnight.

"Let's go see what we can see." Losing the propane wouldn't worry him if it was just him and Rachel, but the babies upped the ante.

In the bedroom he pushed aside her smoky-blue curtains and pulled the cord to lift the mini blinds.

Rachel joined him, using a tissue to clear the condensation from the glass. She pointed to the left. "Over there."

They both looked out on a cloud-darkened world of white on white, with the wicked storm spewing snow and ice through the air.

"It's buried under snow," she said.

He took in the placement, the proximity to the house, the flow and depth of the snowbanks, the visible foliage, making note of the wind direction and velocity. "I see branches between the house and the tank. Do you have something planted there?"

"No. I keep it clear." She shivered. "If it's that cold, maybe you shouldn't be going outside. You don't have the proper gear. That Macintosh isn't going to protect you from the cold and none of my other coats will fit."

"I'll be fine. It shouldn't take more than a few minutes to check things out and decide if there's anything to be done."

Hugging herself, she unconsciously rubbed her upper arms in a warming motion. "It doesn't take long to get frostbite or hypothermia, either. If something happens to you out there, I'm not sure I can get you back to the house by myself. Maybe it's not worth the effort."

He tugged on a short wisp of her blond hair. "You're worried about me."

She ducked her head, pulling away from his touch. She backed clear up to the bed and abruptly sat when the back of her knees hit the mattress. In a flash she sprung to her feet and headed for the door, leading them away from the intimacy of the bedroom.

Over her shoulder she said, "I may be a loner, but I'm not a monster. Yes, I'm worried, especially if the risk isn't necessary."

He followed her to the end of the hall, propped a shoulder against the wall and watched her pace the living room carpet. For such a tough cookie, she had a marshmallow center.

"Even though I'm the enemy?"

She slanted a glare his way. He probably shouldn't take such pleasure in teasing her, but she riled so easily. Her shows of emotion just pulled him in.

"Yes," she hissed the word then stopped, crossed her arms and cocked a hip, the picture of indignation. "And I don't appreciate being made to feel concern when I'm trying not to like you."

"You might have to give up on that project. I'm a pretty likable guy."

Her eyes narrowed. "You're bossy, nosy and you're planning to take my family away. I think I can resist your questionable wit and charm."

Ouch. That stung more than it should. Time to get back on point.

"We're already low on fuel for electricity, if we lose the propane, too, it's going to get very primitive around here very fast." He notched his head toward the playpen where the twins played. "That would be tough enough if it were just you and me, but with the babies—"

As if cued, Cody's sneeze punctuated Ford's point.

Rachel held up a hand. "I get the picture. I'll go with you."

He started shaking his head before she finished speaking. "Don't even think it. I'll be out and back before you even realize I'm gone."

"Storms are unpredictable. What if something happens to you out there? It's best if we go as a team, like yesterday."

"No. When I went with you to the barn, the babies were asleep. They'll freak out if you leave them alone."

He knew he had her, but she didn't relent until he agreed to a signal system, which made a lot of sense. Every ten minutes she'd yank twice on the snow line and he'd yank back. If he didn't respond, she'd come find him. Then she insisted on giving him one of her large sweatshirts to put under the yellow slicker. He wore extra large so they had to cut out the sleeves to make it fit, but it gave him an added layer of warmth. And the feeling didn't just come from the sweatshirt.

As soon as the door closed behind Ford, time slowed so every minute lasted an eternity.

Rachel tried to convince herself her worry factor would be the same for whoever was out there. The trouble with that was, she was no good at lying to herself. She'd stopped that practice a long time ago.

What insanity gripped her that she suddenly loved

the whole world? Okay, that was an exaggeration. But not by far. Not by nearly far enough.

She'd allowed Sullivan to get entirely too close for comfort. As if by letting the twins into her heart, she'd left a breach for others to slide in, too.

Standing at the sink, her gaze trained on the path Ford would traverse back to the house, she made sandwiches and determined—absolutely—to shore up her defenses.

Just as soon as he got back safely.

He came into view and, breath hitching in relief, she went to the back porch to greet him. He burst through the back door along with a cloud of snow and sleet. She brushed at his head and shoulders as he stamped his feet.

"Good news. The connection is sound. A large tree limb fell, but the tank took the brunt of it." His large shoulders shuddered as his body combated the freezing elements.

"I have a towel and blankets here. Let's get you out of this wet gear." She reached up to help free him of the slicker, but he shook his head.

"I'm going back out. The gauge showed you're at a little over a quarter tank. That's probably why it's freezing. Less mass, and the tree dropped a load of snow and ice on and under the tank. I want to dig it out, create a windbreak to shelter it through the rest of the storm. Where's your shovel?"

"You're half frozen," she protested. "You can't go back out there."

"The exertion will warm me up." He spied her snow shovel in the corner of the porch.

While he gathered it and looked over her other equipment, she rushed to get the coffee she had heating up by the fireplace. She poured a mug and then filled a thermos, dumping in lots of sugar.

She reached the door at the same time he did. He carried a shovel in one hand, an ice hatchet in the other.

"Here—" she thrust the mug at him "—drink this before you go."

She got no argument this time. He drank the coffee in one swallow while she slipped the thermos into the deep pocket of the slicker.

"Be careful," she urged him.

"I will." He wrapped his hands around hers on the mug and squeezed. "Thanks."

The look in his eyes shot right through her, threatening her new resolution. Stepping back, she indicated the door with her head.

"Every ten minutes," she reminded him.

"Two tugs." He confirmed before sliding out of the door, tools in hand.

Rachel's gaze immediately went to the clock marking the time. She needed something to occupy her thoughts or she'd go crazy while she waited. First, check on the babies. Then, more coffee.

She threw another log on the fire before going to the playpen. Jolie slept on her side, a teddy pillowed her head and she still held a toy car clutched in her little fist.

Cody began to cry when he saw her. His nose was

running and his eyes looked glazed. He held up his arms and she bent to pick him up.

"Poor tyke. You're not feeling well, are you?" Kissing his forehead, she felt the heat coming off him. "And you're a little warm. Let's get you some medicine. That'll make you feel better."

After cleaning Cody's nose with a tissue, she covered Jolie with a blanket, checked the time and headed for the medicine cabinet.

She spent the next hour cuddling a fussy Cody, tugging on the snow line and watching for sightings of Ford through her bedroom window. Once he had the tank cleared, the sightings became fewer and fewer, but the heater kicked in after forty-five minutes. So whatever he'd done, it had worked.

Thank goodness. Without the heater, the fireplace would have been their sole source of heat, which would have held them all captive in the living room. Tight quarters for four people, two of whom were at odds with each other.

Ford returned the shovel and ice hatchet to the corner of the porch then pulled off his gloves. When he turned toward the kitchen door, Rachel was there in front of him. Without a word she began helping him out of the wet clothing.

His fingers refused to work the buttons on the slicker. He welcomed her help and took the towel she handed him to dry his neck and hair.

"I've managed to boil enough water to run a warm bath

for you." She removed the thermos, placed it on the washer then dragged the yellow plastic garment off his shoulders.

After the roar of the storm outside, the quiet inside struck him as odd and was offset by a low-grade whine. He finally realized the sound came from inside the house. A baby was crying.

"Wh-what's wrong with Cody?" he asked through chattering teeth.

"He's running a low-grade fever. His cold's come back. He'll be all right until we can get you into the tub. Sit." She pushed him into a kitchen chair.

A mug of coffee appeared in his hand, which shook so badly he wrapped the second hand around it as well. The bite of a brandy chaser sent heat rolling through his body.

"Oh my God." He savored the warmth of the brew, the invigorating burn of alcohol. "I think I love you."

She looked up from where she worked on his boot-laces. "Careful, Sullivan. Someone might think you're easy."

"An-anything you want," he stuttered. "Name it, and for another c-cup of this c-coffee it's y-yours."

"Really?" Her eyes turned wistful. "Maybe now is the time to talk about custody."

"Uh-huh." He shook a finger at her. "Truce, remember? No talk of c-custody while we're sn-snowed in."

"Right." Ducking her head so he couldn't see her eyes, she finished removing his boots and socks. Then she refilled his mug, including another shot of brandy. "We'll just put this on account."

She tugged him to his feet and headed him toward the bathroom. "Come on, you can drink that in the tub, you need to get warmed up. I've already put a change of clothes in there for you. The water's lukewarm now, but I can boil more and add it as you start to thaw out. At least until the propane kicks in and we have hot water again."

"Thanks." He stopped at the bathroom door. "I can take it from here."

"Right. Sorry." Color flowed up her neck and into her cheeks. She swung on her heel and crossed the room to a teary-eyed Cody.

A moment later Ford sank into the tub cursing as he lowered his frozen body into the water. His skin came alive with a million stinging prickles. He went from shudders to shivers to chills, which was when he reached for the kettle of hot water.

Sipping from the mug he began to experience a warm sense of well-being. Hearing the heater kick in, he sighed and relaxed back in the tub.

At least his efforts had succeeded. Heck, even if the heater hadn't come back on, the effort would have been worth it. He didn't do idle well. And considering every unoccupied moment allowed guilt-ridden thoughts of Tony's and Crystal's deaths to worm away at his conscience, Ford prayed they'd see a break in the storm soon.

Logically he understood there was no way he could

have predicted an earthquake when he purchased the tickets for his friends' vacation. But the bottom line was they'd still be alive if he hadn't bought the tickets, hadn't butted into their business.

And he'd never have met Rachel Adams.

Truthfully he hadn't made any such agreement not to talk custody while the storm held them captive, but he was reluctant to bring it up when they were stuck in such close proximity with each other.

He expected the conversation would get heated, and they may both need fallback room.

The more time he spent with Rachel, the less he wanted to hurt her, but he had to do what was best for the babies.

Ford loved his five brothers, hell, as the youngest, he'd spent his life emulating them or competing for a place among them. It hadn't been good enough to match their efforts, he'd had to do more, do better. He'd earned their respect and a spot on the SEAL team because of the drive and ambition he'd learned early in life. Tony had been a brother of the soul. They'd worked the trenches together, saved each other's hides.

He owed Tony in ways the average person could never understand.

Tony had made it clear he wanted the twins raised with Ford's family, and Ford had had to agree an extended family with aunts, uncles, cousins and a grandmother was a better support team than a lone aunt.

Not to mention San Diego offered cultural, educational and employment opportunities unavailable in Scobey, Montana.

Plus, with the income Ford got from his share in the family jewelry store in addition to his military pay, he had the money to give the babies advantages Rachel wouldn't be able to provide. At least not without touching the life insurance from the loss of their parents.

No matter how he looked at it, he still thought the best plan was for the twins to come home with him. If Rachel wanted to take them occasionally for holidays or vacations, he had no problem working something out with her.

Now he just needed to convince Rachel.

Dressed in jeans and a navy T-shirt and sweater he opened the bathroom door to a prime view of Rachel's heart-shaped butt as she bent to put something in the bottom drawer of her nightstand.

Flush from the tub, the vision of her lush derriere ignited his blood. The sight of a satin and lace fuchsia thong peeping over the top of her jeans shot him right to boiling point.

Making short work of the hallway and bedroom, he advanced on her so that when she stood and turned it was into his arms. Surprised, her gaze flew up to his. Slowly he cupped her cheek in his left hand, giving her plenty of time to pull away.

"I have to do this," he whispered, "I have to taste you." And lowering his head, he claimed her lips with his.

Oh, yes, so sweet, so hot, she fit against him perfectly ratcheting his blood pressure up another notch. He shifted his head and took the kiss deeper, longer.

Groaning softly, she melted into him and circled his

neck with her arms, anchoring herself to his length. She opened her mouth and invited him in, tongues meeting and mating in a sassy dance of give and take.

The intoxicating scents of soap, baby powder and woman wove around him, teasing his senses so he longed for more.

"Closer." Spreading his stance, he pulled her between his legs, pressing her soft breasts to his chest and reaching down with his right hand to trace the flirty line of her thong.

Her breath hitched and a shudder ran through her body, rocking her against him. Murmuring her approval, she tightened her arms around him, and hiked up on her toes aligning her body with his.

He trailed his fingers up to the small of her back and found the softest patch of fine velvet skin. A low moan told him he'd discovered one of her sweet spots. So of course he played his thumb over it again and she went up in flames.

One second she was as lost in the moment as he, the next she'd pushed him away.

"I can't do this." Her voice shook. Taking a step back she tucked her hands behind her, an obvious move to prevent her reaching for him again. "Not with you."

"Rachel." He lifted a hand, needing to touch her, needing to ease the torment in eyes more blue than green.

"No." She sidestepped. "I can't. If you have your way, you're going to take the twins. And that's going to tear me apart. I can't give you this, too."

His hand fell to his side as he watched her walk away.

* * *

The next morning the quiet woke Rachel. For a moment she snuggled under her blankets and thought ahead to her day. She'd be done at the clinic by four. Maybe she'd treat herself to dinner at the diner tonight, save time and effort so she could get right to work on her book when she got home.

The sound of a whimper disrupted her thoughts bringing reality rushing back.

The twins.

The storm.

The wolf in hunk's clothing.

Remembering Ford, and the time spent in his arms yesterday, she groaned and buried her head under her pillow. What had she been thinking?

Problem was she hadn't been thinking at all. Tasting, touching, feeling, she'd been doing all of those and more. In fact, her senses had suffered overload at his first touch, and it became all physical after that.

Intensely, mind-blowingly, wonderfully physical.

And it had been sheer insanity.

Really. The man may smell like heaven, but giving into the temptation of his passionate embrace lay the direction of hell.

She'd never forgive herself if she let her libido interfere with her bid for custody. Because make no mistake, he was a warrior, and he'd use every weapon at his disposal to get his way. She'd be a fool not to think that included any perceived affection for him.

Already she'd given too much away by letting him know he possessed the ability to hurt her.

Last night the tension between them could have been cleaved with a hatchet. Cody's fretfulness kept them both busy but only added to the already tense atmosphere. The poor baby just didn't feel good. And she felt for him, but she'd also been grateful for something to focus on besides the blunder of letting go in Ford's arms.

The silence outdoors meant the conversation they'd both avoided could no longer be put off.

About time. In retrospect she wished it had happened before she'd gotten to know him, to like him, to want him. But she'd have to deal with it.

And no time like the present. Tossing aside her pillow, she threw back the blankets and climbed out of bed. She checked on Cody. Because of his restlessness last night, Jolie had slept in the playpen out in the living room with Ford.

Despite a restless night and the whimper she'd just heard, Cody slept peacefully in his cot. She brushed the back of her fingers over his forehead feeling for a fever. Pleased to find him normal, she tucked the blanket around him and escaped to the bathroom for a shower.

Twenty minutes later she left her room to find Ford and Jolie still asleep. Jolie looked like a little angel. Bare chested with dark stubble and a scowl on his face, Ford looked like a disreputable pirate. Oh, yeah, even sleeping he had that dangerous edge that drew her.

He'd let her sleep in yesterday, so he deserved a sleep in today.

In the kitchen she put on coffee and started pancakes. Jolie woke up first and Rachel snagged her up before she woke Ford. Then she heard Cody through the baby monitor. She changed and dressed both babies then set them up in their high chairs with bowls of pancakes cut into tiny pieces and dusted with powdered sugar.

She glanced into the living room, surprised Ford hadn't stirred yet. She'd heard him cough a couple of times but nothing more. He'd proven to be an early riser. And he didn't strike her as the type to sleep through all the morning activity.

Leaving the twins happily eating their pancakes with their fingers, Rachel slipped into the living room to stand over the couch.

Still sleeping, at some point Ford had pushed the blankets further down his chest so they ringed his waist. He'd also kicked his feet free. This worried her, because even with the heater working, a chill lingered in the air. She wondered if he had a fever? Perhaps he'd caught Cody's cold.

After yesterday morning's lesson in hand-to-hand combat, she knew better than to startle him.

"I'm awake," the words came out in a deep, raspy growl.

"Good, then you won't jump me when I do this." She brushed the backs of her fingers over his forehead and along his cheek, feeling the heat of his skin and the scratch of his beard.

"No promises." He reached up and grabbed her hand, pressing her palm to his cheek. "That feels good."

"You're burning up. How do you feel?"

"I'm fine," he said in the same gravel pit voice. "I don't get sick."

"Uh-huh, Mr. Temperature of 102. I'm going to get you some aspirin, some vitamin C and a cup of tea with Echinacea."

"Don't bother. I just need a shower and I'll be good to go." He sat up and the blankets pooled in his lap.

"No arguments. Think of it as preventative maintenance if it helps. I can't afford for you to be sick when I have two babies to look after."

"I said I'm fine." The denial held a bite.

She propped her hands on her hips. "Fever and grouchy. You'll take what I give you, or we're going to go a few rounds. Then I have pancakes if you're hungry."

"We lost the fire." His glazed blue eyes were angled toward the empty fireplace.

"Yeah. I put the last of the wood on about an hour ago. The good news is that it stopped snowing overnight."

"That's what's different. No wind." He stood and wrapped the blanket around his hips, ran a hand through his disheveled hair. "Good. I'll go out later and fill the wood reservoir."

She sent him a wry glance. "One of us will."

He lifted a dark brow and advanced on her. Suddenly there was nothing debilitating or tame about him. He was hard eyed, hard bodied, hard edged.

With an effort she stood her ground.

"Don't attempt to mother me, dynamite," he breathed

against her ear as he walked by her. "That's not a relationship either of us wants."

Wow, she mouthed after he disappeared into the
bathroom. Too bad all that male intensity was attached
to a totally inappropriate man. The sooner the snow
melted and she could send him on his way the better.

The twins belonged with family. She would care and
provide for them not out of a sense of duty but out of a
sense of love.

Now she just needed to convince Ford.

CHAPTER SIX

FORD placed a piece of wood on the block and cleaved it in two with one swing of the ax. He then quartered the pieces and tossed them into his done pile.

After a morning moping around eating Rachel's cold remedies, he felt well enough—and desperate enough—to escape outside. Cutting wood fit his mood to a T.

Being snowed in gave a man too much time to think, too much time to admire the long, soft curves of his reluctant hostess. To admire her quiet strength and loyalty, her perseverance in the face of uncertainty and her infinite patience when dealing with the twins. Her tolerance of a stranger bent on tearing her world to pieces.

Instead of tasting those luscious lips, instead of dwelling on how he paid for the vacation that had claimed his friends' lives, Ford worked off his frustration and his guilt by swinging an ax.

The very idea of Rachel out here wielding an ax tore his gut to pieces. Not that she wasn't fully capable. That wasn't the point.

Not that it mattered. Because it was none of his

business. The only thing that mattered was getting the roads cleared so he and the twins could get on their way to San Diego.

Another log went on the block.

He had arrangements to make. A nanny to hire, a nursery to set up.

Lift and swing.

He always figured he'd wait to start a family until he retired from the team. Now the decision had been taken from him.

But damn. He wasn't ready to hang up his wet suit.

Crack.

Two months ago Tony had signed up for another four years. Ford had planned to do the same when his commission came up in another couple of months.

If the twins' dad could be a SEAL, Ford could be a SEAL.

New log.

All right so that theory held some flaws. Like the fact that Tony hadn't been living with his children. The twins had lived with their mother. And Tony had been in a bad place with Crystal when he'd reenlisted. She'd been adamantly opposed to his SEAL career, which in Ford's opinion had spurred Tony's recommitment for four years.

Lift and swing.

But there was no lying to himself. Ford had disapproved of Tony's decision.

Crash.

Ford believed if you had a family, you owed it to

them to be around. Any military position involved risk to some degree. Obviously some more than others. SEALs were at the extreme end of that category. Which was why he'd been waiting to settle down.

And that brought him full circle.

Guilt, resentment, uncertainty and resolution made for a confusing jumble of emotions spurring on his efforts. In the end it came down to one truth. He owed his friend not only for his solidarity on the battlefield but because Tony would be alive today if Ford hadn't butted into his business.

Ford had a reputation for always following through. With the twins' future on the line, he couldn't fail now.

He stopped, braced the ax handle against his thigh and swiped the back of his wrist over his sweaty brow. The crunch of footsteps heralded the approach of someone.

Rachel was headed his way. Dressed in jeans and a brown parka she moved with athletic grace. In the sun her eyes sparkled more blue than green and the cold weather brought a flush out on her cheeks. Her blond hair contrasted against the fur of her jacket framing her face like a halo.

"Hey, that's quite a pile you have there." She greeted him. "I won't have to chop wood for a month."

"That's the plan." He set a new log on the block. "What about the twins?"

She pulled the baby monitor out of her coat pocket. "They're sleeping."

He nodded toward the monitor she'd tucked back in her pocket. "That's pretty handy."

"Yeah, it's been invaluable. The receptionist at the clinic gave them to me. Everyone's been incredibly kind. When I picked up the twins in San Diego, they gave me one diaper bag with the minimum of essentials included. I had to outfit a nursery from scratch. People at work, my neighbors, they gave me a lot."

"And that's hard for you."

She ducked her head, peeked at him through her lashes. "A little, yeah. I can't help who I am."

"No. We are who we are. Whatever good intentions we have."

Rachel glanced at the pile of wood that would have taken her days to chop. She'd say his good intentions had cost him quite a lot. Remembering his rage of yesterday, she hazarded a guess. "That sounds like guilt talking."

"Yeah." He picked up the ax, but his gaze moved off to the distance.

She went still, touched by his distress. He obviously felt the loss of his friend deeply. Whatever their differences she understood his sorrow. "I'm sorry about your friend."

His grip on the ax handle tightened until his knuckles whitened. "And I'm sorry about your sister. It's hard to believe they're gone."

Rachel swallowed a snowball-size lump. Her relationship with her sister had been so new. In a way, that added to her heartache.

"People say things happen for a reason."

"Eternal optimists." His words had the quality of crushed glass. "People who've never seen the horrific things I have… Death is nothing new to me."

"No, but it sounds like grief is." She gently took the ax from him, set it aside. Clearly she'd hit a raw nerve. "Your job must require a huge amount of skill and bravery, but I imagine in order to see the things you have you'd have had to develop a pretty thick skin."

"Impartiality is necessary, yes. That doesn't mean we don't care." He stood, fists clenched at his sides, his profile a portrait of stubborn pride.

"I can see you do care." No doubt more deeply than he let most people see, which spoke to the level of his torment. "But that's all part of the job. This was different. This was your friends, and there was nothing you could do to save them."

His jaw clenched. "I don't like feeling helpless."

The problem with not interacting with people very often was that she lacked the words to comfort him. So she just spoke from the heart. "We have to think of the babies now, that's what they'd want us to do."

"It's because of me the twins no longer have parents." The confession seemed torn out of him. "How am I supposed to face them every day for the rest of our lives knowing what I cost them?"

"What are you talking about? Tony and Crystal died in an earthquake in Mexico."

"Yeah, and I sent them there. Hell, I paid for the tickets and practically escorted them to their deaths."

He began to pace, snow crunching under the heavy weight of his boots.

She'd never seen him so agitated. "I don't understand."

He drilled her with an anguished glare. "Me. I'm the one who sent them to Mexico. Tony and Crystal were constantly at odds. They never agreed on anything to do with the twins. I thought if they could get away from the problems of everyday life for a while, be together as a family, they might settle some things. Come to an understanding."

"And instead they died."

"Yeah."

And he blamed himself. Which was ridiculous, but he'd brooded about it for so long that simply saying so would have little impact. So that's not what she'd say.

"Wow. No wonder you feel guilty."

He blinked at her, shock in his blue eyes.

"What?" She feigned innocence. "Were you expecting sympathy? This is my sister we're talking about."

"No. Right." He sank down on the chopping block, scrubbed both hands over his face "You're right, I deserve the recrimination."

"Damn straight." She purposely struck a hard note. "This whole thing is your fault."

"Now wait a minute." His head and shoulders went back.

"You owe me." Beginning to circle him, she laid on the guilt. "You owe the twins. Because of you our only family was taken from us. The only honorable thing to do is sign over custody to me so we can keep what's left of our family together."

"The hell you say." He surged to his feet, placing himself directly in her path.

"Hell yes." She propped her hands on her hips and met him chin to chin. "You can also give me the winning numbers for the lottery this week."

His dark brows drew together and he shook his head as if trying to clear his confusion. "What are you talking about now?"

"I'm talking about winning the lottery. The twins and I could use the money. I mean you are psychic right? Otherwise how could you know about the earthquake in Mexico?"

The tension went out of him. "No, I'm not psychic."

She pouted. "No lottery numbers?"

He stepped closer, lifted her chin with the edge of his hand. "No lottery numbers."

"And you're not to blame for Tony and Crystal's deaths?"

"As I have no psychic ability, I guess not." He stared into her eyes, and she saw a lightening of his spirit. "You think you're so smart, don't you?"

"Pretty much." She grinned, then grew serious. "You aren't at fault here, Ford. Don't let it haunt you."

He turned her toward the house, and draping an arm over her shoulders started walking. "We should check on the twins before Cody wakes up and finds something to finger paint with."

"At least I got smart and started separating them for naps."

"Good idea. Yeah, that boy gets into everything, nothing is out of his reach."

"He got you, didn't he?" She giggled and slanted him a look through her lashes. "When you had the kids the other day, he got you."

"I'm not admitting to anything."

"Coward."

"Hey, that there is a fighting word to a SEAL."

She bumped her shoulder into him. "I'm not afraid of you."

"No." He laughed. "You're one tough little cookie." They reached the front of the house. "Thanks for talking trash to me."

She stopped on the first step of the porch, which she'd shoveled clear before going in search of him. Facing Ford now she saw the pain still shadowing his fathomless blue eyes. "But you still feel responsible, don't you?"

"Let's say, you've given me something to think about." His gaze swept her face and he leaned forward.

She saw the kiss coming and lowered her head. "Don't."

"You're a special woman, Rachel Adams." Gently he lifted her chin, and touched her heart by pressing a warm kiss to her cheek. "I wish things could be different."

Ford came awake in an instant. Unmoving he scoped out his environment to determine what had alerted him.

The first thing that struck him was the warm weight and sweet scent of the woman in his arms.

He opened his eyes to find he was reclined on the couch, not unusual, as that's where he'd been sleeping, but his bed hadn't been made up and he was still fully clothed. A pity considering the woman cuddled up to him, was—to his disappointment—also fully clothed.

He sure wouldn't mind seeing more of her colorful, sexy lingerie.

A log fell in the fireplace shooting sparks through the grate. He recognized the sound as the one that had awakened him. He should get up, stoke the fire, toss on another log.

He had no intention of moving.

Not while Rachel slept so peacefully against him.

They'd had a busy day between his chopping wood, her shoveling the porch and looking after the kids. After dinner he and Rachel had settled on the couch, a respectful distance apart, and watched Cody and Jolie play in the playpen while discussing the events of the day.

Cody's cold appeared to be on the mend again, and good-natured Jolie put up with his high energy antics with stoic patience. The conversation moved from the kids to films and books, current events and war stories. He told her of the time he'd night-dropped into foreign territory only to get treetopped fifteen feet off the ground. She shared some outrageous animal tales that had him laughing out loud.

It turned out she wrote a syndicated column about

animal antics, and had even been offered a book deal she was waiting to hear on.

Yeah, they talked about everything under the sun but what really mattered.

Which was totally out of character for him. He lacked the patience for prevarication.

Tonight had been different.

He'd never spent a more domestic evening with a woman. Didn't usually want to. But tonight, with Rachel, he'd enjoyed a quiet, fun, invigorating and peaceful interlude. She had a biting wit that both challenged and amused him. Even the occasional silences had been comfortable.

During one of those silences they must have fallen asleep. And as the fire died down and the room grew chillier, they'd gravitated together for warmth. Now he was lying with one leg up, one foot on the floor and she lay tucked between him and the back of the couch.

She felt good in his arms, every breath she exhaled whispered over his skin teasing the hair at the opening of his shirt. Her silky hair feathered his cheek and smelled of peach blossoms. And he pillowed their clasped hands, her left in his right, on his stomach.

Giving into temptation he ran his thumb over the petal soft skin of her palm. He longed to touch more of her, all of her. To taste every inch of her and have her ignite in his arms like she did yesterday. Her responsiveness, so sweet and sassy, so genuine, undid him.

The tiny movement of his thumb finally penetrated her subconscious because her hold tightened into a fist around him.

He liked that feeling. He'd hold her close and let tomorrow take care of itself.

Rachel sighed as the tension drained from Ford's body. The even flow of his breathing meant he'd fallen asleep or was close to it.

The stirring of the fire had woken her. How surprising to find herself in Ford's arms. She should have moved, put space and sense between them. Just gotten up and gone to bed.

Instead she'd stolen this time. Illicitly taken advantage of the peace and safety of being held by a strong, gentle man. For these uncounted moments she pretended he didn't want something from her. That he wouldn't be leaving in a matter of days.

For these cherished moments she just lay in the strength of his warm embrace and let herself be.

When he'd started caressing her palm, she'd thought he might try to touch her further, might try to wake her and turn so she was under him.

Her body clenched with need as she imagined welcoming him into her arms and her body.

She inhaled, loving the smell of him, the scents of man and soap with a hint of wood smoke. Oh, how the woman in her wished he'd woken her.

But she couldn't make the move herself. The mother in her couldn't forget the babies even for the length of time it would take to shatter in his arms.

But the woman in her, the one who longed for a man's touch, the one weakened by Ford's thoughtfulness and the tender way he handled the twins, that woman would have succumbed to a midnight seduction.

It wasn't to be.

Sigh. Rachel closed her eyes, content to savor these unplanned hours.

Tomorrow was soon enough for regrets.

The next morning Ford walked the quarter mile down to the main road. The intermittent sunshine yesterday and this morning had started a thaw. He could see patches of the driveway and when he reached the road it had been cleared.

They'd be able to make it into town today to replenish supplies. And the way to San Diego had been opened up.

"I don't know how much longer I'll be," he said into his cell in answer to his older brother's question. "My commander gave me thirty days leave to handle the situation. Now the snow has stopped, I'll be able to get on the road once we resolve the custody issue."

"What's the hold up there? I thought you said she wasn't interested in taking on the twins."

"The picture Crystal painted of her sister was off. Way off. She's already bonded with the kids and she's refusing to sign off on custody."

"So if she's willing and able to take on the task, why don't you let her?"

"Tony made them my responsibility. I can't do my duty by them if they're in Montana and I'm in California."

"I know you don't want to hear it, but you can't do

it by jet setting all over the world, either. Maybe they'd be better off in Montana."

"I'm not exactly hopping the globe on pleasure trips. It's my job. And you were singing a different song about responsibility when you took Gabe from Samantha. She was willing and able and you still went after custody."

"Different scenario. Gabe is my son. The twins are not your family."

"They are now. I owe Tony in ways I can't define. I can no more deny his request than I could if something happened to you and Samantha and you left your boys in my care."

"I've always admired your loyalty, little bro. You know we'll support you any way we can."

"Yeah, I know. That's what Tony was counting on." After promising to keep his brother posted, Ford disconnected the call.

He sighed, his breath crystallizing in the air. He and Rachel were long overdue for a conversation on custody. Today he'd get her to sign the papers and tomorrow he and the twins would be on the road.

No more excuses.

As he approached the house he heard a ringing. Sounded like phone service had been restored.

He opened the front door to see Rachel waving her arms in the air and shimmying her hips. A tantalizing strip of creamy flesh showed between her low-cut black jeans and the turquoise sweater that matched her eyes. She danced around the kitchen; making the twins who were strapped into their high chairs, giggle.

"Was that the phone I heard?" he asked.

She whipped around at the sound of his voice and he saw the smile lighting up her face.

"Yes, it was." She shimmied toward him, threw herself into his arms. "The phones are working."

"That is good news. And if you like that…" He waltzed her around the table, twirled her around once and dropped her into a dip. "You'll want to do a jig when you hear the road is clear."

Her eyes laughed up into his. He grinned, taking delight in her happiness. And unable to resist while he had her dipped and at his mercy, he cupped her head in his hand and lowered his head to claim her mouth.

She immediately opened to him. Tightening her arms around him, she returned the kiss with a passion to match his.

Reluctantly he pulled back, brought her upright and twirled her around again.

"Whew." She swayed on her feet, her cheeks burning red. She licked her lips and blinked away the lust glaze from her dazzling eyes. "They want the book."

"Your book on animal manners?" he asked.

"Yes." Excitement made her glow. "That was my agent on the phone. They want my book. The publisher made an official offer."

"Hey." Absurdly proud of her, he swooped her up and swung her around. "That's great news."

She threw her head back and laughed. Joy radiated from her.

The babies shrieked in glee.

Ford realized he'd seen little happiness in her. Passion, resolve, sadness, determination, anger, sorrow. He'd seen all those and more. And certainly love for Cody and Jolie. Yet simple happiness and joy had been missing.

Slowly he lowered her to the floor. When she reached eye level, she sobered. He expected her to push him away as her sense of self-preservation demanded every time he got too close.

She surprised him by throwing her arms around his neck and laying one on him.

The kiss didn't last long but held a punch. Because it was the first overture she'd made to him. When she pulled back, he let her slip the rest of the way to the floor.

She framed his face between her hands. "You made this moment more special by being here. Thank you."

"Hey, this is a big deal." Something bloomed in his chest at her words. Some feel-good emotion that he didn't recognize filled him up. He liked making her feel good even if it meant putting off talking about custody issues. It would take a lesser man than him to spoil her pleasure.

"In fact we need to celebrate. Let me take you to dinner."

"Oh." Flustered, and clearly pleased, a flush added to her glow. But she flittered away, began fussing over the twins. "That's not necessary."

"Of course it is. You deserve a party. And the twins and I are just the ones to give it to you."

She hesitated for another moment, but her excitement couldn't be contained. She grinned. "All right. It's a date."

CHAPTER SEVEN

IT'S a date. How lame was that?

Rachel surveyed her reflection in the mirrorlike surface of the restaurant door. Looking beyond the little girl in her arms, she saw a woman dressed in a calf length brown suede skirt with brown boots and an ivory sweater under a black leather duster. Too dressy?

Not for a date. Oh God.

Stepping through the door Ford held open, she inhaled the spicy aromas of onion, garlic and tomatoes. Decorated in dark woods and red vinyl with a video arcade and jukebox for entertainment, the Pizza Pit catered to families, sports teams and bored teenagers.

She'd directed Ford to the pizza joint knowing the twins were likely to be excitable after being cooped up for days. And maybe the loud, boisterous crowd, with kids popping up and down and all around, would make it less like a date.

Where had her head been? Answer: In the stratosphere.

Oh, yeah, she'd kept her cool while talking to her

agent. But let Ford suggest something simple like a celebratory dinner, and she blew it all out of proportion.

Proximity was the problem.

The enforced intimacy of the last few days gave her subconscious ideas. Working together, sharing the responsibility of the twins, sleeping in each other's arms all played into her dream of having a family.

Ford with his intelligent blue eyes, muscle-ripped body and dangerous edge spoke to every female particle in her. But even more than his skillful fingers and sinful mouth, she responded to his willingness to listen, his patience and generosity, his loyalty and sorrow for his friend and his stubborn sense of duty.

Ideal mating material, or so her subconscious would have her believe.

But it was impossible.

Even if she decided to act on the amazing attraction between them, too many obstacles blocked the goal. He lived a thousand miles away. He was big city, big family, bigger than life. She was small town, family-poor and self-contained. He was a warrior who traveled the world; she was a loner, comfortable in her little corner of Montana.

She followed Ford to a booth not far from the video arcade. Hitching Jolie higher on her hip, Rachel looked around for the high chairs. Spying them by the salad bar, she pointed them out to Ford.

"I'll get them. Here, take Cody." Ford set the boy in her lap next to his sister.

Bouncing the babies on her knees, she watched Ford

cross the room, his stride long and graceful. Yum, he looked fine in black jeans, a black T-shirt and black boots.

Out of her league fine.

Heck, he probably had a whole slew of beach bunnies waiting for him back in California. A prime military man with dark good looks and fatal charm, he probably had them lining up and down the pier.

She'd be delusional to think they had a chance in purgatory of being together.

Not only did they not have a future together, he had every intention of tearing her world apart. She'd do well to remember that.

He came back with the high chairs and they got the twins settled. A waitress arrived and Ford ordered the pizza. Pasting on a smile, Rachel tried to keep up her end of the conversation, to get into celebration mode. It was her party after all.

And she did appreciate his gesture. More than she could ever say, but she couldn't pretend any longer.

"It's okay you know," she said after about twenty minutes. "We can talk about the custody plans for the twins."

Clearly startled, he sat back and eyed her. "No." He shook his head. "We're here to celebrate your book. I don't want to spoil it for you."

"I appreciate that, I do." Rather than meet his quizzical gaze, she picked up her discarded straw wrapper. "But I can't sit here and pretend you're not plotting the best way to get my signature on the custody papers so you can pack up Cody and Jolie and truck on back to San Diego."

His features tightened. He almost looked hurt. "Is that what you think I'm doing, sitting here plotting against you?"

"Yes. No. I don't know." Confused, she bought some time by digging in her purse for some crackers to give the twins.

But she'd started this conversation she needed to see it through. "Look, we both know you wouldn't be here with me if not for your interest in the twins, so we might as well deal with the issue."

"I'm in Montana because of the twins." He reached across the table and took her hand. "Tonight I'm with you because I want to be with you."

"Don't." She pulled her hand back, scattering shredded wrapper pieces, her emotions seeming to scatter in the same way. "Please don't say things like that. There's no point. Let's just decide what we're going to do about the twins so we can get on with our lives."

He set his drink aside and leaned forward with concern in his eyes. "Not until I understand what's happening here. Why are you so upset?"

I can't afford to care for you. And I'm afraid it's already too late. But she'd give him too much ammunition by admitting that out loud. "You want to take the twins from me, isn't that reason enough to be upset?"

"I'm not taking them from you," he said carefully. "I'm bringing them into my family. There's a difference."

"They can live with me and still be a part of your family. They can visit you in the summer and on holidays."

"If I thought that would work, I'd go for it in a heart-beat. But we both know that they'd feel like outsiders visiting strangers. My family will embrace them, they'll have aunts and uncles and cousins. They've already played with my brother's boys. They'll have a grand-mother. Love will grow and surround them but only by being in the midst of the family."

"I already love them." Her gut clenched in fear. Everything he said made horrible sense. "All of the people you mentioned are the strangers. I'm their family."

"And you can have all the visitations you want. The twins can come here. You can come to San Diego. We'll work it out."

"I don't know how." She glanced at the twins and her heart bloomed with such love she choked up. Swal-mlowing with difficulty she informed Ford, "I won't sign away my rights. I won't. I've thought and thought on how we can make this work because obviously neither of us is going to give up full custody, but nothing makes sense.

"We live too far apart to share custody unless it's for six months at a time. I'd be willing to consider that but honestly I don't think it's best for the babies. It would be disorienting for them when they're this young, es-pecially after losing their parents."

"And when they get older and start school, they'd

have to change school every six months." He shook his head. "That's every kid's worst nightmare."

A shadow loomed over the table. Rachel looked up into Sheriff Mitchell's chiseled features. "Evening, folks. Is everything all right here?"

"Sheriff." Ford acknowledged the other man. "I imagine you've been busy these last few days."

"Some." Mitch turned his attention to her, a question in his eyes. "Rachel, how are you doing?"

Rachel sighed; the last thing she needed was a macho contest between the two men. Summoning patience—no easy task—she flashed a smile.

"We're fine, Mitch. I hope no one was seriously hurt by the storm."

"No serious damage, no." His eyes narrowed suspiciously and his gaze shifted from her to Ford and back.

Oops. Maybe she'd overdone the friendliness a bit.

Cody chose that moment to make a grab for Mitch's shiny steal handcuffs.

"Cody, no," she chided and reached to grab his hand.

Too late. Feeling the pull on his belt, Mitch slapped his hand down, connecting smartly with Cody's fingers. Stung, the boy began to cry.

Lightning fast Ford shoved to his feet, shouldering Mitch aside. "Back off."

"I'm sorry." Mitch held up both hands in a conciliatory gesture. "He startled me."

Rachel tensed, ready to jump between the two men if necessary. But Ford simply nodded and picked up Cody, quietly murmuring to soothe the distraught boy.

Mitch quickly made his excuses and left.

"I'm going to go run cold water on his fingers." Ford hefted Cody to his shoulder. "We'll be back in a minute."

Left at the table, Rachel and Jolie looked at each other. Big eyed, the little girl chewed on a cracker.

"Get used to it, babe," Rachel advised. "Boys never change."

The pizza arrived just ahead of Ford and Cody's return to the table. By unspoken agreement they ate in silence.

After a few minutes Jolie began to fidget and whine. Rachel grabbed the diaper bag and escaped to the rest room. Besides being wet the baby had developed a rash on her butt and along the waistline of the diaper. Rachel lathered on ointment, finished changing Jolie and rejoined the boys.

She'd barely regained her seat before Ford tossed out a new suggestion.

"What about split custody?"

As soon as he said the words, Ford wanted to pull them back. For so many reasons. In the short time he'd been around the twins he'd observed how they drew strength from each other. His older brothers, Rick and Rett, identical twins, would beat him to a pulp if they'd heard him voice the suggestion. He couldn't conceive of them being parted and the same went for Cody and Jolie.

"Split them up? Like you take Cody and I take Jolie?" She sounded both appalled and fascinated by the prospect. Her gaze went from him to the twins. Without breaking stride she casually removed a paper napkin from Jolie's mouth and handed Cody another piece of crust.

"That would probably be the best division of custody." Why was he pursuing the outrageous option? "What do you think?"

But she was no longer listening.

"Ford." The urgency in her voice caused him to tense. She set her pizza down and nodded toward the video arcade.

He looked over, spotted a pretty brown haired girl about fourteen or fifteen playing a video game. He also noted the young punk, dirty blond hair, oversize clothes, hassling her. The girl tried to walk away, but the boy blocked her retreat.

"I'll take care of it." He slid to the edge of the booth.

"Wait." Rachel's hand on his arm stopped him. "Look."

Another kid—Ford could tell it was the girl's older brother by the resemblance between them—jumped into the fray. He stepped between the punk and the girl, said something that had the punk backing off, then he took the girl's arm and escorted her back to their table.

Ford settled back into the booth. The whole incident lasted only a few minutes. Such a small envelope of time to deliver such a huge emotional impact. How could they possibly separate brother from sister after witnessing such a scene?

He met Rachel's blue-green gaze, saw she'd come to

the same conclusion as him. "If I believed in signs, I'd say fate just slapped us with one hell of a lesson."

She arched a delicate brow. "You think?"

"It was a bad idea anyway."

"At last. Something we agree on."

Back at the house, Ford put away the groceries while Rachel got the kids ready for bed. Because she'd been fussy on the way home, Rachel had given Jolie a bottle while she changed Cody and dressed him in his pajamas.

Once he was settled in the crib with his bottle, Rachel reached for Jolie.

"What's wrong, baby doll?" Though she'd taken the bottle the little girl had continued to whine the whole time Rachel had been dealing with Cody. Usually the mellower of the two children, Jolie's distress began to worry Rachel.

Once she'd stripped Jolie down and seen the raw red welts covering her torso and bottom Rachel's uneasiness turned to apprehension.

"Ford," she called as she inspected the nasty irritation. She felt awful that the baby had suffered all evening. "Oh, poor baby, I'm so sorry. I should have realized something was wrong when I saw the rash earlier."

Ford appeared in the bedroom doorway. "What's up?"

"Jolie has a bad rash. It was only a little red earlier. I thought it was diaper rash. But now she has red welts."

"Let me see." He moved to her side, his features tightening when he saw the livid marks on the girl's delicate skin. "Probably just an allergic reaction. But it looks so bad."

"I want to take her to emergency. Will you stay with Cody?"

He shook his head. "We'll go together."

"There's no need to take Cody out, too. It's better if you stay here with him."

"Forget it." He wore his stubborn expression. "I'm no good at waiting. And I'm not letting you go alone."

"Fine." She could have argued, but she saw the concern under his obstinate façade. And she really would welcome his company. "Let's get going then."

They quickly bundled the babies up and Ford drove them to Daniels Memorial Hospital, where despite Ford's aversion, they spent time waiting. Cody was out like a light in the stroller. Jolie dozed intermittently but the welts obviously bothered her as she woke often. At those times she wanted to be held and walked.

Time dragged, worry escalated, nerves were strung tight, while Rachel lashed herself with self-recriminations. She should have acted sooner. She should have known the rash meant something more.

But no, she'd been too caught up in denying her attraction to Ford and claiming her rights to the twins.

Maybe this was another sign. Maybe Rachel wasn't meant to raise Cody and Jolie.

She'd rather give them up than see them harmed in any way.

"Stop beating yourself up," Ford whispered, his breath warm on her temple as he wrapped his arms around her, helping her to support Jolie's weight. "Kids get rashes, upset stomachs and colds. It's nobody's fault."

Rachel nodded unable to speak for the tears that threatened. His reassurances warmed her icy core. He'd been a rock. For a moment she allowed herself to absorb his strength, to lean just a little.

When they finally got in to see the doctor, a slim woman with blue-black hair and horn-rimmed glasses, they learned Ford had been right. It was an allergic reaction.

Jolie announced her displeasure at being stripped and inspected by screaming at the top of her lungs and trying to twist away. It broke Rachel's heart to have to hold her still for the doctor's examination.

The cries woke Cody. Ford had his hands full keeping the boy from following his sister's example.

"Has Jolie eaten or touched anything new over the past twelve hours?" Dr. Wilcox asked.

"I've racked my brain trying to remember if I fed them something different." Rachel heard the waver in her voice. Determined to keep the tears at bay, she took a deep breath. "We've been snowed in, so we've been eating what we've had on hand. Nothing new."

"It doesn't have to be something she ingested," the doctor clarified. "It could be something applied to her skin or that she's worn. Like soaps, lotions and softeners. It could even be something in the air."

Rachel tried to focus her thoughts. "I'm sorry, Doctor, nothing comes to mind."

"I opened a new laundry detergent when I washed the sheets this morning," Ford said. "She took her nap on those sheets this afternoon."

"Yeah." Rachel wearily pushed her hair back from her face. "I've used that brand before, but not since the twins have been with me."

"You've probably found the culprit, but you should see her pediatrician for allergy tests." The doctor advised. "In the meantime, I'll give her a shot. The welts should go down quickly."

"Thank you, Doctor." Ford settled Cody against his shoulder. "Can I take my family home now?"

A miracle happened on the way home. The twins fell asleep and stayed asleep until Rachel and Ford tucked them into bed. In the playpen. Too late to rewash the sheets tonight, so they'd decided to pile in a couple of blankets for padding and let Cody and Jolie sleep in the living room.

Rachel stood over the playpen watching the babies slumber peacefully. Thank God it hadn't been any more serious than allergies. Even so, she felt as though she'd been put through the spin cycle and hung out to dry.

Ford came out of the bathroom, ready for bed in pajama bottoms and a T-shirt.

"Thank you for coming with me tonight. You made a difficult trip easier."

His gaze ran over her as he rounded the couch. She

tucked a strand of hair behind her ear, knowing any glamour she'd managed earlier had long disappeared. She'd already had her turn in the bathroom so she lacked a lick of makeup. And her flannel pajama bottoms and long sleeved thermal underwear were a long way from date material.

Undeterred he stepped right up to her, wrapped a hand around the back of her neck and laid his forehead against hers.

"I'm glad I was there, too." His fingers worked magic on the sensitive skin of her neck. "But you would have handled it. You're one tough lady. You were amazing."

"Oh heavens, Ford. I never want to go through that again." Too weak to resist the lure of his comfort and strength, she relaxed against him.

"Me, neither." He ran his hands down the backs of her arms until his fingers tangled with hers then he stepped back pulling her with him. "You've had a tough day. Come lie down. I want to hold you."

"Oh. I shouldn't." She let him go until their arms were stretched full-length, but her resistance stopped there. When he continued walking she followed step for step. Sleeping in his arms sounded like heaven. But oh, she shouldn't. "You said it yourself, I'm tough. I don't need to be held."

"I do." He drew her down to the couch and into his arms. "Just for a while. Hold me."

When he lay back and took her with him, she let him. And oh it felt so good, so right to lie in his arms.

She snuggled her cheek over his heart, sighed and closed her eyes.

"All right. But just for a little while."

CHAPTER EIGHT

FOR the second day in a row Rachel awoke on the couch alone. How Ford had managed to slide away without waking her she didn't know. The man had skills.

Not least of which was sneaking past her defenses.

The harder she tried to create distance between them, the closer he seemed to get. He'd claimed to be a likable guy and she had to agree. Damn it.

He'd be much easier to resist if he were a selfish jerk, which considering his insistence on taking the twins should have qualified him hands down. Unfortunately he carried his weight and more with household chores. His patience and gentleness with the twins never wavered. Heck, he even changed diapers without complaining.

His loyalty and sense of duty were the biggest bane of her life. And confirmed the honor his commanding officer proclaimed he had in spades.

He made her think, he made her laugh, he made her want.

But she couldn't—wouldn't—give in to the insanity

of falling for him. Of all the mistakes she could make, that would be the biggest.

Hearing giggles from the kitchen motivated her to get up and get going. She hopped into the shower, brushed her teeth, and then dressed in jeans and a flannel shirt over a navy T-shirt.

In the kitchen she found a fresh pot of coffee, Ford kicked back reading the paper, and the twins covered from the waist up in applesauce as they pounded the trays of their high chairs with spoons. The bigger the mess they made the more they giggled.

Rachel shook her head and moved to pour herself a cup of coffee. She leaned back against the counter and sipped.

"Having fun?"

Ford lowered the paper far enough to meet her gaze. "Good morning."

Approval shone in his eyes even after his gaze had swept her from head to foot. Here she stood without a lick of makeup, and he'd made her feel as if he'd never seen a more beautiful sight in the morning.

The man had to go, and the sooner the better.

Before she did something foolish, like do more than sleep in his arms.

Like fall in love.

She hitched her chin toward the twins. "They're dangerous with those spoons. You know they haven't learned to feed themselves yet."

He folded the paper and set it on the table then flicked a glance at Cody and Jolie. "It'll wash off. And they won't learn if they don't try."

"Huh. It's good to hear them laughing."

"Yes. The welts are down on Jolie. She's looking much better." He got up and punched some numbers on the microwave. Next he dropped bread in the toaster. "Sit down, I made breakfast."

"You spoil me." She took a seat at the table just as he set down a plate of scrambled eggs and smoked sausage.

"You make that sound like a bad thing." He went back to the counter for the toast.

"It is. I'm used to doing things for myself. I prefer it that way."

"Maybe that's why I like doing things for you." He sat down and pushed a plate of buttered toast toward her. "Because it's not expected."

"Huh." She flashed him an exasperated glare.

He grinned. "Eat up. I have a surprise for you."

She lifted her brows at him. "All this and a surprise, too? Are you sure you don't want to quit the Navy and move to Montana?"

The levity left his expression and his eyes turned pensive. "My brother thinks I should give up the SEALs now that I'm guardian of the twins."

"And you're not ready to?"

"Honestly? I don't know. My current commission is up in a couple of months, so I don't have long to think about it. I do know I want it to be my decision. Not something forced on me by circumstances or told to me by my brother."

"That would be ideal, wouldn't it? If outside influences and well intentioned advice didn't play a part in our decisions."

The exasperation boomeranged back to her. "Very funny."

"You're just upset because you have to think about this before you were ready to. Let me ask you this, does your brother expect you to quit because he voiced an opinion?"

"No, if anything, he'd expect the reverse."

"Why's that, because you're the youngest of six and you've been bucking the system since the day you learned to say no?"

His eyes narrowed in speculation. "How do you know that about me?"

"Please, I've known you what, a week? And I already know you can find Ford as a synonym for stubborn in a thesaurus. You haven't accepted no for an answer since you got here and when you have compromised, it's been on your terms." She reached for the grape jelly for her last piece of toast. "Your brothers must know you are your own man."

"Yeah, we all know that about each other." He reached over, took her toast, bit the end off and handed it back to her.

A smear of jelly clung to the corner of his mouth. Rachel bit her lip to keep from acting on the impulse to lean over and lick the sweet treat from his skin. Instead she sank her teeth into the same end of the bread he had and lectured herself on forgetting the physical attraction to concentrate on the conversation.

"So the decision is yours to make. Whether you allow the circumstances to influence you or not is up to you."

He looked at her for a long moment, his expression giving nothing away.

"You're not going to suggest you keep custody of the twins so I can re-up as a SEAL? We both know you want to."

"You mean because it makes perfect sense for me to take the kids while you pursue your career?"

Yes, it had occurred to her. And yes, she wanted to keep the twins. But begging would weaken her position. She'd learned that lesson too well, and too early in life to forget it when it mattered the most.

"No, I'm not going to suggest that. You're smart enough to come up with it on your own."

"Right. My brother mentioned the arrangements for Tony and Crystal's memorial service were set for the week before Thanksgiving. Will you come?"

"Your family made arrangements for Crystal?" The thoughtfulness of the gesture staggered her.

"It's what I thought you'd like. If you prefer to make other arrangements, I can let my brother know."

"No. No. She'd want to share this last rite with Tony. Of course I'll come."

Jolie called for her attention, breaking the growing tension.

"Good morning, baby. You're feeling better aren't you? I'm so glad." Rachel grabbed a napkin and swiped at Jolie's face. "But oh my. Uncle Ford let you make one big mess, didn't he?"

"Da na da." Cody pointed his dripping spoon toward Ford and grinned showing two bottom teeth.

Rachel's gaze met Ford's. He looked shell-shocked for a moment before shutting off all expression.

She knew how he felt. The first time she thought the twins called her mama both broke her heart and mended it back all at the same time. The incongruity along with the inherent acceptance struck right to the core of you. And revived the sorrow of loss all over again.

"Just coincidence." She crossed her arms over her chest. "They don't know what they're saying yet." But she knew the day wasn't far away.

Thinking of Ford being called daddy made her gut clutch. She loved the idea the twins were starting to adjust, that they felt loved enough to accept her and Ford in their parents' stead. But that meant they would be hurt again by whatever custody settlement she and Ford decided on.

Sometimes life just sucked.

"Hey, bud, let's get you cleaned." Ford reached for a dish towel and wrapped it around Cody. Ford carefully didn't look at Rachel when he asked, "Bath?"

Rachel stepped out onto the porch, a bundled up Cody riding her hip, to find old Mr. Brown from next door sitting on the perch of a shiny red sleigh drawn by a well-groomed, gray speckled horse.

"Ms. Adams," he greeted her with a huge grin and a tip of his red plaid hat. "Beautiful day for a ride."

"Mr. Brown." Determined to be neighborly she

answered his good cheer with a smile. "I hope you and Mrs. Brown survived the storm in tact."

"What ya say there? Sorry lass, don't hear as good as I used to."

Rachel walked to the top of the stairs and, raising her voice. repeated her question.

"That we did, young lady. The Mrs., though, she caught a chill. I've been feeding her chicken gravy and biscuits, so she should be feeling better right soon."

"Chicken gravy and biscuits?"

"Yeah, yeah. Chicken noodle soup is more than an old wives' tale. It really works to help cure a cold. Don't know how to make chicken noodle soup, but I can make chicken gravy and biscuits. I figure it's close enough."

"I'm sure she appreciates your efforts." Rachel didn't know how well his heavy meal worked on the cold but at least it wouldn't hurt the woman. Rachel made a note to send some Echinacea tea home with him.

"Oh, the Mrs. always appreciates my efforts," he said and winked.

"Mr. Brown." Rachel chided him.

He cackled, pleased to get a rise out of her.

"Here now, that little guy wants to come say hello to Betsy. You bring him on down here." Spry for a man in his sixties, he hopped to the ground. He took Cody from her to gently instruct the little boy on how to pet the horse.

"I had Betsy out for a ride this morning. Met your young man down by the road. He thought you and the little ones might like to get out of the house and go for a ride."

Her "young man" was simply diabolical.

"Yes, I think we'll all enjoy a trip through the snow. This is a beautiful sleigh."

"She is a beauty isn't she?" He beamed. "I got it out yesterday to get it cleaned up and ready for Santa."

She blinked at him. "Santa?"

"Yeah, I've driven Santa's sleigh in the Thanksgiving Day parade for the last eight years. I'm sure you've seen it."

She shook her head. "I'm not much for crowds. I don't go to parades."

He laughed. "Lass, there are more people in the parade than watching it. The little ones would enjoy it."

Ford joined them saving her from having to reply. But Mr. Brown had a point. From now on she had to think beyond her own comfort zone to accommodate the twins.

"John, thanks for giving us a ride." Ford shifted Jolie to shake hands with Mr. Brown. "The kids are going to love it."

"My pleasure. Let's get you folks loaded up."

The men continued to exchange pleasantries while they all got settled, Mr. Brown on the perch, Rachel and Ford with the twins between them in the back.

And then they were off, gliding over pristine snow to the merry jingle of bells. Tucked beneath blankets, the cool air invigorated rather than chilled.

The twins took in everything red cheeked and bright eyed. Rachel figured she looked much the same. It was beautiful and fun. And never before had anyone ever done anything so special for her. For the twins, too, of course, but she knew Ford had done this mostly for her.

The scenery shimmered into crystal brilliance as moisture swelled in her eyes.

"Hey." Ford cupped the back of her neck and ran his thumb over her cheek. His touch felt especially warm against her wind-chilled skin. "Are you crying?"

"No, of course not." She blinked away the tears. "It's just the wind."

"It's more than the wind." He insisted. "Talk to me, Rachel. This was meant to be a treat, to make you happy not sad."

"I am happy." She assured him. "This is wonderful. The twins are loving it."

"And you? Are you loving it?" The intensity in his blue eyes convinced her the answer really mattered to him.

"I am," she confirmed. Hearing the huskiness in her voice, she cleared her throat, met his gaze. "Thank you for arranging this adventure. Nobody's ever done anything like this for me."

"You mean planned a surprise for you?" He gently tugged on a lock of her hair.

"That, or done something for me just because they thought I'd enjoy it." The confession didn't come easily. She didn't talk about her childhood, ever. But Ford had shared his guilt and sorrow with her and he'd put together this lovely surprise. He deserved some consideration from her.

"I had a strict upbringing." Okay, slight understatement there.

"Is that why you left home so young?" he asked.

She hesitated, glanced at Mr. Brown. He hadn't tried to participate in the conversation. His poor hearing along with the cheerful bells ensured their privacy.

"Yeah, and because I learned I wasn't my father's daughter." Funny, she'd thought the words would be harder to say. But here, with Ford, she said them for the first time and felt lighter.

"Wow. Heavy. How'd you find out?"

"My mother told me. I had to get a job when I was fourteen to help with expenses. My expenses, as it turned out. I didn't get an allowance, but I got to keep part of my paycheck. My senior year of high school, I wanted to buy a car. I'd saved my money. It wasn't hard considering I was never allowed to do anything.

"Mom said I'd need the money when I graduated because I'd no longer be welcome to live with them. I was shocked. That's when she told me she'd been pregnant when she'd married my dad. She'd lied and told him I was his. He'd found out and their marriage survived the truth, but he never accepted me, never loved me."

"Your mom sacrificed you for her own comfort." Ford cut to the heart of her past, the harsh edge in his tone criticizing her mother's choices. Too bad she had no excuses for her mom.

"I didn't wait to graduate. I packed up and left the next day. I bought a one-way ticket to Scobey and started a new life."

"It must have been difficult." The simple sympathy almost undid her.

"It was a relief to be free. I never felt loved in that house. Except by Crystal." She looked down at her hands clasped together in her lap. "Why do you suppose she misled Tony about me?"

He caught her chin and turned her head to face him. Bending, he sealed his warm mouth over hers, telling her with lips, teeth and tongue of his admiration and affection. Sealing the kiss with his lips, he pulled back.

"Whatever her reasons, you have nothing to be ashamed of. You're a strong woman who's made a good life from a bad beginning."

"Thank you." She cupped his cheek in her hand and showed her gratitude with a soft kiss in return. "I know that's true, but it's easy to believe the worst when someone you love bad-mouths you."

"I can only speculate. Tony didn't talk much about his relationship with Crystal, but I know it was tempestuous. They loved each other, but they weren't compatible."

Rachel recalled the e-mails where Crystal poured out her fears of losing Tony. She'd despised that he was a SEAL. "I know she hated it when Tony went out of the country."

"Yeah, that was tough on Tony. Being a SEAL defined who he was. His parents were alcoholics and they really did a job on his self-esteem. He was one of the best men I knew, but he had no sense of self-worth except on the job."

"I told her she needed to make peace with his job or let him go. It wasn't fair for her to impose her fears on him."

Not that Rachel was an expert on relationships, but one lesson she'd learned, and learned well, was you couldn't make someone love you. And if you weren't true to yourself, you'd have nothing to hold on to when you realized the truth.

Ford nodded his agreement. "They did break up for a while before she found out she was pregnant."

"Really? I didn't hear from her for several months. Then she called to tell me she was expecting a baby. She was so happy. I thought she'd made her peace. Now I realize she probably just stopped sharing her fears with me."

"The pregnancy did bring them closer. Until Tony made out his will. I knew there was no love lost between him and his parents, which is why I agreed when he asked me to watch over the kids if anything ever happened to him."

He lifted his hand to cover hers. "Crystal was young, only twenty-one. She was in love with a man she didn't really understand and couldn't control. I've been thinking about it and I think part of it was my fault."

"How could that be?"

"She didn't like that Tony named a guardian without consulting her. She didn't like that he chose a bachelor, hated that it was another SEAL. I was her worst nightmare."

"Mustang, wild and free." Rachel began to see what motivated her sister's actions. She still didn't like it, but a mother's concern accounted for a lot.

"Pretty much." Ford agreed. "My guess is she set up

her own will listing you as guardian then played up the negative aspect of your life to teach Tony a lesson, both for leaving her out of the process and for choosing an inappropriate guardian. Being so young, she probably figured they had plenty of time to deal with the whole issue. It's the only reason I can think of."

She gave him a sad half smile. "I guess we didn't get as close as I thought."

The twins objected to being squeezed between them by squirming and pushing against them. When Rachel settled back into her corner, Jolie pulled on Rachel's sleeve and hauled herself to her feet. The better view and the wind in Jolie's face made her grin and clap her hands. Soon Cody stood next to her.

Turning to better anchor Jolie in place, Rachel noted Ford did the same with Cody and they were suddenly facing each other. Rachel felt as if they were in an oversize snow globe, an intimate cocoon with the beauty of a winter wonderland passing in the background.

Too bad the intensity of the conversation didn't match the splendor of the scenery.

Jolie laid her head on Rachel's shoulder. The excitement had worn her out. As always the acceptance and trust of Jolie's slight weight resting against Rachel sent warmth flooding through her. She settled the sleepy baby in her lap and wished Jolie could have grown up knowing her mother.

"Poor Crystal and Tony, they just wanted to take care of their kids. But instead of working together they worked against each other and didn't resolve anything."

"That would be my take." Ford stopped Cody from climbing into Rachel's lap along with his sister. He lifted Cody into his lap instead. "Hey, buddy. Let's get you warmed up." Ford tucked a blanket around the boy.

"And now here we are," Rachel said, "trying to make sense of their mess. At least Tony's parents are out of the picture."

"For now anyway."

That sounded ominous. "What's that mean?"

"It means if we don't work out a solid home situation for the twins, it'll leave room for Tony's parents to sue for custody."

"But they couldn't win." Her heart sank at the thought of the twins in the hands of the abusive couple. "A court's not going to give custody of small children to alcoholics."

Ford shrugged, his expression grimmer than she'd ever seen it. "They're closet drinkers. As an established couple making decent wages living in a nice neighborhood, the courts may find them eminently better than two single people living a thousand miles apart splitting or sharing custody."

"Oh my God." Put like that their chances did sound bad. "Why didn't you mention this before?"

"Because I didn't intend to split or share custody. I intended to take the twins and surround them with the strength and support of my family."

Her heart latched onto one word. "Intended? Does that mean you no longer have that intention?"

"It means I want you to move to San Diego."

CHAPTER NINE

THE cold must be getting to her because she thought he'd just asked her to move to California.

She looked askance at him and pounded the side of her head a couple of times. "I don't think I heard right. Did you just say move to San Diego?"

"Yeah, think about it. It makes perfect sense."

"It makes no sense whatsoever."

His somber expression didn't lighten. "I'm serious."

"No." The cold must be getting to him, too. "You're delusional."

"That's a knee-jerk reaction. Don't dismiss the idea without thinking about it."

"What's to think about? This is my home."

"No, it's where your house is." He delivered the harsh decree with utmost gentleness. "You've built a life here, but by your own admission you've isolated yourself from the community. I haven't heard you mention another woman's name besides Crystal. Who's your best friend?"

Ouch. The question cut deep.

And then her spinning thoughts spit out the words, you are.

The instinctive response irritated her almost as much as his question. And how revealing that in the short time she'd known him, she'd become closer to him than people she'd known for thirteen years.

"Just because I prefer my own company doesn't mean I don't have c-connections here." Hating the break in her voice, she buried her nose in Jolie's soft brown curls.

Ford slid closer. Once again she felt the tensile strength of his hand on her neck. Massaging soothingly, he melted her.

"I'm not suggesting there won't be sacrifices, but this could be the solution to our custody dilemma. You're going to have to move anyway. The three of you won't fit in a one-bedroom house for long. You can write anywhere, and there are bound to be plenty of opportunities to work with animals in San Diego.

"Look, you don't have to make a decision right now. You're coming to California for the memorial service, right? I'm just asking you to keep an open mind. Check out the area and consider staying."

Mr. Brown pulled the sleigh to a stop in front of Rachel's house effectively ending the conversation. Between expressing her appreciation to Mr. Brown, running inside for the Echinacea tea for Mrs. Brown and getting the kids inside and settled down for their afternoon naps, Rachel kept busy.

But for all the activity, her mind revved around one thing. The possibility of moving to California.

But it wasn't the practicalities that snagged her attention. It wasn't even the fear of leaving the comfort and safety of small town Scobey for the cosmopolitan metropolis of San Diego.

Although those concerns niggled at her psyche, what occupied her mind was being so close to Ford. She'd known him a week and already her emotions were way too involved. And, much as she'd fought it, not at all platonic.

The attraction went both ways but that only made the situation more dangerous.

If it had been anyone other than Ford, she'd seriously contemplate jumping his fine bod and riding the electric blaze until it caught fire or fizzled out. But a fling with her co-guardian? Not a smart move.

It opened up too many options for sticky relations down the line.

Moving across country may well solve their custody issues, but could she live so near him and just be friends? Could she watch him date other women, cut their wood, surprise them with sleigh rides and still maintain a personal relationship for the twins' sake?

The part of her that had learned not to trust emotions saw no problems ahead. But every other feminine instinct she possessed shouted out a warning.

And were his motives for asking strictly to make things easier with the twins? Or did he have a more personal reason for wanting her in California? He hadn't inferred any kind of intimate relationship in his request.

Yet he hadn't exactly kept his hands to himself, either.

After taking all that angst into account, none of it really counted. The twins mattered. What was best for them mattered.

Like her, they'd fallen under Ford's charming spell. If a resolution to the custody issue let her keep the twins and allowed them to be closer to Ford, how could she deny them the opportunity?

Ford wanted her to think about moving? Ha, she'd be lucky if she could focus on anything else.

A cheerful fire crackled in the hearth. Soft jazz played in the background. A nice red wine was breathing on the counter. The furniture had been pushed back, and Ford had spread a plush blanket on the carpet in front of the fire. Rachel tossed down several overstuffed pillows.

A more romantic scene would be hard to find.

Until Rachel sprinkled the area with a handful of plastic toys.

Sighing, Ford lifted Cody from the playpen and set him in the middle of the blanket. He shouldn't be thinking about seduction anyway.

Rachel set Jolie next to her brother and then settled against one of the big pillows. Pretty in a soft pink sweater topping black jeans, she looked sexy as hell. She glowed in the flicker of the fire, her appeal due more to good health and hair that looked like she'd just climbed out of bed than makeup or hair gel.

On this, his last night in Montana, they'd decided on a fireside picnic. The twins loved it when he and Rachel got down on the floor and played with them. He wanted tonight to be fun and carefree.

Too bad he didn't feel in the least lighthearted.

A week ago he'd thought he'd come in, save Tony's kids from the clutches of their evil aunt and shoot back to San Diego where he'd leave them in the capable care of his family. Now he dreaded walking out the door, dreaded leaving Rachel and the twins behind.

"You're sure you'll be all right traveling with both kids? They're going to be quite a handful." He dropped to the ground and stretched out.

A flash of panic came and went in her incredibly expressive eyes. "Don't remind me or I may change my mind. I love them so much even though I've only had them a couple of weeks. And they're just two little babies, but they're a lot of work." She cringed. "I mean—"

He held up a hand, shook his head. "I've only been here a week." A ball bounced off him and he rolled it back to Cody, enjoyed the boy's laugh. "I understand too well."

"The idea of traveling with two babies is daunting, but the flight's only a few hours. And you'll be waiting at the other end."

"Right, piece of cake. You'll be in San Diego before you know it."

Again the flash of panic reached her eyes. To distract her, Ford offered to get their dinner, a fragrant stew she'd been slow cooking all day. She waved him off and immediately jumped up to get the meal.

Ford winked at Cody who'd pulled himself up to lean against Ford. "Works every time. Keep it between us men."

He rewarded Cody's cooperation with a cookie and handed one to Jolie. They'd already eaten pasta and peaches. The cookies were a treat that Rachel had set within reach to keep the kids occupied while the two of them ate.

She came back with two steaming bowls of stew, a plate piled high with golden brown biscuits and two glasses of wine. Setting the tray on the ottoman coffee table, she handed him a cloth napkin.

"Sit." He told her. "You did the rest. I'll serve you."

"Okay." She sank down across from him and smiled as he fussed over her dinner.

He liked doing things for her. Talking to her. Looking at her.

They finished the stew, and the wine. He polished off the biscuits and a couple of cookies. All the while chatting and watching the twins play.

Time flew when he wanted each moment to stretch into forever. There was a lesson in relativity for you. Put him in the middle of a nest of terrorists and every minute lasted an hour. Yet tonight, in a room with a lovely, intelligent, witty woman playing with his delightful wards and every hour rushed by in a blink.

He felt his departure looming closer and closer.

Jolie crawled over and he helped her to climb up. Leaning forward she gave him an openmouthed kiss.

"Ah, baby." He wrapped her in a hug, kissing her soft curls. She laid her head on his shoulder breaking his heart with her love and trust.

In the next moment she wiggled to be set free. He sat up and held her fingers as she walked to Rachel who held her arms up ready for the trade off.

Suddenly Jolie let go and took two steps on her own straight into Rachel's arms.

"Oh my God, Ford," Rachel exclaimed. "She walked. Did you see her? Jolie walked. How smart you are." She covered the baby's face in kisses.

"I sure did." Ford clapped to show his pride in the girl. "Isn't she clever."

Cody, seated on the blanket between Ford and the fireplace, clapped, too. And added a gleeful shriek for good measure. He didn't understand what happened, but he felt the excitement.

Proud of herself, Jolie pushed away and turned to face Ford wanting to repeat her new trick.

Grinning ear to ear, he held out his arms and wiggled his fingers. "Come on, baby, come to Ford."

She toddled three steps and he grabbed her before she fell. The game continued with love and laughter. Cody wanted to take his turn, too. He couldn't quite keep his balance, but Ford shared a look with Rachel, they both knew it wouldn't be long.

Finally Rachel called for bedtime. Working together he and Rachel made short work of bathing, changing and tucking the two exhausted babies into their crib. They were asleep before Ford and Rachel backed out of the room.

Back in front of the fire, Ford handed Rachel a second glass of wine. He tapped his rim against hers. "To Jolie."

"I'm glad you were here to share the moment." She sipped around a grin.

"Me, too."

"You're wonderful with the kids." She leaned back against a pillow. "How come some lucky girl hasn't dragged you down the aisle?"

He shrugged. "There have been some special women along the way. But I wasn't ready to give up being a SEAL and they weren't willing to wait."

"No room for compromise? Then it must not have been love."

He cocked a brow. "Don't look now, but your cynicism is showing. You say that like you don't believe in love."

"Hard to believe in something you've never known." She turned her gaze to the fire but not before he saw the wistfulness in the aqua depths.

"You're right, I didn't love them enough to be tempted to break my rule."

She eyed him over her wineglass. "What rule is that?"

"My friends call it Mustang's rule. Basically I've never thought it would be fair to commit to a permanent relationship while I'm a SEAL. Not only for the woman, but for me. I'm not the type to forget my family back home, which is necessary in order to get the job done."

"I suppose it's good to know yourself so well. Being a SEAL obviously means a lot to you."

The admiration in her voice bolstered his confidence. Naturally reticent, the closeness they'd developed encouraged him to share feelings he usually kept hidden.

"Yeah, it does. It means I'm one of the best."

"No," she waved her wineglass back and forth in a negative gesture, "the training did that. What does the job mean to you?"

Nobody had ever made such a distinction before. He had to think for a moment.

"Justice."

"Justice? In what way?"

"There's a lot wrong in the world. A lot of evil people doing evil deeds. As a SEAL, I make a difference. It's not black and white. But nothing ever is."

"You fight for those who can't fight for themselves." She toasted him. "Commendable. But you won't be a SEAL forever. What comes next?"

So intense. Her skin looked translucent in the golden glow of the fire. He traced the gentle curve of her cheek. "You ask some tough questions."

"They're only tough if you don't have the answers."

"Ouch." The woman pulled no punches.

She turned on her side to face him. Her fingers found his on the blanket between them. She traced and played, warming him with her touch.

"Have you thought about training?" She suggested. "I think you'd be very good as an instructor."

His commander had asked the same question. Disdain curled the corner of Ford's lip. "Haven't you ever heard the expression those that can do, and those that can't teach? In this case, those that no longer can, teach."

"You don't believe that." But after meeting his gaze straight on, she changed her tune. "I see you do. Why? Do you have so little respect for those who trained you?"

Her question took him back to BUDS training, to the extreme tests of endurance, lack of sleep and larger than life trainers. He hadn't doubted their skill at the time, hadn't dared. So why did he now?

Because he didn't feel up to the challenge? Or because others would know he could no longer handle the heat of active duty?

"Hum." The low sound in her throat shouted a warning: facetious comment coming. "Surprising you got to be the best with such inferior teachers." She laced her fingers through his, anchoring him even as she challenged him. "Maybe your condescension isn't so much what you believe, but what you think others will believe."

How did she do that, zero right in on the heart of his fears before he'd even recognized them himself?

"You mean disparaging the job is a self-defense against considering it as an option for the future. The great subconscious at work."

"It makes sense. You're a man of action obviously torn about settling down. What better way to put off a decision than to find something wrong with your choices?"

He flopped down on his back. Self-examination was a bitch. "So basically, I'm being a wimp."

"Not at all." She crawled over so she looked into his eyes, compassion rained down on him. "It just proves you're human like the rest of us."

She traced the rasp of his beard with a curved knuckle. For a sassy, standoffish loner, she'd become quite the toucher. He liked it.

"I'm pretty sure they don't let wimps in the SEALs."

He grinned. "Damn straight. You're right about one thing. It's wrong to disrespect my trainers. They put us through hell, but we were ready when we hit the field."

The concern in her eyes lingered. "Just remember if you decide to pursue training. When you were ready, the instructors let you go. What happens after that belongs in the field not in your conscious."

"Heavens." She was talking about his guilt over buying the trip for Tony. In this she was wrong. They weren't the same thing at all. SEALs were ready for anything and everything when they hit the ground. They planned and trained for best and worst case scenarios.

Tony hadn't been prepared, his training hadn't helped him because he couldn't know an earthquake was going to hit. He couldn't save himself or Crystal because an earthquake provided no warning before raining down horrific destruction.

Ford ran his hands over his face, trying to scrub away the senseless helplessness. *Tony couldn't have known an earthquake was going to hit.* So how could Ford?

If only letting go of his guilt was that easy.

He looped his arm around Rachel, tucked her into his side. "How did you get to be so wise?"

"I don't know about wise." She placed her hand on his chest, and he covered it with his, pressing her palm over his heart. "I admit I'm a loner. But I'm also an observer. People and animals, we're not so different. We give love and loyalty until we learn the pain of rejection, we fight when cornered, and we shy away from what scares or hurts us."

Maybe that was Ford's problem, he'd never run scared. From the day he was born sixth in a family of sons, he'd been fighting for his place in the world. Which explained why he didn't recognize his subconscious at work.

And why he kept finding ways to put his hands on Rachel.

He understood the sense in keeping their interaction platonic. But in learning to fight for what he wanted, he pretty much got what he aimed for. Everything in him demanded more than the feel of her in his arms.

He desired all of her, and not for the sake of the twins.

When he got her to San Diego, she'd be his. And he wouldn't let her go until she agreed to stay.

CHAPTER TEN

A NEW storm came in delaying Rachel's flight by a day and a half. She fretted all the way to San Diego. Thankfully the twins behaved beautifully because nothing else was going as planned.

Because of the delay they'd have to go straight to the memorial service. There'd be no time, or place, to change once she arrived so Rachel wore the new black dress she'd bought onto the plane. She counted it a blessing she'd be attending in wrinkled splendor. Better that than not attend at all, which had been her worst and most likely fear until the wheels of the aircraft had left the tarmac.

The past week had been harder than Rachel had ever anticipated. The kids missed Ford, especially Cody. The two had really bonded over the last week. What Rachel hadn't expected was that *she* was missing Ford just as much.

How quickly she'd become accustomed to his presence, his help, his touch.

I wasn't that she hadn't had contact with him. She'd talked to him on the phone every day, sometimes more than once. And Ford had talked to the twins. Okay, so the kids couldn't talk and they usually tired of the conversation long before the adults disconnected, but she and Ford had had things to discuss, travel arrangements to make. They'd done a lot by e-mail but it wasn't the same.

Not the same as hearing his voice, his laugh, his concerns. She liked that he felt able to talk to her. Especially since she'd become a regular Chatty Cathy around him.

This week had taught her two things. One, she loved Cody and Jolie too much not to be a part of their lives. Whatever it took, she'd find a way to retain custody. And two, she was already way too attached to Ford. If she were smart, she'd forget her promise to think about moving to California and hotfoot it back to Montana as fast as possible.

Two insights and both put her heart on the line. Too bad they were at complete odds.

With the airline's help she made it through the San Diego airport with little trouble. A young sailor with a Southern accent and a shy smile met her in the baggage claim. He had a picture of her and an e-mail from Ford introducing Dawson as her driver. He took control of the luggage, and they were soon on the road to Paradise Pines and the memorial service.

Flying in, the plane had seemed to dodge skyscrapers. Now pulling out of the parking lot she saw those buildings across a harbor view framed by palm trees and a bright blue sky.

The third week of November in San Diego looked, and at seventy-eight degrees, felt a lot different than Scobey, Montana.

"Thirty minutes before the service starts." Rachel checked her watch, pulled it off to reset the time. "Mr. Dawson, how long before we get to Paradise Pines?"

He shot her a grin. "Ma'am, no need for the Mr. It's just Dawson."

"Okay. Please call me Rachel. Do you think we'll make the service on time?"

"We're sure going to try. It's early enough we'll miss traffic, and the church is in Alpine, which is about twelve miles this side of Paradise Pines. You just sit back and relax. I'll have you there in a jiffy."

"Thank you, Dawson. Do you have a cell phone so I can check in with Ford?"

"You don't have a cell?" He sounded shocked.

"No." Not much need for one in Scobey. Heck she rarely used her house phone. "May I borrow yours?"

"Sure, but when I tried Mustang twenty minutes ago to tell him your plane was on time, I got an out of service message. It can be sketchy close to the mountains."

Rachel received the same message. Disappointed, she returned the phone to Dawson.

Once on the road both babies fell asleep. Rachel used the time to freshen her makeup and hair. Dabbing perspiration from her temple, she realized her plan to hide the worst of the wrinkles in her dress under a fitted sweater jacket were out the window.

"Y'all want the air on?" Dawson pressed a few buttons on the console, and blessed cool air flowed from the vents.

"Thanks, I'm overdressed for this heat. It was ten degrees when I left Montana this morning. It sure is beautiful here."

Forty minutes after leaving the airport, they pulled to a stop in front of Queen of Angels church in Alpine.

"Here ya'll go. You want help with the little ones?"

"Please." Rachel climbed from the SUV and removed Jolie from her seat. Still sleepy, she laid her head on Rachel's shoulder and whined quietly.

"Shh, baby. It's okay." Rachel soothed Jolie while Dawson came around the car with Cody. When he saw her, Cody held his arms out to Rachel. She quickly distracted him with a teething ring.

Tears stung the back of her throat as she approached the church doors. Sadness welled up inside her. Focused on the logistics of the trip, the purpose had receded to the back of her mind. Now it rushed forward intensified by her disappointment in being too late to sit with Ford.

She'd so wanted to get here in time for the twins to be with Ford. For the four of them to be together to support each other in this time of sorrow.

It touched her to see the small church almost filled to capacity. Quaint colored light filtered down on the mourners from beautiful stained-glass windows.

Ford sat on the aisle in the front row. Rachel longed to go to him, but the service had begun. Not wanting to disturb the ceremony, she directed Dawson into the last row of chairs across the aisle from Ford. At least she could take comfort in seeing him and knowing he was near.

A lot cranky and a whole lot less impressed by the proceedings, Cody immediately protested with an annoyed wail.

Ford knew Cody's cry. He swung around, and across the expanse of the small church, he met Rachel's aqua-blue gaze.

Immediately something in him eased. She was here. Finally. It felt as if a lifetime had passed since he'd last seen her.

And here, mourning the loss of his friend, reliving his part in the untimely deaths of these young, vital loved ones, he needed her by his side.

Nobody understood like Rachel. Nobody was as close to the departed as they were, except the twins. And today more than ever he and Rachel stood for the orphaned siblings.

Uncaring of the assemblage, he rose and went to her, watching as Cody, not content to stay with Dawson, climbed into Rachel's lap so she held both twins.

He stopped in front of her. Jolie looked up, saw him and practically leaped into his arms. Rachel rose with a struggling Cody in her arms. Holding Jolie against his heart, Ford drew the other two into his embrace. For a moment he closed his eyes and rested his forehead against Rachel's, absorbing the peace of her presence, the sheer rightness of them being together again.

This, the four of them standing as a family, was the biggest honor they could bestow on Tony and Crystal's memories.

When the quiet of the church registered, Ford looked up to realize the priest had paused out of respect for them. Taking Rachel's hand, he led her to the front row where his family had shifted to make a seat for her.

"This is my grandmother." He whispered the introduction of the petite, gray-haired woman with alert blue eyes.

"My dear." Gram reached for Rachel's hand, squeezed and held on. "I'm so glad you made it."

Ford held Cody in one arm and placed his other around Rachel's shoulders. She held Jolie on her lap. With his family linked in love and support, he nodded to the priest to continue.

A reception at the Sullivan estate in Paradise Pines followed the service. Many of the mourners, plus a few who couldn't attend the service flowed over to Gram's place. A soft blue color with white gingerbread trim, the large Victorian manor sat on a couple of acres of lush green grass and flowering gardens.

A crush of people filled the living room, parlor and kitchen. Rachel quickly lost track of names and faces. She made an effort to note Ford's brothers, a chore made easier by the resemblance between them. She'd met and liked his sister-in-law, Samantha, a green-eyed blonde, who Rachel learned was a school nurse.

The twins were swept away, oohed and aahed over and pretty much spoiled by everyone.

A self-proclaimed loner, Rachel felt a little out of her element and a lot overwhelmed. If not for the twins, she'd have found a quiet corner to escape to. She felt a tug on her hand and turned to find Ford.

"Come, walk with me." He drew her toward the kitchen and the back door. "Samantha has agreed to watch the twins for a while."

"Oh—" she hung back at that news "—I can't let her do that. She has her own boys to watch. It's too much."

"Look around you." He swept a hand out to indicate the crush of people in the kitchen and beyond to the parlor. "She has plenty of help."

Seeing the babies bouncing on the knees of their uncles, she conceded he was right. The twins were in good hands. With them taken care of, the thought of spending time with Ford held great appeal.

"Okay, for a little while."

He grinned and led her outside. "The last time you said that, you slept in my arms."

"Oh snap." Laughing, she chided him. "That was your fault. You were supposed to wake me." Better to make light than to dwell on the peace and rightness she had felt being in his arms.

She'd found she had little impartiality when it came to him.

"Now you tell me." Stopping in the middle of a garden pathway, he wrapped an arm around her waist and pulled her close. "Let me warn you right now, if you're leaving it up to me to watch out for your virtue, there's an old adage that covers this situation."

"Oh?" Breathless at his nearness, at the intensity in his eyes, she was reminded of his dangerous edge. His sexy, seductive, uncompromising appeal. "What's that?"

"All is fair in love and war." Dipping his head, he claimed her lips in an urgent melding of their mouths. Unlike the slow and dreamy kiss he'd stolen on her porch before leaving Montana, this kiss demanded a response. She answered by rising onto her toes and opening to his sensual assault.

He angled his head, cupped her neck in a sure hand and took the caress deeper. The heat of his passion, the desperation of his touch showed her how much he'd missed her.

She savored the moment as she conveyed her own fierce loneliness.

When he stepped back, she blinked up at him slightly disoriented. His blue eyes were dilated and a red flush stained his earlobes. He glanced behind him, and she realized they still stood in the middle of the garden in full view of the house.

"This way." He led her past the garden and across a green lawn to a small cottage tucked into the back corner of the estate.

"What's this place?" she asked as he foraged for a key in the planter beside the door.

"Guest house." He opened the door and drew her inside. Overstuffed furniture and neutral colors offset with splashes of deep wine gave the room a comfortable feel. "We can talk in here."

Despite his predatory stance and the heat radiating from him, for all his body's readiness to finish what they'd started in the yard, he made no move toward her. Out of respect, she knew, for her. Because she'd made it clear how insane a physical relationship would be in their situation.

Right, sheer lunacy, she thought, as she advanced on him. Just call her crazy.

"Talk?" she asked as he watched her warily. "I think I'm ready to do more than talk."

"It's not that simple between us." He caught her hand when she would have touched him. Holding their clasped hands to his heart, he fought for clarity. "Are you sure this is what you want?"

"Yes." She turned her hand to press against his heavy pounding heart. "I feel alive when you touch me. I feel connected like I never have before." She pushed him toward the couch conveniently located behind him. "I need to feel alive today."

Six feet two inches of hard muscle and bone-deep honor, he didn't budge an inch. "All the more reason I shouldn't take advantage of you."

His resistance should have brought Rachel to her senses. After all, she'd been the one to fight against the attraction between them from the beginning. Except she hadn't lied. Sitting through the memorial service had opened a raw emptiness in her.

Her parents were gone. Her younger sister was gone.

Yes, she'd walked away from them in her youth. She'd had her reasons, and she wouldn't really change her decision if she had it to do again. But she'd always known they were there. That she had family out there somewhere. Now she was alone, except for two young babies.

Her sister's children. Crystal had been young but she'd taken chances. She'd lived, she'd loved, she'd created life.

Today Rachel wanted to take chances, she wanted to live, and she wanted to make love with Ford. If that meant seducing him, she was up to the challenge.

And she promised herself, no regrets.

"You won't be taking advantage of me," she assured him as she slipped behind him where he couldn't hold her off with his superior strength. Twining her arms around his waist she leaned into him, her breasts flat against his back, her cheek between his shoulder blades. "I intend to take advantage of you."

He laughed and she smiled as she felt the rumble vibrate through his body. She wanted this man, this body, this moment more than she'd ever longed for anyone else in her life.

"Am I going to have to get rough with you?" She let her hands wander, enjoyed touching him, thrilled at the tactile contrast between soft silk and hard muscles. He caught her hands when they reached his belt buckle.

He turned around, caught her face in his hands and kissed her with burning urgency.

"Rough can be fun," he whispered against her open mouth, "but it's not necessary. As long as you're sure."

Satisfaction and anticipation ignited her blood. Melting against him, she met his mouth, sank into the kiss. She felt more than alive in his arms, she felt energized, vitalized.

"Ford, we said goodbye to Crystal and Tony today. If life were fair at all, they would have lived to see the twins' first steps, to walk them to kindergarten, to teach them to drive. Tony would have escorted Jolie down the aisle and coached Cody on the finer points of throwing a football.

"But life isn't even close to fair. It's a kick in the teeth. So instead of Tony and Crystal, the twins are stuck with us. I love the twins. I can't even remember what life was like without them, but I'd give them up quick as a heartbeat if it would bring my sister back."

"Shh." Ford pressed a finger to her lips, followed the gesture with a soft kiss. "Don't go there. It's useless speculation, and you're the one who kicked my butt about second-guessing fate."

"I know. I'm sorry." She wiped away a tear she'd sworn to keep locked away and almost lost it when he captured her finger to absorb the tear with his kiss. She cleared her throat. "I didn't mean to get maudlin. My point is I'm beyond sure. I want to be with you. More, I need the comfort and escape I'll find in your arms."

To show him just how certain, her fingers went to the buttons of her new black dress. She'd been looking for a reason to get out of the dress since she landed in San Diego. No better reason than this.

"Make me forget that they're gone, Ford. Let me remind you why it's good to be alive."

She released the third button, revealing the first rise of cleavage before Ford took over.

"Dynamite, you did that the minute you opened your door in Scobey." He made short work of the rest of the buttons. "Lucky for both of us, I'm a SEAL. The Boy Scouts have nothing on us for being prepared."

He was talking about birth control, telling her he had it covered. His assurance warmed her. She'd been running on emotion, hadn't thought that far ahead. Thank goodness his cool head ruled.

The heat of his breath caressed the curve of her neck as the dress fell off her shoulders and to the floor, leaving her in nothing but a black bra and thong.

The sexy lingerie was another new purchase. Obviously her subconscious at work.

His eyes cherished her before his mouth began the same downward journey. Time slowed and lengthened while desire bloomed.

Suddenly her clothes were gone and he lowered her to the downy softness of a bed. Sensation replaced all else as he took her to heights she'd never known before. Precious, he made her feel so precious, using his mouth, fingers, and body to worship every inch of her.

She reciprocated touch for touch, kiss for kiss, stroke for stroke, thrilling when she drew groans of satisfaction from him. Wrapping her arms around him, she clung on tightly and followed him to the explosive realm of completion.

* * *

Ford sighed, contentment flowing through him along with the soft peach scent of Rachel's shampoo. He tightened his arm around her and buried his nose in her hair.

She smelled so good, felt so good. He'd known they'd be volatile in bed, but he'd been wrong. Oh, there'd been explosive chemistry between them, bursting gratification. But what they'd just shared went beyond the physical.

He cared about her and that infused the act with a special sense of fulfillment. She'd talked about being connected. He now knew what she'd meant. He couldn't remember the last time he'd felt so close to another human being.

She slipped past his defenses with her sassy attitude and fragile vulnerability. Yet he hadn't realized how much he missed her until she hadn't made it to the church before the start of the memorial service.

Even surrounded by family and friends, he'd felt as if he were all alone. Then she arrived and seeing her and the twins had grounded him, allowed him to make it through the emotional ceremony.

Now more than ever he wanted her to move to San Diego. With her here he wouldn't worry about Cody and Jolie. He'd have felt good about leaving them with his family, but as she'd pointed out, Rachel was their family. The twins wouldn't have to earn her love. She gave it unconditionally.

And he liked the thought of her being here when he came home between assignments. It was the best of both worlds.

* * *

This time Rachel slid away from a sleeping Ford. She barely breathed until she'd retrieved her clothes and ducked into the bathroom.

No regrets. That's what she promised herself. She'd taken a chance and received glorious results. Being with Ford exceeded all her fantasies. And revealed a scary new facet to their relationship.

She loved him.

She loved his honor, his gentleness, his generosity. She loved that he knew the sound of Cody's cry, that he had shed tears at the loss of his friend, that he loved and respected his grandmother. She loved his tough as nails exterior and soft as marshmallow interior. Through him she'd discovered that duty and responsibility weren't always used to squash down those in your care, but sometimes meant dealing with compromise and hard decisions.

All these soft feelings scared her to death. Because she'd be a fool to mistake his passion for anything more than casual affection. She knew the sad truth of unrequited love too well to risk rejection when the twins' future hung in the balance.

No doubt about it, her best course of action was to pretend this little incident never happened. She slipped out of the bathroom and made it all the way to the front door, when Ford spoke behind her.

"Don't go."

Her hand tightened on the doorknob. Two seconds more and she'd have been on the other side of the door.

"I don't just mean now. I mean for good." She felt

his heat as he came to stand behind her. Snuggling close to her back, he ran his hand down her arm to link his fingers with hers. "Please stay."

The words seemed to echo in the stillness. His request brought her dilemma front and center.

Electing to remain turned away in case any of her newly acknowledged emotions showed on her face, she responded, "I promised I'd think about moving. I know it's the perfect solution to the custody issue, but it's a big decision. I need time."

"I don't mean just move to San Diego." He gently turned her to face him, traced the curve of her cheek with a knuckle. "I mean stay with me, move in with me."

Stay with Ford? The thought both terrified and exhilarated Rachel. Yes, she loved him and she longed to be with him, but her life was in Montana, what she had to offer the twins was in Montana. She could write anywhere, but her home was in Montana.

Dare she give up the life she'd made, which until a month ago was all she'd had to define herself?

"I'm so glad you made it in time for the service." The huskiness in his voice revealed emotions close to the surface. "I was lost until you got there."

"Oh, Ford." His unexpected vulnerability tore her apart.

"It was important to me that you and the twins were there because we've become a family." He kissed her ear, her neck, the corner of her mouth. "Let's make a home together, you, me and the twins. We can move in here until we find a bigger place."

She looked into his eyes, gauged his expression. She saw earnestness along with affection, determination, and desire in his sapphire gaze.

But love? Could what he felt for her grow into something stronger?

She'd taken a huge chance by making love with him, and suffered no regrets. Could she take it one step further?

"It's too complicated. We have to think of the future."

His mouth teased hers. "We won't let it get complicated. We'll take it one day at a time. As long as we're honest with each other and put the twins first, we keep it simple."

Her mind urged caution, but her heart wanted to believe. She threaded her fingers through his silky, dark hair and pulled him down for a kiss.

Against his mouth, she whispered. "I'll stay."

CHAPTER ELEVEN

RACHEL followed Ford into the kitchen of the main house. Only the family remained. His brothers sat around the huge butcher-block table while Gram and Samantha watched over the four children from armchairs near the fireplace in what used to be the parlor. Ford's cousin Mattie stood at the counter making a new pot of coffee.

Laughter and chatter filled the room, happy sounds compared to the somber gathering they'd left behind earlier. The rich scent of brewing coffee added to the homey feel of the room.

"I'll take a cup of that." Ford opened a cupboard and took down a mug. He looked at Rachel and at her nod grabbed a second mug. While he waited for the coffee to finish, he faced the room.

"I have an announcement. Rachel has decided to move to California. We're going to get a place and raise the twins together."

Silence greeted his statement. For five full seconds. Then pandemonium broke out. Everyone started talking at once, well wishes overlapped questions of concern, and advice on buying versus renting.

Unused to such chaos Rachel just let it wash over and around her until Gram came forward and squeezed Rachel's hands.

"My dear, welcome." Gram kissed Rachel's cheek.

Rachel gave her a hug. "Thank you, Mrs. Sullivan. I also want to tell you how much I appreciate all you, and your family, did in arranging the memorial service today."

"Call me Gram." The older woman waved away the formalities. "I was happy to help honor Tony and Crystal. Tony was dear to me. Crystal, I only met a couple of times, but she was full of life, and she loved those babies. Such a loss, for them, for you, for the world."

The simple sympathy caught Rachel unawares. Tears swelled up and overflowed. She'd done so well at maintaining her cool through the day, keeping her tears to the service. But then it all suddenly caught up with her. So much had happened, not least of all discovering her love for Ford, that Gram's words of comfort tipped Rachel over the edge.

"It's okay, you go ahead and cry." Gram pulled Rachel into her arms and rubbed her back soothingly.

Instantly Ford appeared at their sides, but Gram shooed him away. "I've got her, she just needs a little cry is all. Why don't you put together a plate of food to heat when she's ready? I noticed she didn't eat much earlier."

Ford kissed her hair and whispered, "Take your time. I'm here if you need me." Then went off to do as directed.

So gentle, so sweet. Rachel just sobbed harder.

Gram led her to a couch in the quiet of the living room. "I've got you," Gram said, holding Rachel in her arms. "Go ahead and cry."

Unable to resist the comfort of a motherly embrace, something she'd known so little of in her life, Rachel clung to Gram and let the tears flow.

"I like it." Rachel glanced around the medium-size kitchen of the prospective rental in Alpine. She'd insisted on renting at this point. Everything was moving so fast, falling so easily into place, she didn't completely trust it.

She and Ford had looked at houses with larger kitchens, but she liked the openness of this one. It reminded her of the setup of her home in Montana. No island, but a breakfast bar separated the kitchen from the family room. Like Gram's parlor, the family room had a fireplace.

Cautiously optimistic, Rachel could see the four of them spending lots of happy moments in these two rooms.

"I like it, too." Ford opened a pantry door, nodded and closed it again. "Only three bedrooms, but that's enough until the twins get older. The master suite is huge, great walk-in shower."

"We don't really need three bedrooms. We could find a two bedroom for less."

Shaking his head, Ford came to her, curved his arm around her waist and pulled her close. "We're only going to have two bedrooms and an office. I want you to have your own space to write."

"Ford—"

"Shh." He stopped her with a kiss. "I know the rent seems high compared to Scobey, but money is not a problem. We can afford any place we want."

Money wasn't a problem for him. He'd explained he held an interest in the family jewelry store, Sullivans' Jewels. Which apparently did quite well. She found the family's net worth somewhat intimidating.

She had decent savings, by Montana standards, but she couldn't help thinking she'd have been in real trouble if she'd had to fight Ford for custody.

"Money does matter." She wouldn't be a slouch in this relationship. Her independence had been too important to her for too long for her to change now. "I want to pay my share."

"You will." He promised, sweeping his mouth across hers. "You already have with all you bought for the babies. And I promise to let you pay for the utilities."

Her tension eased at his assurances and the look of understanding in his eyes.

"Okay, then." She leaned against him and looked around the kitchen one more time. "So, shall we put in an application for this place?"

"Yeah. We can take it with us to fill out tonight, and you can drop it off tomorrow."

He'd gone back to work the Monday after the

memorial service. And she missed him so much. Gram, Samantha and Mattie kept her company and helped with the twins so Rachel got plenty of time to write. Yet she still lived for the end of the day when he returned home to her arms.

"Sounds like a plan." She agreed. "The ad said available for immediate occupancy. Do you think we'll be able to move in over the long weekend?"

"That's the beauty of city life, babe." He tucked a stray lock of hair behind her ear. "Except for Thanksgiving the rest of the weekend is business as usual."

"Great, then we can move this weekend." She made to move away, but Ford held her in place.

"About this weekend. There's something I have to tell you."

Her heart started to pound, her mouth went dry, and dread grew heavy in her gut. She knew. By the seriousness of his expression and the leeriness shadowing the blue in his eyes.

"You're leaving on assignment."

"Yeah." He rubbed his forehead. "We're already on call. When we go in tomorrow we'll go into lockdown for planning and prep. I don't know when I'll see you again."

Wow, here it was.

Fear for him rose up in a tidal wave. She wanted to scream out a protest, to say no he couldn't go. He couldn't leave her and the twins. But she'd known what she'd been signing up for when she'd agreed to stay, to be a part of his life.

He supported her independence; she owed him the same respect, the freedom to be who he was. It's the advice she'd given Crystal; Rachel would be a fool not to take it herself.

Of course, that didn't stop the emotions from roiling through her. But she refused to give into the worry and dread, instead she chose to make the most of the time she had before he left tomorrow morning.

"Let's go home." Lifting onto her toes, she kissed the frown from his mouth. "Do you think Alex and Samantha would baby-sit? I want you to myself tonight."

In the predawn light Ford stood quietly next to the bed. Already packed, his duffle waited by the front door.

Time to say goodbye.

He didn't want to do it. Which set up all kinds of conflicting emotions inside him, satisfaction at being able to rejoin his SEAL team but reluctance at leaving Rachel. And regret that he'd miss a moment of the twins' development—he just knew Cody would walk any day now.

Ford stood gazing down at Rachel. Her short blond hair curled softly around her face while her long dark lashes fanned across her creamy skin. She looked like an angel tucked beneath the sheets. The last of the moonlight slanted a dim glow over an alabaster shoulder.

He grinned. A naked angel.

She'd slept little if at all during the night. His smile

lingered at the corner of his mouth. They'd spent hours making love, from hard and fast, to sweet and sassy, to heart wrenchingly slow.

Only when they were both exhausted did he wrap her in his arms to sleep. Even with all the expended energy he knew she'd slept little. She'd pretended to sleep, as she was doing now.

To save them from the moment of goodbye.

He'd done that in the past, slipped out after a sensuous farewell. Because it was easier for everyone that way. More anonymous, less intense, especially when the emotions didn't run that deep.

Rachel deserved better than a hit-and-run. Standing over her, with death a true possibility on the other side of the door, saying goodbye rated as the hardest thing he'd ever done.

For that reason, it had to be face-to-face, eye-to-eye.

As if her thoughts brought her to the same conclusion at the same time, her stunning aqua eyes opened. All the anxiety and uncertainty she felt showed in her gleaming gaze.

"Hey," she said softly, sitting up so the sheet pulled tight across her breasts.

"Hey." Ford sat down next to her. Needing to touch, he cupped the back of her neck and ran his thumb over the silkiness of her cheek.

Because the words wouldn't come, he bent and put his feelings in a kiss, all his adoration, passion and torment. Her response equaled his in emotional impact.

When it reached the point where he needed to climb

into bed or pull back, he lifted his head. "Promise me you'll let my family help you."

That earned him a wan smile. "I promise."

Knowing the time had come, he stood. He held out a hand. "Walk me out?"

She slipped out of bed, wrapped the sheet around herself and laced her fingers through his. He led her to the front door where his duffle waited.

Pulling her into his arms, he pressed his nose into her mussed curls. "Kiss the twins for me."

"I will." She looked up, framed his face in trembling hands. "Wild Mustang, come back to me."

I will, the words were on the tip of his tongue, but they both knew it was a promise he couldn't make. Instead he gave her one last, hard kiss and stepped out the door.

"Oh my goodness, Cody is walking," Samantha called out, drawing everyone's attention to where she and Rachel were sitting on the floor in front of the parlor fireplace.

Gathered together for Thanksgiving Day. Rachel sat among Ford's family in Gram's house and clapped along with the others as Cody wobbled from her hold to Samantha's. Her pride in Cody's accomplishment only suffered from Ford's absence. She knew he'd regret missing this special moment.

"Hey, little buddy, walk to Uncle Cole."

The Sullivans were a rowdy crowd, boisterous and giving. They'd welcomed her and the twins into their midst with warmth and generosity. The twins thrived in the loving environment, which showed in Cody's zigzag journey around the room as he walked from uncle to aunt to uncle.

Rachel did her best to fit in, but too many years on her own gave her a reticence that couldn't be shrugged aside so easily. Ford's brothers, bless them, gave her both space and casual affection.

Gram, Samantha and Ford's cousin Mattie drew her in and made her one of the crowd. No distance allowed here. Rachel accepted their good-hearted advice and interference with surprising tolerance.

Leaving the twins in the capable hands of the family, Rachel slipped out to the front porch. Last week's heat had given way to a cold front, and the nip in the air made her wish she'd grabbed her sweater.

In moments like this one she missed Ford all the more, not just for her sake but for his as well. His excitement when Jolie had walked had matched Rachel's. She knew he'd be disappointed to miss this milestone in Cody's life.

The door opened behind her and Ford's oldest brother Alex stepped out on the porch. Tall, dark and broad, with the Sullivan blue eyes, the resemblance between him and Ford was striking. But there were differences, too. Alex carried more weight and showed the beginnings of gray in his hair and he lacked Ford's dangerous edge.

"I guess you're missing Ford about now." Alex came to stand beside her.

"Yeah." She leaned her hip against the railing and faced him. "And I guess you've come out to give me the third degree."

He shrugged and propped a shoulder against a post. "What makes you think that?"

"I know animals. This is your pack. You need to check out the new member."

"I won't apologize for protecting my family." Totally confident, neither his stance nor his expression changed.

"I don't expect you to," she assured him, though she didn't back down. "Now I'm responsible for the twins, I have a whole new respect for what a parent will do to protect their family."

"And how far will you go for the twins, Rachel?"

A half smile tugged at the corner of her mouth. "Somehow I don't think you're referring to the distance between Montana and San Diego."

"Once Ford sets his mind to something, it takes dynamite to change his course. He left here intending to bring the twins back, to raise them within the family. And that's exactly what he did. But you, you're a surprise."

She lifted a brow. "And you want to know if I'm taking advantage of him?"

"You've known my brother for little more than a month, yet you're living with him, raising children together. That's damn fast work."

"Do you think it would be so easy to make Ford do something he didn't want to do?"

He rolled his eyes. "You're a beautiful woman,

what's not to want. You should know Ford isn't ready to settle down. For a commitment. He's not called Mustang for nothing."

"I don't think you give him enough credit, which is a shame, because I know your opinion matters to him." She crossed her arms over her chest. "Ford is the most generous, caring man I know."

Alex cocked a dark brow. "He's my brother, I think I know him better than you."

"You should, but you don't. You ought to know by now he doesn't like to be told what to do. The two most important things in his life are the SEALs and his family. He's committed to both. Having to choose between them is tearing him apart. A little support from you would be helpful, and I'm not talking about giving advice. I'm talking about supporting whatever decision he makes regardless of whether you approve or not."

By Alex's stark expression she saw she'd hit a nerve, had given him something to think about. Rachel drew in a deep breath, breathed out. She needed to compose herself. Being with Ford meant being a part of his family.

"It's hard as hell," she said more calmly. "But that's what I'm offering him, because it's what I'd want from him, and I respect him too much to force my fears on him." She forced a smile. "It may reassure you to know no promises have been made between us. None are necessary."

Pensive, Alex stuffed his hands in his pockets. He frowned as he focused on her.

"Is that fair to you?" he asked.

Now she smiled for real. "You can't help yourself, can you? You have to take care of everyone." She moved to him, watched the wariness come into his eyes, but all she did was give him a kiss on the cheek. "You're sweet, but this is where Ford and I are right now. As you said, we've only known each other for a month. We'll work it out."

"And that's good enough for you?"

"Oh, yeah. Mustangs are famous for being wild and free, but they make great domestic animals if you don't break their spirit." And because she'd reached the limit on what she felt comfortable revealing to him, she turned to the house. At the door she stopped and glanced back at him. "Alex?"

He looked over his shoulder at her, one dark brow lifted in query.

"Ford has a nickname for me, do you know what it is?"

Alex shook his head. "What?"

"Dynamite." With a wink and a grin, she stepped into the house.

Rachel spent Friday and Saturday packing and shopping for furniture. Before he left, Ford had arranged for the baby furniture at her place in Montana to be packed up and shipped to Alpine. The rest of the stuff could wait until she had time to make a trip.

In the meantime Samantha volunteered to help so they left the children in the care of Sami's regular baby-sitter and set out to put a home together.

The first course of action was to inventory Ford's condo in downtown San Diego to see what they wanted to take and what they'd need to buy new.

"I like this dining room set, but I think I prefer using the living room furniture from the cottage to this black leather." Rachel stood hands on her hips surveying the setup.

"I agree and Gram said you were welcome to use whatever you need." Sami swept a long length of blond hair behind her ear. "What's Ford going to do with this place?"

"He talked about renting it. I told him we could stay here, but he wanted the twins and me to be closer to the family when he was gone." Rachel walked down the hall into the master bedroom. "Oh, this is beautiful."

A lovely king-size mahogany framed bed dominated the room. Matching bedside tables and a large bureau completed the set. The comforter was a scrumptious red satin with oriental motifs.

Rachel loved it, but only one thing came to mind when she looked at it. She met Sami's gaze.

"New bedroom set," they both said at the same time.

CHAPTER TWELVE

BY SHEER force of will and instincts honed by years of experience, Ford made it through the assignment without getting anyone killed. Himself included.

Rachel invaded his mind every minute of every day. And the twins, he couldn't help wondering whether they were all safe and sound.

While the team worked to rescue a politician's daughter from a hostage situation, he worried about his little corner of the world.

Lord, he thought, he'd missed Rachel in the week between leaving Montana and her arrival in San Diego. The whole world had seemed dimmer that week.

He'd known before she'd even got to San Diego, he wouldn't be letting her leave. He'd been prepared for a fight, and to do whatever it took to win.

Instead she'd surprised him with a soft and giving acceptance he knew had cost her hugely in trust and independence. The next week he'd literally and figuratively lived in Paradise.

Everything fell into place. He went back to work.

Gram helped Rachel with the twins during the day so she had time for her writing. And at night they'd been together as a family until they closed the bedroom door and he had Rachel all to himself.

"Hey man, how you doing?" Hoss, massive, dark skinned, bald headed, and a straight shooter on and off assignment sat down next to Ford.

"Not good." Ford bent his head, scrubbed at his eyes with the heels of his hands. "I was a mess out there."

"You held it together."

"Barely. And that kind of distraction gets people killed." A SEAL always knew danger was an inherent part of any assignment, but they put that out of their mind and did the job.

In the past Ford had embraced the impartiality needed to accomplish the task. This time he couldn't forget he had people at home counting on his safe return. People he longed to see again, to hold in his arms, to cherish.

"So what *are* you going to do?" Hoss asked.

Ford summoned a grin he didn't feel. "I called ahead, got a meeting with the CO to explore my options."

"You know Intelligence would scoop you up in a heartbeat."

Ford rubbed a weary hand over the tight muscles of his neck. "Yeah. Man, you remember BUDS training?"

"Hell, yeah. You thinking of training? Those instructors are tough bastards." Hoss eyed Ford thoughtfully, nodded. "You'd be great."

"You think? Rachel suggested it. The idea is growing on me."

"Woman knows her man." Hoss held up his hand and they bumped knuckles. "Good luck, Mustang."

When he reached the base, Ford went straight to the commander's office. He knocked, and then stepped inside at his CO's wave.

Ford saluted. "Sir. I'm here to request a transfer."

With all the excitement of the move and ending the day in a new house, the twins were over excited and refused to settle down on Sunday night. Rachel glanced at her watch. After nine. She'd hoped to get some unpacking done, instead she threw pillows down on the living room carpet and let the kids loose.

Restrained most of the day both of them immediately climbed up to practice their new favorite thing, walking.

"You two are tired, so be careful." Rachel perched on the edge of the sofa ready to spring into action if needed.

Jolie grinned and walked straight to Rachel.

"Hey, beautiful. You're getting good at this aren't you? Cody has some catching up to do doesn't he?"

Hearing his name Cody turned from where he stood by the coffee table and waved his arms. His weight shifted and he started to fall.

"No." Rachel saw it happening, saw it and couldn't stop it. She jumped up but couldn't reach Cody before he fell hard against the edge of the hardwood table. He twisted trying to compensate, but instead of saving himself he hit the table hard splitting his forehead open.

Cody screamed.

Blood spurted everywhere.

Jolie began to cry.

"Oh God. Oh God." Heart in her throat Rachel scooped Cody up in one arm and Jolie in the other and rushed to the bathroom. She put Jolie in the dry tub and took Cody to the sink.

"It's okay, baby, it's okay." God she prayed it was okay.

She tried to wash the wound but the gash was deep and wouldn't stop bleeding. Her mind spun as she considered what to do. She tore a new pillowcase into strips and wrapped a makeshift bandage around his head.

The hospital, she needed to get Cody to the hospital.

Grabbing a baby in each arm she carried them both to the crib, and then went to the kitchen to call Alex and Samantha. They'd left an hour ago. She hated to drag them back, but she didn't know where the hospital was, and if they could watch Jolie...

"Shoot." No answer. And no time to keep trying. She tried Cole's number, but again received no reply. She elected not to leave messages because they'd only worry and there'd be no way for them to reach her.

Damn. First thing tomorrow morning she was getting a cell phone.

It was after two when Ford reached home. He'd decided to stop off in Alpine in case Rachel had managed to arrange the move over the long weekend as she'd wanted to do. And sure enough lights blazed from several rooms.

He didn't have a key yet so he knocked. Then knocked louder. No answer. Utilizing skills he usually restricted to national security, he unlocked the door and stepped inside.

He immediately spotted the blood in the hall, in the living room. Adrenaline shot through his system.

"Rachel," he called out, following the blood trail down the hall. His stomach flipped when he spied the mess in the bathroom. "Rachel!"

He pulled out his phone, called Gram. She hadn't heard from Rachel since early evening. Next he tried Alex and Sami. Alex reported they'd left Rachel and the twins around eight-thirty. Everyone had been fine. They had a missed call from her a little after nine, but she hadn't left a message.

"Grossmont is the nearest hospital," Alex reasoned.

"I'm on my way." Ford was already climbing into his Jeep.

"I'll call and see if I can learn anything. Don't worry, Ford, we'll find them. Was Rachel's SUV in the driveway?"

"No." Ford cursed. "And I didn't stop to check the garage."

"It was in the driveway when we left, that means Rachel was able to drive them wherever they went. That's something at least."

"Yeah." Ford disconnected. His stomach churned. Bloody scenarios raced through his head. The fact that Rachel had been able to drive offered little consolation. He just wanted to find them all safe.

Then he'd talk to Rachel about taking off without letting anyone know where she was going or what had happened.

He made the twenty-mile drive to Grossmont Hospital in twelve minutes. He stormed up to the nurse's station. "I'm looking for Rachel Adams. Are they here?"

"Ford?" The voice came from behind him. "Ford!" He turned in time to catch Rachel as she launched herself into his arms. "I'm so glad you're here."

"Rachel." He breathed her name, more a prayer of thanksgiving than a greeting. He squeezed her to him, buried his face in her hair. "Tell me you're all right."

Rachel wrapped her arms around Ford and held on tight. For the first time in hours her world felt right. Tears held at bay for so long broke free. She clung to Ford, wanting nothing more than to burrow into the safety of his arms.

"Rachel!" He pushed her away, held her at arm's length. Concern bleached his features of color. "Talk to me. What happened?"

Swiping tears from her face she struggled for composure. "Cody—" She hiccupped and a fresh wave of tears flowed as she remembered her panic and fear when he hurt himself.

"What about Cody?" Ford walked around her to get to the twins in their double stroller. Both babies slept. Cody sported a white bandage across the length of his forehead. "My God." Ford crouched down by the boy. "Tell me what happened."

"He fell." Her breath hitched; again she brushed the wetness from her cheeks. "It was after everyone left. Th-they, the twins wouldn't settle down so I l-let them out to walk around."

"Cody is walking?"

She nodded, breathed deep. "On Thanksgiving. He fell tonight, hit his head on the coffee table. It took six stitches to close the gash."

"Good God." Ford shot to his feet and rolled the stroller outside. He stopped and confronted her. "Alex said you were moving all weekend, that they didn't leave until after eight. You all had to be exhausted. How could you be so careless?"

Stunned Rachel backed up a step. She blinked away the last of the tears. "What?"

Ford's cell phone rang. He took it out, flipped it open. "Hi, Alex. Thanks, I found them. Cody fell and cut his head. We're taking him home now." He listened. "Yeah, she's fine. Hey can I give you a call tomorrow? Thanks."

He flipped the phone closed, pocketed it. "Let's go. I'll drive. We can leave my Jeep here and pick it up tomorrow." He held out his hand. "Give me your keys."

Chilled inside and out by his cold and accusatory attitude, she led the way to her SUV, helped put the children in their seats, stored the stroller in the back, but when it came to climbing in next to him the tension broke her.

"I don't think so." She crossed her arms under her breasts. "Not until you explain your accusation."

He stalked around the vehicle to confront her. "You're the one that needs to explain a few things." He paced away, then back, his movements jerky, out of control.

"Do you know what it was like to walk into the house tonight and find blood everywhere? To call my brother and find out you couldn't be bothered to leave a message about what happened or to say where you were?" He raked both hands through his hair, shook his head. "On top of that selfishness I find out this could all have been avoided if you'd used a little common sense."

"Enough," she demanded. Not since he'd first landed on her doorstep had he been so critical of her. So cold. She'd spent the last hours wishing he were here to help her, to hold her. To make everything all right. How cruel of fate to grant her wish only to deliver this antagonistic stranger.

"I've just spent four hours beating myself up over Cody's accident, but I'll be damned if I'll stand here and take criticism from you when you don't know what you're talking about." She shook with anger, with disappointment, with betrayal.

She spread her arms wide, exhibiting the rust-colored bloodstains on her blue shirt and jeans. "Yeah, there was blood in the house, lots of it, so excuse me if I chose to get Cody to the hospital rather than chase down your family, who'd already spent the weekend helping us move. And no I didn't leave a message because I couldn't wait for them to respond, and I didn't know where I was going so why worry them unnecessarily?"

Beyond weary, she swayed where she stood.

He'd gone still and quiet during her diatribe, now seeing signs of her weakness, he reached for her arm. "Come on, let's go home, we'll talk about this tomorrow."

"I'm not going anywhere with you." She dodged his touch, rounded the hood of the SUV and got behind the wheel. He followed her, but when he reached for the door handle she hit the locks.

"Rachel, open the door." He knocked on the window. A frown drew his dark brows together. He looked tired and drawn. "You're upset. Let me drive."

Tears came back, blurring her vision. She blinked them away and put the car in gear. She drove away without a backward glance.

Rachel was greeted for the empty streets—it compensated for the fact that her full attention wasn't on the road. On a lonely stretch of Freeway 8 at 2:55 in the morning reality hit her square in the face. Ford only asked her to stay so he could leave. By agreeing to stay she'd only set herself up for a repeat of her childhood, to live where she was valued more for what she did— care for the twins—than for who she was—a strong and independent woman.

A strong and independent woman foolishly in love.

Shame on her for dropping her guard, for believing, even for a moment, something special had developed between her and Ford. Love of the self-sacrificing, unconditional variety didn't exist between men and women.

Giving up her home, setting aside the protection of her loner ways had earned her nothing more than a broken heart.

Disillusioned, angry with him and herself, she realized she couldn't stay in San Diego. When Cody was well enough to travel she'd take the twins and fly back to Montana. With the decision made she went numb, her emotions and subconscious shutting down to protect her from the too familiar sense of loss and betrayal.

Aware of Ford following behind her, she almost didn't go to the house in Alpine, the house she'd taken such joy in preparing for their family, but it took more energy than she possessed to think where else to go.

She parked in the driveway, released Jolie from her seat and carried her to her crib, carefully avoiding any sight of the blood throughout the house. Cleanup could wait until later.

Ford arrived with Cody, gently lowering the baby into his crib. Rachel felt his gaze as she changed Jolie and got the little girl situated. She ignored him, unable to deal with him any further tonight.

She breathed easier when he moved to the door without speaking. She'd be even happier if he'd left the room entirely, but he lingered by the door watching her.

Forcing herself to focus, she went to Cody and woke him as instructed, checking his pupils and level of alertness. Both seemed fine so she changed him and then lifted him and pointed to Ford, because regardless of what was or wasn't between the two of them, she knew he cared about the twins.

"Look who's here," she said.

A grin broke across Cody's face and he held out his little arms.

Ford cradled Cody against his chest and felt something click into place deep inside. Cody and Jolie had pulled on his heartstrings until his heart had grown big enough to embrace them both. He had a lifetime love affair going on here.

Trailing Rachel to the kitchen where she prepared a bottle, Ford knew she was part of the package. More, she was the heart of it.

Boy he'd blown it big time tonight. An overload of adrenaline had caused him to come out blazing when he should have provided a strong, comforting refuge in the face of her ordeal.

Rachel had told him how she'd left home at such a young age because she'd felt unwelcome within her own family, and what did he do but make her feel an outsider again by putting more importance on informing his family of the emergency than of praising her for her handling of the distressing incident.

"I'm sorry," he said to her back as she stood waiting for the microwave to heat Cody's bottle.

Her shoulders tensed; otherwise she gave no sign of hearing him.

"I'm an idiot. No, that's not strong enough." He crossed the room to stand behind her. "I'm an insensitive ass."

"If you're waiting for an argument from me, you won't get it." The microwave dinged. She made no move to remove the bottle. Or to face Ford.

Not a problem, Cody was already sleeping on Ford's shoulder.

"I've decided to return to Montana." With the declaration, Rachel turned to look him in the eye. "And I'm taking the twins with me."

"No." The hurt and lack of hope in her gaze tore him apart. He'd done that to her.

For a man of action he'd sure been slacking. He'd failed to tell her of his feelings, been afraid to admit his love just as he'd been afraid to give up the excitement of his job. It was time he stepped up. "You can't go. I won't let you leave. I love you."

Rachel frantically shook her head, sidestepped away from Ford, and wrapped her arms around herself.

"You have no say." She completely disregarded his declaration of love as too late, too convenient. "I'll pay for the month's rent. The furnishings can be returned. You're right, your family is special, the twins are lucky to have them in their lives, but I'm keeping them until you leave the SEALs behind. And you're going to let me because it's the decent thing to do."

Her throat tightened before she finished, a sure sign tears threatened. Refusing to break down in front of him now, she started for the kitchen door.

"Please put Cody in his crib. I have to wake him every hour but first I have to get out of these bloody clothes."

"Rachel, wait—"

"No, just no." She escaped before he tempted her with his easy charm.

In her room she grabbed clean clothes and locked herself in the bathroom where she let the shower wash away the tears. She'd started the day with so much joy, with such anticipation of finally living her dream of love and a family. Hearing Ford announce his love should have been the ultimate high of the day instead of a devastating betrayal of everything good between them.

Unable to stay hidden forever, she dressed and opened the door.

Ford leaned against the doorjamb. He held up a packet of folded papers.

"What's this?"

"Transfer forms. I talked to my CO when we reached base. A master chief instructor at the training facility is retiring next month. I'll be taking his place."

"Why?" She took the papers, opened them to read. "I thought you wanted to finish on your own terms."

"These are my terms." He led her over to the bed, sat down beside her. "I was a mess in the field. I couldn't get you or the twins out of my head. I love you, Rachel. Nothing is more important to me than building a life with you, Jolie and Cody. And maybe a baby of our own someday."

Oh, unfair. Longing and fear battled inside her. "I can't. Tonight—"

"Tonight I overreacted. I was so scared. When I

found you all safe I went into an adrenaline crash and I lashed out. But I was wrong. You were smart, and brave, and you made all the right choices."

She shook her head, she wanted to believe but she didn't dare.

"It's no use, you know." He brought her hand to his mouth and kissed her palm. "I know you love me."

That burned her; she snatched her hand away. "You think you know what?"

"You don't fool me. Not once during the argument at the hospital did you throw my job up at me. No reference to missing the twins' first Thanksgiving, to having to handle the move on your own, or to blaming me for not being there when Cody fell. All kill shots. But you didn't make them, why not?"

She looked away from him. "It was already ugly enough."

"Uh-huh, my little piece of dynamite. You never held back when it came to protecting the twins. You could have decimated me, but you didn't." He lifted her chin, forcing her to meet his gaze. "For two reasons. First you love me, and second because of your past. Subconsciously you believe all the nonsense I was spewing. But I was wrong, so wrong."

She swallowed the lump in her throat as she realized she'd fallen into her old familiar role. Drawing in a deep breath, she let the tension go. She refused to give the past power over the future.

"You truly think I was brave?"

"Very brave." He leaned in for a kiss, keeping it slow

and gentle. "I'm the SEAL, but you're the one with all the courage. You gave up your home to move here, to be with me, to make a home for the twins. Don't give up on us now."

"If you're transferring to training, you'll be here for the twins. You don't need me to stay."

"I never needed you to stay for the twins. It was always for me."

"Really?"

He pressed her back into the bed. "Oh, yeah."

Rachel looked up into his blue eyes; saw the love shining there for her. "I stayed for you."

"I know." He claimed her mouth, and her love with a passionate sweep of his tongue, deepening the kiss when she wrapped her arms around his neck and lifted into his embrace. "Let's make it permanent."

She pulled back, threaded her fingers through his silky hair. He made her feel so cherished. Yet… "Ford, we didn't make it through our first day in our own home."

"Because I didn't respect what we have. Love is both simple and complicated, easy and hard. Heartache and joy. As long as we stay true to love, as long as we don't give up on each other, we'll make it together. Forget one day at a time, I want forever. Marry me."

Oh God, she wanted to believe him. In truth she'd changed over the last month. Ford and Cody and Jolie had collectively shattered the barrier she had used to buffer herself from the rest of the world. She was stronger because of the love they'd brought to her life.

Her mind urged her to run, but her heart begged her

to stay. Deciding to take a risk on love, she pulled him down for a kiss.

"Yes," she whispered against his mouth. "I'll stay. Forever."